# THE FOREVER MAN
## Gordon R. Dickson

"DELIGHTFUL . . . HIGH DRAMA . . . *The Forever Man* embodies many of the attributes which have characterized his previous work, and should find an eager audience!"

—*Locus*

"One of the long-lasting pros of science fiction has given us a typical fast-paced space-adventure, first-contact novel that zips along!"

—*Isaac Asimov's Science Fiction Magazine*

"A lighter and brisker-than-usual adventure . . . The tantalizing exploration of alien cultures moves this adventure forward rapidly as the protagonists keep readjusting and expanding their ideas to meet new, challenging situations."

—*Publishers Weekly*

"Since the beginning of his career, Dickson has been searching for new literary forms . . . providing readers with some of science fiction's finest moments!"

—*Omni*

# GORDON R. DICKSON

# THE FOREVER MAN

ACE BOOKS, NEW YORK

THE FOREVER MAN

An Ace Book / published by arrangement with
the author

PRINTING HISTORY
Ace hardcover edition / September 1986
Ace edition / February 1988

ISBN: 0-441-24713-X

Ace Books are published by
The Berkley Publishing Group,
200 Madison Avenue, New York, New York 10016.
The name "ACE" and the "A" logo are
trademarks belonging to
Charter Communications, Inc.
PRINTED IN THE UNITED STATES OF AMERICA

10  9  8  7  6  5  4  3  2  1

# CHAPTER

# 1

THE PHONE WAS RINGING. HE CAME UP OUT OF A SLEEP AS DARK as death, fumbled at the glowing button in the phone's base with numb fingers and punched it. The ringing ceased.

"Wander here," he mumbled. An officer he did not recognize showed on the screen.

"Major, this is Assignment. Lieutenant Van Lee. Laagi showing upward of thirty ships facing our sector of the Frontier. Scramble, sir."

"Right," he muttered.

There was no reason for the Laagi to start putting extra ships into that part of their territory that faced the North American Sector, and necessitate an all-personnel call-out of the ship-handling crews—including people like himself who had just come back in off patrol out there six hours ago.

But then, attacking or running, the Laagi made no sense. They never had.

"You're to show in Conference Room K at four hundred hours. Bring your personals."

"Right." Groggily he rolled over on his stomach and squinted at his watch in the glow from the button on the phone. In the pale light, the figures on his wrist-com stood at twelve minutes after three—three hundred twelve hours. Enough time.

"Understood, sir?"

"Understood, Lieutenant," he said.

"Very good, sir. Out."

The phone went dead. For a moment the desire for sleep sucked at Jim Wander like some great black bog; then with a convulsive jerk he threw it and the covers off him in one motion and sat up on the edge of his bed in the darkness, scrubbing at his face with an awkward hand.

After a second, he turned the light on, got up, showered and dressed. As he shaved, he watched his face in the mirror. It was still made up of the same roughly squarish, large-boned features he remembered, but the lines about the mouth and between the eyebrows seemed deepened with the sleep, under the tousled black hair, coarsely curling up from his forehead. It could not be drink, he thought. He never drank except on leave, nowadays. Alcohol at other times did nothing for him anymore. It was just that now he slept like a log—like a log watersoaked and drowning in some bottomless lake.

He had not gone stale. Out on the Frontier he was as good as ever. But he needed something—what, he could not specify. He felt the lack of it, like the emptiness of a long-empty stomach inside him. But it was not hunger, because he was fed regularly; and it was not women, as his friends suggested, because he had no trouble finding women on his leaves from duty. What he wanted was to come to grips with something. That was it, to have a wall behind him he could set his back against and a job to do in front of him, where he could see himself getting it done—instead of fighting an endless war and getting nowhere, surrounded by those who found simply being in the war enough to justify their existence.

He needed to accomplish something and find someone who understood what it was like to have that need.

He got up and started getting himself ready for duty.

When he was finally dressed, he strapped on last of all his "personals"—his sidearm, the painkiller kit, the little green thumbnail-square box holding the x-capsule. Then he left his room, went down the long, sleeping corridor of the officers' quarters and out a side door into the darkness of predawn and the rain.

He could have gone around by the interior corridors to the Operations building, but it was a short cut across the quadrangle and the rain and chill would wake him, drive the last longing for sleep from his bones. As he stepped out of the door the invisible rain, driven by a light wind, hit him in the face. Beyond were the blurred lights of the Operations building across the quadrangle.

Far off to his left thunder rolled. Tinny thunder—the kind heard at high altitudes, in the mountains. Beyond the rain and darkness were the Rockies. Above the Rockies, the clouds. And beyond the clouds, space, stretching light-years of distance to the Frontier.

—To where he would doubtless be before the dawn rose, above this quadrangle, above these buildings, these mountains, and this Earth.

He entered the Operations building, showed his identification to the Officer of the Day, and took the lift tube up to the fourth floor. The frosted pane of the door to Conference Room F glowed with a brisk, interior light. He knocked on the door and went in without waiting for an answer. Inside, the room was half-full of pilots like himself and their gunners.

"Oh, Jim!" said the colonel behind the briefing desk. "Not here. They want you in Conference Room K, this time."

Jim grunted. He had forgotten. He went out. One floor down and halfway down the corridor to the right was Conference K. Jim went in this time without even knocking—and stopped. Like all conference rooms in Operations, it had one desk and many chairs. This room also had two people, one of whom was General Louis Mollen, Sub-Chief of Operations, and the other was a woman Jim did not know.

Mollen, round and hard-bodied as a medicine ball, with a head to match, sat behind the desk; and in a chair half-facing him was a woman in military flight clothes, in her midtwenties, lean and high-foreheaded, with the fresh skin and clear eyes of someone who has spent most of her years inside walls, sheltered from the weather. Under reddish blond hair her eyes were blue-green, in a face that was rectangular, with the jawlines sloping straight down to a small, square chin. It was not a remarkable face. Nor was it unremarkable. It was a strong, determined face.

"Sorry, sir. I should have knocked," said Jim.

"Not important," said Mollen. "Come in."

Jim came in and both the other two stood up as he approached the desk. They watched him closely, and Jim found himself examining the woman. The flight coveralls she wore had been fitted to her, which meant she was not just a civilian fitted out by the supply depot for this occasion. At the same time something about her did not belong in the Operations building; and Jim, out of the dullness of the fatigue that was still on him and the emptiness in him, found himself twinged by a sudden and reasonless resentment at her presence here, at the moment of a scramble. She looked unnaturally wide-awake and competent for this dark hour of the morning. Of course, so did Mollen; but that was different.

Jim stopped in front of the desk.

"Jim," said the general, deep-voiced, his round, snub-nosed, pugnacious face unsmiling. "I want you to meet Dr. Mary Gallegher. She's from the Geriatrics Bureau."

She would be, thought Jim sourly, reaching out to shake hands with her. Mary Gallegher was almost as tall as Jim himself, who at five feet ten was near the upper limit in height for the cramped quarters of the pilot's com seat of a fighter ship, and her handshake was not weak. But still . . . here she was, thought Jim, still resenting her for being someone as young as Jim himself, full of the juices of living, and with all her attention focused on the gray and tottering end-years of life. A bodysnatcher—a snatcher of old bodies from the brink of the grave for a few months or a few years.

"Pleased to meet you, Mary," he said.

"Good to meet you, Jim."

"Sit down," said the general. Jim pulled up a chair and they all sat down once more around the desk.

"What's up, sir?" asked Jim. "They told me it was a general call-out."

"The call-out's a fake. Just an excuse to put extra ships on the Frontier for something special," answered Mollen. "The something special's why Mary's here. And you. What do you remember about the Sixty Ships Battle?"

"It was right after we found we had a frontier in common with the Laagi, wasn't it?" said Jim, slightly puzzled. "Over one hundred years ago or so. Back before we found out logistics made mass spaceship battles unworkable. Sixty of ours met forty-some of theirs beyond the Frontier, as it is now, and theirs were better. What about it?"

"Do you remember how the battle came out?" It was the civilian, Mary Gallegher, leaning forward with an intensity that puzzled him.

Jim shrugged.

"They were better, as I say. Our ships were slower then. We hadn't started to design them for guarding a frontier, instead of fighting pitched battles. They cut us up and suckered what was left into staying clumped together while they set off a nova explosion," he said. He looked into her eyes and spoke deliberately. "The ships on the edge of the explosion were burned up like paper cutouts. The ones in the center just disappeared."

"Disappeared," said Mary Gallegher. She did not seem disturbed by Jim's description of the explosion. "That's the right word. How long ago did you say this was?"

"Over a hundred years ago," said Jim. He turned and looked at General Mollen, with a glance that said plainly— What is this, sir?

"Look here, Jim," said the general. "We've got something to show you."

He pushed aside the few papers on the surface of the table in front of him and touched some studs on the control console near the edge of the top. The overhead lights dimmed. The surface of the table became transparent and gave way to a scene of stars. To the three seated around the desk top it was as if they looked down and out into an area of space a thousand light-years across. To the civilian, Jim was thinking, the stars would be only a maze. To Jim himself, the image was long familiar.

Mollen's hands did things with the studs. Two hazy spheres of dim light, each about a hundred and fifty light-years in diameter along its longest axis, sprang into view— bright enough to establish their position and volume, not so bright as to hide the stars they enclosed. The center of one of the spheres was the sun of Earth, and the farthest extent of this sphere in one direction intermixed with an edge of the other.

"Our area of space," said Mollen's voice, out of the dimness around the table. "—And the Laagi's, Mary. They block our expansion in that direction, and we block theirs in this. The distribution of the stars in this view being what it is, it's not practical for either race to go around the other. You see the Frontier area, Mary?"

"Where the two come together, yes," said Mary.

"Now Jim—" said Mollen. "Jim commands a Wing of our Frontier Guard ships, and he knows that area well. But nothing but unmanned drones of ours have ever gotten deep into Laagi territory beyond the Frontier and come back out again. Agreed, Jim?"

"Agreed, sir," said Jim. "More than twenty, thirty light-years deep is suicide."

"Well, perhaps," said Mollen. "But let me go on. The Sixty Ships Battle was fought a hundred and twelve years ago—here." A bright point of light sprang into existence in the Frontier area. "One of the ships engaged in it was a one-man vessel with a semianimate automatic control system, named by its pilot *La Chasse Gallerie*—you said something, Jim?"

The exclamation had emerged from Jim's lips involuntarily. And at the same time, foolishly, a slight shiver had run down his back. It had been years since he had run across the old tale as a boy.

"It's a French-Canadian ghost legend, sir," he said. "The legend was that *voyageurs* who had left their homes in Eastern Canada to go out on the fur trade routes and who had died out there would be able to come back home one night of the year. New Year's night. They'd come sailing in through the storms and snow in ghost canoes, to join the people back home and kiss the girls they now wouldn't ever be seeing again. —That's what they called the story, 'La Chasse Gallerie.' It means the hunting of a type of butterfly that invades beehives to steal honey."

"The pilot of this ship was a Canadian," said Mollen. "Raoul Penard." He coughed dryly. "He was greatly attached to his home. *La Chasse Gallerie* was one of the ships near the center of the nova explosion, one of the ones that disappeared. At that time we didn't realize that the nova explosion was merely a destructive application of the principle used in phase-shift drive. —You've heard of the statistical chance that a ship caught just right by a nova explosion could be transported instead of destroyed, Jim?"

"I'd hate to count on it, sir," said Jim. "Anyway, what's the difference? Modern ships can't be anticipated or held still long enough for any kind of explosion to be effective. The Laagi haven't used the nova for eighty years. Neither have we."

"True enough," said Mollen. "But we aren't talking about modern ships. Look at the desk schema, Jim. Forty-three hours ago, one of our deep, unmanned probes returned from far into Laagi territory with pictures of a ship. Look."

Jim heard a stud click. The stars shifted and drew back. Floating against a backdrop of unknown stars he saw the old-fashioned cone shape of a one-man space battlecraft, of a type forgotten eighty years before. The view moved in close and he saw a name, abraded by dust and dimmed, but readable on the hull.

*La Chasse Gallerie*—The breath caught in his throat.

"It's been floating around in Laagi territory all this time?" Jim said. "I can't believe—"

"More than that"—Mollen interrupted him—"that ship's under pilotage and moving." A stud clicked. The original scene came back. A bright line began at the extreme edge of the desk and began to creep toward the back limits of Laagi territory. It entered the territory and began to pass through.

"You see," said Mollen's voice out of the dimness, "it's coming back from wherever the nova explosion kicked it to, over one hundred years ago. It's headed back toward our own territory. It's headed back, toward Earth."

Jim stared at the line in fascination.

"No," he heard himself saying. "It can't be. It's some sort of Laagi trick. They've got a Laagi pilot aboard—"

"Listen," said Mollen. "The probe heard talking inside the ship. And it recorded. Listen—"

Again, there was the faint snap of a stud. A voice, a human

voice, singing raggedly, almost absentmindedly to itself, entered the air of the room and rang on Jim's ears.

> . . . en roulant ma boule, roulant—
> en roulant ma boule, roulant . . .

The singing broke off and the voice dropped into a mutter of a voice that switched back and forth between French and English, speaking to itself. Jim, who had all but forgotten the little French he had picked up as a boy in Quebec, was barely able to make out that the owner of the voice was carrying on a running commentary on the housekeeping duties he was doing about the ship. Talking to himself after the fashion of hermits and lonely men.

"All right," said Jim, even while he wondered why he was protesting such strong evidence at all. "Didn't you say they had the early semianimate control systems then? They used brain tissue grown in a culture, didn't they? It's just the control system, parroting what it's heard, following out an early order to bring the ship back."

"Look again," said Mollen. The view changed once more to a close-up of *La Chasse Gallerie*. Jim looked and saw wounds in the dust-scarred hull—the slashing cuts of modern light weapons, refinements of the ancient laser beam-guns.

"The ship's already had its first encounter with the Laagi on its way home. It met three ships of a Laagi patrol—and fought them off."

"Fought them off? That old hulk?" Jim stared into the dimness where Mollen's face should be. "Three modern Laagi ships?"

"That's right," said Mollen. "It killed two and escaped from the third—and by rights it ought to be dead itself, but it's still coming, on ordinary drive, evidently. It's not phase-shifting. Now, a control system might record a voice and head a ship home, but it can't fight off odds of three to one. That takes a living mind."

A stud clicked. Dazzling overhead light sprang on again and the desk top was only a desk top. Blinking in the illumination, Jim saw Mollen looking across at him.

"Jim," said the general, "this is a volunteer mission. That

ship is still well in Laagi territory and it's going to be hit again before it reaches the Frontier. Next time it'll be cut to ribbons, or captured. We can't afford to have that happen. Its pilot, this Raoul Penard, has got too much to tell us, even beginning with the fact of how he happens to be alive in space at well over a hundred years of age." He watched Jim closely. "Jim, I'm asking you to take a section of four ships in to meet *La Chasse Gallerie* and bring her out."

Jim stared at him. He found himself involuntarily wetting his lips and stopped the gesture.

"How deep?" he asked.

"At least eighty light-years in toward the heart of Laagi territory," said Mollen bluntly. "If you want to turn it down, Jim, say so now. The man who pulls this off has got to go into it believing he can make it back out again."

"That's me," said Jim. He laughed, the bare husk of a laugh. "That's the way I operate, General. I volunteer."

"Good," said Mollen. He sat back in his chair. "There's just one more thing, then. Raoul Penard is older than any human being has a right to be and he's pretty certainly senile, if not out-and-out insane. We'll want a trained observer along to get as much information out of contact with the man as we can, in case you lose him and his ship, getting back. That calls for someone with a unique background and experience in geriatrics and all the knowledge of the aging process. So Mary, here, is going to be that observer. She'll replace your regular gunner and ride in a two-man ship with you."

It was like a hard punch in the belly. Jim sucked in air and found he had jerked erect. Both of the others watched him. He waited a second, to get his voice under control. He spoke first to the general.

"Sir, I'll need a gunner. If there was ever a job where I'd need a gunner, it'd be this one."

"As a matter of fact," said Mollen slowly—and Jim could feel that this answer had been ready and waiting for him—"Mary, here, is a gunner—a good one. She's a captain in the Reserve, Forty-second Training Squadron. With a ninety-two point six efficiency rating."

"But she's still a weekend warrior—" Jim swung about to face her. "Have you even done a tour of duty? Real duty? On the Frontier?"

"I think you know I haven't, Major," said Mary evenly. "If I had you'd have recognized me. We're about the same age and there aren't that many on Frontier duty."

"Then do you know what it's like, Captain—what it can be like out there?" raged Jim. He was trying to keep the edge out of his voice but he could hear it there in spite of all he could do. "Do you know how the Laagi can come out of nowhere? Do you know you can be hit before you know anyone's anywhere near around? Or the ship next to you can be hit and the screens have to stay open—that's regulation, in case of the one-in-a-million chance that there's something can be done for whoever's in the hit ship? Do you know what it's like to sit there and watch someone you've lived with burning to death in a cabin he can't get out of? —Or spilled out of a ship cut wide open, and lost back there somewhere . . . alive but lost . . . where you'll never be able to find him? Do you know what it might be like to be spilled out and lost yourself, and faced with the choice of living three weeks, a month, two months in your suit in the one-in-a-million chance of being found after all—or of taking your x-capsule? Do you know what that's like?"

"I know of it," said Mary. Her face had not changed. "The same way you do, as a series of possibilities, for the most part. I've seen visual and audible recordings of what you talk about. I know it as well as I can without having been wounded or killed myself."

"I don't think you do!" snapped Jim raggedly. His voice was shaking. He saw Mary turn to look at the general.

"Louis," she said, "perhaps we should ask for another volunteer?"

"Jim's our best man," said Mollen. He had not moved, or changed his expression, watching them both from behind the desk. "If I had a better Wing Cee—or an equal one who was fresher—I'd have called on him or her instead. But what you're after is just about impossible; and only someone who can do the impossible has a hope of bringing it off. That's Jim. It's like athletic skills. Every so often a champion comes along, one in billions of people, who isn't just one notch up from the next contenders, but ten notches up from the nearest best. There's no point in sending you and five ships into Laagi territory with anyone else in command. You simply wouldn't come back. With Jim, you might."

"I see," said Mary. She looked at Jim. "Regardless, I'm going."

"And you're taking her, Jim," said Mollen, "or turning down the mission."

"And if I turn it down?" Jim darted a glance at the general.

"I'll answer that," said Mary. Jim looked back at her. "If necessary, my Bureau will requisition a ship and I'll go alone."

Jim stared back at her for a long moment, and felt the rage drain slowly away from him, to be replaced by a great weariness.

"All right," he said. "All right, Mary—General. I'll head the mission." He breathed deeply and glanced over Mary's coveralls. "How long'll it take you to get ready?"

"I'm ready now," said Mary. She reached down to the floor behind the desk and came up with a package of personals—sidearm, med-kit and x-box. "The sooner the better."

"All right. The five ships of the Section are manned and waiting for you," said Mollen. He stood up behind the desk and the other two got to their feet facing him. "I'll walk down to Transmission Section with you."

# CHAPTER

# 2

THEY WENT OUT TOGETHER INTO THE CORRIDOR AND ALONG IT and down an elevator tube to a tunnel with a moving floorway. They stepped onto the gently rolling strip, which carried them forward onto a slightly faster strip, and then to a faster, and so on until they were flashing down the tunnel surrounded by air pumped at a hundred and twenty miles an hour in the same direction they traveled, so that they would not be blown off their feet. In a few minutes they came to the end, and air and strips decelerated so that they slowed and stepped at last into what looked like an ordinary office, but which was deep in the heart of a mountain. —This, the memory returned to Jim, in case the Transmission Section blew up on one of its attempts to transmit. The statistical chance was always there. Perhaps, this time . . . ?

Mollen had cleared them with the officer of the duty guard and they were moving on through other rooms to the suiting room, where Jim and Mary climbed into the unbelievably barrel-bodied space suits that were actually small spaceships in themselves and in which—if they who wore them were unlucky and still would not take their x-pills—they might drift in space, living on recycled air and nourishments until they went mad, or died of natural causes.

—Or were found and brought back. The one-in-a-million chance. Jim, now fully inside his suit, locked it closed.

"All set?" It was Mollen's voice coming at him over the aud circuit of the suit. Through the transparent window of the headpiece he saw the older man watching him.

"All set, General." He looked over at Mary and saw her already suited and waiting. For a moment it struck Jim that she might have been trying to suit up fast to show she was something more than a weekend warrior, and he felt a tinge of sympathy toward her. With the putting on of his own suit, the old feeling of sureness had begun to flow back into him, and he felt released. "Let's go, Captain."

"Stick with —'Mary,'" she said, "and I'll stick with 'Jim.'"

"Good luck," said Mollen. Together, Jim and Mary clumped across the room, waited for the tons-heavy explosion door to swing open, then clumped through.

On the floor of the vast cavern that was the takeoff area, five two-man ships sat like gray-white darts, waiting. Red "manned" lights glowed by each sealed port on the first four they passed. Jim read their names as he stumped on forward toward the open port of the lead ship, his ship, the *AndFriend*. The other four ships were the *Swallow,* the *Fair Maid,* the *Lela* and the *Fourth Helen*. He knew their pilots and gunners well. The *Swallow* and the *Fourth Helen* were ships from his own command. They and the other two were good ships handled by good people. The best.

Jim led the way aboard *AndFriend* and fitted himself into the forward seat facing the controls. Through his suit's receptors, he heard Mary sliding into the gunner's seat, behind and to the left of him. Already, in spite of the efficiency of the suit, he thought he could smell the faint, enclosed stink of his own sweat; and, responding to the habit of many missions, his brain began to clear and come alive. He plugged his suit into the controls.

"Report," he said. One by one, in order, the *Swallow,* the *Fair Maid,* the *Lela* and the *Fourth Helen* replied. "—Transmission Section," said Jim, "this is Wander Section, ready and waiting for transmission."

"Acknowledged," replied the voice of the Transmission Section. There followed a short wait, during which as always

Jim was conscious, as if through some extra sense, of the many-tons weight of the collapsed magnesium alloy of the ships' hulls bearing down on the specially reinforced concrete of the takeoff area. "Ready to transmit."

"Acknowledged," said Jim.

"On the count of four, then," said Transmission Section's calm, disembodied voice. "For Picket Nine, L Sector, Frontier Area, transmission of Wander Section, five ships. Ready to phase-shift. Counting now. Four . . . three . . ." The unimaginable tension that always preceded transmission from one established point to another began to build, a gearing-up of nerves that affected all the men on all the ships alike. "Two . . ." The voice of Transmission Section seemed to thunder at them along their overwrought nerves. "One . . ."

" . . . *Transmit!*"

Abruptly, a wave of disorientation and nausea broke through them, and was gone. They floated in dark and empty interstellar space, with the stars of the Frontier area surrounding them, and a new voice spoke in their ear.

"Identify yourself," it said. "Identify yourself. This is *Formidable*, command ship for Picket Nine Sector, requesting identification."

"Wander Section. Five ships." Jim did not bother to look at his instruments to find the space-floating sphere that was *Formidable*. It was out there somewhere, with twenty ships scattered around, up to five and a half light-years away, but all zeroed in on this reception point where he and the other four ships had emerged. Had Jim been a Laagi Wing or Picket Commander, he would not have transmitted into this area with twenty ships—no, nor with twice that many. "Confirm transmission notice from Earth? Five ship section for deep probe Laagi territory. Wander Section Leader, speaking."

"Transmission notice confirmed, Wander Section Leader," crackled back the voice from Picket Nine. "Mission confirmed. You will not deship. Repeat, not deship. Local Frontier area has been scouted for slipover, and data prepared for flash transmission to you. You will accept data and leave immediately. Please key to receive data."

"Major—" began the voice of Mary, behind him.

"Shut up," said Jim. He said it casually, without rancor, as if he was speaking to his regular gunner, Leif Molloy. For a moment he had forgotten that he was carrying a passenger instead of a proper gunman. And there was no time to think about it now. "Acknowledge," he said to Picket Nine. "Transmit data, please."

He pressed the data key and the light above it sprang into being and glowed for nearly a full second before going dark again. That, thought Jim, was a lot of data—at the high-speed transmission at which such information was pumped into his ship's computing center. That was one of the reasons the new mind-units were evolved out of solid-state physics instead of following up the development of the older, semianimate brains such as the one aboard the ancient *La Chasse Gallerie*. The semianimate brains—living tissue in a nutrient solution—could not accept the modern need for sudden high-speed packing of sixteen hours' worth of data into the space of a second or so.

Also, such living tissue had to be specially protected against high accelerations, needed to be fed and trimmed—and it died on you at the wrong times.

All the time Jim was turning this over with one part of his mind, the other and larger part of his thinking process was driving the gloved fingers of his right hand. These moved over a bank of one hundred and twenty small black buttons, ten across and twelve down, like the stops on a piano-accordion, and with the unthinking speed and skill of the trained operator, he punched them, requesting information out of the body of data just pumped into his ship's computing center, building up from this a picture of the situation, and constructing a pattern of action to be taken as a result.

Evoked by the intricate code set up by combinations of the black buttons under his fingers, the ghost voice of the mind-unit whispered in his ear in a code of words and numbers hardly less intricate.

" . . . transmit destination area one-eighty Ell Wye, Lag Sector L 49C at point 12.5, 13.2, 64.5. Proceeding jumps 10 Ell Wye, R inclination Z49 degrees Frontier midpoint. Optimum jumps twelve, .03 error correctable on the first shift . . ."

He worked steadily. The picture began to emerge. It would not be hard getting in. It was never hard to do that. They could reach *La Chasse Gallerie* in twelve phase-shift transmissions or jumps across some hundred and eighty light-years of distance, and locate her in the area where she should then be, within an hour or so. Then they could—theoretically at least—surround her, lock on, and try to improve on the ten light-years of jump it seemed was the practical limit of her pilot's or her control center's computing possibilities.

With modern phase-shift drive, the problem was not the ability to jump any required distance, but the ability to compute correctly, in a reasonable time, the direction and distance in which the move should be made. Phase-shifting was an outgrowth of the Heisenberg Uncertainty Principle of physics that had enunciated the fact that it was possible to establish either the position of an electron, or its speed of movement, but not both at the same time. When a ship activated a phase-shift it did not move in the ordinary sense of that word. Effectively, for a timeless moment its speed became zero and its position universal. It was everywhere and no particular place. Then its position was established at the destination point which had been calculated for it and its speed became relative to its position at that point.

The problem with phase-shifting lay in that calculation. Of necessity, it had to take into account the position and current movement of the ship about to make the jump and the position and movement of the destination area—this in a galaxy where everything was in relative movement, and only a mathematical fiction, the theoretical centerpoint of the galaxy from which all distances were marked and measured, was fixed.

The greater the distance, the more involved and time-consuming the calculations. The law of diminishing returns would set in, and the process broke down of its own weight—it took a lifetime to calculate a single jump to a destination it would not take quite a lifetime to reach by smaller, more easily calculable jumps. Even with today's ships it was the necessary calculation time-factor that made it impractical for the human and Laagi races to go around each others' spatial territory. If we were all Raoul Penards, thought Jim grimly, with two hundred and more years of life coming, it'd be different. —The thought chilled him; he did not know why. He put it out of his mind and went back to the calculations.

The picture grew and completed. He keyed his voice to the other ships floating in dark space around him.

"Wander Leader to Wander Section," he said. "Wander

Leader to Wander Section. Prepare to shift into Laagi territory. Key for calculations pattern for first of twelve shifts. Acknowledge, all ships of Wander Section."

The transmit section of his control board glowed briefly as the *Swallow,* the *Fair Maid,* the *Lela* and the *Fourth Helen* pumped into their own computing centers the situation and calculations he had worked out with his. Their voices came back, acknowledging.

"Lock to destination," said Jim. "Dispersal pattern K at destination. Repeat, pattern K, tight, hundred kilometer interval. Hundred kilometer interval." He glanced at the sweep second hand of the clock before him on his control board. "Transmit in six seconds. Counting. Five. Four. Three. Two. One. Transmit—"

Again, the disorientation, and the nausea.

Strange stars were around them. The mind-unit's lights glowed while it verified their position and adjusted the figures for the precalculated next jump. After a time it whispered in Jim's ear again, and—

"Check Ten," whispered Jim. It was the code for "make next jump immediately."

"Three. Two. One. Transmit—"

Once again the wrench of dislocation. Nausea. Lights glowed in silence as time passed again—

"Check Ten . . ."

Ten more times they shifted, silent tension reflecting the waits for calculations while they floated, only lights in the silent darkness. Then they were there.

In darkness. They were alone amongst the enemy's stars. None of the other ships registered on the instruments.

"Report," ordered Jim to the universe at large.

"*Swallow . . .*" came a whisper in his earphones as from somewhere unseen a tight beam touched the outside of the *AndFriend,* carrying its message to his ears. "*Fair Maid . . . Lela . . .*" A slightly longer pause. "*Fourth Helen.*"

*Fourth Helen* was always a laggard. Jim had braced her pilot about it a dozen times. But now was not the hour for reprimands. They were deep in Laagi territory, and the alien alert posts would have already picked up the burst of energy not only from their initial transmit from Picket Nine, which had been precalculated by the com-ship there over the hours since *La Chasse Gallerie* had been discovered—and which consequently had been able to send them with some accuracy half the distance to her—but from the succeeding jumps that had brought them light-years deep into Laagi territory. Communication between the ships of the Section must be held to a minimum while the aliens were still trying to figure out where the chain of shifts had landed the intruders.

Shortly, since they must know of the approximate position of *La Chasse Gallerie,* and have ships on the way to try to kill her again, they would put two and two together and expect to find the intruders in the same area. But for the moment Wander Section, if it lay low and quiet, could feel it was safely hidden in the immensities of enemy space.

Jim blocked off outside transmission, and spoke over the intercom to Mary.

"All right, Mary," he said. "What was it you wanted to say to me back at Frontier?"

There was a slight pause before the other's voice came back.

"Major—"

"Nevermind that," said Jim. "You had it right before; let's not go all formal now we're in space. I apologize for the 'Captain,' earlier. What was it you wanted, Mary?"

"All right, Jim," said the voice of Mary. "I won't bother about military manners either, then." There was a slight grimness to the humor in her voice. "I wanted to say—I'd like to get in close enough to *La Chasse Gallerie,* so that we can keep a tight-beam connection with her hull at all times and I can record everything Penard says from the time of contact on. It'll be important."

"Don't worry," said Jim. "We're spread out and searching on instruments for him now. If Picket Nine did a reasonable job of calculating his progress, we should have him alongside in a few minutes. And I'll put you right up next to him. We're going to surround him with our ships, lock him in the middle of us with magnetics, and try to shift out as a unit, since he doesn't seem capable of anything more than regular acceleration on his own."

"You say he'll be along?" said Mary. "Why didn't we go directly to him?"

"And make it absolutely clear to the Laagi he's what we're

after?" answered Jim. "As long as they don't know for sure, they have to assume we don't even know of his existence. So we stop ahead in his line of travel—lucky he's just plugging straight ahead without trying any dodges—and wait for him. We might even make it look like an accidental meeting to the Laagi—" Jim smiled inside the privacy of his suit's headpiece without much humor. "—But don't bet on it."

"Do you think you can lock on to him without too much trouble—"

"Depends," answered Jim, "on how fast he starts shooting at us when he sees us."

"Shooting at us?" There was incredulity in Mary's voice. "Why should he—oh." Her voice dropped. "I see."

"That's right," said Jim. "We don't look like any human ship he ever knew about, and he's in territory where he's going to be expecting aliens, not friends."

"But what're you going to do, to stop him shooting?"

"They dug up the recognition signals of the Sixty Ships Battle," said Jim. "Just pray he remembers them. And they've given me a voice signal that my blinker lights can translate and flash at him in the code he was working under at the time of the battle. Maybe it'll work, maybe it won't."

"It will," said Mary calmly.

"Oh?" Jim felt harshness in his chest. "What makes you so sure?"

"It's my field, Jim. It's my business to know how the aged react. And one of their common reactions is to forget recent events and remember the events of long ago. Their childhood. High points of their early life—and the Sixty Ships Battle will have been one of those."

"So you think Penard will remember?"

"I think so," said Mary.

Jim grinned again, mirthlessly, privately in his suit.

"You'd better be right," he said. "It's one order of impossibility to pick him up and take him home. It's another to fight off the Laagi while we're doing it. To fight Penard at the same time would be a third order—and that's beyond ordinary mortals."

"Yes," said Mary. "You don't like to think of being mortal, do you, Major—Jim?"

Jim opened his mouth to answer and shut it quickly. He sat

rigid and sweating in his suit. This—this professional—he thought, who doesn't know what it's like to see men and women you know, die . . . ! The shockingly murderous reaction passed, after a moment, leaving him trembling and spent. There was the sour taste of stomach acids in his mouth.

"Perhaps not," he said shakily over the intercom. "Perhaps not."

"Why put it in the future, Jim?" said the voice of the other. "Why not tell me plainly that you don't like people who work in geriatrics?"

"Nothing," said Jim. "It's nothing to do with me. Let them live as long as they can."

"Something wrong with that?"

"I don't see the point of it," said Jim. "You've got the average age up pushing a hundred. What good does it do?" His throat went a little dry. I shouldn't talk so much, he thought. But he went on and said it anyway. "What's the use of it?"

"People are pretty vigorous up through their nineties. If we can push it further . . . Here's Penard who's far over one hundred—"

"And what's the use of it? Vigorous!" said Jim, the words breaking out of him. "Vigorous enough to totter around and sit in the sunlight —What do you think's the retirement age from Frontier duty?"

"I know what it is," said Mary. "It's thirty-two."

"Thirty-two." Jim sneered. "So you've got all these extra vigorous years of life for people, have you? If they're all that vigorous, why can't they ride a Frontier ship after thirty-two? I'll tell you why. It's because they're too old—too old physically, too old in the reflexes and the nerves! Snatch all the ancient bodies back from the brink of the grave, but you can't change that. So what good's your extra sixty-eight years?"

"Maybe you ought to ask Raoul Penard that," said Mary softly.

A dark wave of pain and unhappiness rose inside Jim, so that he had to clench his teeth to hold it back from coming out in words.

"Nevermind him," Jim said huskily. For a second it was as if he had been through it himself, all the endless years, refusing to die, beating his ship back toward the Frontier, and the solar system, without being able to phase-shift—on his long, long way home. I'll get him home, thought Jim to himself— I'll get Penard to the home he's been after for more than a hundred years, if I have to take him through every Laagi Picket area between here and the Frontier. "Nevermind him," Jim said again to Mary. "He was a fighter."

"He still is—" Mary was cut suddenly short by the ringing of the contact alarm. Jim's fingers slapped by reflex down on his bank of buttons and some moments later their ship swam up beside a dust-scarred cone shape with the faded legend *La Chasse Gallerie* visible on its side.

# C H A P T E R

# 3

IN THE SAME MOMENT, THE OTHER SHIPS OF WANDER SECTION were appearing around the ancient spaceship. Their magnetic beams licked out and locked—and held—a fraction of a second before *La Chasse Gallerie* bucked like a wild horse and tried to escape with a surge at many gravities of acceleration.

Taken by surprise by a power kick that should have killed any human aboard the long-lost vessel, the mass of the five other ships still managed to hold her back.

"Hold—" Jim was whispering into the headpiece of his suit and circuits were translating his old-fashioned phrases into blinking signal lights beamed at the cone-shaped ship. "Hold, *La Chasse Gallerie*. This is a Government Rescue Contingent, title Wander Section. Do not resist. We are taking you in tow—" The unfitness of the ancient word jarred in Jim's mouth as he said it. "We're taking you in tow to return you to your Base Headquarters. Repeat . . ."

The flashing lights went on spelling the message out, over and over again. *La Chasse Gallerie* ceased fighting and hung docilely in the net of magnetic forces. Jim got a talk beam touching on the aged hull.

" . . . home," a voice was saying, the same voice he had heard recorded in Mollen's office. *"Chez moi . . ."* It broke into a tangle of French that Jim could not follow, and emerged in accented English with the cadence of poetry. " . . . *Poleon, hees sojer never fight—more brave as dem poor habitants—Chenier, he try for broke de rank—Chenier come dead immédiatement . . .*"

"*La Chasse Gallerie. La Chasse Gallerie,*" Jim was saying over and over, while the blinking lights on his hull transformed the words into a ship's code over a century dead. "Can you understand me? Repeat, can you understand me? If so, acknowledge. Acknowledge . . ."

There was no response from the dust-scarred hull, slashed by the Laagi weapons. Only the voice, reciting what Jim now recognized as a poem by William Henry Drummond, one of the early poets to write in the French-accented English of the Canadian habitant in the nineteenth century.

" . . . *De gun dey rattle lak' tonnere*—" muttered on the voice. "*Just bang, bang, bang! Dat's way she go*—" Abruptly the voice of Raoul Penard shifted to poetry; in the pure French of another poem by a medieval prisoner looking out the tower window of his prison on the springtime, the shift was in perfect cadence and rhyme with the earlier line.

"*Le temps a laissé ton manteau—de vent, de froidure, et de pluie . . .*"

"It's no use," said Mary. "We'll have to get him back to Earth and treatment before you'll be able to get through to him."

"All right," said Jim. "Then we'll head—"

The moan of an interior siren blasted through his suit.

"Laagi!" yelped the voice of *Fourth Helen*. "Five bandits, sector six—"

"Bandits. Two bandits, sector two, fifteen hundred kilometers—" broke in the voice of *Lela*.

Jim swore and slapped his fingers down on the buttons. With all ships locked together, his phase-shift impulse was sorted automatically through the computer center of each one, so that they all shifted together in the direction and distance he had programmed. There was the wrench of shift-feeling—and sudden silence.

The siren had cut off. The voices were silent. Automatic dispersal had taken place, and the other four ships were spreading out rapidly to distances up to a thousand kilometers on all sides, their receptors probing the empty space for half a light-year in each direction, quivering, seeking, while *And-Friend* stayed locked to *La Chasse Gallerie*.

"Looks like we got away." Mary's voice was eerie in its naturalness, breaking the stillness in Jim's headpiece. "Looks like they lost us."

"The hell they did!" said Jim savagely. "They'll have unmanned detector probes strung out all the way from here to the Frontier. They know we're not going anyplace else."

"Then we better jump again—"

"Not yet! Shut up, will you!" Jim bit the words off hard at his lips. "The more they collect to hit us with here, the more we leave behind when we jump again. Sit still back there and keep your mouth shut. You're a gunner now, not a talker."

"Yes sir." There was no mockery in Mary's voice. This time Jim did not comment on the "sir."

The seconds moved slowly with the sweep hand of the clock in front of Jim. The mind-unit had made its calculations and was ready to move. He waited. Inside the headpiece, his face was dripping with perspiration. The blood creaked in his ears—

Moan of siren!

"Laagi!" shouted *Fair Maid*. "Four bandits—"

"Bandits!"

"Bandits!"

Suddenly the helmet was full of warning cries from all the ships. The telltale sphere in front of Jim came alive with the green dots of Laagi ships, over and beyond the white dots of his own Section.

They came on, the green dots, with the illusion of seeming to spread apart as they advanced. They came on and . . .

Suddenly they were gone. They had winked out, disappeared as if they had never been there in the first place.

"Formation Charlie," said Jim tonelessly to the other four ships. They shifted their relative positions. Jim sat silent, sweat dripping off his chin inside his suit. He could feel the growing tension in the woman behind him.

"Jump!" It was a whisper torn from a raw throat in Mary. "Why don't you jump?"

"Where to?" whispered back Jim. "They'll have planet-based computers the size of small cities working on our probabilities of movement now. Anywhere we jump now in a straight line for the Frontier, they'll be waiting for us."

"Then jump to a side point. Evade them!"

"If we do that," whispered Jim, "we'll have to recalculate." He suddenly realized the other's whispering had brought him to lower his own voice to a thread. Deliberately he spoke out loud, but with transmission of the conversation to the other ships of the Section blocked off. "Recalculation takes time. They'll be using that time to find us—and they've got bigger and better equipment for it than the computing centers aboard these little ships of ours."

"But what're we waiting for? Why'd they go away? Shouldn't we go now—"

"No!" snarled Jim. "They went away because they thought there weren't enough of them."

"Not enough? There were twice our number—"

"Not enough," said Jim. "They want to kill us all at one swat. They don't want any of us to escape. It's not just *La Chasse Gallerie*. Enemy ships can't be allowed to get this deep into their territory and live. We'd do the same thing if Laagi ships came into our space. We'd have to make an object lesson of them—so they wouldn't be tempted to try again."

"But—"

"Laagi—Laagi! Laagi!—"

Suddenly the pilots of all the vessels were shouting at once. Jim's hand slammed down on a button and four screens woke to life, showing the interior of the other four ships. The sight and sound of the other pilots and gunners were there before his eyes.

The spherical telltale was alive with green dots, closing in from all sectors of the area, racing to englobe Wander Section.

"Hector! Pattern Hector!" Jim heard his own voice shouting to the other ships. "Hector! Hit, break out, and Check Ten. Check Ten. . . ."

They were driving toward one group of the approaching green lights. *La Chasse Gallerie* was driving with them. Over the shouting back and forth of the Wander Section pilots came the voice of Raoul Penard, shouting, singing—a strange, lugubrious tune but in the cadence and tone of a battle song. As if through the winds of a nightmare, Jim heard him. . . .

*Frenchman, he don't lak to die in de fall!*
*When de mairsh she am so full of de game!*
*An de little bool-frog, he's roll veree fat . . .*
*An de leetle mooshrat, he's jus' de same! . . .*

The feeble lasers of the old ship reached out toward the oncoming Laagi lights that were ships, pathetically wide of their mark. Something winked up ahead and suddenly the soft, uncollapsed point of the primitive, dust-scarred hull was no longer there. Then Wander Section had closed with some eight of the enemy.

*AndFriend* suddenly bucked and screamed. Her internal temperature shot up momentarily to nearly two hundred degrees as a glancing blow from the light-weapon of one of the Laagi brushed her. There was a moment of insanity. Flame flickered suddenly in the interior of *Fair Maid*, obscuring the picture of it on the screen before Jim. Then they were all past the enemy ships and Jim cried "Transmit!" at the same time that he locked his own magnetic beams on the chopped hull of *La Chasse Gallerie* and tried to take her through the jump alone.

It should not have been possible. But some sixth sense in the singing, crazed mind of Raoul Penard seemed to understand what Jim was trying. The two ships jumped together under *AndFriend*'s control, and suddenly all six ships floated within sight of each other amid the peace and darkness of empty space and the alien stars.

Into this silence came a soft sob from one of the other vessels. Jim looked and saw the charred interior of the *Fair Maid*. Her pilot was out of his seat and half-crouched before the equally charred, barrel-suited figure in the gunner's chair.

"*Fair Maid*!" Jim had to repeat the call, more sharply. "*Fair Maid*! Acknowledge!"

The pilot's headpiece lifted. The sobbing stopped.

"*Fair Maid* here." The voice was thick-tongued, drugged-sounding. "I had to shoot my gunner, Wander Leader. She was burning up inside her suit. I had to shoot my gunner. She was burning up inside her—"

"*Fair Maid*!" snapped Jim. "Can you still compute and jump?"

"Yes . . ." said the drugged voice. "I can compute and jump, Wander Leader."

"All right, *Fair Maid*," said Jim. "You're to jump wide—angle off outside Laagi territory and then make your own way back to our side of the Frontier. We're close enough to outside both territories for that now. Have you got it? Jump wide, and make your own way back. Jump far enough so that it won't be worth the trouble to the Laagi to go after you."

"No!" The voice lost some of its druggedness. "I'm staying, Wander Leader. I'm going to kill some—"

"*Fair Maid*!" Jim heard his own voice snarling into his headpiece. "This Section has a mission—to bring back the ship we've just picked up in Laagi territory! You're no good on that mission—you're no good to this Section without a gunner. Jump wide and go home! Do you hear me? That's an order. Jump wide and go home!"

There was a moment's silence, and then the pilot's figure moved and turned slowly back to sit down before his controls.

"Acknowledge, *Fair Maid*!" snapped Jim.

"Acknowledge," came the lifeless voice of the pilot in the burned interior of the ship. "Jumping wide and going home."

"Out then," said Jim in a calmer voice. "Good luck getting back. So long, Jerry."

"So long, Wander Leader," came the numb reply. The gloved hands moved on the singed controls. *Fair Maid* vanished.

Jim sat back wearily in his pilot's chair. Hammering into his ears came the voice of Raoul Penard, now crooning another verse of his battle song. . . .

> . . . *Come all you beeg Canada man* .
> *Who want find work on Meeshegan,*
> *Dere's beeg log drive all troo our lan',*
> *You sure fin' work on Meesh—*

In a sudden reflex of rage, Jim's hand slapped down on a button, cutting off in midword the song from *La Chasse Gallerie*.

"Jim!"

The word was like a whip cracking across his back. Jim started awake to the fact of his passenger-gunner behind him.

"What?" he asked.

"I think I've got my second wind in this race," answered the even, cold voice of Mary. "Meanwhile, how about turning Penard back on? My job's to record everything I can get from him, and I can't do that with the talk beam between his ship and ours shut off."

"The *Fair Maid*'s gunner just died—"

"Turn the talk beam on!"

Jim reached out and turned it on, wondering a little at himself. I should feel like shooting her at this moment, he thought. Why don't I? Penard's voice sang at him once again.

"Look," Jim began. "When a woman dies and a ship may be lost—"

"Have you looked at Penard's ship, Major?" interrupted the voice of Mary. "Take a look. Then maybe you'll understand why I want the talk beam on just as long as there's any use."

Jim turned and looked at the screen that showed the cone-shaped vessel. He stared.

If *La Chasse Gallerie* had been badly cut up before, she was a floating chunk of scrap now. She had been slashed deep in half a dozen directions by the light beams of the Laagi ships. And the old-fashioned ceramet material of her hull, built before collapsed metals had been possible, had been opened up like cardboard under the edge of red-hot knives. Jim stared, hearing the voice of Penard singing in his ears, and an icy trickle went down his perspiration-soaked spine.

"He can't be alive," Jim heard himself saying. If a hit that did not even penetrate the collapsed metal hull of the *Fair Maid* could turn that ship's interior into a charred, if workable, area—what must those light-weapons of the enemy have done to the interior of the old ship he looked at now? But Raoul still sang from there his song about lumbering in Mee-shegan.

"—Nobody could be alive in that," Jim said. "I was right. It must be just his semianimate control system parroting him and running the ship. Even at that, it's a miracle it's still working—"

"We don't know," Mary's voice cut in on him. "And until

we know we have to assume it's Raoul himself, still alive. After all, his coming back at all is an impossible miracle. If that could happen, it could happen he's still alive in that ship now. Maybe he's picked up some kind of protection we don't know about."

Jim shook his head, forgetting that probably Mary could not see this silent negative. It was not possible that Penard was alive. But—he roused himself back to his duty. He had a job to do.

His fingers began to dance over the black buttons in their ranks before him, working out the situation, planning his next move.

"K formation," he said automatically to the other ships, but did not even glance at the telltale sphere to make sure they obeyed correctly. Slowly, the situation took form. He was down one ship, from five to four of them, and that reduced the number of practical fighting and maneuvering formations by a factor of better than three. And there was something else. . . .

"Mary," he said slowly.

"Yes, Jim?"

"I want your opinion on something," said Jim. "When we jumped out of the fight area just now, it was a jump off the direct route home and to the side by nearly sixteen light-years; and of course we carried *La Chasse Gallerie* with us, out of the direct route to home she's been on since we first found her. Penard let me do that without fighting me with his own controls. Now, what I want to know is—and it ought to be impossible that he's got power on that hulk, anyway, but he obviously has—will he let me move him from now on without fighting me, once I slap a magnetic on him? In other words, whether he's a man or a semianimate control, was that a fluke last time, or can I count on it happening again?"

Mary did not answer immediately. Then . . .

"I think you can count on him trusting you," she said. "If Raoul Penard is alive in there, the fact that he reacted sensibly once ought to be some indication he'll do it again. And if you're right about it being just a control center driving that ship, then it should react consistently in the same pattern to the same stimulus."

"Yeah . . ." said Jim softly. "But I wonder which it is—is

Penard in there, alive or dead? Is it a man we're trying to get out? Or a control center?"

"Does it matter?" said the level voice of Mary.

Jim looked bleakly into the vision screens fed by his instruments.

"Not to you, does it?" he said. "But I'm the man that has to order men to kill themselves to get that ship home." Something tightened in his throat. "You know that's what hit me when I first saw you in Mollen's office, but I didn't know what it was. You haven't got guts inside you, you've got statistical tables and a computer."

He could hear his own harsh breathing in the headpiece of his suit once he had said it.

"You think so?" said Mary's voice grimly. "And how about you, Jim? The accidents of birth and change while you were growing up gave you a one-in-billions set of mind and reflexes. You grew up to be a white knight and to slay dragons. Now you're in the dragon-slaying business and something's gone wrong with it you can't quite figure out. Something's gone sour, hasn't it?"

Jim did not answer. He was sweating again.

"You know," said Mary, "I think you've got a bad case of combat fatigue; but you won't quit and you're so valuable that people like Mollen won't make you quit."

"Play-party psychiatrist, are you?" demanded Jim through gritted teeth. Mary ignored him.

"You think I didn't have a chance to look at your personal history before I met you?" said Mary. "You ought to know better than to think that. You're a Canadian yourself, and your background is Scotch and French. That, plus the way you've been reacting to hearing Raoul Penard, ought to be all anyone needs to know to read the signs—and the signs all read the same way—"

"Shut up!" husked Jim, the words choking in his throat.

"The signs read dead, Major. All of them, including the fact it upsets you that I'm in the business of trying to make people live longer. You don't want to live a long time. Victory, or death, that's what you've been after; and now that you've been forced to the conclusion that you can't win that victory, you want death. But you're not built to deliberately kill yourself—"

Jim tried to speak, but the strained muscles of his throat let out only a little, wordless rasp of sound.

"—So death has to come and take you," said Mary's relentless voice. There was a trace of something sad also in that voice. "And it's got to come take you against the most of your strength, against all your fighting will. He's got to take you in spite of yourself. —And Death can't do it! That's what's wrong with you, isn't it, Jim?" Mary paused. "That's why you don't want to grow old and be forced to leave out here, where Death lives."

Mary's voice broke off. Jim sat, fighting for breath, his gloved fingers trembling on the access flap to the sidearm. After a little, his breath grew deeper again; and he forced himself to turn back to his computations. Aside from the habit-instructed section of his mind that concerned itself with this problem, the rest of him was mindless.

I've got to do something, he thought. I've got to do something. But nothing would come to mind. Gradually the careening vessel of his mind righted itself, and he came back to a sense of duty—to Wander Section and his mission. Then suddenly a thought woke in him.

"Raoul Penard's dead," he said quite calmly to Mary. "Somehow, what we've been hearing and what we've been watching drive and fight that ship is the semianimate control center. How it got to be another Raoul Penard doesn't matter. The tissue they used kept growing, and no one ever thought to keep one of them in contact with a man twenty-four hours a day for his lifetime. So it's the alter ego, the control center we've got to bring in. And there's a way to do that."

He paused and waited. There was a second of silence, and then Mary's voice spoke.

"Go on. Maybe I underestimated you, Jim."

"Maybe you did," said Jim. "At any rate, here it is. In no more than another half hour we're going to be discovered here. Those planet-based big computers of theirs have been piling up data on our mission here and on me as Leader of the Section, and their picture gets more complete every time we move and they can get new data. If we dodged away from here to hide again, next time they'd find us even faster. And after two more hides they'd hit us almost as soon as we got hid. So there's no choice to it. We've got to go for the Frontier, now."

"Yes," said Mary. "I can see we do."

"You can," said Jim. "And the Laagi can. Everybody can. But they also know I know that they've got most of the area from here to the Frontier covered. Almost anywhere we come out, they'll be ready to hit us within seconds, with ships that are simply sitting there, ready to make jump to wherever we emerge, their computations to the forty or fifty areas within easy jump of them already computed for them by the big planet-based machines. So, there's only one thing left for me to do, as they see it. —Go wide."

"Wide?" said Mary. She sounded a trifle startled.

"Sure," said Jim, grinning mirthlessly to himself in the privacy of his suit. "Like I sent *Fair Maid*. —But there's a difference between us and *Fair Maid*. We've got *La Chasse Gallerie*. And the Laagi'll follow us. And we'll have to keep running—running outward until their edge in data lets them catch up with us. Then their edge in ship numbers'll finish us off. The Laagi ships won't quit on our trail—even if it means they won't get back themselves. As I said a little earlier, enemy ships can't be allowed to get this deep into their territory and get home again."

"Then what's the use of going wide?" asked Mary. "It just puts off the time—"

"I'm not going wide." Jim grinned privately and mirthlessly once more. "That's what the Laagi think I'll do, hoping for a miracle to save us. I'm going instead where no one with any sense would go—right under their weapons. I've computed ten jumps to the Frontier which is the least we can make it in. We'll lock on and carry *La Chasse Gallerie*; and when we come out of the jump, we'll come out shooting. Blind. We'll blast our way through whatever's there and jump again as fast as we can. If one of us survives, that'll be all that's necessary to lock on to *La Chasse Gallerie* and jump her to the Frontier. If none of us does—well, we've done our best."

Once more he paused. Mary said nothing.

"Now," said Jim, grinning like a death's head. "If that was a two-hundred-year-old man aboard that wreck of a ship there, and maybe burned badly or broken up by what he's been through so far, that business of jumping and coming out at fighting accelerations would kill him. But," said Jim, drawing a deep breath, "it's not a man. It's a control center. And a control center ought to be able to take it. —Have you got anything to say, Mary?"

"Yes," said Mary quietly. "Officially I protest your assumption that Raoul Penard is dead, and your choice of an action which might be fatal to him as a result."

Jim felt a kind of awe stir in him.

"By—" He broke off. "Mary, you really expect us to come out of this all right, don't you?"

"Yes," said Mary calmly. "I'm not disappointed with life —the way you are. —You don't know it, Jim, but there's a lot of people like you back home, and I meet them all the time. Ever since we started working toward a longer life for people, they've turned their back on us. They say there's no sense in living a longer time—but the truth is they're afraid of it. Afraid a long life will show them up as failures, that they won't have death for an excuse for not making a go of life."

"Nevermind that!" Jim's throat had gone dry again. "Stand to your guns. We're jumping now—and we'll be coming out shooting." He turned swiftly to punch the data key and inform his three remaining other ships. " . . . Transmitting in five seconds. Five. Four. Three. Two. One. Transmit—"

# CHAPTER

## 4

DISORIENTATION. NAUSEA...

The stars were different for the fifth time. Acceleration hit like a tree trunk ramming into Jim's chest. His fingers danced on the sub-light control buttons. The voice of Raoul Penard was howling his battle song again—

> ... When you come drive de beeg saw log,
> You got to jump jus' lak de frog!
> De foreman come, he say go sak!
> You got in de watair all over your back! ...

Time passed. . . .

"Check Ten!" shouted Jim once again. "All ships Check Ten. Transmit in three seconds. Three. Two—"

No Laagi ships in the telltale sphere again this time. And the next. And the next—

Suddenly *AndFriend* bucked and slammed. Flame flickered for a fraction of a second through the cabin. The telltale was alive with green lights, closing fast.

Fifteen of them or more . . . Directly ahead of *AndFriend*

were three of them in formation, closing on her alone. In Jim's ears rang the wild voice of Penard. . . .

*P'raps you work on drive, tree-four day—*
*You find dat drive dat she don' pay. . .*

"Gunner!" cried Jim, seeing the green lights almost on top of him. It was a desperate cry for help. In a moment—

Two of the green lights flared suddenly and disappeared. The third flashed and veered off.

"Mary!" yelped Jim, suddenly drunk on battle adrenaline. "You're a gunner! A real gunner!"

"More to the left and up—sector ten—" said a thin, calm voice, a voice he could hardly recognize as Mary's, in his ear. He veered, saw two more green lights. Saw one flare and vanish—saw suddenly one of his own white lights flare and vanish as the scream of torn metal sounded from one of the screens before him. Glancing at the screens, he saw for the moment the one picturing *Fourth Helen*'s cabin, showing the cabin split open, emptied and flattened for a second before the screen went dark and blank.

Grief tore at him. And rage.

"Transmit now!" he howled at the other ships. "Check Ten! Check Ten—"

He slapped a magnetic on the battered cone shape that fled by a miracle still beside him and punched for the jump—

Disorientation. Nausea. And—

The stars of the Frontier were ahead of them. Jim stared into his screens. They floated in empty space, three gray-white dart shapes and the ravaged shape of *La Chasse Gallerie*. *Lela* rode level with Jim's ship, but *Swallow* was slowly turning sideways like a dying fish drifting in the ocean currents. Jim stared into the small screen showing the *Swallow*'s interior. The two suited figures sat in a blackened cabin, unmoving.

"*Swallow!*" said Jim hoarsely. "Are you all right? Acknowledge. Acknowledge!"

But there was no answer from the two figures, and the *Swallow* continued to drift, turning, as if she was sliding off some invisible slope into the endless depths of the universe.

Jim shook with a cold, inner sickness like a chill. They're just unconscious, he thought. They have to be just unconscious. Otherwise they wouldn't have been able to make the jump to here.

"—*Brigadier!*" the voice of Penard was singing with strange softness—

> . . . *repondit Pandore*
> *Brigadier! Vous avez raison.*
> *Brigadier! repondit Pandore*
> *Brigadier! Vous avez raison!*—

Jim turned slowly to look into the screen showing *La Chasse Gallerie*. He stared at what he saw. If the old ship had been badly slashed before, she was a ruin now. Nothing could be alive in such a wreck. Nothing. But the voice of Penard sang on.

"No . . . " muttered Jim out loud, unbelievingly. "Not even a semianimate control center could come through that. It couldn't—" He stirred himself and shifted once more, pushing for speed by settling for any location in the general direction of the Frontier's other side. . . .

"Identify yourself!" crackled a voice suddenly on Jim's ears. "Identify yourself! This is Picket Six, B Sector, Frontier area."

"Wander Section—" muttered Jim, still staring at the tattered form of *La Chasse Gallerie*. He remembered the original legend about the return of the dead *voyageurs* in their ghost canoes, and a shiver went down his back. "Wander Section, returning from deep probe and rescue mission into Laagi territory. Five ships with two lost and one sent wide and home, separately. Wander Leader, speaking."

"Wander Leader!" crackled the voice from Picket Six. "Alert has been passed all along the Frontier for you and your ships and orders issued for your return. Congratulations, Wander Section, and welcome back."

"Thanks, Picket Six," said Jim wearily. "It's good to be back, safe on this side of the Frontier. We had half the Laagi forces breathing down our—"

A siren howled from the control board, cutting him off.

Unbelieving, Jim jerked his head about to stare at the telltale sphere. It was filled with the white lights of the ships of Picket Six in formation spread out over a half light-year of distance. But, as he watched, green lights began to wink into existence all about his own battered Section. By sixes, by dozens, they were jumping into the area of Picket Six on the human side of the Frontier.

"Formation B! Formation B!" Jim found himself shouting at the *Lela* and the *Swallow*. But he'd forgotten that *Swallow* had fallen away on the other side of the Frontier, and only the *Lela* was here to respond. The *Swallow,* he knew, was still on its long, drowning fall into nothingness. "Cancel that. *Lela,* follow me. Help me carry *La Chasse*—"

His voice was all but drowned out by transmissions from Picket Six.

"Alert General! Alert General! All Pickets, all Sectors!" Picket Six was calling. "Full fleet Laagi attack. Three Wings enemy forces already in this area. We are overmatched! Repeat. We are overmatched! Alert General—"

At maximum normal acceleration, *AndFriend* and *Lela,* with *La Chasse Gallerie* caught in a magnetic grip between them, were running from the enemy ships, while Jim computed frantically for a jump to any safe area, his fingers dancing on the black buttons.

"Alert General! All ships Picket Six hold until relieved. All ships hold! Under fire here at Picket Six. We are under—" The voice of Picket Six went dead. There was a moment's silence and then a new voice broke in.

"—This is Picket Five. Acknowledge, Picket Six. Acknowledge!" Another moment of silence, then the new voice went on. "All ships Picket Six. This is Picket Five taking over. Picket Five taking over. Our ships are on the way to you now, and the ships from other Sectors. Hold until relieved! Hold until relieved—"

Jim fought the black buttons, too busy even to swear.

"Wander Section! Wander Section!" shouted the voice of Picket Five. "Acknowledge!"

"Wander Section. Acknowledging!" grunted Jim.

"Wander Section! Jump for home. Wander Leader, key for data. Key to receive data, and Check Ten. Check Ten."

"Acknowledge!" snapped Jim, dropping his own slow

computing. He keyed for data, saw the data light flash and knew he had received into his computing center the information for the jump back to Earth. "Hang on *Lela*!" he shouted. "Here we go—"

He punched for jump.

Disorientation. Nausea. And . . .

Peace.

*AndFriend* lay without moving under the landing lights of a concrete pad in the open, under the nighttime sky and the stars of Earth. The daylight hours had passed while Wander Section had been gone. Next to *AndFriend* lay the dark, torn shape of *La Chasse Gallerie,* and beyond the ancient ship lay *Lela*. A hundred light-years away the Frontier battle would still be raging. Laagi and men were out there dying, and they would go on dying until the Laagi realized that Wander Section had finally made good its escape. Then the Laagi ships would withdraw from an assault against a Frontier line that well over a hundred years of fighting had taught was permanently unbreachable by either side. But how many, thought Jim with a dry and bitter soul, would die before the withdrawal was made?

He punched the button to open the port of *AndFriend* and got clumsily to his feet in the bulky suit. During the hours just past, he had forgotten he was wearing it. Now, it was like being swaddled in a mattress. He was as thoroughly soaked with sweat as if he had been in swimming with his clothes on.

There was no sound coming from *La Chasse Gallerie*. Had the voice of Raoul Penard finally been silenced? Sodden with weariness, Jim could not summon up the energy even to wonder about it. He turned clumsily around and stumbled back through the ship four steps and out the open port, vaguely hearing Mary Gallegher rising and following behind him.

He stumped heavy-footed across the concrete toward the lights of the Receiving Section, lifting like an ocean liner out of a sea of night. It seemed to him that he was a long time reaching the door of the Section, but he kept on stolidly, and at last he passed through and into a desuiting room. Then attendants were helping him off with his suit.

In a sort of dream he stripped off his soaked clothing and showered, and put on a fresh jumper suit. The cloth felt strange and harsh against his arms and legs as if his body, as well as what was inside him, had been rubbed raw by what he had just been through. He walked heavily on into the debriefing room, and dropped heavily into one of the lounge chairs.

A debriefing officer came up to him and sat down in a chair opposite, turning on the little black recorder pickup he wore at his belt. The debriefing officer began asking questions in the safe, quiet monotone that had been found least likely to trigger off emotional outbursts in the returned pilots. Jim answered slowly, too drained for emotion.

" . . . No," he said at last. "I didn't see *Swallow* again. She didn't acknowledge when I called for Formation B, and I had to go on without her. No, she never answered after we reached the Frontier."

"Thank you, Major." The debriefing officer got to his feet, clicking off his recorder pickup, and went off. An enlisted man came around with a tray of glasses half-filled with brown whisky. He offered it first to the pilot and the gunner of the *Lela*, who were standing together on the other side of the room with a debriefing officer. The two men took their glasses absentmindedly and drank from them without reaction, as if the straight liquor was water. The enlisted man brought his tray over to where Jim sat.

Jim shook his head. The enlisted man hesitated.

"You're supposed to drink it, sir," he said. "Surgeon's orders."

Jim shook his head again. The enlisted man went away. A moment later he came back followed by a major with the caduceus of the Medical Corps on his jacket lapel.

"Here, Major," he said to Jim, taking a glass from the tray and holding it out to Jim. "Down the hatch."

Jim shook his head, rolling the back of it against the top of the chair he sat in.

"It's no good," he said. "It doesn't do any good."

The Medical Corps major put the glass back on the tray and leaned forward. He put his thumb gently under Jim's right eye and lifted the lid with his forefinger. He looked for a second, then let go and turned to the enlisted man.

"That's all right," he said. "You can go on."

The enlisted man took his tray of glasses away. The doctor reached into the inside pocket of his uniform jacket and took out a small silver tube with a button on its side. He rolled up Jim's right sleeve, put the end of the tube against it and pressed the button.

Jim felt what seemed like a cooling spray against the skin of his arm. And something woke in him after all.

"What're you doing?" he shouted, struggling to his feet. "You can't knock me out now! I've got two ships not in yet. The *Fair Maid* and the *Swallow*—" The room began to tilt around him. "You can't—" His tongue thickened into unintelligibility. The room swung grandly around him and he felt the medical major's arms catching him. And unconsciousness closed upon him like a trap of darkness.

He slept, evidently for a long time, and when he woke he was not in the bed of his own quarters but in the bed of a hospital room. Nor did they let him leave it for the better part of a week. He had had time, lying there in the peaceful, uneventful hospital bed, to come to an understanding with himself. When he got out he went looking for Mary Gallegher.

He located the geriatrics woman finally on the secret site where *La Chasse Gallerie* was being probed and examined by the Geriatrics Bureau. Mary was at work with the crew that was doing this, and for some little time word could not be gotten to her; and without her authorization, Jim could not be let in to see her.

Jim waited patiently in a shiny, unlit lounge until a young man came to guide him into the interior of a vast building where *La Chasse Gallerie* lay dwarfed by her surroundings and surrounded by complicated items of equipment. It was apparently a break period for most of the people working on the old ship, for only one or two figures were to be seen doing things with this equipment outside the ship. The young man shouted in through the open port of *La Chasse Gallerie*, and left. Mary came out and shook hands with Jim.

There were dark circles under Mary's eyes and she seemed thinner under the loose shirt and slacks she wore.

"Sorry to hear about *Swallow*," she said.

"Yes," said Jim, a little bleakly. "They think she must have drifted back farther into Laagi territory. The unmanned probes couldn't locate her, and the Laagi may have taken her in."

Mary looked steadily at him.

"That's what chews on you, isn't it?" she said. "Not knowing if her pilot and gunner were dead or not. If they were, then there's nothing to think about. But if they weren't ... we never know what becomes of them—"

He shook his head at her in a silent plea and she broke off.

"*Fair Maid* made it in, safely," he said hoarsely. "Anyway, it wasn't about the Section I came to see you."

"No." Mary looked at him with a gentleness he had not seen in her before. "It was about Raoul Penard you came, wasn't it?"

"I couldn't find out anything. Is it—is he alive?"

"Yes," said Mary. "He's alive."

"Can you get through to him?—What came to me," said Jim quickly, "while I was resting up in the hospital, was that I finally began to understand the reason behind all his poetry-quoting, and such. It struck me he must have started all that deliberately. To remind himself of where he was trying to get back to. To make it sharp and clear in his mind so he couldn't forget it."

"Yes," said Mary nodding. "You're right. He wanted insurance against quitting, against giving up."

"I thought so. You were right." Jim grinned with a slight grimness at her. "I'd been trying to quit myself. Or find something that could quit me. You were right all the way down the line. I'm a dragon-slayer. I was born that way, I'm stuck with it and I can't change it. I want to go through the Laagi, or around them and end this damn murderous stalemate. But I can't live long enough. None of us can. And so I wanted to give up."

"And you don't now?"

"No," said Jim slowly. "It's still no use, but I'm going to keep hoping—for a miracle."

"Miracles are a matter of time," said Mary. "To make yourself a millionaire in two minutes is just about impossible. To make it in two hundred years is practically a certainty. That's what people like me are after. If we could all live as long as Penard, all sorts of things could be possible."

"And he's alive!" said Jim, shaking his head slowly. "He's really alive! I didn't even want to believe it, it was so far-fetched." Jim broke off. "Is he—"

"Sane? No," said Mary. "And I don't think we'll ever be able to make him so. But maybe I'm wrong. As I say, with time, most near-impossibilities become practicabilities." She stepped back from the open port of *La Chasse Gallerie,* and gestured to the interior. "Want to come in?"

Jim hesitated.

"I don't have a Secret clearance for this project—" he began.

"Don't worry about it," interrupted Mary. "That's just to keep the news people off our necks until we decide how to handle this. Come on."

She led the way inside. Jim followed her. Within, the ancient metal corridor leading to the pilot's compartment seemed swept clean and dusted shiny, like some exhibit in a museum. The interior had been hung with magnetic lights, but the gaps and tears made by Laagi weapons let almost as much light in. The pilot's compartment was a shambles that had been tidied and cleaned. The instruments and control panel were all but obliterated and the pilot's com-chair half gone. A black box stood in the center of the floor, an incongruous piece of modern equipment, connected by a thick, gray cable to a bulkhead behind it.

"I wasn't wrong, then," said Jim, looking around him. "No human body could have lived through this. It was the semianimate control center that was running the ship as Penard's alter ego, then, wasn't it? The man isn't really alive?"

"Yes," said Mary, "and no. You were right about the control center somehow absorbing the living personality of Penard. —But look again. Could a control center like that, centered in living tissue floating and growing in a nutrient solution with no human hands to care for it—could something like that have survived this, either?"

Jim looked around at the slashed and ruined interior. A coldness crept into him and he thought once more of the legend of a great ghost cargo canoe sailing through the snow-filled skies with its dead crew, home to the New Year's feast of the living.

"No . . ." he said slowly, through stiff lips. "Then . . . where is he?"

"Here!" said Mary, reaching out with her fist to strike the metal bulkhead to which the gray cable was attached. The dull boom of the struck metal reverberated in Jim's ears. Mary looked penetratingly at Jim.

"You were right," said Mary, "when you said that the control center had become Penard—that it was Penard, after the man died. Not just a record full of memories, but something holding the vital, decision-making spark of the living man himself. —But that was only half the miracle. Because the tissue living in the heart of the control center had to die, too, and just as the original Penard knew he would die, long before he could get home, the tissue Penard knew it, too. But their determination, Penard's determination, to do something, solved the problem."

She stopped and stood staring at Jim, as if waiting for some sign that she had been understood.

"Go on," said Jim.

"The control system," said Mary, "was connected to the controls of the ship itself through an intermediate solid state element which was the grandfather of the wholly inanimate solid-state computing centers in the ships you drive nowadays. The link was from living tissue through the area of solid-state physics to gross electronic and mechanical controls."

"I know that," said Jim. "Part of our training—"

"The living spark of Raoul Penard, driven by his absolute determination to get home, passed from him into the living tissue of the semianimate controls system," went on Mary, as if Jim had not spoken. "From there it bridged the gap by a sort of neurobiotaxis into the flow of impulse taking place in the solid-state elements. Once there, below all gross levels, there was nothing to stop it infusing every connected solid part of the ship."

Mary swept her hand around the ruined pilot's compartment.

"This," she said, "is Raoul Penard. And this!" Once more she struck the bulkhead above the black box. "The human body died. The tissue activating the control center died. But Raoul came home just as he had been determined to do!"

Mary stopped talking. Her voice seemed to echo away into the silence of the compartment.

"And doing it," said Mary more quietly, "he brought home the key we've been hunting for in the Bureau all this time. We pulled the plug on a dam behind which there's been piling up a flood of theory and research. What we needed to know was that the living human essence could exist independently of the normal human biochemical machinery. Now, we know it. It'll take time, but someday it won't be necessary for the vital element of anyone to admit extinction, unless whoever it is wants to."

But Jim was only half-listening. Something else had occurred to him, something so poignant it contracted his throat painfully.

"Does he know?" Jim asked. "You said he's insane. But does he know he finally got here? Does he know he made it home?"

"Yes," said Mary. "We're sure he does. Listen . . ."

She turned a little away from Jim and spoke out loud, as if Raoul was right around a corner, hiding there in the ship's interior.

"Raoul?" she said.

. . . And softly the voice of Raoul Penard spoke from the ship's hull all around them, as if the man was talking to himself. But it was a quieter, happier talking to himself than Jim had heard before. Raoul was quoting one of the poems of William Henry Drummond again. But this time it was a poem entirely in English and there was no trace of accent in the words at all. . . .

> *O, Spirit of the mountain that speaks to us to-night,*
> *Your voice is sad, yet still recalls past visions of delight,*
> *When 'mid the grand old Laurentides, old when the*
>   *Earth was new,*
> *With flying feet we followed the moose and caribou.*
>
> *And backward rush sweet memories, like fragments of a*
>   *dream,*
> *We hear the dip of paddles . . .*

Raoul's voice went on, almost whispering, contentedly to itself. Jim looked up from listening, and saw Mary's eyes fixed on him with a strange, hard look he had not seen before.

"You didn't seem to follow me, just now," said Mary. "You didn't seem to understand what I meant. You're one of our most valuable lives, the true white knight that all of us dream of being at one time or another, but only one in billions actually succeeds in being born to be."

Jim stared back at her.

"I told you," he said, "I can't help it."

"That's not what I'm talking about," said Mary. "You wanted to go out and fight the dragons, but life was too short. But what about now?"

"Now?" echoed Jim, staring at her. "You mean—me?"

"Yes," said Mary. Her face was strange and intense, and her voice seemed to float on the soft river of words flowing from the black box. "I mean you. What are you going to be doing, a thousand years from today?"

# CHAPTER

## 5

JIM HAD MORE THAN A MONTH OF ACCUMULATED LEAVE TIME coming and he took it. He wanted to go someplace with the feel of hot sand under his bare feet and the smell of sea in the breeze. He wanted to forget about space and about Raoul Penard and *La Chasse Gallerie;* he wanted to forget about the old Canadian poems and songs, and about Mary Gallegher. Above all, he wanted to forget what she had said the last time they had talked. Instead he wanted to fill his mind with wine, women and song. But he lied to himself.

So he went off, relying on sand, salt-smelling breezes and the touch of women to burn all he wanted to forget out of his mind. He went to a place in Baja California called Barres de Hijo and signed in at a resort there. It had everything he was looking for, including charterboat fishing for sailfish and tarpon. It also—or rather the resort hotel he stayed at—had a swimming pool at which he met a fellow vacationer named Barbie Novak, who did fit his ideas of beauty and liked him even better when she found out he was one of the Frontier Guard pilots, on leave.

The days and nights, consequently, were a pleasant blur with Barbie for a companion, until she had to go home; and following that there was a girl named Joan Takari. But the morning after she had left he found himself lying alone on the beach, hoping she had gotten home all right; and he could not remember her face.

So instead of looking around for more women to companion him, he took to sitting and walking by himself, lying on the beach and listening to the waves or seated up on the rocks overlooking a part of the shore that had no beach, watching the surf crash on the blue-black boulders below in white foam.

It was not, he concluded, that he wanted to live forever. But nonetheless Mary's words from their last meeting stuck in his mind. In a way they had taken the place of the emptiness inside him—which was still there, but was now like a dark cavern into which a small aperture had broken, letting in a single ray of light.

He had dreamed of space and wanted it from the first time he had realized it was out there—which was earlier than he could remember. All his life had pointed him at it. It was his arena in which he could do something . . . something of lasting effect. What he would do and how he would do it, he had no idea. But he was like someone who dreams of a much-wanted place, in a mountain so far off it was like a blue cloud on the horizon of his babyhood, but always there, day after day. And one day he had started to walk toward that mountain.

He had had no idea what roads led to it, what waited for him along the way, or how he would find his path and keep from going astray. But he had been determined to keep heading toward it until he reached it; and then he was determined to find on it the place of which he dreamed. It was a case of just always going forward. That way he could never go wrong because all roads led there eventually. All roads, in fact, were one road as long as he kept searching—the Forever Road, he had named it in his mind.

So, he left the resort one morning and went back to the Base, to his duty station, in the mountains outside Denver. When he checked into the Bachelor Officers' Quarters, he found a phone message waiting for him from General Mollen.

"As soon as you get in, call me," the message read.

He did so, and, after a certain length of time got put through to the general.

"Well," said Mollen, "and how was the fishing?"

"Good, sir," said Jim. "I meant to stay longer, but I found I got filled up sooner than I thought, on time off. I want to get back to work."

"Glad to hear it," said Mollen. "And I want to talk to you about that. So why don't we have dinner at the Officers' Club tonight?"

What does a major say when a general invites him to dinner?

"Thank you, sir. I'd appreciate that. When, sir?"

"Nineteen hundred hours. Meet you in the bar."

"Yes sir. Thank you."

Jim had bet himself that the general would be at least fifteen minutes, and perhaps as much as an hour, late. But he, himself, was at the Officers' Club fifteen minutes ahead of the time set, just to be on the safe side. It was a busy part of the day for the bar, and the lounge which held it was full. Jim was lucky enough to get a stool on the curve of the horseshoe-shaped bar that was farthest from the lounge entrance, from which he faced not only that entrance, but beyond it the front door of the Club.

"Good to see you again, Major," said the sergeant on duty behind the bar.

"You, too, Lee," answered Jim. They knew each other; but that particular verbal exchange was routine between the barman and anyone who flew the Frontier, since none of the pilots who did that ever knew for sure that they would see the Club again.

"Ginger ale," said Jim. "On the rocks."

"Coming right up, sir."

Jim sat, sipping the ginger ale, and watching the entrances to the Club and the lounge, for Mollen. Jeremy Tickler, who also captained a Wing on the Frontier and had gone through final training with Jim, came by. They fell into shoptalk.

But it was at exactly 1900 hours that the entrance door opened and Mollen came through.

"—Excuse me, Tick," said Jim, interrupting the other. "Here he is now. I'll see you again, soon."

"We shall wish," said Tickler, who was a little drunk, but who had been told by Jim about the latter's dinner with the general. Tickler lifted his glass to Jim as Jim departed to intercept Mollen.

He caught the general just outside the door of the lounge.

"Oh, you're already here. Good," said Mollen, changing direction. "In that case, let's go right into the dining room."

He led the way to the dining room entrance, where the mess attendant on duty took them to the quiet table in a corner that was of course waiting for the general and his guest.

"I'll have a bourbon. A single-mash bourbon, no ice, no water, no soda, no anything," said the general.

"Yes sir," said the mess attendant and went off, to return with the drink himself in a few minutes. A waiter was at his heels.

"We don't want dinner just yet," Mollen said. He looked over the attendant's shoulder at the waiter. "Come back in about twenty minutes."

Attendant and waiter departed.

"Well, here's to the hope the fishing was good," said Mollen, lifting his glass. Jim drank with him, politely.

They talked fishing until they were halfway through the general's second bourbon; and by the time the first one had been finished, Jim was beginning to be pretty sure that for some reason Mollen was stalling. However, there was nothing much he could do about that but wait for his superior to get to the point.

"—There's Mary Gallegher," the general interrupted himself midway through the second drink. He nodded across the dance floor, which the dining area surrounded.

Jim looked and saw her, just as Mollen had said. She was with some major Jim did not know who was wearing the aiguillette, or dress shoulder cord looped through one epaulet, that marked him as an aide to some high-ranking officer; and the two of them were just sitting down at a table at the dance floor's edge, in plain view.

"She's got a working area of her own on Base here, with *La Chasse Gallerie* and a staff of her own," said Mollen.

"Yes sir," said Jim. They looked away from Mary and her companion and back across the table at each other.

"There's a lot of politics involved in it," said Mollen. He drank from his glass. "Ever have much to do with politicians, Jim?"

"Happily, sir, they're above my range," said Jim.

"Don't be so sure," said Mollen. Below the still-dark hair on his round head, his bulldog face was somber. "Dealing with them's supposed to be above my range, too. But the fact is every one of us is affected by what they do to the Service, generally. In this case, the fact we've got Mary and her lab, as it's called, here on Base is all a matter of politics."

"Is that so, sir?" He had not known anything about Mary and a lab. He was being more polite than anything. It seemed to him the general was still just making conversation.

"Yes, that's so. And it's something that concerns you and me, particularly," said Mollen. "They raised hell with me when they discovered I'd let you go off on leave. Luckily, they were ready to listen when I said that it might attract more attention to call you back, suddenly, than it would be to let you come back in your own time. I didn't think you'd stay much longer than you did, anyway, knowing you."

"Yes sir," said Jim, not understanding this at all.

"Well, I was right. You're back safely and now you're here, I'm afraid you're going to stay here. If you go off Base from now on, it'll be with a couple of Secret Service types riding shotgun on you."

Jim stared.

"Can I ask the general why?"

"I told you. Politics. It just happened that the *Chasse Gallerie* came home through the North American Sector of the Frontier. That makes Raoul Penard and all the potentially valuable scientific possibilities of his existence in the metal of his ship a piece of property belonging to this continent. It also makes him, it, Mary Gallegher—and you—items of considerable potential value to our partners who guard the other Sections of the Frontier. That is, if they know about him yet—but the general feeling is that if any of them don't by now, they will shortly. Also, the general feeling among those few who know about this is that there's too much at stake to take any chances at all. There's the possibility of immortality which Mary may have mentioned to you—or at least a lifetime that isn't dependent on a body that can wear out. But beyond that, there's unlimited possibilities of having ships and other things that don't have to take into account the necessity of being designed to protect the life of a breakable human inside them, while they maneuver at high accelerations."

He took a swallow from his glass. "The war with the Laagi," he said, "may have brought all the nations of Earth into alliance, but the national rivalries are still there, and the business of looking forward to a day in which they'll find themselves competing, once again. So you're all under special guard from now on."

"But all I did was listen to Penard when we escorted him back."

"And saw his ship. And heard him again after he got here. And had Mary Gallegher riding with you, in which case some of her educated understanding of the nature and possibilities of Penard may have rubbed off on you. No, Jim, the people up top, the politicians up where decisions like this are made, have decided you're under wraps from now on; and under wraps you're going to be."

"But I can go off Base, if I want to, as long as some Secret Service people go with me?"

"I didn't say that," Mollen answered. "In fact, I'm not so sure you'll be allowed off under any circumstances, unless it's for something like going to Washington and reporting to the higher-ups; or something of that nature."

"I see, sir," said Jim glumly.

"Brace yourself," said Mollen. "So far I've only shown you the tip of the iceberg. Not only are you going to be restricted in the matter of leaving the Base, your movements and contacts are going to be restricted here on the Base, too. From now on you live in special quarters in that lab of Mary's I was talking about, just as she and her staff does; and during your waking hours I'll be keeping you under my eye, since I'm personally responsible for you."

"But you can't ride with me when I take the Wing out to the Frontier, sir," protested Jim. "It'd be ridiculous, having a general riding as gunner. These people up top you talk about can't expect anything like that."

"They don't," grunted Mollen. "I'm not going to join you; you're going to join me."

It took a long moment for the implications of this remark to sink into Jim's mind. When it did, he stared at the older man.

"Sir? You mean—you can't mean I'm grounded!"

"That's the size of it," said Mollen. "Beginning tomorrow morning you move into an office at my headquarters and behind a desk as Chief of Section."

"But sir," said Jim, "there has to be some other way of

working this. I'm a ship man. I don't know anything about a desk job. Can't I—"

But Mollen was not listening. His gaze was roving the room as if in search of a waiter. There was no waiter to be seen, but in a minute the mess attendant had abandoned his customary post by the entrance to the room and come hurrying over.

"Oh, Sven," said Mollen. "I'm sorry to bother you with this, but would you just step across to Mary Gallegher—you know who she is? Good. Ask her if she'll join us for a few minutes. We won't keep her long. Tell her that."

"Yes, General."

The mess attendant went off. They could see him talking to Mary Gallegher, and a second after, both she and her escort pushed their chairs back and got to their feet.

"Damn it, I don't want her hound dog, too!" said Mollen.

But the major with the aiguillette was simply being polite. As Mary started across the empty dance floor toward them, the major sat down again. Jim and Mollen got to their feet in turn. Mary came up and they all sat down.

"Jim, here, just got back from leave," said Mollen to Mary. "I've been telling him he's going to be housed with you people from now on and ride a desk as Chief of Section. Of course, Jim, we'll be making you a colonel while we're about it."

"If you don't mind, sir, I'd rather stay a major," said Jim.

"Still dreaming of getting back with your Wing?" said Mollen. "Don't worry, if the chance comes, we'll send you back as you are, even if you're the only lieutenant colonel-led, five-ship Wing on the Frontier."

"Thank you, sir," said Jim. But his mind was really not on what the general had just said. He was looking at Mary, who was wearing a light blue cocktail frock with irregularly shaped chunks of aquamarinelike earrings under her reddish blond hair.

The combination became her. She had a good body and Jim found himself once again up against the fact that she was simply not his type of woman. It was just that rectangular face of hers, with its straight bones and her blue-green eyes seemed always to be challenging the world, including him—even when there was no apparent reason.

She was looking tired, though.

"I take it you've been busy," he said to her, for something to say. Mollen had caught a waiter at last and was sending him off for a duplicate of the glass of white wine Mary had been drinking with her major.

"We have," said Mary. "But we're set up now and things are moving. I won't be bothering you too often, but from time to time there'll be parts of the work we'll want to bring you in on, if that's all right?"

"It'll be all right," said Mollen. "More than that, he'll be glad to get away from that desk."

"How's Raoul?" asked Jim.

"Still happy to be back, I think," said Mary. "He doesn't talk as often, anymore, but that's because I think what's left of him in that ship spends most of its time dreaming. You see, we don't have the whole man—I should say we don't have the mind of the whole man, but just the part that wanted so badly to get home. That's one of the things our work's turned up. It isn't necessarily a matter of the whole mind being transferred to something inanimate—"

She broke off. The waiter had just come up with her glass of white wine.

"Thank you."

"A pleasure, ma'am."

". . . You see," she went on, "what we seem to be coming to is the beginning of a theory that could explain a lot that's been part of folklore for centuries, but generally put down to superstition. The poltergeist phenomenon, for example, and haunted houses . . . that sort of thing."

"Tell him why," said Mollen.

She glanced around.

"It's a little public . . ."

"Don't worry. This corner's clean and it's in a scrambler zone. Anyone even three feet from us would hear our voices, but not be able to make out what we're talking about. Also notice the empty tables around us, and the ones beyond that with just one or two officers at each of them, sitting with drinks instead of food. Believe me, we're covered; and I want him to learn this before he steps into that Aladdin's cave of yours."

"If that's what you want—sir." The "sir" was a slight afterthought. Clearly, Mary had not yet acquired an automatic use of military manners. "You see, Jim, we established one thing just by Penard's existence in that ship—the fact that the mind can have an existence away from anything material; though its instinct is to find something material as a vehicle if it can."

Jim nodded.

"But our discovery since then's a blockbuster. It's that the mind, existing separately, doesn't have to be the complete mind. The mind'll go to almost any extremes normally rather than leave the body it first grew in, from the first spark of consciousness in the womb to a full-fledged, unique human or animal individual. In fact, it'll go right up to the point of dying with the body, ordinarily, rather than leaving it. But under certain overwhelming, particular stresses, it or a part of it will leave an intolerable situation. Is what I'm saying making sense to you?"

"You mean do I follow you?" said Jim. "I do."

She made a little grimace of discomfort.

"Please . . . ?" she said.

"Goddamn right!" said Mollen. "Cut out the prickly business, Jim. We've no time or place for that anymore."

"Yes sir . . . I'm sorry," said Jim to Mary. "I really am. I don't know what gets into me sometimes. Go ahead. I'm interested, as well as ready to listen."

"It's most important you understand," Mary said. "I was using the poltergeist phenomenon as an example. Most poltergism has been tied to young females. It's been checked in a number of cases and pretty well taken for granted in the others that the girl causing such phenomena was unhappy. No one I know of ever found a way of measuring how unhappy."

"I'd heard or read something like that," said Jim.

"Well," she said, "Raoul's case gives us a new slant on what might be happening in the case of poltergeist activity if it actually is caused by unhappy, pre-adolescent girls. According to what we've found with Raoul, one possibility is to assume that it's not the whole mind, but just a portion of it, that breaks loose from the rest under the strain of what, to the person involved, is an intolerable situation. This part that breaks loose, not being a full mind, is—effectively—crippled. It reacts like a mindless animal, or like an insane person, simply reacting to whatever triggers it. That's only a guess and it may be completely wrong."

"But it'd make sense," said Jim.

"The same theory could even be pushed to help explain certain types of insanity in general," said Mary. "But that's way out on a limb, and not what we're concerned with first and foremost, which is duplicating the Penard phenomenon. The problem with Raoul is that there's absolutely nothing in the way of previous work or speculation to build on. The most we can find to stand on is the fact that, as his case proves, the human mind's not only able to exist apart from the body; but it can bond to and control material objects. Whether it controls them directly or by means of their own machinery, is a pure guess."

"You mean, whether Raoul's dead mind drove his engines, or he just pushed it through interstellar space by mind-power alone?"

"Maybe he was able to do both," said Mary. "Actually, in Raoul's case, there seems to be some evidence he used his mind alone to move the ship where he wanted. Particularly on the last stages of the trip home, that ship had no ability left to drive itself mechanically. By the way, I wish you wouldn't talk about Raoul as if he was dead. To me, he certainly isn't; or to anyone working with me."

"All right," said Jim.

"You mean, it's not all right at all," said Mary, on what sounded very close to a note of exasperation. "When you set your jaw like that and look nobly at the ceiling, I know exactly what you're thinking. I tell you it's important that those of us working with him—and you're going to be one of those from time to time, though we'll try to disturb you as little as possible—don't think of him as dead, at all; any more than we go around thinking of ourselves as particularly alive. We're just in one state. He's in another."

"He's not a whole mind, I thought, according to what you said," murmured Jim. Nonetheless he was embarrassed. "Sorry again, though. I'll make a point of thinking of him as a living person, all the time, from now on."

"Good," she said. "We'll all appreciate that."

"What exactly," asked Jim, "are you likely to want me to

do? I was saying to General Mollen that I didn't know what use I could be."

"We don't know—yet," she said. "What we're going to be doing is flying blind, trying out first this theory, then that one. On some of the theories we may need your help to test them. For example, one of the things that seems to be deeply involved with what happened is Raoul's literal love for his ship. Would you say you loved your *AndFriend*, Jim?"

The question was asked in a tone that was almost too serious.

"Like a sailor loves his ship. You bet," said Jim. "Possibly even a little more, since *AndFriend*'s practically an extension of my own body when we're out in space together. Maybe it's almost like loving your own dog. Haven't you ever done anything like that, Mary? Loved the first bike you ever owned or some pet you once had."

"No," said Mary. "Loving a piece of machinery sounds almost a little abnormal; and I never was much for having a pet, let alone loving one."

"You said you need me to test these theories?" Jim asked.

"Yes."

"On Raoul?"

"On Raoul. Possibly on you, too, as a sort of control subject since you seem to respond to your ship very much the way he did to his. We can compare reactions and hopefully discover something."

"I thought you said he doesn't talk as much nowadays. Will he answer when you speak to him?"

"We think so, sometimes," Mary said. "It seems to depend on whether what we ask ties in to what he's thinking—or dreaming—about at the time. Sometimes we can recreate a sort of ship-on-the-Frontier situation for him, and that helps us to get through to him and get his cooperation. You may be able to help us in that area."

"I'll do what I can, of course."

"Well, you're due to have dinner; and we haven't had ours yet, either," said Mary. "What about if when you finish, you come over and get me and I'll take you through the lab we've set up?"

"Fine," said Jim.

"Very fine," said Mollen, "because if no one else is, I'm

starving to death. We'll be ordering right away, Mary. Why don't you come over when you're through with your own meal, because my hunch is we'll be finished first."

"All right, if you think that'd be better."

She rose, and they got up with her. She went back across the dance floor and they sat down. The waiter, who seemed to be hovering in the wings, was with them almost as soon as they were reseated.

After Jim and Mollen had eaten, they talked for about half an hour, while Mary and her escort finished their own meal across the dance floor. Happily, it was a weekday night and no band was playing, so that the floor stayed empty and the view clear—though Jim suspected that something would have been organized to let them know how dinner was going at the other table if the dance floor had been full of dancers.

At any rate, after a bit, Mary sat back from her plate, said a few words to the major across from her and got up. She came across and got Jim, and together they walked down the lit streets of the Base and over a few blocks into its older section.

She stopped at one of the older office buildings, a four-story structure of wood, rowed with tall windows, with only a few of them lighted, and one equally tall wooden door, which Mary now unlocked.

Here, they were away from most of the street lights, and it was possible for Jim, when he looked up for a moment before going in, to see the stars over the mountain peaks on this cloudless night. For a second the thought of space tugged at him with a poignancy that was a stabbing pain. Then he followed Mary into the lighted interior, and the door closed behind them.

The room they stepped into was tiny and brilliantly lit. No, it was two rooms; for even its small space was divided, front to back, from beside the entrance to beside a door in the back wall by a floor-to-ceiling transparency behind which was a single desk, a single chair and a single sergeant with holstered sidearm. The feeling of closeness was increased by the bright light, the lowness of the ceiling and a faint smell of varnish.

"Credentials, ma'am? Sir?"

The voice of the sergeant came at them through some speaker system in the roof overhead. Mary fished in the large tan handbag slung by a strap from her left shoulder and produced two silver-colored identification-type cards complete with pictures.

"Thank you, ma'am. Sir."

The door in the farther wall swung open. Mary handed one of the cards to Jim before leading the way farther into the building.

"Here, you'd probably better keep that with you from now on."

Jim took it. The picture on it was the same as that on his regular Base ID. He tucked it in his wallet as he went after her through the door, which closed behind them.

They stepped into an area which to Jim, at first glance, seemed enormous. To his surprise, the wooden front wall of the building, and presumably the side walls also, had been backed by a four-feet thickness of concrete blocks solidly cemented together, so that the effect was like being in some enormous cavern. Lights at some distance from each other were burning three stories overhead, reinforcing the illusion of vast, empty space.

To Jim's left was a chunk of the building still divided into rooms and offices, so that it looked like a tower built inside the cave and going up the full four stories of the original structure. Inside here, all of these enclosed spaces had lights on within them but no sign of people. Mary reached out to the wall beside her and touched it. The existing illumination was suddenly reinforced by a blaze of lights in the open cavern area, not only at the third story level of those now burning, but also now at ceiling level, a story higher up.

The increase in brightness was so intense that for a moment Jim's eyes were dazzled and he saw nothing. Then, looking up, he became aware that in the fourth story of space of the open area hung all sorts of cranes and heavy slings; and the reason for reinforcing the walls became obvious. Support would be needed if instruments like these were going to lift the sort of loads they had been designed to lift.

But it was when he looked down again, at the vast open space of the floor, that he reacted. Because there sat not only *La Chasse Gallerie,* the ship that literally now was Raoul Penard, but beside it another ship that he recognized at first glance.

"You've got *AndFriend* here!"

It came out of him as an exclamation that was magnified by the echoes of the large open space into a shout.

"Of course," said Mary. "Your ship's also part of everything that's concerned with our rescue of Raoul. In a situation where we don't know anything, we work with anything that could possibly help give us a key."

Jim went unthinkingly toward *AndFriend* and laid a hand flat on the polished curve of her nose.

"Is she taking good care of you, baby?" he whispered, too low for even the echoes here to make it audible to Mary Gallegher's ears. He thought he felt reassurance from the metal he touched.

He turned to look at *La Chasse Gallerie*. In contrast with her interior, nothing had been done to repair or even clean her up, outside.

"I suppose," he said over his shoulder to Mary, his voice sounding loud in the stillness in spite of his conversational tones, "you didn't want to risk touching Penard's ship any more than you had to. It looks the way it looked when we first saw it, out beyond the Frontier."

"Yes," said Mary. She had drawn close until she stood only a step from him and his ship and only half a dozen steps from Raoul's. "We had to take some very small lab samples so we'd have something to work on. Otherwise it hasn't been touched."

An intense longing suddenly gripped him to sit once more in *AndFriend's* command chair. He had not seen his ship from the moment of landing with Penard's vessel alongside here at Base. He had tried to get to her half a dozen times, and been turned back with the excuse that *AndFriend*, like *La Chasse Gallerie*, was off-limits until it had been thoroughly checked out by all those departments from Intelligence on down who felt they might have something there to check.

In the same moment he thought he caught a glimpse of something, there and almost instantly gone again, in Mary's eyes as she watched him. What it could have been, if in fact it had not been something he had imagined, he could not tell. It might almost have been a look of pity, except that there was no reason for Mary to look at him that way; and in fact he was not sure she was capable of feeling that particular emotion.

But the longing to sit in the pilot's com-chair again had put him in movement even as he was noticing this. He swung about, walked three steps down *AndFriend*'s side and laid his hand on the operating button of her entry port.

"I'll have a look inside while I'm here—"

"No!" said Mary, so sharply that he stopped in spite of himself.

He swung around to face her.

"It's my ship."

"I'm sorry," said Mary. "But it's part of the red tape—you know how these things are. It hasn't been released for entry by anyone but me and my staff."

She smiled a little sadly at him.

"I'm sorry," she said—and she really sounded as if she meant it. "You know. Orders."

But the Frontier pilots were not book people. If they had been, most of those who had lived would have died before this.

"Orders may be orders," he said lightly, turning back to the button, "still—"

"Still, you'll obey them!" said the voice of Mollen harshly, and Jim swung around again to see that not only the general, but also either the sergeant at the entrance or his double, had together come around the nose of *La Chasse Gallerie*.

Jim's hand fell helplessly at his side.

"I came by to see if you could use a ride back to the BOQ," Mollen went on to him. "You'll be moving into the resident wing in this building tomorrow, but tonight you might as well be in a bed you're used to."

"Thank you, sir," said Jim. He looked at Mary. "If Mary's finished showing me around . . . ? We'd just got in here. . . ."

"I'm afraid there's not much more I can show you, anyway," Mary said. "All the labs are locked and most of the people out of them at this hour. I just thought you'd like to see where your own ship and Raoul's are being kept."

"I appreciate it," said Jim to her. He turned to the general. "Thank you again, sir. I'll come right along."

"Good," said Mollen.

He turned and led the way to the entrance and into the street outside. It was so dark by contrast that for a moment Jim could hardly make out Mollen's limousine, floating just above the pavement, a step from the door. Mary had not followed them out. Mollen gestured and Jim followed him into the back seat.

"Bachelor Officers' Quarters, Building K247," Mollen told his driver. They moved off.

"For God's sake," the general said after a bit, breaking the silence as they drove toward the part of the Base where the unmarried officers were quartered, "don't look like you're going to be shot. I promise, I'll get you back into space, eventually."

Jim looked up, hope waking in him after all.

"It actually is a promise, sir?" he said, and held his breath.

"It's a promise," grunted Mollen. "The only one who'll stop you from getting back into space will be you. But you'll have to stick it out, meanwhile."

"I'll stick," said Jim.

# C H A P T E R

# 6

SO HE BEGAN WAITING IT OUT.

They gave him a first lieutenant and a sergeant who knew everything that was needed to know to keep his office running. There were about fifteen minutes' worth of decisions he had to make daily; after that there was nothing for him to do. He was in Procurement and Supplies, and very junior in that, as far as decisions went, anyway. The paperwork he put his signature to was either for things that obviously had to be ordered, or for things that, if they represented a bad decision, it was a bad decision that would not prove itself to be so for months or even years. He listened to the advice of his lieutenant and his sergeant, especially that of the sergeant, and in consequence he could have done the job in his sleep.

Like all Frontier pilots, he was used to playing hard, fast and furious during his time off. But now, for all practical purposes, almost all his time was time off. He could run, swim, play tennis or golf, go to the gym and work out, or go and camp in the Officers' Club night and day, if that was what he wanted.

He did it all. The Officers' Club was not empty in the daylight hours of the ordinary work week, because there were always people working night and off-shifts of various kinds, and people coming and going from the Base. But by comparison to the 5 P.M. to closing hours, it was deserted. Of course, there were likely to be Frontier pilots in there at almost any time of the night or day; and when he ran into those he had instant companionship.

But his pleasure in even this grew thin. As the weeks went by, and he became more and more removed from his own time of being out on the Frontier, he became less and less one of them. Also, they were out for the same reasons he had been out, to play, to find women and raise hell generally, as a relief from a tension he no longer shared; and he found that what once had been rare and precious, became dull and tasteless when it was available all the time.

He could not go off Base with the other pilots, which cancelled him out of most of their adventures and the chance of finding female playmates, anyway. He learned that Mollen had been only too correct in forecasting that only a need to report to someone in Washington or an equal occasion of duty was considered sufficiently important a reason to allow him past the gates of the Base. And he also found, gradually, that he did not really enjoy being with half-drunk friends before noon, even with his Frontier sidekicks—that he did not enjoy being with them before dinner time—that, indeed, he no longer enjoyed being in the usual sort of Earthside celebration of survival at any time at all. He, at least, had nothing to celebrate.

He became more and more solitary. The physical activities remained open to him, and he found himself retreating more and more into them. He had set himself a solid program of activity to make sure he stayed in physical shape to be let back into space. But with time on his hands, this program expanded. He ran fifteen miles instead of five. Swam five miles instead of one. Worked out on the exercise equipment for two hours instead of half an hour.

At the same time he began to discover an indifference in him to food. He was active enough to want to eat, but from being the satisfaction of a keen appetite, his eating became simply another duty that had to be performed. On paper he stayed in excellent physical shape, but visibly, he began to grow lean and stringy, solitary and withdrawn.

His fellow pilots, led by those who had been in his Wing,

worried about him and tried to come up with ways to lighten his mood. They diagnosed his trouble as being primarily due to a lack of women. Being what they were, with a Frontier pilot's attitude toward rules and regulations, they concocted elaborate schemes to circumvent regulations; and, first, to get him off Base so they could get him to bed with some attractive female; and, second—when he proved to be too tightly under observation for that—to smuggle some likely lady on Base for him and provide the proper quarters and privacy for them.

His lack of enthusiasm for this and their other schemes for him worried them even more. In any case, they were unsuccessful, for he was truly guarded like a national treasure—to which, perhaps, in some minds he was. He had been made lieutenant colonel, as Mollen had promised, shortly after his return with *La Chasse Gallerie*. After a little more than half a year he was promoted to full bird colonel—interestingly, Mollen had become a two-star general just a few months before—and his pilot friends seized the opportunity to put on an elaborate celebration for him at the Officers' Club and in the Bachelor Officers' Quarters.

At this celebration he presided like a ghost at a banquet. In vain they kept trying to spike his ginger ale with vodka and trick him into empty rooms with attractive females who had been given the mission of seducing him.

After that, they pretty well gave up and left him alone. On his part, he increased his solitary exercising and became stringier and more somber than ever.

In fact, they had been using the wrong bait.

His first month after he had moved into the building that held the residence quarters that were part of Mary Gallegher's lab—but completely apart from the lab and served by an entirely separate entrance from outside—he had heard nothing more from her in spite of her suggestion that she might need him from time to time for experimental purposes. At the end of the first month he had felt relieved rather than otherwise. He did not relish the role of laboratory rat.

But when the second month began to trickle away without a summons from her, he began to wait and watch for one. It was not, he told himself, that he had a particular interest in her using him, but that his being called into the laboratory proper where she worked might give him a chance to get to *And-*

*Friend* once again. Finally, toward the end of the second month, a call came, and he reported happily, only to find himself hustled directly up into one of the lab rooms in the inner tower of the building.

He had only a glimpse from a second-story balcony walkway, down into the main open area of the building where he had seen the two ships on his previous visit. To his disappointment, what seemed to be a large tent of opaque plastic fabric had been erected over the section of the floor where they lay, so that he could see nothing of either one of them.

It turned out he had only been wanted to wear his space suit while a couple of Mary's staff made some tests of either him or it— the two women doing it were not informative and he had no idea what they were up to. Being once more enclosed in the suit with its familiar, ancient smells brought on him a nostalgia almost too strong to bear.

After that he was called in about once a week for different tests, but the plastic tent was always in place and he was unable to learn for certain even whether the two ships were there, let alone in the same positions and conditions in which he had last seen them.

The back of his head began to evolve wild dreams in which he somehow got into the lab, stole *AndFriend* and took off into space. Eventually he literally began to dream such dreams, when sleeping. Meanwhile, he was working himself physically to the bone, to pass the days and bring about sleep of any kind—which had been harder and harder to come by, in the same measure as his disinterest in food grew.

He could and did hide from his friends that it was not wine, women and song he needed, but *AndFriend* and space. He was certain he had also hidden it successfully from Mollen, and from Mary—whom, in any case, he had not seen in person since that first night in the lab. What concerned him more was whether he was being successful in keeping the depth of his need hidden from the physician to whom he had to report almost daily.

It was evidently part of the whole package of surveillance, control and so forth set up around him, that his state of health be monitored and recorded on what was effectively a twenty-four hour a day basis. The Medical Officer, also a full colonel, who examined him three times a week or more, was probably the one person to whom Jim talked at all openly.

Part of this was because there was no one else Jim felt safe talking to about himself. The other part was that whatever the physician's actual specialty was—and he had told Jim once, when the visits had first started, but Jim had since forgotten —Jim gradually came to feel that there was something about the other that hinted at a touch of the psychiatrist in him. Not that Jim had any experience with psychiatrists; but there was a way the other man had of listening to him that seemed different from the listening of other doctors to whom Jim had gone.

He told himself he had an unduly suspicious mind. Nonetheless, he found himself saying more than he had intended, so that he was surprised to hear the words coming from his own mouth.

The procedures during Jim's visits were ordinarily routine. Unless there were lab samples to be taken from him, it was merely a matter of Jim's being scanned by a number of esoteric instruments, after which he sat down for a few words with the physician before being turned loose once more.

"You're losing weight again," said the physician, checking through the papers that were the hard copy of Jim's file and lay on the desk before him. He was a tall, gangling man in his early fifties with a high forehead, a straight nose and a surprisingly gentle, small smile that came at unexpected moments.

"All right, Doc," said Jim. "I'll eat more."

The doctor glanced up at him from the papers.

"You could try exercising less," he said.

"And then what'd I do with my time?"

"There's always your job," said the doctor.

"What job?"

The doctor smiled his small smile.

"I don't know what to do with you," he said, sitting back with a sigh. "The first person I've ever treated who tried to kill himself with good health. But, you know, I'm serious about your cutting back on the physical activity."

"For God's sake, Doc," said Jim. "Don't ask me to do that. The only time I can forget about things is when I'm running or swimming or sweating it out to the point where I haven't got any energy left over to think with. I'll get more food down me. I don't mind eating; it's just that it's kind of a chore these days."

The doctor scribbled on a prescription pad, tore off the sheet he had written on and handed it to Jim.

"Take these, two a day, when you get up and when you go to bed," he said. "They ought to increase your appetite."

Jim looked at the piece of paper in his hand, dubiously. He was not a pill-taker by preference.

"It won't make me dopey, will it, Doc?" he asked. "I mean, it isn't some sort of tranquilizer?"

"I guarantee it won't make you dopey. Let's just hope it makes you more interested in food," said the physician. "Well, that's it, then. See you Thursday."

"Right," said Jim, getting up.

He left.

At first it did seem that the pills gave him a little more appetite. At any rate, he made a point of getting more food inside him whether his body craved it or not, and his weight came back up a few pounds. But then he leveled off and stayed where he was on the scale in the doctor's office each time he came in. He suggested once to the doc—since the pills had given him no feeling from taking them at all—that he was willing to up the dosage, if that would do any good.

"I think not," said the physician. "You're taking about what you should of that, right now."

So, he kept forcing the food. It was a problem, because he did not sleep better. Sometime about this period, also, his hours of slumber began to be occupied not so much by dreams of his stealing *AndFriend* and escaping into space, as with nightmares in which the lab suddenly burnt down and people would not let him go in and help keep the fire away from *AndFriend*—which bothered him even though he knew an ordinary fire would not harm the ship. Or he would dream that there had been a sudden earthquake that opened a fissure right under Mary's lab. All that was needed was someone to go in and hook a cable around *AndFriend* to keep her from being dropped into the lava-hot interior of the earth, but they held him back from doing so because it was "too dangerous."

Meanwhile, Mary's staff—he still had not seen her in person since that first visit to the lab—began to call him in more and more frequently. They were on a new kick now, as he entered the ninth month of his captivity on the Base. This one had him still wearing his space suit while listening, over and over again, to the voice recordings of himself, Mary and Raoul Penard when they had taken his Wing out to meet *La Chasse Gallerie* in Laagi territory, and convoy her home here to the Base. When he had listened to it all the way through, they would ask him questions about who had said what to who. It was like being on the witness stand in an endless court trial.

When they got him to the point where he knew the recordings by heart, they switched to having him work with recordings in which one of the voices was edited out, and he spoke the words of that speaker; and it finally ended with him playing, over and over again, the part of Raoul.

They kept it up until, among his other dreams, he began to dream that he actually was Raoul; or rather what was left of Raoul as a mind, locked in the sliced and broken metal that was *La Chasse Gallerie*. Curiously, these dreams were not unpleasant. But finally his appetite gave up for good. He would get to sleep, sleep for about two or three hours, dreaming nightmares, and then wake. Only getting out under the night sky in his running gear and covering four or five miles would rub out the memories of those dreams and let him get to solid sleep for a few hours. He even tried the desperate measure of getting drunk to make himself sleep, but that did not work either.

"Alcohol may help put you out," his doctor told him, "but after a few hours, it turns around and makes you wakeful again."

"I've got to do something. Can't you just give me a sleeping pill, Doc?"

"That's only a temporary solution and this is a continuing problem," said the doctor. "Maybe that medication I gave you for your appetite is working against you now, instead of for you. Let's try taking you off it."

So Jim went off the pills. The first night he slept marvelously, the next night not so well. By the end of a week he was back with the dreams and the starlit runs again. He could feel himself beginning to lose his grip; and he found himself taking it out on the physician in a way he would never have considered doing, a year previously.

"It's this goddamned bird-in-a-gilded-cage life they've got me living!" he said. "I could take it if I could only get a taste, just a taste of space, once in a while. If they'd only let me take *AndFriend* out once a week—once a month, even! If they'd only let me see her!"

"You might be right," said the doctor. "But I don't have any say about that. Have you tried putting in a formal request to visit your former ship?"

"Ever since this thing started. Ten months now!" said Jim. "I put in a written request through channels two and three times a week. All they do is come back disapproved."

"Bring the next one to me. I'll add a letter and sign it," said the doctor.

Jim did.

It came back disapproved.

He called Mollen and was told that the general could not be reached right now, but that his request to talk to the general would be passed on to the general.

Mollen did not call back that day or the next.

Jim called again.

That day Mollen did not call back, either.

Jim called again. Still, there was no call-back from Mollen's office, and Mollen had made no other effort to contact him.

That night, after one more of the innumerable sessions in Mary's lab in which Jim was made again to play through the conversation of Raoul's rescue, saying what Raoul had been heard to say while this was going on, he had a new nightmare.

This time when he was Raoul, however, on becoming aware of *AndFriend* and the rest of the Wander Wing that was convoying him back to Base, he broke off his litany of poetry and recitation.

"No, you don't!" he howled out the earphones of all their suits, swung *La Chasse Gallerie* in a hundred and eighty degree turn and headed away from Earth, back into enemy territory.

The dream changed, without reason but without surprising Jim, as dreams have a habit of doing. He found himself still in his space suit, standing on the observation platform of one of the big command ships on the Frontier, watching in a screen as *AndFriend* drove across into Laagi territory.

"What're you doing?" Jim shouted at the gunnery command officer, standing next to him and also watching. "There's a whole flight of Laagi ships coming up on her!"

"Oh, I thought they told you," the gunnery command officer answered cheerfully. "They were through with her in the lab, so they decided to get some use out of her as an unmanned drone to draw Laagi fire, so we can make a study of how the aliens attack. Look at them now, will you? They're moving in, now. Now they're really starting to slice her up."

"Unmanned? No!" cried Jim. His gaze was back on the screen, which now showed *AndFriend* being killed and destroyed. "Baby, don't just run straight like that. Cut! Cut and run! Fire back. . . ."

In his mind's eye he saw his own empty command chair, with the buttons he could have touched if he was there, the controls he could have used, if he was in the seat. Sweat sprang out all over him; and meanwhile, beside him, the gunnery command officer continued his cheerful chatter about how badly *AndFriend* was being destroyed, as if it was a game, an entertainment. . . .

Jim woke, throwing off the bedcovers in one wild movement. The underwear which years of ship's duty had conditioned him to use as nightwear was glued to him by the perspiration that soaked it. Still caught up in the emotions of seeing *AndFriend* destroyed while he ached to save her, he stripped off the sodden T shirt and shorts and stumbled into the shower to pour gallons of water on his shaking body. After which he dressed in his running clothes and went out under the unchanging stars to run the streets through the Base until he was limp with exhaustion.

The next day he went in person to Mollen's offices.

The general was out, he was told.

He said he would wait.

He was told politely that he was not allowed to wait.

"Then send for the Military Police," he told them, taking a chair, "because I'm waiting!"

He waited. There was a good deal of excitement with officers of various ranks up to and including a one-star general who came and told him he could not stay. He did not answer, merely sat.

Eventually they left him as he was.

The day wore on. No one came out or went in through the door to Mollen's inner, private office. Clearly he was not there. He did not come in from the corridor door, either. The afternoon passed. Jim was not conscious of the hours passing either slowly or fast. It was simply time to be put in. He did not read. He did not think. He simply sat and waited. At last, with the afternoon far advanced, the captain on at the desk in the outer office got up and went out briefly.

When he returned, he was accompanied by two tall MPs with holstered sidearms and the flaps buttoned down. No nightsticks. The captain cleared up his desk. He went out and the door closed behind him. The two MPs took positions, standing one on each side of the closed door. Jim hardly paid them any attention.

Together the three of them spent the night. On the rare occasions when Jim got up to go to the men's room down the corridor, one of the MPs went with him and came back with him. Toward morning, Jim may have dozed in his chair. But he was not conscious of having slept, and if he had, he had not dreamed while he was asleep.

At dawn two other MPs replaced the Military Police who had been there all night. One of them brought a plastic cup of coffee and put it on the chair next to Jim's. Jim looked at it and realized he was thirsty. He drank it; but he could not have said, a second after finishing it, whether it had been black, or whether it had had cream and sugar in it.

A little before 7 A.M., the corridor outside began to sound with the feet of incoming workers. At a little after seven, the corridor door opened between the two MPs and Mollen strode in, followed by the same captain who had sat at the outer desk yesterday.

Mollen jerked his head at Jim.

Jim got to his feet, awkwardly. He was dully surprised to find how stiff his body was after his long sitting. He followed the general into the private office.

This office had padded armchairs before its one large desk. Mollen took the chair behind the desk and gestured Jim to one of the facing, padded ones.

They looked at each other.

"Well?" said Mollen. "You ready to go back into space again?"

Jim stared at him dumbly and the silence lengthened out between them, until Jim realized that the question had been for the record. And for the record, which was undoubtedly a voice and picture recording going on at the moment, he would have to give an answer.

"Yes sir," he croaked.

Mollen opened the wide drawer in the middle of his desk, fished around and came up with a document that seemed to consist of half a dozen or so sheets of paper, heat-stapled together. He passed it across to Jim.

"Sign this."

Jim took it and blinked at it. He tried to read through it, but his brain was almost as numb as his body. It read something like the document he had been required to sign upon getting his commission, about the Official Secrets Act and penalties for his disregarding it. Essentially these papers before him, once signed, put him completely at his government's disposal —which seemed like doing the thing twice-over, since as a Frontier pilot he was already the government's, to use or throw away.

In any case, it did not matter. *AndFriend* and space were all that mattered. He signed it with a pen the general handed him and passed both pen and document back. Mollen waved it for a second in the air.

"You can have another look at the file storing this any time you want to," the general said, "unless you ever become a civilian again or you're put on a different status. Then that file'll be closed to you. Understand?"

"I understand, sir."

"Good." Mollen's voice became more gentle. "From now on you report every morning to the lab proper—Mary's work area. For now, for God's sake get back to your quarters and get some sleep."

# CHAPTER

# 7

JIM DID GO BACK TO HIS QUARTERS. AND HE DID SLEEP—FOR about seven hours. At the end of which time he woke up feeling terrible generally, but very happy for reasons he could not, in the first minute or two, remember. Then he recalled the long wait in Mollen's office and what had happened after the general had showed up; and his sensations of feeling terrible settled down to the recognition that he was merely very hungry, ready to eat anything digestible—in large quantities.

He checked his wrist-com. It was midafternoon. He got up, showered, dressed and went to the Officers' Club, where he found the menu available at that hour to consist only of sandwiches. He proceeded to eat perhaps a dozen of these and wash them down with several bottles of ginger ale—no great amount, but the food and drink together in his stomach acted on him like knockout pills. He made his way heavily back to his quarters, undressed and fell asleep again . . . and this time he slept until after five-thirty the following morning.

His body had become used to running. It wanted to get out and move, but he was once again as hungry as a bear in spring. He had breakfast, put aside the desire to run and went directly to Mary's lab.

"Credentials, sir?"

It was a different face beyond the transparency, but the uniform and the routine were as usual. Except that this time, for the first time in months, there were no lab workers waiting to take him off for their eternal tests. He showed his credentials.

"You'll have to wait for the Head of Lab, sir. If you'll take a seat, she ought to be here in the next ten or fifteen minutes," said the guard.

He found a hard seat on a bench built into the wall across from the transparency. He grinned. From cooling his heels in Mollen's outer office to cooling his heels in Mary's surveillance entrance. That was progress.

It was, however, nearly three-quarters of an hour before Mary showed up. Jim did not care. He was this far and he did not intend to move unless they carried him out. When at last Mary did come in from the street, she had Mollen with her.

"Told you he'd be here at the crack of dawn!" said Mollen. If Jim had not been feeling so happy, he might have allowed himself a small sense of injury. Dawn had been a good three hours earlier.

"I'm sorry I haven't had more time to talk to you myself all these past months," Mary said directly to Jim. She looked at him, he thought, sympathetically. "You've lost weight."

"Nonsense!" said Mollen. "He's in top shape. Aren't you, Jim?"

"Yes sir. Top shape," said Jim. He grinned at Mary. Today he even loved her.

"Come along." Mary and Mollen showed their credentials to the guard in movements that betrayed an infinity of repetitions.

"Please go on in, ma'am, sirs."

Mary led them through the inner door, and for the second time Jim stepped into the enormous room that he had looked down into only from galleries for nearly twelve months. It was the same as it had been, the last time he had seen it. The plastic tent was still in place. But Mary led them to it, pulled back a flap of the plastic and let them into the enclosed interior which was lit by its own lamps hanging just under the fabric of its roof.

By that light, the two ships Jim had seen on his first trip here still lay, side by side. *La Chasse Gallerie* was still a slashed and broken wreck. *AndFriend* was also exactly as she had been when he had last seen her. Or was she? She looked the same but there was an air about her as if she had just been washed or, at least, dusted.

All Jim's emotions called on him to head for her closed entry port at a run. But he was almost superstitiously afraid of something going wrong with his new right of access to her if he even showed his eagerness to be back inside her.

"She looks good," he commented, stopping because Mary and Mollen had both stopped, a good ten paces from either ship.

"She's been updated," said Mollen. "You're going to have to learn a lot of new things about her. And no, you can't go aboard her now."

Jim had half-expected it, but the disappointment nonetheless was like a fist, hard, in the face.

"Oh?" he said. "When can I, then, sir?"

He looked at Mollen and then at Mary.

"You'll need some retraining first. We've got a special job for you to do," Mary answered. "That's one of the reasons *AndFriend's* been improved the way she has. I'm afraid it could be a few weeks or more yet—"

"A few weeks!" In spite of his good intentions, the words, in just the tone he had told himself he would avoid, popped out of Jim's mouth.

"I'm afraid so." Mary turned. "Come along to my office, where we can talk."

They went out through a flap in another side of the tent and crossed the open floor to the bottom level of offices in the tower. Mary entered one of these, which had a trim, white-haired lady behind a desk, and chairs set up plainly for visitors, chairs which were presently empty.

"There've been a number of phone calls," said the lady.

"No calls for a little while yet," said Mary. "Tell anyone with urgencies it'll be an hour or so before I can start making calls back. Come on, Jim, General."

She led them to an inner office which was spacious, with a desk even larger than Mollen's and padded chairs even more comfortable and spacious than those in the general's office. But every available surface in the office except the floor itself was stacked with papers, and the chairs did not face the desk as they had in Mollen's private office, but were in a rough circle facing each other.

Mary took one of these, the general slipped into the one next to her, and Jim took one across from the two of them.

"Do you want to talk to him first, Louis?" said Mary to the general. "Or shall I?"

"I'll say a few words first," Mollen answered. He looked hard at Jim. "Jim, we've got plans to send you into space farther, faster, and for a longer time than anyone human—except Raoul—ever went. But it's not going to be easy."

"I didn't sign up for the Frontier thinking any part of it'd be easy, sir," said Jim. "Where's this you want me to go?"

"That, you won't be told until just before you're ready to leave," said Mollen. "But I'll tell you this much. You're going out around Laagi territory, and your ship's been adapted accordingly. For one thing we've gone back to fusion engines for her."

"Fusion?" said Jim.

Fusion engines had been discarded nearly forty years before when an improved fission engine design made them no longer necessary. The drawback to fusion engines was that there was no possible way to shield them completely in something as small as a fighter ship; they had caused some bad physical effects in the pilots that flew ships with them, the least of which had been guaranteed sterility after a relatively few number of missions.

"You're going to make a Raoul Penard out of me, then, are you, sir?" said Jim, grinning.

"I wish we could," answered Mollen somberly. "Believe me, if it was possible for me to snap my fingers and turn you into something like Raoul, I'd do it. But we still don't know how his mind got into the actual nonliving body of that ship of his, and maybe we'll never know."

Jim himself sobered. He had automatically assumed that they would not be sending him out in a fusion ship unless they could do so safely, without the harmful effects the older ships of that type had had on their pilots. For the first time it occurred to him that the mission might be important enough so that they would expect him to put up with the effects. He thought of the paper he had signed in Mollen's office.

"It's not as bad as you may be thinking, Jim," said Mary.

"We haven't found out how Raoul Penard became part of a ship, and I don't know when we will. I'm sure some people will someday—that is, provided Raoul stays around long enough. But while we haven't answered that question, we've found out a number of valuable things we didn't know before. Things that'll make your mission possible."

"What things?"

"I'm sorry," Mary answered. "I'm going to have to answer you pretty much the way Louis just did, when you asked where you'd be going. You'll get answers to most questions like that only when you've reached the point of needing to know. Everything about this is as secret as it's possible to make it. Specifically, in answer to what you just asked, you'll be finding out about these things as we work with you to get you ready for the mission."

"I can tell you a little more," said Mollen. "Most of the past year's been spent trying to find out what happened to Raoul from the last time the other pilots in his Wing saw him to the time we picked up his signals coming back through Laagi territory. But we know now he found something, in that time. Wherever he went, he ended up by finding something very interesting there; and our guesses about what it is are secret as hell. But we're pretty sure it's beyond the far side of Laagi space territory—in the other direction. Down-galaxy."

"And I'm to go see what it was and come back to tell you?" Jim said.

"That's about the size of it," said Mollen. "Something else. We can't be sure, but we think he was—that is, *La Chasse Gallerie*, with him being part of it, was—actually in Laagi hands for a while."

"They had him?" Jim stared. "What makes you think that?"

Mollen looked at Mary, who nodded. A procedure that jarred on Jim, slightly, since it seemed to him it should be the other way around.

"We've found a route of communication, so to speak, with him, with Raoul," Mollen said. "Or rather, with what there is of him, which is mainly memories. The problem's been that he suppressed the bad memories and remembered only the good ones. But Mary's people did finally find a way to stimulate him to remember some of the things he'd rather forget—

and one of those was of being on the surface of a planet, and examined by Laagi."

Mollen stopped, and looked at Mary again. She took over the conversation, briskly. "Possibly they had him on show there, in a sense. At any rate, we finally got him to reminisce about it, but what we could learn was limited. The trouble is, as you know, the part of his mind that came back isn't capable of direct communication. The best we can do is stimulate him to talk out loud to himself. So the most we achieved that way was to prod his memory about this, and listen while he relived it, in his own mind."

"But that could be quite a bit," said Jim.

"It was. But with parts missing. Tantalizing parts," Mary said.

The arch of her eyebrows straightened out as the inner ends of them came together in a small frown when she concentrated. Jim had had a third grade teacher who had done the same thing.

"He was talking to himself, so he only referred to things that happened. He didn't describe them or spell them out in any way. We can be fairly sure that for a while at least, he was essentially a Laagi prisoner. They'd be as fascinated as we are with the question of how a ship could absorb the mind of its pilot. They're probably the ones who removed his dead body for examination. Which means that now, if they didn't before, they're one up on us by knowing what we're like physically; and, since Laagi ships always destroy themselves if it looks like they're going to be captured, we still don't have any idea of their physical make-up."

"But you said he got away from them," prodded Jim, more interested in what Raoul had done than in what the Laagi might have found out about him.

"Well, probably," said Mary, "they didn't realize he could move the ship with his mind alone—and that's something else we also haven't yet found out; how he could do that. But his engines had almost certainly been destroyed before the Laagi got him; and so it undoubtedly took them by surprise when he suddenly simply decided to go home, lifted off from wherever he was, and headed back."

Jim shook his head.

"This . . ." he began and ran out of words. "How does this all tie in with me?"

"As I say," said Mary, "we've found a way to stimulate his memory. . . ."

She touched one of the keys on her desk top console and they heard sounds of bird songs, leaves rustling in the wind, branches creaking against each other and, under all, the chuckling of running water.

"What we did was record noises from up around the part of Canada where he grew up as a boy," she said. "It was a sort of sonic, or if you like the word better, electronic way of medicating him, so he'd tell us what he remembered. From what we heard, we isolated more and more sound-cues until at last we were able to trigger off memories like the one that we think refers to his being in Laagi hands."

Jim nodded, still unsure about what this might have to do with him.

"We'll be using a developed version of the same techniques to put your mind as much in touch with his as possible," Mary went on.

"We want you to be able to think like Penard—think as if you were him," said Mollen.

"At the same time," said Mary, "we're going to use a variant of the same techniques to put your mind and mine as much in touch as possible. Now, with living human bodies like the two of us have, we can be given chemical medication by already established means—"

She broke off, pressed a button of her desk console and spoke into the communications grill beside the console.

"Ola," she said, "has Dr. Neiss come in yet?"

The voice of the white-haired lady said something unintelligible from the grille.

"Dr. Neiss?" said Mary sharply. "He's not there yet?"

More unintelligible response from the grille.

"Well, call me when Dr. Neiss gets here." Once more the emphasis on the title of "doctor" could be heard in Mary's voice. "Thanks, Ola. Yes. No, that's all right. Just remember to announce him as I said."

She looked from the grille back at Jim and Mollen.

"Dr. Neiss is someone you'll meet in a moment, Jim. He'll be taking care of you from now on. You go to him for anything medical—even if it's just a finger you cut on a piece of paper opening an envelope."

"You hear that, Jim?" said Mollen. "That's an order. Come to think of it, you'd better remember that anything Mary tells you to do from now on has the effect of a military order from me."

"Yes sir," said Jim. "But—"

He broke off, went back and tried again.

"Forgive me," he said to Mary, "but I don't understand why you and I need to have our minds put together, or however you say it?"

"Simply so I can monitor your contact with Penard as fully as possible—" She broke off as the speaker grille on her console made noises again.

"Yes?" Mary said. "Well, send him in, then."

The door from the outer office opened and a short, thin man in his late twenties or early thirties, with straight black hair and a sharp face, walked into the office. He leaned a little forward with his upper body as he walked, as if he would pugnaciously make the most of his height.

"This is Dr. Amos Neiss," said Mary. Jim got to his feet, uncertain as to how he should greet the newcomer. Neiss came up to him and they shook hands. Neiss's grip was firm and energetic to the point of nervousness, like the rest of his appearance.

"So you're Jim Wander," Neiss said. His voice had a slight upper East Coast edge to it.

"That's right," said Jim.

They sat down, Neiss in the chair at Jim's right.

"I take it we're ready to go, then?" Neiss asked Mary.

"Ready, yes," said Mary. "That doesn't mean we can start in the next five minutes—"

The speaker grille interrupted her again.

"Oh yes," said Mary to it. "I forgot to tell you I'd asked him to come in this morning, too. Send him in."

The door opened once more. This time the man that came in was large-framed and a little overweight, even for his size. His face was square and blunt-nosed, under graying brown hair.

"Colin, take a seat, will you?" Mary said, with more warmth in her voice than when she had introduced Neiss.

"This is Jim Wander. Jim, this is Colin Eastoi. He'll be sitting at my desk here while I'm spending time working with you and the doctor."

Colin walked heavily over to shake hands with Jim and take the chair on Jim's other side.

"So," he said. He had an unexpected bass voice that seemed at odds with his easy-going face. "We're all ready to start?"

"That's what Amos was just asking," answered Mary. "So I'm glad you're here. How soon can you pick up the reins for me?"

"Right this moment, if you want," said Colin. "My department's been running itself for the past few weeks. Oh, you'll have to bring me up-to-date on the last twenty-four hours or so, I suppose, if there's things there I've got a need to know."

"We can do that the rest of today," said Mary. "Tomorrow—"

She switched her gaze to Amos Neiss.

"—we'll begin the lab work, Jim and I, with you," she said.

"I could make some preliminary tests on Colonel Wander today," said Neiss. "That way—"

"No, I don't think so," said Mary. "He's a human being and he needs a little time, just like the rest of us, to make the transition. What you can do is have lunch with him and lay out our work schedule for him, so if he has any suggestions, he can make them. Jim—you've got to give this work your wholehearted efforts. So if there's something about what Amos has in mind you don't like, tell us; and if it's adjustable, we'll adjust it. You remember that, Amos—we tailor around Jim, not around me, let alone around you and your staff."

"Whatever you say," said Amos.

Jim was watching the other man out of the corner of his eyes. Amos Neiss's general appearance and the tone of his voice did not promise as easy an agreement as his words did.

"Then," said Mary—she looked at Mollen—"as far as I'm concerned, we can break up this meeting. General?"

"Fine, far as I'm concerned," Mollen grunted, getting to his feet. He was looking more tired than Jim had ever seen him look, and older.

So Jim spent the morning happily running and working

out, topping it all off with a game of handball. Then, feeling full of glowing good health, he went off to the Club to lunch with Amos Neiss.

He was more than a little curious about the man, under whose auspices, apparently, both he and Mary were to be put through a training period. But when he actually came to the lunch he found Amos Neiss as sharp-faced as ever and concerned with talking about only one topic—the things he would require of Jim.

"You've got it all straight, then?" said Neiss after what amounted to a monologue, and which had lasted through the main course of the meal to the point where they had just ordered dessert.

"Right. There's only one problem," Jim said. "You'll have to make some time for me each day, for exercising."

"Exercising? Well," said Neiss, "well, I suppose. We could give you an hour before we begin in the morning."

"I'll need more like three hours," Jim said. He knew a bargainer when he met one.

"We can't possibly let you play for that much time," said Neiss. "You don't understand how crucial these tests and routines are. Oh, by the way, speaking of tests, I talked to Mary this morning after you left. You can come in after we leave here and we can use this afternoon to get some of the tests done for your preliminary profile—"

"Oh? Fine," said Jim. "Would you excuse me for a minute? I just remembered I forgot to tell the switchboard operator at the front desk of the Club that I'd be here in the dining room. I'm expecting a call. It may have come, and there may be a message for me there. Be right back."

He got up and vanished before Neiss could object. Outside the dining room, however, he headed for a row of phones, and put through a call to Mary's office.

"I'm sorry, Colonel, she's at lunch," said the voice of the white-haired lady.

"Look," said Jim, "just in case she's there and just not taking calls, will you tell her it's vital I speak to her now? This is Jim Wander. She knows I wouldn't call like this without good reason."

"Well . . . just a minute. . . ."

Silence took over at the far end of the line. The screen that had lit up to show the white-haired lady went suddenly back to a silvery-gray opaqueness. Jim waited.

Abruptly the screen cleared to show the face of Mary.

"What is it, Jim?" She sounded annoyed.

"Amos Neiss just told me that you'd agreed with him he could start making some tests on me this afternoon. I just thought I'd check and make sure you actually did agree. He was careful not to say specifically that he'd got your permission."

"Oh, he told you that, did he? Damn him!" said Mary. "This is one thing he's going to get straight right from the beginning. Where are you now?"

"Still at lunch in the Officers' Club. At the phones. I left him at the table and told him I had to go look for a message for me at the front desk."

"Good. When you get back to the table, tell Amos they also told you there was a message for him to call me."

"I'll do that."

"Fine. And do what you want this afternoon. That's from me!"

"Thanks," said Jim.

Mary broke the connection and he went back to Neiss.

"Oh, by the way," he said, sitting down. "There was a message there for you, too. You're to call Mary at the lab, immediately."

"Oh my God!" said Neiss, jumping to his feet. "Something wrong with the equipment? Did she say?"

"I don't know," said Jim innocently. "There was just the message to call her."

Neiss went out of the dining room literally at a run. When he returned he was not exactly scowling, but he was not happy.

"It looks like we'll have to put off those tests on you this afternoon after all," he said abruptly, sitting down again.

"Ah," said Jim.

Amos looked at him. It was not a friendly look, but the unfriendliness was impersonal, the way a bear stung by a deer fly will turn and clout the bear eating blueberries next to him.

They began in earnest the next day. Apparently, Neiss needed, or at least wanted, a complete physical report made on Jim by his own staff. He was not interested when Jim volunteered the information, as he did once, that most of these scans and examination of physical samples from him merely duplicated what the Medical Section of the Base kept up-to-date on all Frontier pilots, active or inactive. The first few days were given completely over to simply testing Jim. If they tested Mary equally, they did it somewhere else and with a different team. Neiss's staff seemed fully occupied with Jim.

But once the testing was over, they got down to work. To Jim's surprise, this turned out to be the same old business of rehearsing what had been said by Penard, Mary and himself on the mission to convoy Penard home. Only this time, when Jim spoke his own words as they had been taped, Mary was there and also spoke hers. The only voice that was not live was that of Raoul.

Jim had no great objection to this, now that he was close to being reunited with *AndFriend*. But he did object—without success—when Amos began a different stage of work in which he and his staff occupied themselves with Jim alone, and used drugs. They were, apparently, now that they had finished building a physical profile of him, engaged in building a mental one.

This consisted of electrically probing his brain cells for reflexes and memories, and of searching his unconscious, particularly his dream patterns. Jim found himself hating the thought that someone like Amos had access to his mind and could see the evidence of his love for *AndFriend* and space. Also, the business of using the drugs was itself unpleasant. Jim did not like pills, and being under their influence. He liked injectable chemicals even less; and many of the unnamed substances Amos's staff put into his bloodstream or flesh had side effects that clouded his mind or disorganized his body for up to twenty-four hours—and on rare occasions, even longer.

He had been allowed an hour and a half in the morning by Mary for his physical conditioning, plus as much of his free time as he wanted to use for it. The latter allowance was really the best, because Mary was adamant, even in the face of disagreement by Mollen, against the idea of working Jim any more than an ordinary eight hours a day. And evidently she had the final say in such matters, for Jim found himself turned loose at no later than five o'clock every evening.

He still could not leave the Base without special permission, which was just as hard to come by. But he had, if he wanted, enough evening hours to satisfy anyone, as he thought. The only drawbacks were the side effects of the drugs, which sometimes made him unable or unwilling to exercise in the evening hours as usual, plus something he had not expected.

That was that it was he, now, who hated to waste the hours exercising. He no longer wanted to kill time; he wanted to get a particular task done as swiftly as possible, and that particular task was the business of finishing the training that Mary, Mollen and the rest required of him.

The shape of the work was beginning to become apparent to him. He was, indeed, beginning to feel closer to Penard every day. It was not so much that he was establishing an identity with the mind of the man in *La Chasse Gallerie*—to whose audible wanderings, received from a voice transmitter that had been set up in place of the one that no longer existed in the torn ruins of the fighter ship, they now let him listen regularly. It was more as if it was beginning to be that he and Raoul were alone together in a universe of other people who did not understand; and it seemed to him, from time to time, that he comprehended things in what Raoul said of which none of the others listening were aware and for which there were no words.

# C H A P T E R

# 8

SHE LIKED WALNUTS, SLEEPING LATE IN THE MORNING, ALMOST any chicken dish, horseback riding, poetry, candlelight, Mozart and Prokofiev among classical composers, Degas and Chagall among classical painters—also the pointillist painters in general. She did not like green peppers, steak (much), most abstract art, music playing while she worked—or any distraction, however slight, from the task at hand—and any failure to get things correct.

She also, Jim thought, was in love with Raoul but recognized the emotion as a hopeless one. If she was in love, it was with the image of a man she had largely fashioned for herself from the sound of his voice and the choice of the poetry he quoted. All these understandings came to Jim little by little as he and Mary worked together, or were worked together under the direction and treatments of the staff of Amos. They came not as something directly sought for by Mary, Amos, or even by himself, but as inevitable bits of knowledge unavoidably attached to information about her understanding of Penard and her own field of work—all of which it was necessary that he come to know.

The result was that somewhere along in the process he found he had completely ceased to dislike her. He still felt no great kinship for her, but there was a sympathy for her in him that he would not have thought possible before he staged the sit-in in Mollen's outer office.

What she had deduced about him he had no idea and felt that he would rather not know. At least, he felt he could trust her to keep the information to herself, as he would keep the information he had gained about her to himself.

It was a silent pact that both recognized and which drew them closer together. Another cause for a bond between them grew from their habit of having lunch together—just the two of them. The announced reason for this, by Mary, was so she could continue briefing Jim on some of the matters that were secret even from Amos and his staff. The unofficial reason, clearly understood by Jim, was to give them both a break from the company of Neiss, who, though he probably could not help it, seemed to have an irritating effect on anyone with whom he came in contact.

This personality quirk in Neiss was one of the topics they talked about, one day in the third week of their lunching together in Mary's quarters, which were spacious enough, and evidently designed to be able to, hold official entertainment functions.

". . . All he has to do," said Mary, "is stop pushing people around for five minutes. Give them a chance to relax."

"He doesn't dare, I think," said Jim. "I'll bet he'd scare himself to death if he didn't keep the pressure on himself, as well as on everybody else, all the time. My guess is he doesn't feel safe unless he's being aggressive."

"A little aggressiveness is all to the good in just about everyone," said Mary. "A little more than a little, you can put up with. But he'll wear you down, just defending yourself."

"Unless he wears himself down first," said Jim. "You're the one who gets the brunt of it."

"Because I'm a woman," said Mary moodily.

"Because you're his superior," said Jim. "I think it's more than that, than your being a woman."

"Because I'm a woman and his superior," said Mary. "One compounds the other as far as he's concerned. But you seem to be able to disarm him, almost. He picks on you, but only as if from a sense of duty."

"I let a lot of what he does bounce off. That robs him of the emotional reward, and tires him out," said Jim. "You can exhaust yourself a lot faster punching hard at thin air than you can punching something solid."

"And it doesn't take it out of you?" She looked keenly across the small table between them.

"A little," said Jim. They were getting uncomfortably close to the fact that he would put up with anything to get back into space, even if the anything consisted of a platoon of Amos Neisses taking turns working him over. He suspected Mary knew this, just as he had come to know things about her.

"When can I see *AndFriend* again?" he asked.

"Taking a page from Amos's book, are you?" Mary deliberately helped herself from a dish on the table, offered it to him, then pulled it back. "That's right, you don't like broccoli."

"When can I—"

"You can't, not now or for some time to come," said Mary flatly. "There're reasons. I can't tell you why you can't. I'm sorry. If there weren't reasons, you could see her this minute."

"What do you want from me?" Jim heard the weariness in his own voice. "I know everything Raoul said forward and backward. I know everything you said, and I said, after we picked up the *Chasse Gallerie*. I know as much about what you'd want done with anything I might find as you do, yourself. When does this stupid business of drug, drug, drug and question, question, question, stop?"

"You love that ship," said Mary.

"You know that already," Jim answered.

"Would you die for her?"

The question caught Jim unprepared. He floundered in silence for a moment.

"Die for her?" he echoed finally. "If you mean if some idiot was trying to blow her up or some such thing, would I take a risk to try to stop him? Sure, I would! But how do you die for a ship? There isn't any way to do anything like that."

Mary nodded. Which, Jim thought, was no kind of answer at all.

"Well, tell me!" he said. "Is there some sort of danger to *AndFriend*? What're you talking about?"

"No. And I won't talk about it anymore, either," she said.

"I've got your answer; and for any more information, you're going to have to wait."

And, true to her word, she refused to say any more on the subject.

That one question of hers, however, had the effect of unlocking the door to the closet of Jim's anxieties all over again. For some time he had been conscious of a growing, nagging discomfort. He had assumed when Mollen had told him that he was to be given a chance to get back into space that it would be only a matter of time before he was there. And he had assumed after being let in to see *AndFriend* that first morning with Mollen and Mary that from this point on he would no longer be refused access to the ship.

But he had been. He had not been let inside the tent that hid her, since. Gradually, in consequence, he had begun to slip back into the state of mind he had been in before he sat down in Mollen's outer office and refused to budge; only now the state was worse because the effects of the drugs they were always pumping into him made him imagine and dream more vividly than ever.

His nightmares began to return. His appetite went, then his sleep began to suffer; and this time all his running, swimming and other activity brought him no relief. A worry about *And-Friend* grew in the back of his mind and stayed with him, awake and asleep.

He began to fumble his answers and forget things during the sessions with Mary and Neiss's crew. A new fear awoke in him and grew. It was a fear that somehow he had become unfit, or was in the process of becoming unfit to take a ship like *AndFriend* into space—let alone beyond the Frontier.

He got into a blazing argument one lunchtime with Mary in her quarters, as a result.

"Of course I'm not doing well!" he shouted at her. "I had about three hours of real sleep last night. That was all. If you'd let me at *AndFriend*, or at least give me some idea of what all this is about, maybe I could sleep nights. You and Neiss—yes, and Mollen, too—are deliberately wrecking me in the name of trying to build me into something. What? And why? Goddamn it, tell me why! Tell me!"

He heard himself repeating the words like a three-year-old

in a tantrum and with a great effort made himself stop. Mary was sitting across the table looking at him.

"And don't look at me like that!" he broke out all over again. "What's the use of looking at me as if you feel sorry for me, when you're the one who's putting me through it? I went a year—almost a year—before you even got me into this present crazy program. We've been at it three months, and I'm worse off than ever, and I can't see where you've got a thing from me to pay for it."

He was shaking, shaking all over.

"Either let me in on what's up or turn me loose," he said. "One way or another."

"And what would you do if we turned you loose?" asked Mary softly.

"Probably blow my brains out!" He slumped in his chair. "How do I know what I'd do? I don't know anything anymore. I hardly know who I am; and in a couple more weeks or months I won't even know that!"

He stopped talking. Mary said nothing; they sat in silence, while the fury gradually drained out of him and the shaking slowed into stillness.

"I know what we're putting you through," said Mary at last, gently. "I know it. Louis Mollen knows it—and we both hate it. Amos doesn't hate it, of course. He's not capable of seeing you as anything but a lab animal. But Louis and I—you may not believe this, but it's the truth—have been suffering right along with you from the start. Believe me, we're doing this because we've got no choice. Can you believe that?"

"Not really," he said dully. "It's gone on too long."

"See if you believe this, then," she said, "and in telling it to you, I'm breaking security, because I'm telling you more than you realize. It's been necessary to bring you right up to the breaking point—and you haven't broken easily. But the human mind can only take so much . . . and now I think you've had it."

He stared at her. It was more nonsense.

"What I'm saying is, hang on a little longer. Hang on to your sanity. It won't be long, now."

He did not know whether to believe her or not; but in fact, there was no place else for him to go, nothing else for him to do but keep on with her, with Neiss and the whole business. But it not only continued as if she had never given him any promise of the fact they were nearing an end, at all; it got worse.

The drugs they were using in the lab sessions now seemed to leave him foggy-minded and at least a little disoriented all the time. So that the very days themselves ceased to exist separately, but strung themselves together in a long chain of links, each link exactly like and part of, the link preceding and the one following.

As a result, he hardly reacted when the whole process transferred location. He, Mary, Neiss and his staff were all loaded aboard one of the big command ships scheduled to go on post and phase-shifted out to the Frontier.

The last week's lack of sleep and drug-disorientation had been particularly hard on him—or perhaps he was beginning to be weakened, Jim thought, to the point where what would ordinarily not bother him, bothered him noticeably. Whatever the reason, he who had never had shift-sickness during all his time in space, was thrown into a paroxysm of nausea by the shift out to the Frontier. The attack was bad enough so that they had been on station at the Frontier for at least a couple of hours before he was able to get up out of his bed and leave the cabin. And Mary had told him to come to the bridge as soon as they were on station.

He still felt a steady, low-level sickness in the pit of his stomach; and both his vision and his balance were not normal. As a result, even under the ship's artificial gravity that was less than nine-tenths of Earth's, it took effort on his part to make the trip up five levels and along half the length of the vessel to get to the bridge. His legs gave at the knees with weakness and all his senses were distorted, so that even though he knew it was not physically so, he felt as if the deck slanted to either the right or left under his feet as he walked. Any attempt to adjust to a slant to the right found him feeling as if the floor now tilted left; and the ship-green walls on either side of him seemed to lean with their tops either inward or outward from him.

But he made it, and the shipman on guard duty at the port giving entrance to the bridge examined his credentials and then let him through. He stepped unsteadily into a room less than five paces from back to front but running the full width of the ship. Two multi-instrumented control positions, both of them empty as the ship was now holding station and on auto-direction, were to his right and left, perhaps four full meters apart and right up against the vision screen that ran the full length of the forward wall.

This vision screen displayed a number of "windows." The full left half of it was a single window that looked across the Frontier into the Sector guarded by the fighter ships under this ship's command. The right half of the screen was displaying a number of windows showing close-ups of the fighter ships in the Wings under command here, some of them, Jim knew, more than five light-years distant from where he stood.

A command officer of the ship stood before the large left segment of the screen, watching. A hand-control in his right palm blinked with code lights from the various instruments at the com positions, and this hand-control was now emitting a steady buzzing that warned of Laagi ships coming out toward this Sector, though they were evidently still too far off to be shown in the screen.

The buzzing ground away irritatingly on Jim's eardrums, and the red coveralls uniform of the command officer seemed unnaturally garish against the green of the walls and the black of the screen with its thick sprinkling of starlights. In fact, everything in the command room, seen with his present distortion of vision, seemed to stand out in ugly fashion from everything else there, as if an emphasized three-dimensional space was in effect. There was an unnaturalness about all of it; and the buzzing of the hand-control, irritatingly, sounded far louder than it should have in Jim's ears.

He turned toward Mary and Mollen, on his right. They were both, it seemed to his unnatural vision, looking at him oddly; but everything was so distorted he could not trust himself to interpret fine details like the expressions on faces. He started toward them.

He had barely taken his first step, however, when he saw their eyes leave him and go to the left half of the screen in front of the command officer. Jim stopped and turned back to look in that direction himself. A new window had just been displayed in part of the left half of the screen, directly in front of the officer; and something, he was not at first sure what, drew Jim's gaze to the single ship displayed there on close view.

He squinted at the ship, then stared.

Forgetting all about Mary and Mollen he tacked across the slanting floor of the bridge at the closest approach to a run that his unsteady balance would permit, until he was beside the command officer and joining him in staring at the ship shown in the new window—staring at it in utter disbelief.

"That's my ship!" he said.

The command officer appeared not to hear him. The buzzing that warned of the oncoming Laagi vessels seemed to roar in Jim's ears.

"I said—that's my ship!" he shouted over the buzzing in the officer's ear.

A second, smaller window suddenly sprang into existence alongside the one that showed *AndFriend*. The squat, dark shapes of oncoming Laagi ships were now displayed in it, like potbellied, heavy salmon ready to spawn.

"It's just some old hulk they want to get rid of," the officer said without taking his eyes off the screen. He seemed to have only half-heard what Jim had said. "Don't worry. There's no one aboard her."

"No one aboard her!" cried Jim.

"No, they're just using her as a drone target. They want to find out what parts of a ship the Laagi direct their fire on when it simply comes straight on and doesn't defend itself—"

Even as he spoke, there was something—no more than a flicker on the screen showing *AndFriend*. It was the strike of a weapon from one of the Laagi ships, which were still too far away to be seen in the same screen as *AndFriend*. A slantingly vertical gash opened the side of *AndFriend*. She rolled a quarter-turn to port, like a wounded animal, then righted herself and continued onward into the fire of the oncoming aliens.

"Turn her back! Bring her back here!" Jim grabbed the arm of the officer. "Don't you understand? That's *AndFriend*, my ship—the one they've been studying for a year now, the one that escorted back Raoul Penard's ship. She's too valuable to lose, don't you understand me? Get her back!"

"No, no," said the officer soothingly, pulling away from him. "You're right about what ship it is, but they've got all they want from her. She's just an old hulk good for this kind of target practice, now. Say, will you look at the way they're cutting her up?"

"I'm dreaming this!" said Jim frantically. "It isn't true. It's my dream!"

But it was not a dream. In his dream it had not been like this, with Mary and Mollen, who had now drawn close and were also watching. There was nothing dreamlike about the solidity of the crazily tilted deck under his feet, the details of the images in the windows. *AndFriend* was slashed again and again by the power weapons of the Laagi, but she continued on toward them, not trying to evade, not fighting back, just continuing to her destruction.

"Baby, baby, cut and run. Shift clear. Shift and fire back. Baby—" Jim heard his own voice like the voice of some other man at prayer. In his mind he saw the empty command chair in *AndFriend*. His fingers twitched, reaching to touch firing and control buttons that were hundreds of thousands of miles distant in the dying fighter.

Again and again, *AndFriend* shuddered to the direct lashing of the Laagi power weapons that opened her metal sides like tissue paper under red-hot knives. In his mind Jim could see her empty pilot room, with the empty pilot com-chair, the lights winking unseen on her board, signaling the oncoming of the Laagi ships, signaling her own weapons were on target, waiting for the orders to fire and to evade fire; but there was no one there to order her to respond.

He grabbed desperately at the hand-control in the officer's grasp, but the drug-clumsiness in him betrayed him. The other pulled away. Jim's hands grasped spasmodically at empty air and he lost his balance on the treacherously angled deck beneath his feet.

He fell and struggled to get back on his feet. But the apparent slope of the deck, a great wave of nausea and an increased loss of balance, as if his space-shift sickness was suddenly running wild within him, frustrated him. He made it to his knees and then fell sprawling again.

"Baby, baby . . . " he prayed, rolling on his back on the sloping floor. His eyes saw a corner of green ceiling and a corner of black space and stars that was the screen—as they would be showing on *AndFriend*'s screen, right now. He reached upward with both arms as if he could reach out across the thousands of miles to the buttons before that empty com-chair. He saw only the pilot room. . . .

He was in the com-chair. He was invisible but he was there. His invisible body was taking charge. His invisible fingers were finding the drive buttons and the firing buttons. He saw them depressing before him and felt *AndFriend* responding with movement and weapons. A strike by a Laagi weapon came through and destroyed half the pilot room beside his chair. He felt the fraction-of-a-moment's heat-blow through the invisible suit protecting his nonexistent right shoulder. It was too late for him and *AndFriend* to get away now; but at least they could fight. The Laagi would not simply have her for nothing. He and she together would fight back. They would fight. They would fight. . . .

# C H A P T E R

# 9

HE WOKE SURROUNDED BY SILENCE AND DARKNESS. UNBROKEN
silence and unrelieved darkness, as if all the stars had been
taken from the universe, and it stretched away forever around
him, limitless, lightless, and at peace. . . .

"Where am I?" he asked—and heard his own voice hol-
lowly echoing.

"It's all right," said the voice of Mary. There was an anx-
ious tone to it. "You're back at Base. You and *AndFriend*. It's
all right."

"Can you fix her?"

"She's not touched," said the voice of Mollen, "and never
was. She never left here—it was a mock-up, an imitation of
her, you saw out on the Frontier."

Jim pondered this.

"Sir, I don't believe you," he said at last. "I'd know her. It
was *AndFriend*."

"No," said the voice of Mollen. "That's why you were
drugged."

The older man's voice grew harsh.

"Do you think we didn't think of that? That's why we had
you higher'n a kite. Anyone could imitate your ship, but nobody but you could give it a soul."

Jim remembered that Mollen had been a fighter pilot once, himself. The time had to have come for him, too, when he had had to leave his ship. Jim said nothing, considering this and what the other man had just said. He felt clearheaded and natural now—except for the darkness all about him. His slowness in answering was simply because now, for some reason, there seemed all the time in the world to think.

"I'm in *AndFriend* now, like Raoul Penard's in *La Chasse Gallerie,* aren't I?" he said at last.

"Yes," said the voice of Mary. "When you couldn't stand to watch what you thought was *AndFriend* getting killed, you went to her—but you went to the real ship, which was here all the time."

"Yes," said Jim.

"Can you see us?" said a new voice. For a second Jim could not place it; and then he recognized it as the voice of the Base doc he had gone to almost daily before he had finally broken and staged the sit-in at Mollen's office.

"No," said Jim. "I think I'm going to sleep now. I'm very tired."

He must have slept for some time. When he woke the darkness was still there. He stayed where he was in it, replaying in his mind the conversation he had had just before going to sleep.

"Can you see us?" the doc had said. But he had not seen them, or anything else. Could he see if he wanted to? If *And-Friend* was where she had been all this time he must be under the plastic tent in Mary's lab. Surely he could see that.

He could. There was no sudden awareness of light. In fact, he was not really sure how he was seeing, what he was using for eyes or where they might be on *AndFriend*'s hull. He seemed simply to be able to see anything he wanted in any direction, until his gaze was stopped by the dark plastic of the enclosing tent. He told himself that the tent was not there, and abruptly he was able to see the whole inside of the large lab section that housed it, up to the cranes and slings, four stories overhead.

Neither Mary nor Mollen were in sight, let alone the doc. But a thin young man he recognized as one of Neiss's team sat in the tent itself, reading in a folding chair to the right of the nose of his hull.

"I'm awake," said Jim.

The young man lost his book and nearly fell out of his chair.

"Wait, wait . . . " he said, scrambling to his feet. "I'll get them. Just a minute. Wait. I'll be right back. . . . "

He was talking and running backwards at the same time. He turned and kept going, through a flap of the tent that Jim was now holding as invisible in his mind, toward the bottom story of the laboratory tower at the far end of the large open space. Jim followed his movements as he might have followed them on a ship's screen, followed the man to an office and an inner door, on which he pounded with his fist.

"He's awake!"

Jim withdrew his attention and considered himself. He had no idea how he was hearing, speaking or seeing. He simply did these things. It was, he thought, as if each smallest particle of *AndFriend* had ears, eyes, and a voice. His thoughts wandered off into a feeling of happiness over the fact that she had really not been hurt; and that he and she were together again. . . .

"Jim?" It was Mary's voice. He turned his attention to his immediate vicinity again, and saw Mary—in that strange way of seeing he now had—standing close, with Mollen and the doc.

"I could never remember your name," he said to the physician. "I just called you doc. There's been another medical man looking after me lately, but I never felt like calling him doc."

"And I'm sorry about that, Jim," said Mary—and, surprise of surprises, there was a catch in her voice. "Neiss has two doctorates, one in inorganic chemistry, the other in biology, but he's not a medical doctor. We just wanted you to think he was. This is Aram Snyder, who really is a physician and a psychiatrist."

"They sounded me out about working with you, here," said Aram, the doc. "I didn't know what they had in mind then, but from a theoretical point of view, what they were talking about sounded unethical to me, lacking the subject's consent. So they didn't go any farther with me."

"I'm sorry, Jim. I'm sorry, son," said Mollen harshly. "Mary and I, both of us, we didn't like doing this to you, blind. But we didn't have any choice. If there'd been more than one of you, maybe we could have asked for a volunteer. But there was only you; and we couldn't take a chance on your saying no. It's my responsibility, not Mary's."

In the strange calmness in which he now resided, Jim thought about this, turning it over in his mind, examining the words in an effort to understand everything they represented. It occurred to him that if it were not for the calmness—the feeling of being detached from much of what they said, he would be feeling very outraged right now that they should doubt his willingness to volunteer for what had been done to him. He was so long at thinking this over that when his attention came back to the others, he found they had fallen to talking among themselves in the meantime.

" . . . But how is he, Doc?" Mollen was saying.

"How can I tell?" responded Aram, irritably. "He's had a major emotional shock—how major I've no way of measuring. How do I know what it means to find yourself out of your body and into a machine?"

"When Mary did it, she wasn't damaged by it," said Mollen.

"But I knew what I was getting into. I wanted to do it," said Mary. "So I was prepared."

"Mary did this before?" asked Jim.

"She was in *La Chasse Gallerie*," said Mollen. "But she got there by a different route than the one you took."

"We were working on a different premise, then—" Mary broke off, turning to Aram. "Doctor, I'm afraid we're about to talk about things that—"

"I know, I know," said Aram. "Secrecy. You don't have to explain. Just don't put any pressure on him."

He turned and went out through a flap of the tent. They heard his footsteps moving away and the distant slam of a door.

"What different premise?" asked Jim.

"Our samples from *La Chasse Gallerie* showed that part of Raoul's living . . . there's no proper word for it, call it living fabric, had been absorbed by the inner surfaces of some of his ship's walls. We still don't understand how it could work that way, so I can't explain it to you, even if the words were there. But apparently when you get right down to it, matter is matter; and any kind of matter can, under the right conditions, be sensitized to become a vehicle to carry an already developed personality—or soul, if you want to call it that."

"Soul," said Mollen softly. "'Soul' is the word. Mary offered herself as a guinea pig."

"I also had a . . . feeling for Raoul Penard. We thought that might help."

"What did they do, glue you to the inside wall of the pilot's room of *La Chasse Gallerie*?" asked Jim.

The two stared at him.

"Jim," said Mary, "did you mean that as a joke? Or—"

"I didn't mean it literally," said Jim. "Why're you so shocked by that?"

"Because it shows how—how good you are. I mean, how well you are!" said Mary.

"She means," said Mollen bluntly, "how sane. Sane enough to have a sense of humor left."

"Why shouldn't I?" said Jim. "I'm all here, even if I am wearing a ship instead of a body."

To his surprise, the other two were unnaturally silent for a moment.

"Oh, I see," said Jim. "You mean I might have been insane the way Raoul's insane."

"Not insane." Mary spoke with an effort. "Not, anyway, the way we think of insane. That's what I found out when I used myself in that experiment with Raoul and *La Chasse Gallerie*."

Her voice grew more businesslike.

"And to answer you, no, I wasn't glued to one of the inside walls of the ship," she said. "What we did was take a very small amount of material from the ship and implant it under my skin. I lived with it for several months, hoping that this way I'd become sensitized to *La Chasse Gallerie*, too. Then, with the use of hypnotic medications, I was urged to feel that I'd become the ship, with Raoul."

"And it worked?" said Jim, wonderingly.

"It worked—oh, not on the first try or even the fifteenth. But we kept trying different drugs and self-hypnosis instead of someone else hypnotizing me, and so forth; and—we don't know specifically why then and not before—but one day it just worked; and I was in the ship with Raoul."

Mary stopped talking. She looked down at the floor.

"In a sense, then," said Mollen, when it became clear Mary was not going on, "she got the equivalent of a good look at Penard—"

"Yes," Mary interrupted. "That was when we—when I found out he wasn't wholly there."

She paused briefly again, then went on.

"It was just one part of him, the part that remembered his childhood and certain things," she said. "He didn't remember anything about being a pilot. He didn't have any notion of how he'd made *La Chasse Gallerie* fly after her engines were gone, or how he could talk, or anything like that. He was just a sort of bundle of living memories, from his earliest years."

Her voice softened.

"But he's happy with that. That's why we decided to give up trying to do anything more with him. He deserves that happiness after a long century of being lost and finally making it home again. He can stay as *La Chasse Gallerie* as long as he wants to, and he'll always be taken care of."

"But how did I get into this?" Jim said.

"Because Mary found out she couldn't do anything but be there, in *La Chasse Gallerie*," said Mollen. "And maybe you can't either. Try something for me right now—"

"Aram said not to put any pressure on him," Mary interrupted swiftly. "Maybe we should wait—"

"I'm all right," said Jim. "What were you going to say, General?"

"All right, Mary," said Mollen to her. He turned back to Jim. "Jim, I'll leave it up to you. If you don't want to try this, just say so. I'd like you to try to lift *AndFriend*—lift yourself —just off the floor, if you can."

"I see," said Jim. There was a moment in which he considered it, and then he lifted, off the concrete some six inches, the whole length and tons of weight of *AndFriend*, as lightly and effortlessly as a dandelion seed lifted from the ripe blossom by a breath of warm summer breeze. He poised there.

"Fine . . ." said Mollen after a moment. His voice sounded slightly strangled. "You can come down now."

Jim went back to rest on the floor, again gently, silently.

"How did you do that?" demanded Mary.

"I don't know," Jim said, puzzled. "How does someone bend his right arm at the elbow? You want to, so you do."

None of them said anything for a moment.

"So," went on Jim finally, "that was why Mary's way of making herself a part of *La Chasse Gallerie* didn't work for you. It wasn't any good to be part of a ship if you couldn't move it."

"You really don't know how you do it?" demanded Mollen.

Jim shook his head. Then realized he had only thought of shaking his head and that, of course, nothing about *AndFriend* had moved.

"I don't have the slightest idea," said Jim. "I see you, I hear you, I can move. I am—right now, I really am—*AndFriend*. Maybe that's the difference. The only one who could be *La Chasse Gallerie* was Raoul."

"Yes," said Mary somberly. "I think you're right. We finally decided it was something like that, ourselves."

"But it worked with me," said Jim.

"No—" began Mollen.

"No," said Mary in the same moment; and Mollen stopped trying to answer. "I decided the process hadn't worked for me because even when I thought I was part of *La Chasse Gallerie,* I really wasn't. I was part of Raoul. The bonding was based on some sort of emotional tie. Do you remember my mentioning the matter of you loving your ship, when I talked to you at the Officers' Club about this project, long ago?"

"I remember," said Jim.

"I think I also said something about how poltergeist phenomena might be related to Raoul's ability to move a spaceship that no longer had any engines to take off from a planet's surface and move itself through space. I had the idea then that an intolerable situation was the trigger for a parakinetic individual using such abilities. But it wasn't so much the situation as the individual's response to it. A fury at the intolerable situation—which meant some kind of frustrated love as the obverse."

"Raoul's love for his ship—and his home?" said Jim.

"And my—my bond with Raoul."

"Why don't you want to say you loved him?" asked Jim, realizing, strangely, the moment he had said it, that this was as unusual a thing for him to say as Mary's avoidance of the word he had mentioned. "Most women don't have any trouble saying the word 'love.'"

"I'm not 'most women'—I'm me!" flared Mary. "Besides, how would you know?"

"I guess I wouldn't," said Jim, out of the strange painless honesty that was part of him in the place where he now lived.

"Then I'll go on," said Mary. "The point I'm making is that if the joining between the mind of one person and another person or thing requires a powerful love, then simply the mechanical means we'd used to put me in with Raoul wouldn't work to produce a spaceship with only a human mind flying it. A human mind that would not only be in, but be able to control what it was in, had to have three qualifications. It had to know that it was possible for it to be in a ship—and there were only you and me who'd actually experienced Raoul's being in and flying *La Chasse Gallerie*. It also had to be in an intolerable situation; and it had to have the bond of an overpowering love with what it would become part of."

She stopped.

"Am I making sense to you?" she said.

"Yes," said Jim, "I understand."

"If I was right, the hypothesis offered an explanation, not only for poltergeist activity, but for ghosts haunting houses or certain locations, or of human spirits taking over other people, or things, and operating through them."

Again she paused.

"Go on," said Jim.

"It was all we had to work with," she said, almost defensively. "So we set out to try it out on you. We deliberately kept you from *AndFriend;* and we wore you down with frustration. All the time, of course, we were studying you. Under hypnosis, we found what we wanted. It was your dream of *AndFriend* being used as a target drone to study the Laagi responses, and when we thought we had you at the breaking point, we arranged to reenact it for you."

She stopped once more. Jim did not say anything.

"Well, it worked," she said at last. "You're perfectly free to hate me all you like for doing it. I thought it was something that had to be done, and I did it."

"I authorized it," said Mollen. "I told you, Jim, it was my responsibility."

"How did Mary get back into her own body?" asked Jim.

"When I faced the fact that there was no Raoul Penard

there for me to love," Mary used the last word emphatically, "I simply woke up in my own body, where it'd been kept cared for. They'd tried to bring me back by hypnotic signal—I think you know what I mean. I was given an order under hypnosis to come out of that hypnosis when a certain person told me to. It was to be Louis, here, telling me to come back. They tried it. When they found they couldn't communicate with me and Raoul was still going on with his own talking, they had Louis call me back. But I didn't come. Only when I faced the fact there was no real Raoul there—then I came back, of my own accord."

"What you're telling me," said Jim, fascinated by his own calmness, "is that you don't know how I'll ever get back into my own body."

The moment that went by without an answer was long enough so that the truth became obvious.

"It's worse than that, isn't it?" he said. "You don't think I ever will get back?"

"I'm sorry, boy," said Mollen. "It's my responsibility, as I keep saying. But you're right."

"*AndFriend* isn't like Raoul," said Mary. "She's exactly what you knew she was. You'd have to want to leave her . . . enough. And that may—"

"Be impossible," said Jim.

"Yes."

This time the silence was very long indeed. Jim was trying to live with the idea of his situation, to gather in the full meaning of it. The other two said nothing, as people say nothing, watching the critical moment of a medical operation through the glass window of an observation booth.

"You did this all for a purpose," said Jim finally. "You did it because you want me to do something. That reason you had for sending me back into space, General—with the small difference that you didn't tell me you were sending me back this way. No, wait—"

He stopped Mollen as the other was beginning to speak again.

"Don't tell me again it's your responsibility. I've heard that. I know it's your responsibility. And I know you did it because the people who tell you what to do made it your responsibility. It doesn't matter who's responsible. The only thing that matters is why you did it—what's the mission you had for me?"

"Have you looked at yourself? I mean, at *AndFriend*?" asked Mollen. "Can you look at yourself?"

"Yes. You mean the new fusion engines and all the rest of it," answered Jim. "I know it's there, just as you said it would be. But you know, I don't need it, any of it. I can go wherever I need to go the same way Raoul did, the same way I lifted off the floor, just now. Wait a minute, though—I can't phase-shift without using the ship's equipment. But the regular drive equipment you could have just as well left off."

"Perhaps," said Mollen, "but we weren't taking any chances. Also, if you were captured..."

"By the Laagi."

"Yes," said the general with a small sigh, "by the Laagi. If they capture you, we want you to look as if you needed a human being in you, to run you; but the human being just happens to be missing."

"So, you want me to go deep into Laagi territory," Jim said, "deep enough so I could be captured instead of just shot to pieces?"

"Not exactly," said Mollen.

"No?" Jim was surprised, and was startled to realize that it was the first time since his waking as part of *AndFriend* that he had felt that emotion.

"We want you to go out around Laagi territory, just as I said in my office."

"Then why could I be captured?"

"Because we want you to go beyond Laagi territory, around the other side of Laagi territory; and we've no way of knowing how far they've gone on that far side. Since Raoul's already been there, they may be watching for you there. We don't know. But there's that chance. But if you're captured, maybe you'll have a better chance of escaping if they think you need someone to fly you."

"You want me to find whatever it was Penard found," said Jim. "Don't you think you better tell me now what you think it was?"

"We don't know. That's a fact, Jim. It seemed to be some sort of paradise, from Raoul's point of view. The point is, there was this paradise and then there was something else there, too. It's that something else that's got us sending you out there."

"What was it? Animal, vegetable or mineral?"

"That's what we don't know."

"I don't understand," said Jim. "Granted that Raoul thinks it's in a paradise. If nothing more's known about it—"

"Sorry. Back up and start again," said Mollen. "I'm doing a bad job of explaining. It's whatever else it is, and whether or not that's connected with the paradise part, that really interests us. Because we think it might also have something to do with how Raoul got to be part of *La Chasse Gallerie*—and because he claims the Laagi don't know it's there."

"They don't?" said Jim. "Raoul claims they don't?"

"That's what we gather from what he says," replied Mollen.

"How can the Laagi not know it's there if it's right on their back doorstep, if we're on their front doorstep, speaking in interstellar space terms. They ought to be able to see it, too— or at least, I assume the assumption is Raoul saw it."

"I don't know. The best people we've put on it can't guess," said Mollen. "But can you imagine what it'd mean if there was someone or something we could work with, that the Laagi couldn't even imagine, let alone see? It might mean the end of this long war with them after all. It might mean we could open the way we want to the inner parts of the galaxy."

# C H A P T E R

# 10

JIM / *ANDFRIEND* LAY, THINKING. THE HUMAN RACE HAD BEEN at war with the Laagi so long, over five generations, that the contest had become something that was almost as taken for granted as the physical facts of the universe itself. It seemed they had always been at war with the Laagi. They would always be at war with them . . . these aliens, these people no human had ever seen, whose worlds no human had ever seen; but only the hulls of their heavy-bellied space warships. It was almost as if Mollen had suggested altering all the continents of Earth into unfamiliar shapes.

It was not just what he wanted, of course. It was what everyone wanted. No more of this war which had drained Earth's resources and brought her nothing in return—unless it was the feeling of being safely entrenched behind a line of fighting spaceships. But with no more Laagi to fight, what was next?

Hopefully, they could then go out to colonize livable worlds, wherever these could be found, which had been what they had been engaged in when they found that there were no ready-to-live-on planets within practical phase-shifting distances, unless they were the worlds already occupied by the

Laagi or in that area of space to which the Laagi barred the way.

No one even knew why the Laagi fought. They had attacked, on contact, the first unarmed human spaceships that had encountered them. Clearly, they would have followed this up by carrying their attacks against Earth, itself, if the aroused world had not hastily combined to arm and man the defensive line in space that was the Frontier. Clearly, the Laagi wanted colonizable planet-space, too; and in spite of the fact no human had ever seen one, Earth must be enough like their world or worlds to be usable.

In the early years after human and Laagi ships had first encountered each other, their ships had come close enough to be observed just outside Earth's atmosphere. But meanwhile Earth had been frantically building ships fitted for space combat; and by the time the first of these went up in effective numbers, hunting for the Laagi, they had to travel almost as far as the present Frontier before encountering any of them.

But beyond the Frontier all the military strength of Earth had not been able to push, in well over a hundred years. The larger a fleet of fighter ships with which they tried to penetrate, the greater the number of Laagi ships that came to oppose them. Were the Laagi from one world or many? Were they paranoid or reasonable? What were they, physically and mentally?

No Laagi ship ever surrendered. They fought or ran, but once engaged in combat they kept fighting until they were destroyed, or destroyed themselves. Continual efforts to find a way of capturing a Laagi ship had been without success. There seemed to be the equivalent of a dead-man's switch in each of their ships that triggered its destruction if it became too badly crippled either to run or fight any more.

Now Mollen was suggesting that if Jim was lucky in finding what Mollen and Mary seemed to hope was out there, the years of fighting the Laagi might be over. The mountain was far off still on his horizon, but now a road had appeared that might lead him to it.

"Jim?"

It was Mary's voice, speaking to him.

"Yes?" he answered.

"You haven't said a word for nearly an hour," said Mary.

"We thought we'd give you time to think over what Louis just said. But it's been nearly an hour, as I say."

"Has it? I'm sorry," said Jim. "Time feels a little different to me now. Did you say something to me that I didn't answer? What was it?"

"We didn't," said Mollen. "But we were just about to. Do you think you'd have any trouble phase-shifting wide of the Frontier, whether you use your fusion engines or not; and then coming in again, say, fifty light-years farther on, to see if you're beyond Laagi territory?"

"I don't think so," said Jim. "It may take some time, but if time's not important—by the way, where's my body? What's happening to it?"

"It's being cared for," said Mollen. "As long as you come back within an ordinary lifetime, it'll be waiting for you. Actually a straight out, down, in and out again and back shouldn't take you more than a matter of weeks at the outside."

"Then I'm ready to go anytime," said Jim. "It's not as if I need to pack a suitcase, is it? You're talking to a ship, General, not a pilot."

"Louis means, are you mentally ready to go?" Mary asked. "We've been putting you under considerable strain for the last year. No one expects you to just bounce back from that and take off."

"You know," said Jim, "it's strange, but there's nothing to bounce back from. Even if it'd turned out you didn't have a good reason for putting me here, there'd be nothing to bounce back from. I'm different now, that's all, in some way I can't explain. You know, come to think of it, it's almost as if I was thinking like a ship, instead of a man."

"Maybe we should have the doc give him some tests," said Mollen, very nearly under his breath.

"To see if my mind's all here?" Jim said. "It's all here, I promise you. It's just that—it's different, now."

"I don't know. . ." grumbled Mollen.

"Maybe I ought to say it's something like being perfectly free to think without all the body-feelings that used to interfere with thoughts, like static," said Jim. "Anyway, if you want me to leave this minute, I can."

And he once more lifted *AndFriend* a hand's breadth from the floor.

"No. Wait. Come down!" said Mollen.

Jim rested the weight of his ship-body back on the floor.

"There's more to it than you know just yet," Mollen said. "We've got tapes of parts of what Raoul said that we've never let you hear before—tapes about whatever it was he ran into that gave him that idea of a paradise, and that the Laagi didn't know it was there. Are you ready to hear those now?"

"Certainly," said Jim. "Now or anytime. You know, it's funny. Time doesn't seem to mean the same thing to me now. Maybe I don't sleep anymore, like this. No, wait a minute; I did sleep for a while, didn't I? How long was I asleep?"

"Asleep?" said Mollen. "Maybe forty minutes. We thought you'd be out for hours."

"Forty minutes!"

For the first time Jim paid close attention to the faces of Mary and Mollen. They both looked strained and tired. Mollen, perhaps because of his age, looked very tired indeed.

"Just a second," said Jim. "What time is it now?"

"Now? Early morning—" Mollen looked at his wrist-com. "Four hundred thirty-seven."

"Four A.M.! You're the ones who're not up to tapes," said Jim. "Why don't you both go and rest? You can show me the tapes after you've had some sleep."

"And what'll you be doing meantime?" Mary asked.

"Me?" Jim was surprised by the question. He thought for a moment. "I'll think, I guess. Anyway, minutes, hours, days . . . it doesn't make all that much difference to me."

"Why not?" asked Mary. "Can you tell me why not?"

Jim thought about it.

"No," he said. "It just doesn't. It's like the business of my lifting myself off the floor to show you I could do it, earlier. I don't know how I do these things. I seem to be something like a stone-age savage. I know what I can do with my body, but I can't tell you why or how."

"I'd still like to have you try to answer—"

"Mary," said Jim. "If you like, you can stay and we'll talk as long as you want. It won't make any difference to me. You can go until you fall over. But the general's going to fall before you do. And the truth is, you probably need sleep as much as he does. Why don't you go get some, and come back when you're rested. I'll still be here and just the same."

"You're not just trying to get rid of us so you can be alone?" growled Mollen.

"Not particularly," said Jim. "In fact, I don't really know whether I'll think at all while you're gone. I think I'll think, but I won't know until I'm left alone. Did you ever find out whether Penard slept, or just sat there and thought?"

Mollen grunted, wordlessly.

"No," said Mary, "there was no way to check."

"Well, there you are," said Jim. "It's up to you. But why don't you both get some sleep?"

"All right. I'm going, anyway," said Mollen abruptly. "Mary?"

"I suppose"—she looked from Jim to the general and back to Jim—"I really am tired."

"Pleasant dreams," said Jim politely. "Just remember to speak to me when you get back, in case I do sleep myself, or get lost in my own thoughts."

"Good night, then," said Mollen gruffly.

"Good night," said Mary; and it occurred to Jim for the first time in his life how much sweeter the words sounded in a woman's voice than in a man's.

"Good night," he said, and watched as they turned and left.

It turned out that he was never to be sure whether he thought all during the period of hours that passed before he saw Mary and Mollen again, or whether he slept part of it. He was conscious of remembering many things from his own life, the way such things are remembered just before falling asleep, with a particular clarity that almost amounted to reliving them. If he speculated, if he engaged in logical mental attack on any question, he was not conscious of it afterward. He had vaguely intended to try something like that, just to see how his mind would work under these conditions; but there seemed to be all the time in the universe and the question and the experiment were not pressing.

But he understood now how Raoul could lose himself in his memories. He had been so used to the ever-present feelings of his body, its efforts, its weight under gravity or artificial gravity—perhaps even its circadian rhythms—that he had considered his mind totally free for thoughts or dreams when actually it was receiving and noting reports from all over its physical vehicle. It was a pleasant situation to be mind alone. It occurred to him that the condition of being content-edly alone like this might turn out to be useful therapy for some kinds of mental disturbances.

He had rarely felt more contented.

But the question of sleep remained a question. He was conscious neither of falling asleep nor of waking—but with-out body signals to announce them, these things could have happened without his noticing. He could, for example, have slipped from remembering a past experience to dreaming about it without noticing it. He did not, however, remember any of the illogical happenings and transitions that seem to take place, to the dreamer in the dream state. Also, he had been awake as he had watched Mary and Mollen leave him; and he was awake when later they lifted the flap of the tent and came back inside.

"How are you?" Mary asked as they came up to his hull.

"Same as ever," he answered. "There's been no reason for me to change. How about you two? Are you rested?"

"Yes," said Mary.

"You, too, General?"

"Yes. Thanks. I did need some sleep," said Mollen gruffly.

Mary was carrying a small case in her hand. She uncoiled a lead from one end of this and placed the free end against his hull, where it clung.

"These are parts of Raoul's recordings about the paradise and the Laagi," she said.

The sound of Raoul's voice began to resonate in his hull, audible to him but to no one else unless someone had earlier attached a listening device to his hull—and, feeling around himself now, he was sure there was no such thing touching him.

But the recordings were not very informative beyond what he had been told already by Mary and Mollen. Invariably they were fragments of sentences in which mention of the Laagi, or the "paradise" was merely used as a reference.

". . . the Laurentides. Paradise was wonderful, but there's no place like home. . . .

". . . ugly like those Laagi things. All right, maybe not

ugly; but nothing beautiful, just like the Laagi couldn't imagine beautiful . . .

" . . . they didn't even come to watch me. I kept waiting. Just having me there was it, evidently. When I figured that out, I lifted and headed for home. . . . There's no place like home.". . .

". . . but they were all stuck. Crazy Laagi, all stuck in space. Flies on flypaper. Not me . . ."

Jim listened patiently through more than four hours of such excerpts, and ended up not much more informed by these cryptic allusions than he had been before. The sum total of it was what Mary and Mollen had already told him. That somewhere beyond Laagi territory—somewhere reachable in a fusion ship, which could only mean farther in toward the center of the galaxy—there was something Raoul had considered a paradise—or paradises—he seemed to be using the word sometimes to refer to singular places, sometimes to multiple ones.

That these were the Laagi worlds themselves seemed improbable, since Raoul had evidently not found the Laagi home place or places attractive. Also, since it was unmistakably clear that *La Chasse Gallerie* had been in Laagi hands, it was a reasonable assumption that this had been after Raoul had become a part of his ship. Otherwise the Laagi, it was natural to assume, would have made the human pilot, rather than the vessel, their main interest; particularly since their own ships were pretty much on a par with the human ones, judging by how these were able to do in combat.

So, it was at least a reasonable assumption that Raoul had been captured by the Laagi on his way back from wherever this paradise was.

That was all they knew or could guess at with reasonable certainty. The tapes Jim heard now suggested nothing more to him than Mary, Mollen, or anyone else who had been allowed to hear them had concluded and already passed on to him.

Jim said as much, once the playing of the excerpts was over.

"I'll just have to go out there and see," he said.

"Yes," said the general.

"Are there any other reasons why I shouldn't start right away?" asked Jim.

"As a matter of fact, yes," said Mollen. "You may not need to pack a suitcase, or its equivalent. But Mary will; and Mary's going with you."

For the second time since he had found himself wearing a ship for a body, emotion flooded Jim.

"Mary!" he echoed.

"Yes," Mary said. "There's a lot to be learned about the human mind when it's in another vehicle, like this one. My work here's gone as far as I can take it. It can only go on if I go on with you as my subject instead of Raoul, and in space, where it all happened to him."

"But you couldn't come, even if you wanted to. . . ." Jim's mind had already been playing with the highly interesting possibility, particularly with a fusion engine, once he got off by himself in space, of trying some maneuvers of which fighter ships were mechanically capable but which normally, if tried, would reduce their pilots to thin organic smears on the inside of the hull. With no such frail human body to consider, there would be things a fighter ship could do that any fighter pilot would long to try doing. Put a passenger aboard, and such experimentation became open to criticism—from the passenger at least.

"I mean," Jim said, "it's going to be a longer, more dangerous trip into far space than anything that's ever been tried. I may have to try to evade Laagi ships; and with a person on board, I'll be limited in what I can do to get away—"

"You won't have a human on board," said Mary. "I'll be with you the same way I was with Raoul. When we had you under sedation, we used the same technique of implanting a specimen of your living body tissue in mine, of course using immune-reaction suppressants to keep your body from killing it off. It lived; and I'm ready to be with you at any time."

"We'll see about that—" began Jim, getting ready for a shift directly from the floor of the lab to space.

"You couldn't leave me behind if you wanted to," interrupted Mary.

But now she spoke inside his mind. It was as if her words were a thought that had popped spontaneously into his mind. A second later her voice was sounding outside him, normally, once more.

"You see," said Mary, "I'm already with you. I've been

with you for weeks now. Or rather, I've had the capability to be with you for weeks now. I can come whether you want me to or not. I know you don't want me; but it'd make things easier if you reconciled yourself to my coming."

Jim said nothing. But his mind was adding one more point on which they had taken no chances on his objecting, but set things up without asking. Honesty forced him to face the fact that in this case he might very well have objected. But he would not have sustained his objections if they had told him Mary's going along was necessary; and they should have known it.

"I know you don't like me," said Mary a little bitterly. "But this is more important than likes or dislikes. There's too much to be learned not to send someone along to learn it."

"I don't dislike you," said Jim. He thought he growled the words as well as Mollen could have done, but that may have been the self-flattery of his imagination. "I didn't fall in love with you at first sight, that's true. But I don't dislike you now. I like you."

"Oh?" Mary's voice was utterly disbelieving.

"I do. I don't say you're the person I'd pick as the one I'd most like to share a desert island—or a fighter ship—with; because that wouldn't be true. But there's plenty of people I'd put in line behind you as a sidekick, nowadays."

Mary said nothing, but her expression did not change.

"It's the truth," said Jim. He had an inspiration. "Did you ever know a spaceship to tell a lie?"

For a moment the expression on Mary's face held. Then she smiled. Mollen's hoarse chortle joined her.

"All right," said Mary at last. "I'll take your word I'm welcome aboard. Now, we've been preparing for my leaving for weeks now, as soon as we thought you were getting to the point where you'd be able to make the shift into *AndFriend*. But even with all that, there're things still to be done before I go. Figure a couple of days, anyway."

"Which brings up a point," said Mollen. He looked at *AndFriend*. "Jim, what can we do for you to fill in that time? All the physical information you'll need—or as much as we've got to give you up to and around Laagi territory—is in the ship's memory units already, as well as everything else we could think of that might be useful. Is there anything else you can think of you might want?"

"Nothing offhand," said Jim. "I take it, as I sit here now, I can make air connections with the Base and other, outside phone systems—correction, I don't need to ask that. I see I can. No, General, I'm fine. I don't even need a couple of good books to read."

"What'll you do with yourself?" Mary asked, watching him curiously.

"The same thing Raoul does all the time. Daydream," said Jim.

# C H A P T E R

# 11

BUT HE DID NOT SPEND ALL THAT TIME DAYDREAMING—TO HIS own very great surprise. He found himself caught up in other mental exercises.

He had expected no such thing to happen. If anything he was looking forward to a couple of days exploring his more pleasant memories. There was an active pleasure in calling up happy scenes out of his past, and he had been amazed at the detail with which his unconscious recalled them—far beyond what he was used to. Where his ordinary memory would have given him the time, the place, the action and the emotion, this new memory gave him far more. He could study a particular moment he had once lived and simply by looking more closely at it, see the pattern of the fabric on the upholstering of the furniture, the small items scattered about the room, the quality of sunlight coming in the windows. Bit by bit, he had become fascinated, not so much with remembering, as with the capabilities of his memory; and, beyond this, the capabilities and liabilities of his new self.

He had always considered himself in excellent physical shape; and as a result he had simply taken his body so much for granted that most of the time he had been used to forgetting that it had demands of its own. Now that he was out of it, he was astonished to find what a busy and signal-sending creature his body had been. It was not that his mind had not always been getting a multitude of messages from it, from "I'm all in order and working" signals to alarms ranging from fatigue to outright pain. It was that his mind had accepted these as so much a part of the normal process of living that it had, most of the time, handled but ignored them.

Now he could feel what he had been missing, now that he no longer had the static of the body's responses to interfere with his thinking. Now he was not merely capable of day-dreaming with unusual clarity, he was capable of thinking with unusual clarity.

He could switch from one topic of thought to another in-stantly, and, having switched, devote all his attention to the new topic as if the earlier one had not existed. At the same time he was not obsessed by his current topic to the point where he lost awareness of his surroundings or himself.

The liability was that there was now no more of that purely physical pleasure that the body had been capable of giving him in small to large measures as a reward for paying atten-tion to it. Moreover he felt strangely light—not like someone in a lesser gravity, but more like someone with helium-filled balloons attached to his shoes, so that he was being lifted, but from the soles of his feet only; and it required an effort to balance himself when he took a step forward. It was a mental feeling, not a physical one, but "lightness" was the only way he could find of making some description of it.

One of the more curious effects he discovered with his new vision was that he could change the attitudes with which he was normally used to looking at an object, and see it in an entirely new and novel way. Usually, the switch was from a habitual way of seeing something, one which reflected his body's past responses to whatever it was; and the new attitude was one that ignored any connection between it and his body's use for it.

The best example of this turned out to be a reclining chair he had bought for his two-room suite in the Bachelor Officers' Quarters. He had always been very fond of that chair; but now, considering it carefully in memory from a bodiless point of view, he found it one of the most ridiculously engineered objects he had ever seen, and ended up laughing at it.

It was all knobs and angles. It was hard to imagine, just looking at it, what odd-shaped sort of creature would have designed such a monstrosity for its comfort. The seat, leg-support and back planes made sense after a fashion as partial containers for whatever or whoever it was planned to support. But those two strange, horizontal members projecting forward, which had their bases attached halfway up the back portion at its outward edges . . .

"You seem to be in a good humor," said Mollen's voice.

Jim realized suddenly that he had been laughing aloud. He looked outside himself to see that the general was in the process of entering through a flap in the tent. Behind him entered half a dozen men and women in workmen's white coveralls, two of which at least Jim recognized as maintenance workers from the Fighter Ships Unit.

"What's everybody here for?" Jim asked Mollen.

"To check you over before you leave, of course," the general said.

"Oh, no!" said Jim.

"No?" Mollen looked surprised and the maintenance people who were already headed toward Jim's entry port came to a halt. "What do you mean, no?"

"I mean I don't need to be checked over, sir," Jim said. "I can tell you right now that everything about me's all right."

"I see. When did you learn all about fusion engines?" Mollen's scraggly brows pulled together.

"I don't need to learn about them," said Jim. "I can feel that everything's all right inside me."

"So the pilots always say to the doc when they show up for their monthly physical," said Mollen. "I think we better have the experts take a look at you anyway."

He turned to the maintenance people and nodded.

"Go ahead," he said.

They went ahead. Jim made no more protests, although his human experience intruded on his experience as a spaceship, so that—although there was no pain, of course—he had an uncomfortable feeling that he was being operated upon internally without the courtesy of a general anesthetic.

He found that with a little practice he could be aware of where in him every one of the maintenance workers were, and what they were doing. This was a relief, in a way, for it meant that he could be sure nothing could be done to him in the future without his knowledge.

Mollen was still standing outside his hull, hands behind his back, watching the movement of people in and out of Jim's entry port which at the moment was standing wide. Jim became conscious that some of the small cases they had brought aboard were evidently not merely devices for the purpose of checking him out, since they were being stowed in places where they would be prevented from sliding about and left behind when those who brought them in left.

He tried to see inside them, but they were not an integral part of himself and their cases were opaque to his perceptions.

"What're these things they're bringing aboard, sir?" he asked the general.

"Supplemental information units and instruments for Mary," answered Mollen. "She won't be able to read from them directly; but she can direct you on how to go about finding what she wants in them, and once you see what's there, she will, too. Also, there's provision for storage of new information she may be able to collect on the trip."

"How much storage does she think she'll need?" said Jim. For the smallest of the cases could have stored the contents of most public branch libraries.

"I've no idea," said Mollen cheerfully. "That's her department."

And as if summoned like a genie by Mollen's invisible rubbing of a magic lamp, Mary's voice spoke inside Jim's head.

"Are my things aboard?"

"Unless there's more to come," said Jim. "When are you going to be ready to leave?"

"I'm ready now. Can't you tell? I'm in here with you," said Mary.

"I didn't know you were here to stay," he said.

He checked the ship's chronometer record. Sure enough, it had been two days—well, a little over forty hours—since he had last spoken to her. He had marked the time when she and Mollen had left him before just to make sure that they were not pulling any tricks on him about the apparent speed with which time sometimes seemed to pass when he was alone.

"Well, tell Louis I'm here, would you, please?" asked Mary. "You're the only one who can hear me now."

"Mary's here," he told Mollen aloud, suddenly reminded that his verbal exchange with her just now had been strictly on a mental level.

He was abruptly, vastly, relieved of a fear that had concerned him to the point that he had hesitated even to ask about it. It had occurred to him during the hours just past that Mary might be able to read his mind once she was part of him and the ship. Now that fear was laid to rest. For one thing, clearly, he could not read her mind—he had not even known of her presence until she asked that question about her equipment just now. But, secondly, he could now feel her mind, not so much as if it was part of his mental machinery, but as if it was simply another part of the ship which that mental machinery controlled.

Perhaps if he tried, he could control her mind in the same way as he controlled the rest of the ship. . . . He backed away hastily from that thought. It was ghoulish.

"Good to hear you're there, Mary," Mollen had answered when he had passed the word along that she was with him. "The high-hats ought to be along at any minute now; and as soon as they do you two can take off."

"What high-hats?" asked Jim. The term was roughly synonymous with "top brass," except that it referred more specifically to civilian authorities.

"Governmental people who've got the rank to watch you leave," said Mollen. "Doesn't include the President. It was explained to her that it would be too hard maintaining the type of secrecy we've held to this long if she was one of the send-off party."

"Why didn't you tell me people like that were coming?" Jim asked.

"Colonel," said Mollen. "You're a ship-jockey. The only one of your kind, but still just a ship-jockey. You didn't need to know so you weren't told. Nothing personal. If it'd been up to me, I'd have let you know not only about that, but a lot of other things in past months. But the rules were set up and I had to go with them, like everyone else."

"Sorry, sir," said Jim. "I understand."

"I know you do," said Mollen, a little more kindly. "You

might bear in mind while you're gone, though, that Mary—like me—has been a person under rules, and still is. She's been ground between a couple of millstones. You, *La Chasse Gallerie* and Raoul on one hand; and a lot of powerful people on the other. So be decent to her on the mission."

"He will—damn it!" said Mary. "I keep forgetting nobody but you can hear me. Tell Louis for me I've got no doubt you'll be decent to me."

Jim did so. Privately, he spoke to Mary.

"Why didn't you rig up some speaking device so you could talk to someone like him directly?" Jim asked. "Some sort of phone line to the hull that would resonate outside—"

"Because I'm in you, not the ship!" said Mary. "Any phone line I could use has to run through your brain cells and vocal chords, first!"

"Oh," said Jim.

"Yes," said Mary.

"Sorry," said Jim. "I didn't think that through."

He waited for her to tell him it was all right, and that she understood how he could have made such a perfectly natural mistake; but she did not.

"I beg your pardon," said Jim finally. "But I just admitted my error and apologized. It's usual to acknowledge an apology."

"Oh, Lord!" said Mary. "And we aren't even off the ground yet. I'm the one who needs to apologize, Jim. I get wrapped up in what I'm doing and I forget to treat people like people. I'm sorry."

"Honors are even," said Jim gravely.

To his pleased surprise, he got a silent, but actual, laugh from Mary.

"No," she said. "Because you can make me laugh. Nobody's done that for years. I used to think it was because you were a featherbrained flyboy—oh, courageous and daring and all the rest of it, but essentially feather-brained, too. Now, after all these months of studying you, I know you better. Forgive me, Jim; and I'll learn to get this ride-roughshod-over-them attitude of mine under control. And, since I've done everything else I ever set out to do, that's a promise."

"To be truthful," said Jim, "you've got me on the defensive, now. I'm not sure I've always been that easy to live with myself."

"Your excuses for that were better than mine. Anyway, we'll do better from now on?"

"We shall indeed," said Jim solemnly.

"The guests are here."

They had been talking in the privacy of Jim's mind. Now, Jim looked outside his hull and saw that the high-hats, as Mollen had called them, were just now entering through a flap in the tent wall. There were about a dozen of them, all civilians, roughly half of them men and half, women; and every one at least in his or her forties.

"How come," said Jim in one last silent aside to Mary, "if you can't talk unless I talk, you can see something before I see it?"

"You saw them come in. You see everything going on in this ship and outside it all the time. And hear it all," answered Mary. "You know that. You just weren't paying attention to that particular thing. I was."

"I see," said Jim.

He spoke out loud from his hull to Mollen and the newcomers.

"Welcome," he said.

With his back to those entering, Mollen frowned a warning at the hull. Jim fell silent again, and Mollen turned around to personally greet those coming in. When they were all assembled close to the hull and Mollen had spoken and shaken hands with all of them, the general turned to *AndFriend*.

"Colonel," he said. "On this occasion of your leaving with Dr. Gallegher to explore beyond Laagi space, we're honored to have visitors from the highest offices in the land. Mr. Vice President, this is Colonel Jim Wander and Dr. Mary Gallegher."

He had half-turned as he spoke, back toward a tall, athletic looking man in his fifties, in a gray business suit and dark blue weather-cape.

"Hello, Jim—Dr. Gallegher," said the tall man.

"Honored to meet you, sir," said Jim. "Dr. Gallegher joins me in saying that."

"Actually, he makes a good show, but I wouldn't—and

didn't—vote for him," commented Mary silently inside Jim. "Actually, of course, it's a thankless sort of job."

"The best wishes of this nation go with you, Jim and Mary."

"Thank you, sir," said Jim. It was a strange ritual, this, Jim thought. Rather ridiculous, in fact.

"Mr. Secretary, this is Jim Wander and Dr. Gallegher," said Mollen, turning to the next closest figure. "Jim and Mary, this is Secretary of State Jacob Preuss."

The secretary of state was a short, broad man in his sixties or older, looking as if he had too much energy to stand still.

"Take care of yourselves out there," said Preuss. "You've no idea what you're worth to us."

"Twice the man the other one is," was Mary's silent observation.

"We'll take every possible precaution, sir," Jim was saying. "But I imagine you want getting the job done to come first."

"Of course," said Preuss. "Good luck, both of you."

"Thank you, sir."

"Senator, Jim Wander and Dr. Gallegher. Jim and Mary, this is Senator Anita Wong. . . ."

The introductions continued. So did Mary's unheard, internal comments on each person introduced, and some of these were either so pungent or so apposite that Jim had a hard time keeping the proper solemnity of tone in his own audible replies. Finally the round of introductions came to an end. The vice president made a short speech, praising them for going where no humans had ever gone before. Then the visitors all backed up a little, as if there might be something dangerously explosive about *AndFriend*'s departure.

"Good luck," said Mollen under his breath. "Now get out of here."

The whisper in which he spoke was too low-pitched for the dignitaries behind him to hear it; but Jim picked it up with no trouble.

He turned his mind to the phase-shift equipment.

A moment later they were surrounded by space and stars.

# CHAPTER

# 12

"WHY," SAID MARY, "WE HAVEN'T GONE ANYPLACE AT ALL. We're still just a few hundred thousand kilometers from Earth."

"Right," said Jim. "Just as the orders in my command memory specify."

Five other two-person fighter ships suddenly appeared in box formation around them. There were no Wing and no Sector markings on the fighters. They were completely anonymous.

"Our escort," said Jim to Mary. "What do you want to bet they've come in from the Frontier, instead of lifting from someplace else on Earth?"

"*AndFriend,*" said a voice over the ship-to-ship circuit. "This is Wing Cee, *AndFriend* escort. Are you ready to shift?"

"Hear you, Wing Cee," said Jim over the same circuit. "All ready to shift, and thanks for the escort."

"Just following orders. To shift, then. On the count, according to the coordinates in your program, one—two—three—shift!"

They shifted.

A massive command ship swam in space beside them.

"Leaving you, *AndFriend*," said the voice of the Leader of the escort that had brought them here.

"Thanks again, Wing Cee and escort," said Jim.

"Our pleasure, *AndFriend*."

They were gone.

"Now what?" asked Mary.

"Now—I bet you, another escort," said Jim. "It doesn't take a genius to figure it out. Mollen didn't want us to get to the edge of human-held territory without being protected—and observed all the way. But no single ship's company is going to know which direction we go in, or be in a position to make any kind of guess about our mission. Just in case."

"In case of what?" It was almost a grumble from Mary.

"In case of in case," said Jim. "Any avoidable ill chance should be avoided. Rule number sixteen million zip—here's the next team."

Another box of five fighters had appeared around them.

"*AndFriend*, this is Wing Cee speaking, Leader of your escort up to the Frontier in Brazil Sector. Are you ready to shift?"

"Hear you, Wing Cee," said Jim. "*AndFriend* ready to shift; and thanks for the escort."

"Our job. Shift, then. On the count. And . . . two . . . three . . . shift!"

This time they came out in space with no command ship nearby. But their escort left and a few minutes later a new one was with them.

"*AndFriend*," said a voice, speaking English with a noticeable accent, "this is Wing Cee speaking, of the escort for you to next shift point. Are you ready to shift? . . ."

And so it continued.

"What if the instruments of some Laagi patrol over the Frontier pick us up hopping along behind the human line?" Mary asked.

"I'll bet you another bet—that there's a screen of our own ships out just across the Frontier, looking for any Laagi activity and making sure any alien ship is too far off to pick us up on instruments. If they see any sign of aliens, we'll probably get word that our next shift destination point has been changed."

She said nothing, but he suspected her silence of being a doubtful one.

"No, I wasn't told this by the general or anyone else," he said. "But you've got your area of expertise and I've got mine. What I'm suggesting is as elementary a precaution as holding your breath when you put your head under water."

"I could have been told," said Mary.

"What was all that I used to hear so much—about the need to know? As far as being told things—" Jim checked himself before he said too much. People above Mollen and Mary had made the decisions to leave him no options. There was no point in reacting against her.

There was a moment's silence between them.

"Maybe—" began Mary and was interrupted as Jim began to go through the verbal exchange that accompanied another change of escorts.

"Maybe," she said, "I might have had reasons they didn't know about for needing to know."

"Take it up with the general and whoever else was involved, then, when you get back," said Jim.

There was silence from Mary in reply to this. Jim felt a twinge of guilt. He had just told himself he would not take his resentments out on her, and this last remark of his had almost been an invitation to a brannigan. He made a mental note to think before he spoke from now on.

Eventually the last five-ship escort left them with a single ship, the driver of which did not even speak, but flashed a shift signal and countdown on his hull lights. It was like being escorted by a ghost. For some reason Jim was reminded of the Charles Dickens story, *A Christmas Carol*, in which the third ghost—the ghost of Christmas Yet To Come—escorts Scrooge, the main character, into scenes of the future without saying a word, even in answer to Scrooge's questioning.

They were led out beyond the end of the human-defended Frontier by this one ship for four shifts, before their solitary escort finally flashed a "good luck" on its hull lights and disappeared, no doubt on a shift back to the safety of the human side of the Frontier.

"Where are we?" asked Mary, for the vision screens of the ship were showing unfamiliar constellations all around them.

"Where no human has gone before."

"Would you be serious for once?" Mary said; but there was no angry edge to the tone of that question.

"Sometimes it helps not to be serious," said Jim.

"Do you mean you don't know where we are?"

"I do—and I don't," said Jim. "Do you know anything about spatial navigation?"

"No," she answered. "They didn't give us that at Reserve Gunnery School."

"Well, I can't very well explain where we are to you then, unless you take my word for a lot of things," Jim said. "Basically, the earliest navigation in space outside the solar system used our own Sun as a base point for navigation. When we started to get farther out we began to run into errors using that method. So a man named Zee Tai-lin came up with the theoretical centerpoint of our own galaxy, as a base point."

"How did he find that?" Mary's voice was interested.

"Let's not go into that, please," said Jim. "Just take it from me he did establish a theoretical--repeat, theoretical—centerpoint for the galaxy. Someday we may come up with ships which can go in toward the center and come back, and actually establish if he was right about where the centerpoint is, like we finally established the position of the North Pole of Earth—or the South Pole, for that matter."

"You mean we figure all our space-shifts by referencing a point so far away that even a ten-light-year jump is a tiny fraction of our distance to the reference point? Isn't the galaxy something like sixty thousand light-years across? It seems like overdoing things to figure all your spaceship travel—"

"It would be, if that's what we did," said Jim. "No, once a theoretical centerpoint was established, a theoretical line was drawn through it—a diameter of the galaxy—taken as close to Sol as practical. It's that theoretical line we tie to for navigational purposes. That's to say, to travel any real distance from Earth, we go down the line until we're close enough to find on our instruments the star we're interested in. Then we turn off at a sharp angle and go directly from the line to it."

"I remember this now," said Mary. "Yes, it all comes back to me. I had the elements of it in secondary school. The Laagi, of course, are almost right on that line of ours as it goes inward from us toward the theoretical center. That's one reason why going around them's been such a problem."

"That's it," said Jim. "And they evidently either use the same line or one so close to it that we ought to be able to find their home base or bases near or on it, somewhere farther down-galaxy."

"But—" began Mary, and stopped. "We're lost now then, aren't we? How can we find the line again, now that that ship's just led us away out here?"

"The answer to that," said Jim, "is 'not easily.'"

"But—" And Mary got stuck again.

"The point is, it makes it pretty hard for the Laagi to find out where we are, at the same time."

"So how did you plan to get around Laagi space? How did you plan to find your way around to their other side and then back home again?"

"How did Raoul find his way home?"

"We don't know," said Mary.

"And it never occurred to you to ask how you and I were going to do it," said Jim.

"Will you stop that?" snapped Mary. "It may be giving you emotional relief to make a joke out of what I don't know, but you're taking it out of me to get that emotional relief. No, I didn't think to ask how we'd get there and back. I had other things to think of and it wasn't part of my field of expertise. I left it up to those whose field it was. Now either explain yourself, or shut off the funny remarks!"

"Sorry," said Jim. "—Though I might point out that being the one who's got to get us out of this, I could be the one needing emotional relief right at this moment, a little more maybe than you do. No, sorry again. I seem to end up apologizing to you more than I have with anyone else I ever met. No, it's not your fault you didn't ask. But it's somebody's fault you were let come up here not realizing the risks you were running. If and when we get back, I may even say a word to the general about that."

"All right," said Mary. "I forgive you. You forgive me. Now, explain things."

"All right." Jim took a deep breath. "How's your history? Do you remember that before the navigator's sextant came along, there was the cross-staff and the astrolabe and dead reckoning as means for sailors sailing out of sight of land on Earth's oceans to find a particular destination?"

"Yes," she said.

"All right. Pre-sextant navigation, with compass, log, dead reckoning and a ship's clock that might be less than accurate, still allowed people to sail around the world. You just headed for someplace like Africa, say, once upon a time, instead of to a particular town on its east coast; and you sailed along the coast when you hit it until you found what you were after, instead of going directly to it across open ocean from your starting point. It's something like that early level of ocean navigation we're at in galactic space now. So, that's what you and I have to work with from where we sit now."

"You're going to have to be more specific than that," said Mary.

"All right, I will. Now, we've been taken out here and dropped off, out of sight, so to speak, of our galaxy center-line. But we have what the ancient seamen of Earth didn't have, which is a chronometer—in fact three of them, not counting the one in my mind—which are accurate to such a small fraction of a second that for ordinary practical purposes we can ignore the inaccuracy. Also, we have a ship's memory which can recall every phase-shift, how far and where to, and every turn and twist on ordinary drive and calculate all these to tell us where we've gone since we left Earth."

Mary sighed with relief. A mental sigh, observed Jim, was impossible to describe. It was like a promissory note of what would, if there had been a body to do it, have been an exhalation of breath.

"Then we do know where we are right now."

"Well—again, yes and no," said Jim. "Yes, we know where we are right now because in addition to what I've just told you, my memory banks were supplied with the point where that last guide ship dropped us off; although I didn't know it, until his lights flashing farewell released the lock on that section of memory. And, no, because all we know is where we are in relation to Earth, the Frontier and the galactic centerline. What we don't know is where what we're looking for is located."

"But all you have to do—" Mary broke off. "Oh, I see."

"Exactly," said Jim. "The proper course for us would be to head back toward the galactic centerline and follow right down it to the Laagi world or worlds. But if we do that, we'll run into large numbers of their fighting spaceships long before we get to our destination—let alone, beyond it into the unknown territory. Our only hope is to go forward out here, essentially paralleling the centerline until it's safe to turn in toward it again and find ourselves beyond the other side of Laagi territory, in the unknown."

"And if we turn inward toward the line too soon, we run into Laagi warships," said Mary.

"Right. And if we go too far and turn in too late, we'll end up at where the centerline is, according to our calculations, but not knowing where we are in relation to anything but it. Should we assume in that case that we're still short of unknown territory and head on down-galaxy along the line, or figure we've overshot it, and turn back along the centerline—in that case essentially guaranteeing that we'll run into Laagi if we're wrong?"

"There's got to be some way around this," said Mary.

"Oh, I forgot one possibility. What if there's nothing to be found beyond Laagi territory within any practical distance? Do we keep on? Do we turn back—"

"There's a method they used to use for zeroing in artillery fire," began Mary. "You deliberately fired your first shot to strike beyond the target, the second shot short. Then you fired a little short of your long shot or a little farther than your short shot and kept on increasing or decreasing your range until you 'zeroed in,' as they used to say, on the target—"

"Correct, first time out. My compliments. That's exactly the method we'll be using. We deliberately jump for what we are as sure as can be is beyond the Laagi home base—which we estimate to be about as far from the Frontier in its direction as Earth is in its, on the other side of it. We jump beyond the home base, or hope we have, but short of the farther limits of Laagi territory. Then, taking advantage of the fact that we're only one alien ship and in where they'd never expect to find us, we sneak in toward the centerline and see if we can't spot evidence of Laagi space travel or living centers, before whichever it is spots us."

He paused.

"Am I making sense to you so far?"

"Yes," she answered, "go on."

"Well then," he said, "if, by doing all this, we reach the

centerline without running into any such evidence and conclude we've overshot the Laagi territory, we go out away from
the line again, to what we think is a safe distance, and head
back parallel to it, in the direction of the Laagi center, and
then, in again. If we don't find any evidence, we repeat and
go back farther. If we do, we repeat and go outward again,
toward galaxy center but not as far as we went before, and
nose in again. Finally, this way we establish where Laagi territory ends on the down-galaxy side; and we're ready to go
hunting for Raoul's 'Paradise.'"

"Raoul," said Mary almost wistfully, "didn't do all this
inning and outing."

"No, Raoul sailed straight through the heart of Laagi territory and let them cut him to ribbons," said Jim. "The only
reason they didn't blow *La Chasse Gallerie* into cosmic dust
was because somehow, even without drives, he couldn't be
stopped and held still long enough to be blown up. You and I,
we've got a ship to protect, to say nothing of ourselves. Come
to think of it, what does happen to two minds when a ship is
destroyed out from under them? Do they die, too, or are they
left just drifting in space—"

"Let's face that possibility when it comes," said Mary.

"We don't have any choice but to face it when it comes. I
was hoping for a little advance notice."

"Well, I don't have any answer for you. That's why there's
no point in facing it beforehand," replied Mary, almost tran-
quilly. "Shall we begin?"

"We've already begun," said Jim. "I've been setting up an
automatic pattern of jumps to take us forward, in and out, just
in case for some reason I shouldn't be able to command the
ship. So hang on, here we go."

After those words, the actual going was anything but dra-
matic. They shifted ten times—even though they were out of
their bodies, the shifts were perceptible as a sort of hiccup in
attention—and at last swam in what hardly looked any different than the point in galactic space where their last guide ship
had left them.

"Now we try going in . . . very carefully," said Jim.

He mentally ordered about the controls; and Mary was
knowledgeable enough about ship-handling to realize he was
reorienting the hull prior to the shift, so that they would come

out facing in the direction they wanted, which in this case would be toward the centerline. Then he began a series of phase-shifts, shorter and shorter jumps, until he was down to a final shift that was no farther than *AndFriend*'s instruments could see.

"According to the calculations of the instruments—and mine," said Jim, "we ought to be within three light-years' distance of the centerline. If we're right in the assumption of everybody back home, and the Laagi use a centerline very close to ours, then the area we're in ought to have traffic of Laagi ships up and down the line. We'll just have to park here, wait and see."

"And if nothing comes along by the time we get tired of waiting?" Mary asked. "Do we go all the way out again, or do we just edge back up the line?"

"The first way's safe but slow. The second ought to be faster, but risky—assuming we're moving into a higher incidence of Laagi traffic." Jim hesitated. "I know what I'd do. What would you do?"

"Inch back up the line at this distance from it," said Mary without hesitation.

"I was afraid you'd say that."

"Because your choice was going back out again, was it?"

"No," said Jim glumly, "because I'd made the same choice. Now we don't have any excuse for not doing it. And we could stub our toe on a Laagi ship this way before we know it."

They began going up-galaxy. Jim estimated they were now more than half a light-year out from the centerline; and he kept his phase-shifts to just within the limit of the ability of his instruments to spot a Laagi ship. He and Mary fell into a silence with which they both seemed to be content, for it was only briefly and occasionally broken during a period which their ship's chronometer measured as a little over fourteen hours.

The procedure was to make the shift, pause, scan all instrument-visible area and, if anything shiplike was observed, to creep up on this with tiny phase-shifts of no more than a few hundred kilometers until it became clear that what they were seeing was not an alien vessel. Then they would make another jump forward to the limit of their instruments' scanning ability, and another close investigation of the new area if there seemed to be reason for it.

At the end of the slightly more than fourteen hours, however, Jim suddenly grunted and began coding for a shift of a full five light-years more out from the centerline.

"What is it?" demanded Mary. "Did you see something?"

"No," said Jim. "Just back-of-the-head hunch. I can't explain it to you any better than that."

"Come to think of it," said Mary, "you've mentioned several things—a chronometer in your mind, and your own mental calculations as to where we were, in addition to the calculations of the ship's instruments. Now this. Is there something about you I ought to know?"

"Nothing miraculous," said Jim. "You remember my talking about the early days of ocean navigation? Even with a sextant and a good chronometer, it was quite a trick to cross the Atlantic and have the first land you sighted turn out to be the point you were aiming at. But some navigators then seemed to have a knack for it. Some of us space jockeys seem to have a knack for interstellar navigation. That's all."

"That's quite a lot, it seems to me," said Mary. "In fact it's right on the edge of being almost too much to believe."

"Ever hear of a homing instinct in animals—not merely birds but domestic dogs or cats?" said Jim. "The Polynesian navigators watched the action of waves to guide themselves in crossing great stretches of the Pacific in small ships not much bigger than large canoes. The Aleuts up near the North Pole, back home, had something like seventeen different names for different kinds of snow in their language. Their children would play in snowdrifts—but never in the ones that would fall in and bury them. When you asked them why they picked one snowdrift over another, they essentially said it was obvious. I'm one of the ones with a knack for intragalactic navigation—that's one of the reasons it was my Wing that went after Raoul."

"All you're saying, really," said Mary, "is 'trust me.'"

"Right. Trust me. I trust my instinct," said Jim. "While you're at it, remember that all the instruments in Raoul's ship had to have been long gone by the time he started to come back to Earth. But he traveled in the right direction. How do you suppose he knew his way?"

Mary said nothing for a long moment.

"I don't know," she said finally. "But—"

"Hold it!" Jim interrupted suddenly. "Bandit! Straight out!"

Sure enough, there it was on the long-distance screen. Just the barest pinpoint of light at the moment, but with the halo around it that identified it as something radiating as no natural object would.

"How can you tell it's a Laagi? Maybe there's something unknown out here—" began Mary.

"It's Laagi. I can feel it."

"Going away from us? Or coming toward us?"

"That I don't know—yet. I've put the instruments on it. Indications right now are it's traveling parallel to us and about half a light-year in from us. But whether down-galaxy or up-galaxy, I've no way of knowing until we're closer to it."

"Can it see us?"

"I don't know that either," said Jim. "I'd bet a month's pay it hasn't—yet. A lot depends on which way it's going, whether it's facing toward or away from us."

"With screens looking every which way, that shouldn't make any difference," Mary said.

"It does, though. Human—I mean, Laagi nature. Our attention, and theirs, too, seems to be directed most of the time in a ship-forward direction—one of the things that makes us assume they've got eyes looking forward, like animal predators and humans, and not out to each side like birds and prey animals. If it's headed this way, he's going to see us sooner or later, unless we move. And if we move, we're bound to attract the attention of his instruments."

They waited.

"He's traveling down-galaxy. Looking toward our direction," said Jim finally.

They waited a little longer.

"He's seen us. He's turned in our direction. Stand by for him to jump into battle range of us." Jim's mental voice had become remote, businesslike. He felt as well as heard it in his own mind as he was used to hearing it, talking to his Wing on the Frontier, just before contact with an approaching gang of Laagi ships.

"Oh, God!" said Mary. "And we've hardly started."

"Don't worry, baby." Jim could feel that if his body had

been with him, it would be grinning, the same way the combat-recorder films always showed him grinning as he went into battle; and not even he could tell if it was to *AndFriend,* to Mary, or to both of them he spoke: "If he gets close enough to hurt you, I'll kill him."

# CHAPTER

# 13

THE LAAGI SHIP MADE A PHASE-SHIFT JUST AS JIM SAID THIS, and suddenly it was big enough to be pictured as something more than a dot on their longest-looking screen.

"I'm wrong," said Jim. "It's not us he's aimed at. On this angle he'll pass us but only at better than instrument mid-range. Either he's got a destination off to one side of the centerline, or . . ."

He fell silent.

"You mean we could be in among the star systems having Laagi-occupied planets?" Mary asked.

"Your guess on that's as good as mine," said Jim slowly. "But it looks like he's going to pass us by at a distance which could mean his instruments don't see us."

"Don't Laagi instruments see as far as ours?"

"We don't know for sure—just the way we don't know so much about them," said Jim. "But it's a good angle. I mean, like I said, we've noticed that when we're at an angle to them, they don't seem to see us as well as from more head-on angles—or up close; distance helps, too. It's all guesswork because on most things their ships can do as well, or better; and our own ships are under orders to act on that premise. Actually, fighting them, I get the impression there're weak

137

spots in their observation. And that's the way most combat pilots feel. If we're right, it could explain why sometimes they turn and run—if you want to call it running—when you're sure they're ready to joust."

"You're thinking of just letting him go by?" Mary said. "But aren't we a sitting duck here, if he suddenly starts turning toward us?"

"If we move we might attract his attention, as I mentioned," said Jim. "Remember, we're where no Laagi ship is going to expect to run into something like us—particularly just a ship alone, the way we are. If he's really not seen us, and if he's really headed by us, we can sit still and he'll never know we were here. Or if he does, maybe he'll take us for an experimental new design of Laagi ship. Or—oh, I don't know. . . ."

"I've never known you to hesitate like this," Mary said. "Why're you willing to take such a chance he'll go by without seeing us, or even seeing us without attacking us?"

"Because," said Jim slowly, "I don't think he's armed."

There was a second or two of pause.

"Why? What makes you think that?" she said. "More to the point, what makes you think it so strongly you're ready to gamble our whole mission on it?"

"I can't tell you exactly why. It's the way he's acting. Look at him. He's three-quarters on to us—his whole side's a target. Just a little more on that same course and I could cut him wide open with a beam. Then it'd take less than a minute to stand in beside him close enough to drop a mine that'd blow him apart a second after we were out of range of it, ourselves. Why's he taking a chance like that, unless he's unarmed and doesn't see us?"

"You're still gambling," said Mary flatly.

"But with something at stake," muttered Jim. "Suppose he's expected somewhere and they come out looking for him when he doesn't show up . . . and scoop up some dust they can identify as part of his ship? Wouldn't that mean killing him would be like a flag planted to tell them we've been here?"

There was another pause.

"It could be. All right," Mary said. "You're the expert on alien ships. It's up to you."

"We'll sit," said Jim.

They sat.

The Laagi ship went by in one phase-shift and vanished from their instruments with a second.

"Of course," said Mary when it was gone, "you know it might just have pretended to go innocently by because it was unarmed; and it's right now reporting us to the nearest equivalent of military authorities the Laagi have."

"In which case," said Jim, "the sooner we get out of here, the better."

He was setting up a phase-shift for *AndFriend* as he spoke.

"Down-galaxy, I think," he said, "now that we've found Laagi space traffic this far up. As far as his reporting us goes, if you were a Laagi military commander and you heard of a human ship where we just were—just which way do you think that ship might have jumped after it was last seen? And how far away from that point where it was seen could it be, by the time you can get your own fighting ships out after it?"

Mary said nothing.

"So if you were such a military commander," said Jim as they shifted, "wouldn't you find it a lot easier and safer just to file a report and let it get tangled up in the bureaucratic wheels, rather than take a chance on something that might possibly be the figment of a civilian pilot's imagination?"

"You're really assuming they're like humanity," said Mary.

"Well, we've got nothing else to base assumptions on," said Jim. "And a lot of what we've seen of them does parallel what we've got and what we do. We use a theoretical centerline. They seem to, too. Our ships are shaped differently from theirs, but they phase-shift to cover large distances just as we do. They use cutting weapons that seem developed from lasers, like we do. Their fighter ships are only big enough for a crew of two individuals. They seem to think in terms of a Frontier in space, just like we do. . . ."

He got tired of thinking up comparisons and ran down.

"Et cetera," he said.

"All very fine," said Mary. "But you could be wrong because there're things you don't know. And there've got to be things you don't know—that we don't know."

"Right enough," said Jim. "How about it? Drop the subject?"

"Subject dropped."

"I like you, Mary."

There was a long pause.

"If you don't mind," said Mary in a distant voice, "I've got a few things to mull over. Call me if you need me for anything. Otherwise, I'll be in conference with myself, if you don't mind."

"I don't mind," said Jim.

There was no further word from Mary.

They crept down-galaxy, in shift-jumps no farther than their instruments could safely read ahead. Twenty-four hours went by, and no more Laagi ships were encountered. Then another twenty-four hours with the same result. And another twenty-four.

"We must be beyond Laagi space, down-line, by this time, mustn't we?" asked Mary. They had been back in conversation since about an hour following Mary's withdrawal.

"Should be," said Jim. "There's some interesting star systems ahead. I count at least eight G0-type stars within a ten light-year box no more than twenty or thirty light-years down the line. If any of those have got livable worlds, maybe we've found Raoul's Paradise. Maybe we should go all the way in to the line and follow it down."

They had been slowly angling back in toward the centerline as time went by and no more sign of Laagi ships was encountered.

"Any comment?" asked Jim.

"No," said Mary. "I think that's a good idea, Jim."

They had been on considerably warmer terms, lately, for no particular reason Jim could understand. Following Mary's agreement, he made the necessary adjustments in the ship's controls, and took them in a single shift most of the light-year-and-a-half distance that still separated them from the centerline.

"We'll keep a watch, still, though," said Jim. "You watch up-galaxy, I'll watch ahead, down-galaxy. Before I forget to mention it, by the way, I still don't feel the least bit sleepy. How about you?"

They had made an agreement earlier that each of them would let the other know if he or she noticed any sign of tiredness.

"I don't," said Mary. "But I spoke to you twice and caught you sleeping. You had to ask me again what I wanted."

"I did?" said Jim. "I don't remember that. Are you sure?"

"I learned too much about your sleeping patterns in the lab to be mistaken," said Mary.

"Well, that checks out with what I noticed when I first became part of *AndFriend,* back at Base," said Jim. "It also explains how Penard could keep coming steadily that way if he was consciously using his mind to drive *La Chasse Gallerie.* Maybe we don't have to worry about needing sleep for the rest of the trip if we can do it without knowing we do it, and wake up at the first word from the other one of us—at any rate, back to what I was saying. If there're any Laagi moving this far down the line, we're much more likely to run into them from here on, this close to the line."

"Where did you grow up?" Mary asked him unexpectedly.

"Actually, in country a lot like the Base is in," said Jim. "I was born in a hospital in Denver; but my folks lived in Edmonton and that's where I grew up. Every kid's a Frontier pilot when he's five years old. In my case it stuck. I was able to pass the tests—and here I am."

"Have you got any brothers or sisters?"

"Not one," said Jim solemnly.

The solemnity was a fake, but he had forgotten his ability, now that he was only a mind in a ship, of recall. He was suddenly young again, suddenly back among the mountains. Suddenly wondering what it would be like to have a brother or sister to play with. Somehow he always imagined the brother or sister as younger than he was. He remembered now, with painful clarity, being extremely young and telling his mother what very good care he would take of a brother or sister if she would only get him one—or two. It was not until years later that he came to understand that medically what he wanted was not possible; that the circumstances of his own birth had ended his mother's capability to have any more children. All he recognized at the time of his asking was that by doing so, he had made her unhappy.

"We lived outside of Edmonton, a way," he said to Mary now. "My father was a metallurgist with a speciality in metal extraction from water. He was a consultant and gone off somewhere around the world, most of the time."

"Do they still live there?" asked Mary.

"They're both dead," he said. "My father had an accident on an underwater inspection. The oxygen exchanger on his diving mask failed. My mother died a year or two after that in a car accident. She went off the road one night when she was driving home from Edmonton to our place by herself. The officers thought there might have been a hit-and-run accident, some other driver might have nudged her car off the road into a fall down a slope; but they were never able to find anyone who might be responsible. My uncle got me into the Cadet Corps."

"I had no idea," murmured Mary. "It must have been awfully hard for you. Both my parents are still alive."

"Where do you come from?" he asked.

"Los Angeles Complex," she said. "We were actually in San Diego. My folks still live there."

"Good," he said. "You can see them whenever you want."

"I don't, though," she said. "We were always pretty separate in my family. In fact, I couldn't wait to win the scholarship that took me away to Boston to college. One good thing—they let me go."

"Why shouldn't they have?" he said, surprised.

"Why? Oh, I was young," Mary said absently. "I was fifteen when I graduated from high school. I was big for my age, though, and old for my age. I don't just mean I acted old. I'd grown up with a pair of independent adults; and I was an independent adult from the time I could walk. Also, I was good at things. Show me something you can do and I'll bet I can learn to do it better."

"Fly *AndFriend* without the engines, then," said Jim.

"Oh," she said, and laughed. "Of course. You're right and I'm being ridiculous. I know I'm hard to live with. I'm just used to challenging anyone and everything."

"You're not that hard to live with," said Jim—and almost added, "now," but stopped himself in time.

She said nothing for a second. Then she spoke.

"Thank you."

"For what?" said Jim. "I was only stating a fact. Hold it—the instruments are showing something up ahead."

"I don't see . . . oh, there it is. Another Laagi ship?"

"Could be. Let's just sit tight at this range and see whether it moves. We've got all the time we want to take."

They waited, but the pinprick of light with the faint halo around it did not appear to move. Jim took sights on it with the instruments and set up an instrument watch to alert them if it shifted in any direction.

When six hours had gone by with no report of movement by the instruments, Jim took *AndFriend* outward from the centerline on a curve keeping the object they watched just within sight of their instruments; then took a second set of sights and set up a second watch.

When after another six hours, this, also, showed no movement, Jim metaphorically scratched his nonexistent head.

"I don't understand this," he told Mary.

"Could whoever it is be simply planning to outwait us, and just sit there until curiosity brings us close enough to shoot?"

"I've never known of, or heard of, the Laagi showing this kind of patience—or reacting in this way at all. The only ways they've ever shown us are either attack or run, with no hesitation about doing either one."

"Well, then," said Mary, "what's the chance that the instruments are making a mistake and that isn't a Laagi ship at all, but something that looks to them like it?"

"After nearly a hundred and fifty years of our having seen what Laagi ships look like? That doesn't make sense, either."

"So I guess we go in and look," said Mary.

"I guess you guess right," said Jim. "Whatever it is, we'll take a closer look at it."

They began by going even farther away from the centerline, clear out of instrument sight of the object. Then Jim navigated their way back toward it from what should have been the equivalent of a ninety-degree angle to their original approach.

It came on the screen and stayed there. As far as their instruments could tell them, it did not move as they approached. Finally, they were close enough to get a recognizable picture of it on their screen; and it was a typical two-individual Laagi fighter craft, for some unknown reason simply hanging still in space—or hanging still in the sense that it was holding a steady position with regard to the centerline, which—like the galaxy it transversed—was in rotation about the galaxy's theoretical center.

Jim checked *AndFriend* and held her still at that distance from the other vessel.

"I do not—repeat, not—get this at all," he said. "That ship's facing down-galaxy. Unless it's expecting some kind of attack from farther down the line, why should it be here at all? And if it's expecting an attack, why isn't it patrolling whatever segment of whatever Frontier line this is? Just sitting there, it can't watch anything beyond the viewing limit of its instruments. If you wanted to hold a Frontier that way, you'd have to have so many ships . . . "

His mind shook his missing head over the enormity of the thought.

"You'd need thousands of fighter ships like that—no, you'd need several thousand times the total number we estimate they've got facing us on our Frontier; and there can't be that many Laagi worlds, to handle that kind of expense. If there is, they could just run right over our forces on our Frontier without hardly noticing we were there; while actually they've never hit us with more than a hundred or so ships at once—and that was the biggest of the battles we ever had with them."

"It could be abandoned, for some reason," said Mary.

"What reason?"

"I don't know," said Mary. "But, again, we're dealing with nonhuman minds. They may have a lot of things like we have, and act a lot like us, but there could just as easily be a reason for them to abandon one of their ships in space that we humans'd never think of. For example—a religious reason. Or a superstitious reason. Maybe that ship is just a mock-up of a ship, put there to mark the limits of their territory down-galaxy, for example."

"Mary," said Jim, "you'd convince a stone lion. We'll go in and see."

He sent *AndFriend* toward the motionless Laagi vessel.

"Why a stone lion?" said Mary.

"Why? I don't know," answered Jim. "It was just the first thing I could think of—now, don't say anything for just a few minutes, while we get in close. . . ."

"Why any animal, for that matter?"

Jim did not answer. He was concentrating on only two things. First, getting as close as he could safely calculate—or that *AndFriend*'s calculators could safely calculate—to the Laagi ship in one jump, and then taking them on a close pass by it on ordinary drive.

He did so, zipped past it and immediately phase-shifted out of shooting range, then started studying the pictorial record of the other ship that had been made as they passed it.

"No sign of a reaction," he said finally. "Just no sign at all. And that's all wrong."

"Mock-up," said Mary.

"Can you see a technologically advanced society—one as advanced as ours—setting up a mock-up way out here in space for religious or scarecrow reasons?" demanded Jim. "I don't know what we should do now."

"Let's go right up to it, stop, and examine it at arm's length," said Mary.

"Taking one hell of a chance."

"If you were alone, with no one to argue with, what would you do?" asked Mary.

Jim said nothing for a moment.

"I'd go in, of course," he answered finally. "I'd have to "

"Then, may I ask—"

"What we're waiting for?" said Jim. "You may not, because I'm already going in."

In fact, he was.

Fifteen minutes later they were hanging in space, side by side with the Laagi ship and barely fifty kilometers from it.

"Hello! Hey! Do you hear me? Respond if you do. This is *AndFriend* calling Laagi ship . . . " Jim sent his voice out up and down the normal human ship-to-ship communications band.

"Have your people ever contacted Laagi, or overheard them contacting each other, ship-to-ship?" Mary asked.

"Never," said Jim. "As far as we can tell they don't talk to each other. But if this one can hear my voice he may take the fact I'm talking as a sign I'm not about to begin shooting. It's worth a try, anyway. They must have some kind of communication system. When there's several of them they all either attack or run at the same time."

"But you probably aren't going to get anywhere trying to talk to this ship, are you."

"No. But I had to check out the possibility."

"Now what, then?"

"Now what?" Jim echoed. "I don't know. If I was simply piloting *AndFriend* normally, with me in my body and you in yours, as a last resort, we'd put on our space suits and then I'd open the lock and power myself across to that other ship's hull. Then, if necessary, I'd cut my way in through the hull or the entry port. There's the entry port right there, but how does a spaceship like I am now—"

"Like we are now."

"—like we are now, get through it?"

Mary said nothing.

"If you actually touched its hull," she suggested finally, "do you suppose you could see inside it, the way you can see everything inside of *AndFriend*?"

"I don't know. It sounds crazy . . . you're more the expert on this business of mind being in matter. What do you think?"

"I think we need to try it just to check out the possibility."

"You do, do you?" grumbled Jim. "Do you realize what it means to try to move a mass this size up close enough to touch a mass the size of that Laagi ship, without having them do serious damage to each other when they do touch?"

"Of course I know. But what other way is there? Can you think of one?"

"Offhand, no—hang on!" Jim interrupted himself. "There's just a chance I can make some kind of sensory connection across a line connected to that other ship. Now, what do we have in the way of a line or cable to make connection with?"

He fell into a self-examination of everything aboard *And-Friend*. There was, of course, no such article as a line or cable simply aboard waiting to be put to use. It would be a matter of his making one out of material already belonging to the ship.

Theoretically, he thought, any connecting material that was part of the ship would do. The difficulty was that nowhere about a vessel like *AndFriend* was anything resembling such material. After puzzling over the matter for some time, he had an inspiration. What he did have was a repair robot that was independently mobile and could be sent anywhere to do anything.

"What I'm going to do is make a connector out of the hull material," he explained to Mary. "I'll have the repair robot go out the entry port and literally peel off a sliver down the length of the hull. That should give us a good twenty meters of sliver, like a long, very thin rod. The robot can stand in the open entry port—or even on the outside of the hull with the entry port closed, come to think of it, holding out the rod toward the Laagi ship. Then I'll try to move, carefully, as close to the other ship as I can. You watch the screen, in case I don't feel contact when the rod touches the Laagi ship, or the robot fails to report the touching—because I want to stop *AndFriend* moving the moment we touch. At the worst, it'll give us some twenty meters of buffer zone."

So, that was what the robot did and Jim did. Jim found he was conscious of the sliver being peeled off—not as something painful, but as something happening to the general feel of the ship that was unordinary and vaguely discomforting. But there turned out to be a problem when the robot tried to hold the sliver out. It was long enough and thin enough to be extremely flexible; and instead of projecting stiffly toward the other ship, its far end whipped back and forth in extreme arcs, which had begun with the fact that the sliver's farther end had originally lagged behind as the end held by the robot was held out from *AndFriend*'s hull; and once the farther end started moving to catch up, its mass carried it beyond the point of straightness into an arc, bent it the other way until it reached a limit, and then began to oscillate back past the midpoint once more.

Gradually, however, the oscillating slowed. Eventually, when it was down to the point where it was oscillating in an arc of only three or four meters, Jim began to creep *AndFriend* toward the other vessel with both of them lying side by side.

Eventually, the arcing tip of the sliver began to brush the side of the Laagi ship. Jim felt the contact even before Mary announced it.

"It's all right!" he said. "I can feel it—I can feel the other ship. It feels . . . it feels very, very strange. . . ."

He thought he heard Mary saying something, but her voice was at once very far away and muffled; and in any case he had already moved his point of view inside the alien ship and was lost in fascination with what he saw.

# CHAPTER

## 14

THERE WAS ABSOLUTELY NO LIGHT WITHIN THE SEALED INTE-
rior of the alien vessel, so Jim did not see, in the sense of
using his eyes. Rather, he felt everything within it so clearly
that his mind was able to form a picture of what was there as
well as if the interior had been lighted.

It was immediately apparent why the Laagi ships had the
pregnant look that was so characteristic of them. The second
member of the ship's crew did not sit behind the first as in the
human ships, but directly underneath the first. There was
nothing between the two positions and they were close enough
that even humans could have reached down, or up, as the case
might be, and clasped hands with a shipmate.

But whoever had been the pilot and gunner of this ship—if
indeed that was the way the Laagi divided up the duties of the
two who operated the vessel—they were now long dead, even
though Jim felt that the interior of the ship still held an oxy-
gen-bearing but unearthlike atmosphere that his body would
have tolerated only with difficulty. It was a somewhat sul-
phurous atmosphere, as far as his sensing of it could tell him,
but what less odorous gases it held beyond that he had no way
of telling.

The two operating positions in the ship were up front before an open space that was divided into open compartments which could have been bunks or storage spaces. The operating positions consisted essentially of two metallic-looking vertical rings encircling what looked like oversize golf tees. These had their base on flooring behind the rings and angled forward so that the cup of the tee-structure sat in the center of the ring, 'he cup itself tilted so that it sat horizontally—that is, parallel o the floor below.

The inside of the ring was studded with what were easily recognizable as controls, buttons and small levers. On the cup itself sat something almost indescribable; what looked like a pile of hooplike rings of bone or cartilage from a quarter to a half-meter in diameter, enclosed with what might have been a dark, thin, leatherlike skin that was, however, now dried and cracked open under its own weight to show hooplike bones beneath. It was hardly possible to relate the remains of skin that rested on and hung down from the two cup-ends with any imaginable shape of living creature.

The instruments and controls also seemed nonfunctioning. Experimentally, Jim willed some of the buttons and switches into movement, as he was used to doing with those in *And-Friend,* but nothing happened. The ship was dead—powerless. He was left with the enigma of what he had found, plus something else he could not identify and which he was not entirely sure he would have noticed if he had been there in the flesh.

It was a strangeness—a purely nonphysical feeling that compounded the disgust he might have felt in a charnel house with the sadness of a graveside and a feeling of despair. Now that he had noticed it, it grew on him, mounting steadily from a whisper toward a scream in his mind; and he literally fled, in his point of view, to a position on the outside hull of the alien ship.

Back out there, he became conscious of the fact that Mary was still calling him.

"Jim! Can you answer me, Jim? Try to answer me if you can—make any kind of answer. . . ."

There was no note of desperation to be heard in her voice, but he was suddenly conscious of what it might be like for her to find herself alone in a ship, nothing of which she could control, and cut off from contact with the only other person she could possibly reach.

"I'm sorry, Mary!" he called back. "I'm fine. I'll be right back there. Hold on. . . ."

He moved his point of view back across the connecting sliver, through the robot and back into the ship. Mary's presence seemed to him to be gaunt with tension, for all the steadiness of the voice he had heard her using.

"Jim! What happened? What's over there? Why didn't you answer me—"

"I'm sorry," he said again. "I'm really sorry. I didn't realize you weren't with me. Come to think of it, why weren't you with me?"

"I think I was, in a way," she answered. "I could feel something. Something terrible. But I couldn't seem to get you to answer."

"There's what's left of two Laagi there," Jim said. "They and their ship must have been dead a long time. I'll send Fingers over to break open the entry port, go in and make pictorial records of everything there. Then we'll get away from here and look the pictures over and see if we can understand some things—"

He broke off suddenly.

"Now why didn't I think of sending the robot in there in the first place?" he said. "That would've been the sensible thing to do, instead of cutting off a sliver to connect us—"

He interrupted himself.

"No, come to think of it, I'm glad I went the way I did. There's something, a feeling I could feel there that won't be in any pictures. I think it was what those Laagi were feeling when they were there . . . when they died. The record the robot'll make won't give us any of that and we'd never have known it was there. Didn't you say you felt something, too?"

"Yes," said Mary. "Just a touch. But something . . . I can't describe it."

"I can't either," said Jim. "But I'm going to try and so are you. Let's compare notes on it and see if we can't come up with some idea of what it felt like in our human terms."

While he was talking, he was already dispatching the robot to the Laagi ship. The robot, in fact, was effectively an all-purpose tool, one of the most useful bits of equipment aboard a fighter ship. It had been originally designed merely as something that could repair damage to the ship at a time when the pilot and the gunner might be either too occupied in fighting for their lives, or wounded and incapable of making necessary repairs themselves. It was a device with a squat little barrel of a body and numerous flexible arms. The body held, in addition to its independent motive system, the innumerable tools that could be attached by it to any of the arms; it had evolved to the point where it had become the potential solution to any need by pilot or gunner for anything from food and drink to a wound needing emergency medical attention.

It was also used by crew members to find any small thing that might have been accidentally dropped and which had rolled away out of sight into any of the tiny nooks and crannies produced by the equipment tightly crammed into the interior of the vessel.

But none of that was on Jim's mind now. What was concerning him at the moment was a guilty conscience at having let Mary go unanswered and unknowing while he marvelled at his discoveries aboard the Laagi ship. The fact that she had not complained about it, or acknowledged it, except by the momentary expression of the emotion in her mental voice when she once more spoke to her from back aboard *AndFriend*, made it worse.

He found himself wanting her to complain, so he could excuse himself more fully. But whether she understood his reasons or not, complaining seemed to be the one thing she was absolutely refusing to do. It left Jim uncomfortable with the feeling that he was now in debt to her, and he did not see any way by which he might get out.

On the other hand, if she thought that having him in debt to her was going to make him more likely to give in to her wishes . . .

He checked himself on that thought. They had just finally got on good terms with each other and here he was starting to think in terms of an argument. The robot came back aboard with its recording job accomplished and Jim immediately phase-shifted a full light-year from the dead alien ship.

"Look," he said, once they had made the shift. "I didn't mean to ignore you when I was on the Laagi ship. It was just that I was hit so hard by the differences aboard there. Also, I could hardly hear you when I was on the outside of that ship; and inside, I don't think I was hearing you at all."

"It doesn't matter," she said. "Could you move anything in the ship?"

"No," he said. "I didn't try anything but the controls; I could move them—but nothing happened. No telling how long that ship's been sitting there. You'll see what I mean when we look at the pictures Fingers took. I'm sure that ship's engines and everything operable about her's been dead for a long time. What was left of the two Laagi who'd crewed her —well, as I say, you'll see the pictures for yourself. Maybe they've been dead for centuries."

"And the other Laagi never came and got the ship, when we're this close to their civilization centers?" she said.

"Maybe they couldn't find it? Finding just one ship, even if you know its position within something like a couple of times instrument range, can be pretty rough. If this vessel was as much as a light-year out of position, their chances of finding it . . ."

His voice trailed off.

"We found it," said Mary. "In a matter of centuries, you'd think they could do that well if they wanted to."

"We didn't really find it," said Jim. "We stumbled across it."

"Don't split hairs," said Mary. "We were looking for Laagi ships, and it's right on the centerline. If we could stumble across it going right down the centerline, you'd think they'd be bound to find it doing the same thing. What did these Laagi look like? I know I'll be seeing the pictures as soon as the robot gets them stored and on the screen, but what I want to hear is your personal opinion."

"I don't know what they looked like," said Jim, a little irritably. "I didn't see them, you know. I just felt them, along with everything else about the ship. But they were sort of collapsed in on themselves, I'd say. They don't seem to have a structured skeleton inside them, the way we do. You'll have to look at the pictures and make up your own mind about it. Fingers, where are those pictures you just took?"

The robot had been waiting for a specific command to show them. Its first task had been to store what it had recorded from its own memory to the ship's memory, relating it to anything already in the ship's memory to which it seemed pertinent. Jim could merely have "remembered," therefore, what the robot had seen. But Mary, of course, could not do that. She would have to see the actual pictures on the screen.

As soon as Jim spoke, the screen lit up.

The robot had used his own exterior lights to illuminate what he was to record. To Jim, who had felt what was in the alien ship before seeing it, what he looked at now seemed garish under the bright white light in its shapes and strange colors. It was as if some maker of commercial entertainments had created a mock-up of what he had experienced directly.

Gone—he had hardly expected it to be otherwise—was the disgust-charnel house-sadness that had seemed to touch him while he had been in the other ship. But surprisingly also gone was the sense of something built and used by aliens. Besides the impression that what he looked at was a commercial mock-up of something alien was the sense that the film merely showed the interior of a different model of fighter ship, one that could as well have been designed and built by humans.

Because the effect of seeing it was so less than he had expected, therefore, he was taken unprepared by the wave of excitement that reached him from Mary.

"Jim! They're mummified. As if they've been there for centuries!"

He did not say, "That's what I just told you." Suddenly, he was very aware of her reactions. They were a blend of fascination and a curiosity that was so profound in her that it could almost be described as ravenous.

"Jim," she said. "I've got to analyze all this. You'll have to order the controls for me. Tell your robot to give me, up on the screen, the results of his gas samples of the interior atmosphere first, and after that the results of the scrapings he made of every surface, and then after that the measurements and interior views of those two Laagi bodies—"

"Wait a minute!" Jim said. "What do you mean, gas samples, scrapings, all this other stuff? A fighter ship robot—"

"Yours was updated so I could use him as a research tool. Just do what I'm asking you to do, Jim. I'm sorry there wasn't time to tell you everything we'd done to make my end of this trip productive. Now, first the scrapings . . . "

Jim did as she said, ending up by running the ship's artificial intelligence in calculations under her directions using values she had somehow derived from what the robot had reported, on a number of experiments Jim had never suspected it of making on the alien vessel.

"How did you know we'd run into a derelict Laagi ship?" he asked.

"We didn't. This was just general purpose facility built into *AndFriend*, and so forth, so I could investigate anything we did run into. Would you mind holding the questions for the moment, Jim? I'm up to my ears in these calculations."

He gave up and simply waited her out, ordering the ship and its parts to respond to her wishes as she expressed them through him. Eventually, she came to an end of her labors.

"Well," she said in his mind, and he felt a note of satisfaction in her mental voice, "this tells us a lot. Only it raises more questions than it answers."

"Doesn't everything about the Laagi?" said Jim sourly. But his own curiosity was getting the better of him. "What did you find out?"

"Mainly just enough to raise more questions, as I said," she answered. "Call up the list of values I'll give you now, and I can show you a mock-up on the screen of what I think those two Laagi looked like when they were alive."

He did so, and stared with disbelief at what appeared in the tank of the screen before his control chair.

"That?" he said.

"Well, not exactly that," she said. "It's anyone's guess whether they use vision the way we do, or a sense of smell or hearing, or communicate with sound waves. So I haven't tried to put in eyes, a nose or a mouth; but the rest is what the calculations from evidence tell me."

What he saw on the screen looked, more than anything else, like a barrel set up on end and covered with a gray, wrinkled skin like elephant hide. The wrinkles indicated skin so excessive at two points near the top and another two points at the bottom, that it looked as if the Laagi must have at least double the outer covering it needed. There was a small, domelike mound in the center of the top surface of the body that could be imagined as something in the way of a head, unless it was just an unusual bunching of the excess skin.

The whole shape sat like a barrel perched on its base in the cup of the golf-teelike chair in the center of the ring of controls around it. There was nothing about what Jim saw that indicated how the Laagi could even reach the controls in the ring, let alone make use of them to operate a spaceship capable of fighting it out with something like *AndFriend*.

"What bothers me more than anything else—" said Mary, and fell silent. He could imagine her frowning at the screen, the arches of her eyebrows flattening out. The flash of imagination brought up a memory of her whole person, as he had seen her, back on Earth. Animation of her features changed her completely, he thought. If she only realized this, she could do both herself and everyone else a favor by letting her emotions show more often in her expression. Animated, she was attractive. It was almost as if she had developed the severe, unchanging cast of her features as an armor at some time, and it had become habit. Here, where that look frozen on her did not interfere with his perceptions of what she was thinking at him, he was enjoying the sight of an inner Mary Gallegher that was much more human and personal.

"What bothers you?" he asked.

"The neatness of it," she said. She gave him a different set of instructions for the screen; and the gray, featureless, barrel-like image was replaced by one which was a great deal smaller, sitting in the cup of the tee-shaped control seat. This smaller image consisted of a stack of bodily support members —the bones or cartilage of the Laagi body—which were all wheel-shaped with what must be strengthening, rodlike pieces dividing the interior shape of each wheel into triangular sections. There were larger wheellike members in the center of the stack, much smaller wheellike members at the top and bottom of the stack and a sort of skullcap of the same material sitting at the very top, the basis of that mound which Jim had assumed had been the alien's head and which undoubtedly was the equivalent of the human skull itself, as a protection for the Laagi brain or its equivalent.

"I see what you mean," he said. "It looks almost as if those bones, or whatever they were, were stacked up for inspection. But the skin was all over the place."

"It couldn't very well be otherwise. There's twice as much of it, at an estimate, as there was body to cover. But the alignment of those skeletal elements almost has to mean those Laagi were placed in the position we found them in. Or set themselves up. And if they set themselves up, why?"

"I don't know. But that brings me to an important question," said Jim. "Does anything you found out give you any clue as to what killed them—or why they died?"

"No," she said emphatically. "Nothing, whatsoever."

"That's what I was afraid of," said Jim.

At his command, the image they had been watching vanished from the screen and a series of conical, three-dimensional diagrams began to appear.

"What're you doing?" asked Mary.

"My turn to say shut up and don't bother me for the moment," answered Jim. "I'm running a number of possibilities."

"Possibilities? Of what?" asked Mary.

He did not answer. His mind was too busy trying to remember and cover all the variations of the problem he had begun to try out on the screen. Mary did not speak to him again. After a while he blanked the screen.

"Ready to explain?" asked Mary.

"Oh, sure," he said. "Though actually there's not much to tell you. I've been plotting possible approach routes to put that Laagi ship where we found it, and nothing much makes sense except the fact that in that ship these Laagi were traveling directly along the centerline, the way we've been, headed for whatever's down-galaxy from here. If that's what they were doing, why did they stop at just that point? Why did they die here? Or were they killed and their ship stopped?"

"I don't follow you," said Mary. "Killed? By who?"

"That's the question," said Jim. "And you know the only answer I can come up with? If they were killed, it was by somebody from down-galaxy doing the equivalent of coming up the centerline—or firing whatever they fired to stop the Laagi, up the centerline. If that's so, that paradise Raoul kept talking about may have some real snakes in it. Because I don't know of anything, and I can't imagine anything, that would stop a Laagi fighter ship dead, kill its movement, kill its crew, and leave them all looking as if nothing had touched them."

"The same situation could also be an argument that nobody from down-galaxy killed the Laagi."

"Then why are they dead? Why is their ship still here— why didn't other Laagi come and get it and the dead bodies of their own people? What it all adds up to is a very uneasy feeling in me that somewhere beyond where that dead ship floats there may be a civilization that could swat us the way we'd get rid of a fly, and who don't like visitors. Accordingly, I've been looking at ways we could explore around such a civilization's territory without making the mistake of moving too far in on it; just so we, too, don't end up as neat piles of skin and bones."

"We can't," said Mary. "Remember? Our skins and bones are back on Earth, being kept alive as part of live bodies waiting for us to come back to them."

"It was a figure of speech," said Jim. "In any case, *And-Friend* can be killed, the way that Laagi ship was. I mean she can be reduced at least to a gas cloud of her component atoms; and if she is, what happens to you and me, the essential you and me? Do we disperse with the gas or do we simply float forever in the interstellar void?"

"All right," said Mary, "what you're saying is, it may be dangerous down-galaxy; and you want to go out from the centerline and probe for the dimensions of any danger that might be there."

"Right. And we start by finding another derelict Laagi ship, if there are any. In other words, we'll lay back from a position level with that dead ship in relation to the centerline while moving outwards from the centerline and carefully probing ahead with the instruments, to see what we find."

"Great," said Mary.

"I'm serious!" he retorted.

"So am I," said Mary; and he realized there was indeed nothing sarcastic or sardonic about the tone of voice he felt from her. "I think it's a fine idea, Jim."

"Well . . . good then," he said, touched with embarrassment. "Here we go."

He began to shift *AndFriend* out from the centerline, once more in phase-jumps that were just within the limits of the distance at which her instruments could recognize the presence of another ship. Time went by.

"Damn! Look!" he said suddenly. "Right out there at the instrument limit! It looks like another ship."

It was another ship, exactly like the one they had examined before, headed down-galaxy, and showing no sign of life aboard as they approached it. When they came within a hundred meters, Jim sent the robot across.

The pictures it brought back showed no important difference from what they had both seen in the pictorial record of the first derelict.

"It tells us one thing, though," commented Mary as they were looking at the scene displayed in the tank of *AndFriend*'s main screen. "What happened to this one must have been close in time to what happened on the other ship. The two Laagi aboard here are also decomposed to skin and skeletons."

"Maybe they decompose faster than humans," said Jim. "How long does it take the human body to turn into nothing but skin and bones?"

"I don't know. It'd depend on conditions, I suppose," answered Mary. "But these bodies have been dead long enough for all internal soft material—flesh, muscles, tendons, organs, to decay and end up as either dust, or part of the captive atmosphere of the ship. That's got to be a very long time, unless you're right and the Laagi decompose a lot faster than we do. And I don't think that's so."

"Why?"

"Because the samples your robot brought back showed evidence of oxidation, not only in the material left from the soft parts of the bodies, but in the scrapings of metals and other materials from parts of the ship. That means that their atmosphere, like ours, has to have some oxygen in it—though how much is a question. Let's look farther out and see if we can find a ship with bodies that haven't decayed so much."

Jim felt the emotional equivalent of a shudder.

"It's a ghoulish business," he said. Part of his mind was equating these long-dead Laagi with human pilots he had known who had never come back.

They searched outward, and in the next hundred hours of ship's time, they found seven more Laagi ships, all pointed down-galaxy, all with nothing left of their crews but skin and rigid interior body parts.

"And they're all on a line," said Jim, "all level with each other, pointing down-galaxy. What gets me is why they were all killed at this distance from Center and why we can go up alongside them, this way—theoretically as far into the un-known enemy's territory as they did—and not even feel or see anything dangerous."

"Maybe the enemy was here once, but now it's gone," said Mary.

He had found that little by little he had been building a mental image of her from his memory of what she looked like. In the process his imagination had made her look a good deal less severe. It also made their mental conversations more pleasant. It was much easier, he found, not to take offense from the image in his imagination than it had been from the real Mary. Consequently, he answered this last suggestion more tolerantly than he might have if the two of them had been inhabiting *AndFriend* in their proper bodies.

"Then we're back against the question of why their own people haven't come and collected them," he said.

"There could be good reasons from their point of view, that humans wouldn't understand," Mary answered. "There could even be reasons we might. Maybe they left them here to com-memorate something? A battle—"

"It was no battle these ships died in, or their crews," Jim said.

The sudden hoot of a proximity alarm came hard on the heels of his words. He shifted the view in the screen suddenly to show the space up-galaxy behind them.

"Oops," he said. But the lightness of the word did not match the emotion coloring it.

The instruments showed five bright dots with halos, com-ing at *AndFriend* from five different directions, marking out a half-globe of space up-galaxy at the limit of the instruments' views. A half-globe with flat and open side down-galaxy only.

"Laagi?" asked Mary.

"Who else could they be?" Jim considered the screen bleakly. "It crossed my mind they might pick us up on instru-ments, when we started examining these dead ships of theirs. If there's another, enemy civilization down-galaxy, they'd not let their frontier with it go unmonitored. But, idiot that I was, I didn't worry enough about Laagi observers. I actually forgot about that danger—and that's what being all by yourself with a lot of empty space around can do for your sense of alert-ness."

"What are you going to do?"

"Shift out of here—a long jump. A long, long jump; so far they'll need ten years to look through all the space I could have gone into."

The Laagi vessels were closing fast, in ordinary drive at accelerations that must be close to what their pilots could stand. They could reach *AndFriend* in minutes now of her interior ship's time. Unexpectedly, he heard words from Mary that made no sense at all.

"I'm sorry, Jim," he heard her saying. "I'm really very, very sorry. . . ."

# C H A P T E R

# 15

HE WAS LYING ON A FLAT SURFACE.

He was under gravity. He was landed.

Two great, flat hoops, edge-down, of metal, or at least of something that shone like polished steel, were anchored in the hard surface on which *AndFriend* lay and curved over her, at a third of her length in from each end of her. The hoops were five meters wide and narrow, but with their edges that faced down toward *AndFriend* narrowing to a few microns of thickness, so that they were like enclosing, curved knives ready to slice her open if she should try to lift.

In one wild reflex he flung his orders at the phase-drive engines, ordering them to phase-shift immediately, shift a full five light-years away, at once.

Nothing happened. The control studs that should have depressed themselves on the com section in front of his empty control chair did not stir. *AndFriend* did not stir.

He threw all his will, all his longing to escape into a command for the ship to phase-shift; and, when she continued to stay where she was, kept pushing against nothingness, driving, willing *AndFriend* to shift to safety.

And still nothing happened.

"No!" his mind cried.

It was a long, drawn-out cry, like the howl of a trapped animal. Dimly he was aware of Mary trying to speak to him.

"I can't move her!" he shouted voicelessly at Mary. "What's wrong? Where are we? How'd the Laagi do this? How'd they get us here? What happened? What's happened to me?"

" . . . Jim, don't," Mary was saying to him. "Jim, don't fight like that. Please. It won't help and you'll only hurt yourself more. There's nothing you can do. You can't move *And-Friend* now. The Laagi think they have us like they had Raoul—only they didn't try to anchor him down; and we've just got to stay put, for a while at least."

Like a trapped animal crouching in the cage that held him prisoner, he snarled at her.

"What happened? What did they do to me?"

"The Laagi didn't do anything, Jim. Only bring us in and try to lock us down here with those arcs they've set up over *AndFriend*. I'm so sorry, Jim, but I had to. It wasn't them who stopped you from getting away from them, and it's not them that's keeping you from shifting clear now. It was me."

"You?" He raged at her. "You? Have you gone crazy, letting them make prisoners of us?"

"No, Jim. Please. Listen. This was something I had to do. It was planned this way from the start, if it looked like the Laagi might capture us the way they captured Raoul. It was something more important than anything else, if we could find out more about them and then try to bring the information back . . ."

"You just gave them *AndFriend*? You gave them me? Without warning? Without asking? How did you knock me out? What's happened to me that I can't move her?"

It was the third time he had been handled like someone untrustworthy, and it was the limit.

"Oh, Jim!" It was as impossible as the situation they were in now that he could feel from Mary Gallegher an emotion that was the equivalent of tears. But it was so. "It wasn't even Louis who decided to do this; it was the people who give him orders. The only way they agreed to this expedition was if our primary mission was to bring back information about the Laagi."

"What did you do to me?" He hated her now and knew she

was feeling that hate. "How could you come between me and *AndFriend* like this?"

"Jim, try to understand, please...." she said. "I haven't come between you and *AndFriend*. It was just that, during one of the sessions when we had you under hypnosis near the end, you were implanted with a command that could make you unable to use your ability to do anything with her. It was just as if we'd told you about a command that could make one of your arms paralyzed and useless. We couldn't risk you doing what we knew you'd do if we saw something like those Laagi ships coming at us."

"I was going to save us, that's all!" he said fiercely.

"Yes, and that's what we didn't want happening. We needed to let ourselves be captured so that we'd finally have a chance to see the Laagi and understand their civilization, and how they work and why they fight us so—"

"Nevermind that. I don't remember a thing after I said I was going to shift out of danger. Was that command of yours supposed to knock me out, too?"

"Yes," she said. "Oh, yes. Jim, it had to. It was the only safe way. Then I had another command, the one I used just now, once we were safely captured, to bring you back awake again, but still not able to move *AndFriend*."

"Safely captured!" he said savagely. "That's a little bit of a contradiction, isn't it?"

"But we can get away when we want—when we've learned what we came here to learn," she said. "Once you're able to move *AndFriend* again, you can shift right out from under those knives. The Laagi did just what we expected. When they didn't find anybody aboard us, they thought we were a derelict. Just as they thought *La Chasse Gallerie* was a derelict, except that later on she took off under Raoul's power and escaped from them. But they're only expecting that this ship has something automatic about it that doesn't require it to have a pilot to use ordinary drive, and that's what the arcs over us are there to stop happening. They don't realize that we're here and a part of the ship, and that you can phase-shift right out from under this kind of restraint once you're able to move."

"Once I'm able to move," he echoed grimly, mockingly. "Once you take my handcuffs off...which'll be when you've seen enough of the Laagi, which'll be when you're satisfied. I've got no say in the matter, have I—for all your saying you're so sorry about doing this? You want to prove you're really sorry? Turn me loose now and let me have a choice about whether we stay or go!"

"I can't!" she said. "I can't, Jim!"

"You won't—that's what you mean. You don't trust me not to take off the minute you let me go," he said. "You and the general didn't trust me enough to tell me I'd be going into space as a ship rather than a man, you didn't trust me enough to tell me you bought this trip from the higher-ups by promising to let the Laagi capture us if the chance came up. Now you won't trust me with control of the phase-shift equipment aboard my own ship. Let me tell you something, lady. You're either going to have to trust your partner, or you're never going to get back to Earth with anything you learn about the Laagi. And furthermore, I'm going to take back control of myself, the ship, you, and everything else, as soon as I can."

"If we can find out what we need to learn about the Laagi," she said unhappily, "it won't matter, then. But I can't turn you loose, Jim. You just gave the reason yourself."

"That's right. But while you study the Laagi—and I leave that all to you—as I say I'm going to be doing my damnedest to find some way around this lock you've got on me. And what do you want to bet I don't find one?"

"Even if you do," she said, "Jim, please, think before you take us away from here. We've got a chance to learn something we've needed to know for nearly two hundred years. It could save no one knows how many lives and ships. It could even possibly save our whole race. There's no way of telling how much it's worth to study the Laagi up close like this."

He said nothing. The anger in him was like something solid and hard—an anvil upon which he was hammering out thoughts of escape and vengeance.

They were together in silence for a somewhat considerable stretch of time, possibly a few hours, possibly much longer, during which Jim paid attention to nothing beyond *And-Friend*'s interior, and even that he was conscious of only with the periphery of his mind. Events and actions had become largely subjective to his attention as a bodiless mind. Just now he was lost in himself, thinking furiously of everything he had ever read or heard concerning hypnosis, hoping to recall something that would have to do with someone freeing himself or herself from just such a command as Mary had acknowledged putting upon him.

But nothing came out of his memory that was at all helpful. He was still going around and around over what little he knew about the subject when there was an unexpected interruption. The entry port swung outward as the inner door of the airlock between port and door swung open. A breeze of outside atmosphere came into the ship, which, last Jim remembered, had lost its atmosphere with the coming and going of the ship's robot in space. The air was accompanied by a creature a little more than a meter in height and looking like a cross between a small, bent old man wearing a shell bulging outward on his back, and a snail walking—not on a snail's normal, single footpad, but on two very short, thick legs that ended not in feet, but what looked like pads of heavy skin six or eight millimeters in thickness.

The head was like the head of a turtle, with two very small but very bright, black eyes that were closely side by side and facing forward. They seemed, however, to be able to move about considerably as the skin holding them moved; because the first thing the figure did on entering was to pause and direct one eye forward in the ship, while the other eye moved to look toward the back of *AndFriend*'s interior. At the same time a globe the size of a tennis ball that was floating in the air just above the creature's head came alight with a brilliant, yellow illumination that would have made the interior painfully bright if Jim and Mary had been using human eyes to see it with.

The same light made it clear that the shell of the creature was a light tan mottled with irregular black patches, the visible parts of the soft body were dark brown, and the soles of the feet—it appeared from their edges—were a bright red. A second later half a dozen tentacles of the same red color whipped out from under the top edge of the shell, between where the creature's shoulders would be if it had shoulders under there. These tentacles probed the air as if testing the atmosphere.

"Now, what's this?" he said to Mary, startled for the moment into forgetting his anger against her.

"One of the local species that seems to coexist with the Laagi," answered Mary. "They're workers. This one comes about once a week to clean us up."

"Clean us up?"

"I know," said Mary. "There's nothing here that really needs cleaning. But it comes anyway."

"What's it called?" asked Jim, observing in fascination as the creature turned and began to explore the surface of the inner wall of the ship to its right with its tentacles.

"I don't know what the Laagi call it," said Mary. "I call it Squonk, after the janitor of an apartment building where I once lived."

" 'It'?" echoed Jim. "If your janitor was a he, I'd think—"

"We won't guess," said Mary firmly. "There's no indication so far if it's bisexual, unisexual, or what, let alone something else. As I say, I call him Squonk because the janitor in our apartment building was named Skwaconsky—and we all called him Squonk. But it remains to be seen what, if any, sex this creature is."

"Yeah," said Jim. He had remembered his anger toward her and was once more being stirred by it. The tenor of his feelings must have been clear to Mary, for she said nothing more.

For the first time, however, he realized he had not looked beyond the walls of the ship, except for that first view from the center of a flat, empty area of what looked like concrete, except that it was the light brown color of sandy soil on Earth. It was an irregular area, and beyond its borders were dark green strips that seemed to be pathways or roads. Beyond these in turn were beehive-shaped buildings of sizes varying from something the size of a single-family house to something that might have covered the largest sports arena on Earth, all the color of honey. These structures seemed to merge together in the distance, either because they were actually connected or because his unaided vision could no longer see the spaces between them. Overhead the sky had a light greenish cast.

Moving about on the dark green strips were more Squonks and other figures that varied amazingly in size and length of limb but went on two legs and were vaguely human-shaped.

Automatically Jim mentally ordered the main screen in front of his command chair to show the outside scene with telescopic magnification, so that he could get a closer look at the humanlike figures. But nothing happened—and he was suddenly aware that this, too, must be part of what he was blocked off from in his ability to control the ship.

For a second he was tempted to ask Mary to let him at least have control of the screens, if she could without setting him completely free. But the thought was followed almost immediately by a feeling of revulsion at the thought of asking any favors.

Mentally, he forced himself to put his anger aside.

"Are those Laagi, those critters outside there that don't look like Squonk?" he asked her.

"Yes," she said. "Would you like to watch them close up?"

"It doesn't make any difference to me," he said.

"It does to me," she said sadly. "I'd give a lot to be able to see them up close, in the tank of the screen. I'd like to examine the whole city around us that way. But I can't without turning you loose."

"That's right," he answered grimly. "What makes you so sure they're Laagi, then?"

"It was some like that who came aboard us out in space, before they locked *AndFriend* in the midst of them and shifted her here. Only two or three of them have come and looked inside the ship since she's been here. I don't know whether the ones who came and looked at her here were high officials or scientists, or specialists of some kind, or just that the general Laagi public's not interested in us. But those were all who came."

"Specialists or people with rank," said Jim. "I'd bet on it. You don't think we'd let the general public swarm over a Laagi ship we'd captured? And our general public'd certainly be eager to do just that."

"There's always the danger of anthropomorphizing," she answered. "We don't really know them enough even to guess at a reason they'd do anything."

"No reason not to, either," he said.

They went back into silence. Jim because he did not want to talk to her any more than he had to; and she, he presumed, because she knew how he was feeling and did not want to give him any unnecessary chances to tell her what he thought of her—and the general and the people behind him. But most of all of the general and her, who may have been under pressure to do what they had done to him, but who had certainly agreed to betray him.

Squonk continued to go over the interior of the ship, and Jim found himself becoming fascinated with the creature. He had never in his life seen such a thorough search for whatever should not be there. Within the captive atmosphere of the ship—even when that captive atmosphere was that of an alien planet—there was no way for dirt to accumulate. But the almost microscopic search of every surface in the ship by Squonk was as thorough as if it was cleaning an operating theater in a hospital; and, compact as a fighter ship had to be, there were endless niches and crannies to be searched into.

Apparently, while dirt could not find its way onto the surfaces of the ship's interior, tarnish resulting from contact with the unusual atmosphere was possible. Jim saw Squonk several times fish back in under its shell with the end of one tentacle and come out with a small spongy-ended blue rod perhaps fifteen millimeters in length; and that spongy end, rubbed over any metallic surface, made it brighter. Then the blue rod was tucked away again.

Interesting as this was, even more interesting was a fact it took Jim a little while to notice—and that was that Squonk's legs seemed to lengthen or shorten to order, to make it easier for it to get into particular crannies.

"Jim." The voice of Mary interrupted him as he was fascinatedly watching this happen for perhaps the dozenth time.

"What?" he asked absently, his animosity for the moment forgotten.

"Wouldn't you like to know more about these Squonks, and the Laagi, and everything on this world?"

He did not answer immediately, thinking it over. Of course he wanted to know. But saying so would almost sound as if he regretted his words earlier.

"I know, Jim." Mary's voice was sad, but also it was weary. "You're absolutely right. We treated you terribly from the beginning. You don't even know half of what we did to you. We deliberately put you under mental stress; we held you back from the only thing you loved; all of it done deliberately to break you down. We fogged your mind up with drugs, and we finally sent you out under the illusion you were volunteering to do something when actually you were sent to do something entirely different."

He did not answer.

"If it helps—and I know it doesn't," she went on after a while, "I'd never have done it that way, knowing you the way I do now, knowing how much *AndFriend* means to you, how much space means to you. I couldn't do it, if I was asked to do it over again, to anyone. It was the worst sort of misuse of a human being. In a good cause—but misuse all the same—"

"Nevermind," he said. "All right. I feel the way I feel. But we won't talk about it anymore. You want to study the Laagi and you need my help. I won't fight you on the fact that it's a good thing to do. I won't run away from what we can do here. You'll have to trust me that I mean that, meanwhile. You can believe it or not, but if I'd been told the truth from the beginning I'd probably have thought you all were crazy to suppose we could even get to a Laagi world alive, but I'd have agreed to try. It's not that different from what I signed up to do in the first place. It's just sticking my neck way out in a different way."

He stopped. She did not answer immediately.

"Well?" he said. "Did that convince you? Do you trust me enough now to turn me loose?"

"No," she said. The thought from her was like a sigh. "I do believe you, Jim. But I've got my own duty, and I can't let you go just on your word alone. You've got to do something first to prove it."

It took a few seconds for the import of her words to sink in on him.

"Prove it—" he echoed. "How can I do something like that, hogtied the way you've got me?"

"By wanting enough to be a squonk to make something work."

"Wanting to be a squonk?"

"Yes."

His mind whirled.

"Why, for God's sake—even if I could be one, what makes you want me to?"

"So we can really study the Laagi, up close. So we can go into their buildings—into their homes, if they have homes. So we can move around here as invisible observers—"

"Hold on!" he said. Her words had been rising on a tide of enthusiasm that he mistrusted. "I think I know what you've got in mind. You want me to become part of this critter the same sort of way you made me part of *AndFriend,* is that it? So I can travel with him when he leaves this place and we can get a look at what's outside?"

"We, not just you," she said. "Where you go, I'll be going, too, of course."

"All right. We. Just how do you figure to make me part of an alien animal like that, even if I agree? It's not a piece of nonliving metal."

"I'm not sure it'll work, but I think it might if you'll do your part," she said patiently. "You see, we still really don't know how Raoul's mind—what's left of it—became part of *La Chasse Gallerie.* All we ever had was our guess that two things, his love for his ship and his physical contact with it over a period of time, caused the two to blend. Even the physical contact may not have been necessary. That, like the scrapings from *AndFriend* we put under your skin, may be only a sort of black magic, a symbolic sort of thing that helps the mind believe it can migrate to what it's touching. But we do know that the mind has to want to go where it goes—want it badly enough to make the change. Everything else may be so much mumbo jumbo, but you wanted *AndFriend* more than you wanted life."

"That's true enough," he said soberly. For a second, he remembered his exhaustion and his desperation just before he had left his human body behind for what he now was.

"Also," Mary went on, "there could be other factors we can't even guess at. The fact you and Raoul had spent time in interstellar space may have something to do with the ability to move your mind. The fact both of you and your ships had fought for your lives together could have something to do with it. For all those reasons, there's not much more than a hope you can shift your mind into this alien animal, as you call it. But I've got a few things I haven't told you about. We knew I'd be helpless, physically, once I inhibited your command of *AndFriend.* So, the command that took your ability to control away was designed with exceptions—what you could call holes in it; or perhaps "windows" would be a better word. If I turn you loose to use a particular window—and I can with the proper hypnotic command—you can give one, but only one, series of commands through it; and one of those windows lets you use your ship's robot."

"The robot?"

"That's right. But don't get your hopes up," she said. "You'll only be able to tell it to do certain things, none of which are going to help you get back command of the ship as a whole, or do anything to help you to phase-shift it. As it happens, most of what the robot needs to do to try putting your mind into Squonk has already been done. Before we left Earth it was equipped with scrapings from the interior of *And-Friend*, and these've been stored in him all this time. What you'll be able to do if I open one of those windows for you is use Fingers to inject some of that scraping under the skin of Squonk."

"Inject? What makes you think, even if Fingers can do it, that Squonk isn't going to feel the scrapings being injected and immediately head to the Laagi equivalent of a veterinarian to have them taken out?"

"We don't, of course," said Mary. "But the scrapings are microscopic, and the process of injection wouldn't be felt by a human. We just have to hope it won't be felt by Squonk, either."

Jim sat thinking about it.

"Craziest thing I ever heard of," he grumbled. "If, if, and if . . . if right is left and up is down, then maybe we'll all turn into orange trees with the next word I speak."

"That's not the point," said Mary, still patiently. "The point is, will you try it? Will you try, honestly try, to consciously move your mind into Squonk?"

"You'll turn me loose if I do?"

"I didn't say that. I said I'd start to believe that you wanted to stay and find out about the Laagi, if you try—really try. Remember, if you're not trying, I'll know it. That's the advantage of my mind being in yours, the way it is."

"I'll try, of course," said Jim. "I don't have much choice."

"Jim, of course you've got a choice! If you simply sit here refusing to do anything, and I finally become convinced you never are going to help, and so we'll never learn anything more about the Laagi and Squonk and the rest of it than we do now, then I'll turn you loose and we'll go home with that.

Maybe back there there's some other pilot who'll bring me out to be captured again and—"

"That's a low blow," he said.

"Well," she answered, "if you're the one that doesn't want to stay, can you complain if someone else does want to?"

"I told you I wanted to stay," said Jim. "It's just that—forget it. I'm willing to try putting myself into this creature with the maniac housekeeping tendencies. What do I do first?"

"Nothing," she answered. "First, I have to open up the window for you to command Fingers to inject the scrapings. Which I will now do. Go—One! Now, first you'll find you can give the robot the order to inject the material. But it'll have to wait for a chance to do it when Squonk's close but unsuspecting. Second, once the material's in Squonk you try to make the connection. Ready to try it?"

"Ready," answered Jim.

The robot was standing motionless tucked into his storage niche at the back end of *AndFriend*'s interior, as it had been ever since it had last been put to use. Squonk had started its cleaning down the side of the ship from the entry port and would apparently be cleaning up the other side in due course. Before that he would reach the robot and clean it.

Jim concentrated on the small scrapings from *AndFriend* that were to be injected into Squonk. He must, he told himself, have been feeling them there in the robot all the time, but paid no attention to them since Fingers himself was part of *AndFriend*. But now that he knew they were there . . .

With the ability to feel, rather than see the ship around him, he searched the robot for something that was not part of Fingers' normal working equipment. It would be very tiny, but different . . . ah, he had located it. It was in a tiny drawer hidden under the end of one of the multiple arms used by the robot, at the end of the lowest of the extensions at the end of the arm extensions, capable of taking as attachment any number of small tools.

The scrapings were from the control console in front of the pilot's seat; and they were already loaded into a tiny, hollow, diamond-pointed needle that should be able to penetrate any living substance, even horn or bone, to a depth, if necessary, of fifteen millimeters.

Jim's point of view was now within the scrapings themselves, inside the robot. Once he would have told Mary about this, but now there was a barrier between them. If there were things she had seen fit not to tell him, he thought, there could be things he saw fit not to tell her. From the motionless, silent mechanical, Jim watched the alien cleaner getting closer and closer. Even at the slow, careful, deliberate pace Squonk was maintaining, it was now very near to the robot.

"All right," said the voice of Mary. "Prepare the robot to inject the material. Tell it. Say 'on the words "Go in," inject the ship's material, now in the second finger of your lowest right hand, into the living creature before you. Inject to a depth of nine millimeters into the upper part of one of the folds of living tissue on the creature's left leg, just below the shell on its back. Do this as quickly as you can and if possible without attracting the creature's attention. Then return to "Still" position.'"

"I can give the order with a lot less words than that," said Jim, still holding his point of view inside Fingers.

"Just repeat the words I gave you, please," said Mary. "'On the words "Go in," inject . . .'"

"I remember. You don't have to go through it again," said Jim.

"Good," said Mary. "Because unless you use the words I just gave you, the window won't work and the robot won't act. So you've been warned. If your memory does fail you, just pause, and I'll prompt you. I'll also tell you when to start giving the command. So wait for my order."

"Yes, ma'am!" said Jim.

Mary ignored the emphasis on Jim's last word. Together they waited. Squonk finally reached the robot and began to search its head for anything needing cleaning.

"Ready now," Mary's voice sounded in Jim's mind. "All right—say 'Go—One, now!'"

"Go—One, now!" repeated Jim.

Even though he was watching for it, Jim barely saw the movement of the hand with the needle. It was out and in, the finger with the material having seemed to barely approach the back of Squonk's leg—and then the robot continued to stand in perfect stillness for the rest of the grooming being given it by Squonk.

Squonk showed no sign of noticing what had been done to it. It continued with its cleaning.

"Jim?" said Mary. "Jim, did it work? I'm blind, all of a sudden."

"It worked. But we're in a strange country," said Jim. "Now we've got to find our way to the capital city."

"What?"

"Come on, now," said Jim. "A scientist and technologist like you ought to be able to figure out that one. We're in Squonk all right, but its body tissue's not human—it's unfamiliar territory. Now I've got to find my way to wherever its mind lives and in its mind hook up with its vision. You didn't think of this."

"We thought of it, but . . ." Mary's voice was oddly distant, without being any harder to hear for that reason. "We thought it'd either work or not work, since any part of And-Friend acts like eyes and ears for you, like every part of La Chasse Gallerie does for Raoul. So once we got an alien injected, we thought we'd either be able to get the input of its senses right away, or the try'd be a failure."

"Well, it's not a failure. But I can't see, hear, smell or whatever—yet," said Jim. "I'd say that's because I haven't got all the parts connected together, the way I had with And-Friend. Here, I've got a little part of myself buried in opaque, surrounding alien material. What I'm seeing is that opaque, surrounding alien material. Anyway, I think that's it. Sit back and let me work on this."

He was like a man imprisoned in darkness and pressure, caught in a cavern, underground. How to start? He knew nothing about the alien body around him. In fact, the truth was, there was no certainty that it was a body and not some mechanical which had been much more cleverly constructed by the Laagi than Fingers had been by human engineers. Or Squonk could be a biological robot grown to order from cultures of alien flesh belonging to the Laagi or some other species under their control—

He checked himself suddenly. His mind was running wild. The thing to concentrate on, he told himself, was how similar Squonk's body was to the animal bodies of Earth, not let his imagination run to wild imaginings of difference. Alien or not, if it was a body as he knew bodies, it lived and died, it ingested fuel material and excreted wastes. It would need the equivalent of a brain and a heart to circulate the fuel from the ingested material to the living parts of its body needing that fuel. And a liquid circulatory system would be more efficient than any solid manner of delivery . . . which meant it had the equivalent of a blood system. Which meant that if he could just reach that blood—call it the circulatory—system, he could travel it until it led him to the brain. Wherever the brain was, the mind ought to be available.

But first he had to find a conduit of the circulatory system. Like someone lost in a vast continent, he needed to find a river and follow it to the equivalent of the sea, and the sea to a particular place on the shore of the sea. He tried moving the injected material the way he had moved the *AndFriend* when his mind had been free to do so.

He moved, only a tiny distance, but he moved. However —a second later, the material enclosing him moved suddenly, taking him with it; and in panic, he recoiled.

He found himself back in the ship as a whole.

"I can see—oh," said Mary, her voice going from excitement to the flatness of disappointment. "It didn't work."

"No, that's not what happened," he answered. "I panicked. I moved the injected material and—look at Squonk. He's scratching himself. When I felt the pressure of that, inside his skin, I automatically ran."

In fact, Squonk was rubbing the tip of one tentacle energetically at the area on his left leg where the material had been injected.

"I think I can go back into him, all right. . . . " he said, reaching out once more with his mind for the *AndFriend* material lodged in the little alien.

Suddenly it was dark again. He was back.

He tried moving once more, but this time more slowly and carefully. Twice, he was shaken, as a cave-in victim might be shaken by earthquakes in the earth or rock that held him, but he kept going. After a time that he had no way of measuring, he poked the front end of his material into a less solid space.

He explored it. He was all but certain it must be the equivalent of a blood vessel, but it was very small. Still, his material was small enough to fit even into this narrow passage. He slipped all the way in, and tried to sense, by touching the surrounding walls, whether he was being carried along with the fluid that must surround him now.

He was apparently, he decided, being carried backward. He reversed his own point of view in the scrapings and thought of himself as going forward. It was either a long time or a short—once more he had no way of knowing—but he was eventually carried along and into a larger pipeline with a stronger flow.

He had no way of knowing for certain where he was in Squonk's body, but the same sort of feel that had helped him in dead reckoning gave him the general feeling that he was in the body of Squonk, rather than still in the leg where the scrapings had been injected. He oriented his material now to touch the walls of the conduit along which he was being carried by whatever fluid was Squonk's equivalent of a bloodstream. Within the fluid, he was essentially weightless. He could only feel the pressure of its current. If he could just feel the stresses on the solid wall material, however, he ought to be able to tell in what direction gravity was pulling upon them. He blamed himself for not trying to judge, when he was first injected into Squonk's flesh, which way the stress of gravity was pulling on that flesh.

This way would be more difficult. . . . Again he did not know how long he tried to feel what he wanted to feel, but finally he became sure that the stream he was in was flowing horizontally against the pull of gravity—

Without warning, he was tumbled and thrown in a dozen different directions in quick succession. He had come to some intersection, or maybe it was even the equivalent of Squonk's central pumping organ for the circulatory system; Squonk's heart, in short . . .

In desperation he began to move his material in what he conceived to be one steady direction. For a while more he was buffeted, not knowing if he was making any progress or not, and then the maelstrom of forces upon him settled down to a single powerful flow that was clearly against gravity.

He was on his way upward. If Squonk's brain was in his equivalent of a head, as the skullcaplike piece of bone cartilage among the body parts left of the long dead Laagi in their derelict ships had indicated the Laagi brain was, then he was finally on the right track.

It was, perhaps, his lucky day. The flow took him up to a point where it suddenly dispersed itself into innumerable smaller channels.

He nosed into the material surrounding the small conduit into which he had been carried. Beyond the conduit wall, the solid body material was different, softer.

"It could be brain," he said, speaking to Mary for the first time in a long while.

"Then, if you could find an impulse-carrying fiber," Mary said, "you might be able to read whatever message that fiber was carrying, and then spread out your awareness from there."

Smart, thought Jim. But he did not say the complimentary word aloud for her to hear.

"I'll see if I can tell the difference in textures," he said.

He probed the material close about himself.

He touched something, solid within solid. What it was, he did not know at the time and later on it was too late to go back and reconstruct what it was. But suddenly light flooded in around him. He saw the interior of *AndFriend* through Squonk's eyes.

The cleaning was just being finished. As he watched, Squonk turned toward the entry port, carrying the perceptions of Jim and Mary. The entry port opened. They and Squonk went out.

"How do you like that?" he shouted mentally at Mary, his grudge toward her for the moment completely drowned in triumph. "Here we go! Five minutes more and we ought to be close enough to touch some of those Laagilike figures we saw from the ship!"

But he was wrong. Having left *AndFriend* behind it, and once more down upon the concrete of the great stretch surrounding the ship, Squonk was beginning—slowly, painstakingly and industriously, to clean his way toward the distant buildings and the strips of dark green where other, distant figures had been seen moving.

# C H A P T E R

# 16

"THIS IS TERRIBLE!" SAID MARY. "HOW CAN WE SEE ANYTHING IF Squonk won't look at anything but what it's working on at the moment? Why didn't we think of a simple problem like this?"

"Because you didn't know you'd be putting the material from *AndFriend* into a creature that never looks at anything but what it's working at. Though, come to think of it, during work hours, a lot of us humans do the same thing," Jim answered.

"But what are we going to do about it?"

"I don't know," said Jim. "But I'm thinking. If you don't mind, I'd rather do that than talk."

"And another thing—" Mary was beginning; but he shut his mind to her mental voice, something that was easier to do because of the strange effect that made it sound now as if it came from some distance.

He did indeed want to think. In fact his mind had been running along certain lines since he had first started trying to find his way through the body of Squonk to the physical organ that was the seat of its mind.

He had been very lucky, he thought—there was no other word for it—to find the nerve, or conduit as Mary called it, to Squonk's vision. But the prospect of carefully examining, millimeter by millimeter, some distance of sandy-hued pavement as Squonk dusted it was no more attractive to him than it was to Mary.

The first question, therefore, was what could be done about the situation—Mary's question just now. The second, and more important question, was what his own individual relationship was to Squonk in the first place.

Probably the first question could not be answered until the answer to the second question was found and understood. The second question had come to mind when he had suddenly begun to wonder—and this was the sort of thing he would have immediately begun to talk over with Mary under ordinary circumstances, but not now—why, looking out through Squonk's eyes, which were physically different in a large degree from his human eyes, he should still see the interior of *AndFriend* and the pavement outside his ship as a human would see them.

Which raised the interesting question: was he actually seeing what he was seeing through Squonk's eyes, at all?

Now, with *AndFriend,* he had seemed to be able to use the outside surface of its metal hull as eyes. And, come to think of it, not just as one eye or a hundred thousand eyes, covering the ship's outer surface area, but as a pair of human eyes might see. Not only that, hadn't he been able to look right through the opaque plastic of the tent enclosing the ship and *La Chasse Gallerie* when he first woke up as *AndFriend,* back at the Base?

Something was definitely not as he had originally assumed it to be.

Which brought him back to the question of whether he was actually seeing what he thought he was seeing, through Squonk's eyes. How was he actually seeing? Was it mechanical or physical seeing at all? Or was it, perhaps, something entirely different?

Mary herself had said that she and those like her had no idea of how his transfer to *AndFriend* had actually been accomplished. Had he really been sensitized to his ship, or had that been part of what Mary had called possible mumbo jumbo— nonsense masquerading as an explanation for something for which so far there was no known explanation?

Had he actually been in the scrapings that had been injected into Squonk, or had the scrapings been merely an excuse for more of the unexplainable magic that had allowed first Raoul, then him, to move their minds out of their bodies into something else?

Suppose it was all magic—call it "magic" for want of a better word. Or call it excorporal transport, to get away from the connotation that magic was something that had no rational explanation.

If it had nothing to do with the injected material, then perhaps he could do anything he wanted from the viewpoint of Squonk, generally. Look out through Squonk's skin and shell with his own accustomed human vision, as he had with *And-Friend*.

Why not?

It was worth a try.

The first thing to do, he told himself, was eradicate the illusion.

I am not seeing out through Squonk's eyes, he told himself firmly but silently. I am not seeing through Squonk's eyes. I am not connected to Squonk's eyes. . . .

Abruptly, he could see nothing at all.

"Jim!"

It was a cry of alarm from Mary.

"Jim!" she shouted at him again. "What's happened? Jim, can you answer me? Answer me!"

But he had no time to spare at the moment to answer anybody. On the verge of panic he was telling himself—I'm Squonk. I am Squonk. Squonk and I are one thing. I am Squonk. I am Squonk—he was trying very hard to feel like Squonk—Squonk is me. I am Squonk, just like I'm *And-Friend*. *AndFriend*—Squonk, no difference. I am Squonk—"

Equally suddenly and without warning, light flooded back in on him. But now he was able to look around at whatever he wanted to see and see it. With relief, he noticed that they were already a good third of the way to the dark green pathways, on which there were others like Squonk and also . . . his mind boggled. The bipeds he had briefly and distantly seen before, and which he was looking at now, couldn't be Laagis. They simply could not be the same race that had battled with humans so fiercely all these years—

" . . . Jim!" It was pure alarm in Mary's voice. "Oh, my

God, Jim, are you all right? Answer me. If you can answer at all, speak to me!"

"It's all right," he said soothingly. "I just found out how to use all of Squonk's exterior surface as eyes, just as I do on *AndFriend*."

Mary was anything but soothed.

"Why didn't you answer me, if it's so all right?"

"Actually I could, but I was busy just at the moment—"

"Busy, and you let me go on calling and calling—and thinking—how was I to know what'd happened to you? You just left me there imagining all kinds of things had happened to you and never stopped to think how I might be worrying . . . worrying what I was going to do if something had happened to you? You just forgot about me. Did you ever stop to think what it might be like for me, helpless here and calling, calling and still not getting any answer from you? Well, did you?"

"As a matter of fact—"

"As a matter of fact, no. You didn't. All right, I know you've got no reason to worry about me after what we did to you to get you here; but to let me sit in the dark, without any answer, imagining no one knows what had happened . . . you could have said a word, just a word. . . ."

She stopped talking. There was a wave of emotion perceptible from her; and Jim found himself feeling far more guilty than he would have anticipated. Well, he had been busy. Of course, to her . . .

"I'm sorry," he said. "I didn't think—"

"You certainly didn't!"

"But the reason I wasn't answering wasn't because of—well, because of what you and the rest did to get me here. It was because I had my hands full. I didn't know if I'd get sight back, myself. I was putting all my mind to doing that; and, to tell the truth, it never occurred to me you'd be frightened."

"I wasn't frightened! I was—yes, I was frightened. Of course I was frightened. You seem to keep forgetting I've got no control over anything, by myself. I'm completely dependent on you. What was I supposed to imagine when suddenly everything went dark and you wouldn't answer? Not that you condescend to answer me half the time, anyway. . . ."

She broke off suddenly. Her mental voice stopped. He tried

desperately to think of something to say which would mend matters and could think of nothing.

"Oh, Jim," she said after a long moment, while he was still searching and researching his mind for the proper words to make her feel better. "Never, never do that again!"

"I won't," he said.

"It was a lousy thing to do," she said, but less emotionally.

"I won't do it again," he said, trying the magic words for a second time, since they seemed to have had a good effect.

"If you do," she said coldly, in a totally different mental tone, "you might remember that there are things I can do, too, that you might not like. Don't push me too far, Jim. There's only the two of us and it's best for both of us if we're considerate of each other. Now, let's forget it. How did you manage to get this kind of seeing that doesn't use Squonk's eyes?"

"It's . . . well, it's not easy to explain," said Jim cautiously. "I don't know if I have the words. I guess I just exercised whatever it is that lets me use the outer surface of the hull of *AndFriend* to see with, as I said; but I don't know how I do that, so I really don't know how I did this. But about not answering you. If I could just explain to you how it was for me, switching over, just then—"

"I said, let's forget it."

"Well, all right then," he said, "if that's what you want."

"That's what I want," she said.

They fell into silence again. Surreptitiously, Jim tried urging Squonk to abandon his cleaning of the surface and simply go directly to the nearest green path. Nothing happened. He tried again, and still nothing happened.

He considered giving up and simply waiting it out until they got there. He was refusing to look directly at the creatures he had suspected to be Laagi. He wanted a closer view of them before he let his mind acknowledge the unbelievable —that creatures like these were the enemies that he had shaped his whole life to face in space conflict. He concentrated on the minimal facts; that what was left in his mind from that first glimpse was a vague, uncertain image of upright bipeds of various heights with waving arms.

Mary, on her part, was also not saying anything—for which he was grateful. He had the feeling, though he could not pin it down, that she was studying what could be seen ahead of them and lost in that.

They reached the first green path eventually, and Squonk turned to its left and headed off along it at an angle toward the nearest of the beehive-shaped buildings—which, now that they were closer, Jim could see had no windows. Or at least, those close enough for him to get a good look at showed no sign of windows. The doorways into them were apertures in the shape of a triangle with its vertical sides bulging outward, a shape that echoed the shape of the buildings themselves. Squonks and—well, call them Laagi for the moment, anyway, thought Jim—entered and emerged from these doorways to move out along one of the green paths. Between the buildings, he now saw, there was no space except that taken up by the green paths, the surfaces of which seemed to be soft and yielding under the red pads of hard flesh that passed for their own Squonk's feet, like padded carpeting.

"They must really be the Laagi," said Mary's voice in his mind, unexpectedly.

So she had been struggling with herself over believing that to be true, also.

Jim finally let himself look squarely at the closest of the biped figures.

"Yes," he agreed glumly. "But it doesn't make sense, does it?"

"It's certainly hard to believe," she said. "I suppose they could be another tame underspecies like the Squonks, but they don't act like Squonks. They act like this is their world. And look—those doors on the buildings are sized just right for them. The Squonks wouldn't need entrances that tall."

"Yes," said Jim. "But they look like gingerbread men in three dimensions."

"More like big rubber dolls," said Mary.

They were both right, Jim thought. The Laagi either varied in size and length of limb, or were able to vary, but outside of that, they seemed identical, with no differences that would indicate two or more sexes. They were gray-skinned, round-bodied and round-armed. To be more precise, their bodies looked like tanks covered with gray skin, their legs and arms were like thick sections of rubber hose attached two at the bottom of the tank and two at the top; like human legs and arms, but unlike human limbs in that they seemed to have no joints, but to bend like the rubber hoses they resembled. Their legs ended in pads of muscle—but merely a darker gray, not red-colored like those of the Squonks—and their arms either seemed to end in stumps or stubby fingers, depending upon the individual.

They were all in motion, whether they were traveling one way or another on the green strips, or congregated in groups of two to half a dozen, in which case their legs were still, but their arms were in constant motion, waving up and down, stretching out or shrinking to a shorter length. Occasionally, the legs of one of those walking or standing would also lengthen or shorten, for no apparent reason.

Their heads were like small, absolutely round balls, covered by the same colored flesh and half-sunk into the wrinkled skin at the top of the tanklike body. They had, like the Squonks, two tiny but brilliant black eyes side by side and buried in the flesh of what might be called their faces; though they did not seem to move these eyes about individually, as the Squonk's eyes had on its entering *AndFriend*. There were as well a couple of vertical slits, slanting toward each other at the top, where a human nose would be, and a horizontal slit where a human mouth would be. This mouth opened slightly and shut itself again, from time to time, when they were standing congregated together. But their arms in particular were always in motion, waving up and down, bending, extending and shortening. But mostly waving.

And with all this, they made no sound to each other.

It was unnatural by human standards. There were the small noises made by Squonks and of Laagi walking along the paths; there was the sound of wind among the buildings; even something very small that could have been the alien equivalent of either a bird or insect whirred once across the path at about average Laagi height. But the Laagi mouths produced no words, nothing that could be considered sound at all.

"This is your department," said Jim. "I don't get it. Why do they bother getting together that way if they aren't going to talk? How can they be a civilized race in the first place if they don't communicate?"

"They're pretty clearly communicating," Mary's voice in his mind would have sounded almost disinterested if it had not been for its undercurrent of emotion, an almost feverish thread of excitement he could feel from her. "There'd be no point in them getting together like that unless they were communicating. But it's not with sound. My first guess is they're signaling to each other."

"Signaling?" echoed Jim. He stared at the jerking and waving arms of the grouped Laagi. "I suppose you could make a fairly complex language out of body signals. But one good enough to discuss the technological and other aspects of a civilization that could produce fighter ships as good as ours —in some cases better?"

"Most of our own technology isn't really dealt with in verbal terms," said Mary. "We use mathematics, drawings, models—all sorts of means besides our common, everyday spoken language—"

She broke off, for Squonk—their Squonk, THE Squonk, had suddenly turned slightly and headed into the midst of one of the groups of Laagi and to one in particular. It came to a halt before that Laagi and stretched its neck out in an absurd gesture that looked as if it was asking to have its head cut off.

The Laagi it had come to lowered one of its rubbery arms with a swiftness that made it look as if it intended to deliver a blow. But instead of landing heavily on the neck of Squonk, the skin of the descending arm barely touched the neck skin of the smaller creature and vibrated, so that through Squonk's nervous system, the feeling of touch that came to Jim was like that of a feather being rapidly tapped very lightly against the creature's neck.

"What in all the universe . . . ?" said Mary.

"I don't know. But it—Squonk—loves it," said Jim. "It must be—oops!"

The last ejaculation came from the fact that the Squonk had begun to shudder in what seemed an ecstasy of joy. It shortened its legs until its body was touching the ground and suddenly rolled over on its shell with its red feet sticking up in the air. The Laagi vibrated the underside of its arm against the soles of the Squonk's feet in turn, while the Squonk shuddered happily. Then the Laagi gave one of the upturned legs a soft shove, the Squonk rolled back, right side up, lengthened its legs and left the group.

"I think it was just praised," said Jim, after a little silence between himself and Mary.

"Or caressed, petted the way you might pet a dog."

"No, I really think praised is the word," said Jim. "Feel the way it's feeling right now. It's satisfied, like someone who's just done something it felt good about doing."

There was the slightest pause.

"Jim," said Mary, and he got the definite feeling that she was not happy saying it. "I can't feel any kind of emotion from Squonk. Are you sure you can?"

"Of course I'm sure—you can't?" answered Jim, startled.

"I wouldn't say I couldn't if I didn't."

"No, of course not. But that's strange."

"Not so strange." Mary's mental voice was almost bitter. "I'm just a passenger in you, after all. I don't have any direct connection with Squonk."

"Do you with me? I mean, with the way I feel?"

"Some," she said. "Except when you shut yourself off from me."

"I don't do that!"

"You do it all the time!" She hesitated. "Actually, it's probably a good thing we can shut each other out sometimes. You wouldn't want to know what I'm feeling all the time, would you?"

There was something tentative about this last question, as if the question had some hidden purpose.

"Well, no. Of course not," he said. "You're right, of course."

"Well." There was relief in her voice. "There you are. Now what were you about to say when Squonk went to get petted —or praised or whatever?"

"What was I going to say?" He frowned. "I don't think I can remember . . . oh, yes, I was going to say that Squonk was perhaps going to that particular Laagi for orders and we might learn something about how Squonks and Laagi work together by what Squonk does now. But Squonk was only there to get petted, after all."

"Wait a minute—maybe not," said Mary.

"Maybe not?"

"What the Laagi did with his arm in touching Squonk," said Mary. "The Laagi could have been praising it, just as you said. But he could also have been talking to it. In fact, he could have been giving it orders."

"You said you couldn't feel the Squonk's emotions," said Jim. "You should have, then. That Squonk was awfully happy for something just getting orders to do something. It was . . . ecstatic's a good word for what it seemed to me to be feeling."

"Maybe it likes to work."

"That much?"

"How do we know how much Squonks like to work?" demanded Mary. "A sheepdog likes to herd sheep. A sled dog likes to pull a sled with the rest of the team. A Squonk may be like that, only more so. How do we know?"

"We don't," said Jim. "But it's hard to believe."

"So we'll find out."

"Ask it, I suppose," said Jim.

"No. Just observe. What did you do when you were a boy?"

"Went to school. Played games," answered Jim. "What did you do when you were a girl?"

"That's the difference," said Mary. "I began observing and studying from as far back as I can remember. I think I told you I couldn't wait to get away from home. My mother and father—"

She broke off suddenly.

"I talk too much about them," she said.

Jim found himself not knowing what to say.

"I think you only mentioned them to me once before," he told her at last.

"Is that all? Well, it doesn't matter, anyway. All I was going to say was that they were completely useless people. What they did with their lives could have been done by any of millions of other people in the world and nobody would ever have known the difference. I decided as far back as I can remember it wouldn't be that way with me. I'd be a student and a worker; and I've been just that, ever since then. That's one of the differences between me and other people."

"Like me," said Jim.

"Well, if you want the truth, yes. Like you. You just grew up, didn't you? You let things happen?"

"Not exactly," said Jim. "All kids, as I might have said to

you at one time or another, want to be Frontier pilots. I stuck with it."

"That's commendable," said Mary, "that you stuck with it, I mean. There are better things to do than be a fighter pilot. But it's not quite what I'm talking about."

"What made you bring the subject up, then?"

"Because when I said we'll find out how much Squonk really likes working, you made a joke about it, as if it was something that couldn't be done. It can be done. By observation and deduction."

"I see. Sorry. I'll know better next time."

"And you don't need to be flip about it."

"Tell me," said Jim, "just what is it I've done lately to rub you the wrong way?"

"I'm ready to go to work and you're playing!" blazed Mary. "Do you mind shutting up and getting out of my way, if you can't be helpful?"

Jim thought of saying that he thought he had been, then decided saying so would merely continue an argument he could probably not win. Probably, in fact, there was no argument he could hope to win with Mary. So it would be wisest not to get into any. Not that he had planned to get into this one.

At any rate, he had his own plans, and his own work to think about.

"I wonder," said Mary, as if she had completely forgotten her emotion of a moment before, "just where Squonk is taking us."

They did not have long to wait for an answer, because very shortly, Squonk turned into the entrance of one of the larger, beehive-shaped buildings.

# C H A P T E R

## 17

JIM HAD EXPECTED ANYTHING BUT WHAT HE SAW, WHICH WAS, at one and the same time, tidy but enormous. Just inside the entrance and stretching away from it for a large distance, in fact for what must be right to the inner surface of the building's main wall, all the way around it, were long tables or desks perhaps a meter in width and three meters apart and as long as the circular shape of the room permitted them to be, depending on which chord of the circle they struck.

At these desks, on both sides, Laagi stood or sat in cup-shaped seats like those Mary and Jim had found in the derelict alien ships, like assembly workers in a factory, except that their work was not done in part and then passed on. Here, Laagi were building different small mechanisms from a pile of component parts right up to the point of complete assembly. At which time, a squonk, summoned by some means Jim could not make out, would come scurrying over to take the finished work and carry it off.

Some of the workers were not working. These were neither standing nor sitting in the cup-shaped chairs, but had pulled themselves into the smallest possible compass, arms, legs and head retracted almost completely into the body, so that they sat motionless on the base of their trunks looking more like round, skin-covered barrels than anything else.

Mary and Jim's Squonk went directly over to the farthest wall of the room, where it took up a position partway down a long line of squonks who appeared to be waiting there.

"Now what?" said Jim.

Mary did not answer. After a moment, one of the squonks farther down the line suddenly darted out to the nearest bench, took a completed assembly about the size of something that could be enclosed by Jim's two human hands, if he had had them handy, and went off toward the back of the building.

They waited. Other squonks went to pick up completed assemblies from Laagi. Apparently, there was either a specific Laagi that a specific squonk carried for, or else there was a rotational system that took the squonks to be messengers in some particular order.

Mary was silent. She was evidently busy observing and deducing. Jim decided to get busy with his own work in that line, particularly with his private thinking that had to do with his breaking loose of Mary's hypnotic control over him.

He seemed to remember that no hypnotic command lasted forever, but weakened over time. How much time was something he had no means of guessing. In any case he did not intend to wait around for release, if only for the fact that it would be more satisfying to break loose than to wait tamely until he was released.

His mind had fastened on the fact that Mary had said she could not feel the emotions of the squonk. She had also admitted not being able to feel Jim's emotions, some of the time at least. Jim suspected that "some of the time" was any time when they were not in direct mental contact, talking together. It was this apparent inability of Mary's that his mind had fastened on, like the mind of a chess player who has just spotted what he believes to be a weakness on the part of his opponent.

The fact of the matter was, he admitted to himself, it was no longer anger that was driving him, but something like a spirit of competition. In essence he had been challenged by being put under hypnotic control and there was something ancient and stubborn in him that had always risen to a challenge. In fact, as he had discovered one day when he had managed to get a surreptitious look at the results of some tests they had given him while he was being trained to be a Frontier pilot, that response was something that made him good at that particular job. In truth, he operated best, the examiner had noted on them, when under challenge.

The months of mental and other misery Mary, Mollen and others had put him through in the process of getting him to become one with *AndFriend*, he dismissed without another thought. He had deliberately chosen a life that involved hardship and pain, even on the training level. No, what had sparked off the sudden fury in him was something entirely different. It was his own conviction—in fact, he was proud of the fact—that he would have freely volunteered to let himself be captured and held on a Laagi world, so that the aliens could be observed; if all of them, from Mary on up, had only given him the option. The fact that they had not, he read as a fear that he might refuse. They had not trusted him to accept the duty—and that was an insult.

And it was the insult that had made him angry.

But he had always been one of those people who take fire swiftly, only to have trouble nursing the coals of an anger for any great length of time. He simply got tired of being angry with anyone or anything after a while, and forgot what had put a torch to his emotions in the first place. He even had always been a little puzzled by people who could nurse a grievance for years or a lifetime.

So, he was actually no longer angry with any of them— least of all with Mary, who was plainly the kind of person who became obsessed with whatever they put their hands and mind to. But he was acutely conscious now of being in a contest with Mary for control of himself; and he was not in the habit of losing such contests.

He concentrated on the fact that Mary was blind to all of Squonk's emotions and some of his. A part of his mind was insisting that in that fact there was something he could use to set himself free.

What he wanted, he had already told himself, was some way he could control Squonk without Mary knowing he was doing it. How that was to come out of the fact that she could not sense the squonk's feelings, or his under certain conditions, was still obscure. But if there was anything there, it

THE FOREVER MAN  /  193

ought to give up its juices if he chewed it over in his head enough.

He wondered if Squonk could be made to feel his own, human, feelings—

These thoughts were unexpectedly interrupted as they suddenly went into motion at high speed. Squonk had almost leaped forward and was, judging from what they had seen so far from it, doing its kind's equivalent of running headlong toward the solid, vertical panel supporting the long worktable just in front of them. Jim braced himself for an impact against the support, which looked decidedly solid, but something very like a trap door swung up out of Squonk's way a fraction of a second before its nose touched it and Squonk hurtled through the aperture.

At the same pace, it went through trap doors in the supports of the next four tables in order across the room; but after passing through the fourth, it spun left and went down the aisle to a Laagi, who handed it an assemblage of small parts about the size and shape of a loaf of bread.

Squonk's tentacles enclosed it tenderly and lovingly. This Laagi did not touch Squonk in the way that the alien on the path had done, but Jim felt a somewhat lower level of pleasure and pride warming the emotions of the creature he and Mary now inhabited. Squonk turned and, in squonk terms, ran for the back of the building.

The rear of the building turned out not to have tables taking up all possible available space. A section had been reserved there at the very back for two rooms, one being apparently an eating room and one a waste-disposal room. Jim had only a glimpse of these through the portals leading into them, however, for there was something else in the area to which Squonk galloped at full speed, carefully carrying its burden.

It was a large screw-type elevator. An apparently endless, turning spiral of something that might be metal that wound its way vertically up through a hole in the floor to and through the ceiling overhead. Squonk ran up onto this and stopped, letting himself be carried upward. Considering the creature's energy during the last few seconds, Jim had half-expected it to keep running up the turning and climbing platform of the elevator to add its speed to the mechanical lift. But Squonk was evidently satisfied to wait in this instance.

In fact, it let itself be carried through two upper levels of the building before stepping off on the third. Here the available circular expanse of floor held no tables, but groups of Laagi clustered around larger assemblies of whatever it was they built here and of which what Squonk carried was evidently a part, for the creature carried his burden up to one of the groups and waited to have it taken, then turned to head back downstairs once more.

"There ought to be some way we could stop it!" Mary's voice, sharp with frustration, sounded in Jim's head. "I want to see what they're building here, and maybe we could figure out the ultimate use of whatever it is. If we could only get Squonk to stay, somehow!"

Oddly enough, Jim was thinking the same thing, for the same reasons, plus a few of his own. He had long since been caught up in an eagerness like Mary's to find out about the Laagi and everything to do with them. He also would have liked time to examine more closely what was being built on this floor. In addition, however, he was still concerned with the problem of how to communicate with Squonk, with a view to controlling the small alien.

"Did you hear me, Jim?" Mary was asking as Squonk boarded the screw-elevator for the down ride. "If Squonk spends all its time doing nothing but working here and cleaning AndFriend every so often, how are we going to get a look at the Laagi civilization as a whole? Is there any chance, do you think, that we could transfer to another Squonk, or even to one of the Laagi?"

"I wouldn't think trying to transfer to one of the Laagi might be very smart," said Jim slowly. "Squonk might not be aware of us being here in its mind, but a Laagi might—particularly if we started talking to each other. Come to think of it, he might even understand what we're saying."

"I don't see how," said Mary doubtfully. "Our mental concepts have got to be so different from any alien's that they wouldn't make sense to him—or it."

"Are you so certain about that?" asked Jim. "Remember, there's lots of parallels between our civilization and this one. We've got ships, they have ships. We've got buildings, they've got buildings. Just like us, they go places, build things, and so forth. Wasn't it you who said they were probably using something like a body language to communicate? So, we communicate, they communicate. We may translate our thoughts into noises and they translate them into arm jerks, but if the thought's the same—we think of what's underfoot, and what's underfoot to them is what's underfoot to us—wouldn't our thought about it, which we think of as a sound, be seen in the mind we were occupying as an arm jerk that meant 'underfoot'?"

Mary did not answer immediately. Jim found himself feeling a little smug about the success of his argument.

"You're still anthropomorphizing," she said though, when she did answer, "still thinking of them in human terms. The thoughts behind our respective symbols may compare, but we and the Laagi may look at things so differently that our thoughts would be gibberish to them. For example, suppose for the Laagi, there's no specific term for 'underfoot.' The whole concept of something beneath the feet, upholding you, is thought of in terms of who it upholds, or of why it was built, or what color it is . . . or anything."

"Hmm," said Jim. He did not know what else to say. It was disconcerting to make a masterful argument and immediately have someone find a hole in it. Then inspiration came.

"But the point is," he said, "that we don't want to draw the Laagi's attention to the fact we're in its mind at all. Talking gibberish could sound that alarm just as loudly as saying something the Laagi could understand."

"Unless they thought he was crazy."

"Do you want to take the chance?" demanded Jim.

"No," said Mary reluctantly. "I guess not. What's the chance we might be able to transfer to another squonk?"

"I'm still trying to learn about this one," said Jim. "Maybe —but give me some time yet. I understand from our point of view we've got lots of time, so we might as well use it."

Mary did not dignify that final statement with a reply.

Squonk took them back to the waiting line. It was, Jim noticed, glowing all over with satisfaction at what it had just done. Why it should be so pleased with such a simple errand when it had not radiated any unusual happiness over the very careful job it had done of cleaning AndFriend, puzzled Jim. Tentatively, he concluded that the pleasure of a squonk might have something to do with whether one or more of the Laagi was involved in what the squonk did.

They were something like faithful dogs, these squonks. He considered that idea. It was a far-fetched comparison, based only on the pleasure plainly felt by their Squonk on only two instances. Perhaps he should try to go about this more logically.

Item: he could feel strong emotion from Squonk.

Item: he did not know if Squonk could feel any emotion from him or Mary. In fact—

Item: he did not know if the Squonk knew they were in its mind. It could be that it did not feel or hear their presence at all; or it could be feeling or hearing them, but simply ignoring what seemed to have no relation to its ordinary existence.

What he needed was some way of testing out whether Squonk could hear them or not; and preferably it should be a test he could make without Mary knowing he was trying it.

That brought up the question of what Mary could overhear from his mind. He could hear her only when she thought directly at him. Plainly, she could hear him when he thought directly to her. But she had not seemed to hear him when he was simply working out some kind of mental problem, as when he got together with *AndFriend*'s calculating equipment to plot the most promising search pattern to find the second Laagi derelict.

On second thought, it had been plain enough all along that Mary could not hear his thoughts, or he hers, unless they deliberately broadcast them to one another.

Back to squonks, which were a legitimate subject for investigation. Why not try using the image-making part of his mind, imagine himself speaking directly to Squonk as he would to Mary, and see how it would react?

He pictured himself as a Laagi, praising this particular squonk.

He was vibrating his right arm up and down with feather touches on Squonk's outstretched neck. "Good squonk," he was transmitting to it with his feather taps. "Good, good squonk! Hard-working, noble squonk. Fine, industrious squonk . . ."

To his delighted surprise, he was beginning to feel a wave of answering emotion from Squonk. It was responding exactly as if an actual Laagi was praising it with the arm signals. Jim found himself getting into his role as a Laagi, expanding his praise. Working off the feedback of Squonk's emotions he thought he could almost feel, in muscles and tendons he did not have and had never had, the effort behind the touchings that were causing such pleasure in Squonk. He became aware, suddenly, that Squonk was now attracting the attention of its fellow squonks in the waiting line.

Squonk had already begun to extend its neck in delight at being so praised. In a moment it would roll over on its back with both of its red feet stiffly pointing upwards in the air. Hastily, Jim cancelled the image and the thought.

Think about something else, he told himself hastily. But he did not have to work very hard at doing so, because at that moment Mary herself unknowingly lent a helping hand.

"Isn't our Squonk acting rather peculiarly?" she asked.

"Is it?" he said, for the Squonk, praise withdrawn, had already retracted its neck, although its emotions still radiated a joyous feeling. "I didn't notice."

"It was acting the same way it acted when that Laagi petted it, on our way here. It stuck its neck out just the way it was sticking it out before."

"Oh? I'm sorry I didn't notice that," said Jim. "I was thinking."

"I wish you wouldn't go off into these thinking trances," said Mary. "Or at least, tell me how I can rouse you, when you do. Something critical might happen and you wouldn't notice; and I wouldn't be able to get your attention in time — just the way it was now."

"Did you think it was critical? Squonk sticking his neck out?"

"I don't know. But he had the other squonks on both sides of us looking at him as if he was doing something extraordinary."

"Maybe squonks do what he was doing just for exercise — or practice, sometimes even when no Laagi's around. Or he could just be remembering it to the point where he acted it out. The other squonks could be staring at him because they were jealous."

It sounded like a thin explanation, even to Jim.

"Perhaps . . . " said Mary doubtfully.

"You, yourself, said there could be any number of reasons

for the things they do that we'd never guess because their alien minds give them a different understanding of the universe they perceive—or something like that."

"I know," said Mary. "But all the same I'd like to know why Squonk did it. The information might help us to understand the Laagi. Any information could help."

"You're right, of course," said Jim. He hesitated for a second, but then decided it would not be unadvisable to tell her of the possibility.

"I've been playing with our Squonk, with the back of my mind," he told her. "I'm trying to find some way to get through to it so that I can order it the way a Laagi would, to go places and do things. If it works, we can direct him to take us around the city—maybe."

"Good!" said Mary. "That's very good."

"Glad to hear you agree."

"Jim, you do just marvelously, with or without my ideas," she said. "I've been hard to live with, like this. I know it. I always am. I get the bit in my teeth and I'm ready to trample anyone who gets in the way. I'm a louse."

"What of it?" said Jim. "I'm a louse, myself."

You certainly are, said the back of his mind. Jim winced. Happily, winces were one of the things Mary was not able to see.

"Not like me. I tell you, you don't know me," said Mary. "Anyway, I'm ready to dance over the fact you think you might be able to direct Squonk around the city. Will you let me know how it goes—your trying to do that, I mean? Otherwise I'll only keep guessing but not wanting to keep asking you for progress reports."

"I'll keep you up to date."

The conversation broke off, leaving Jim feeling a guilty sensation. He tried to get rid of this by reminding himself of how Mary, General Mollen and the rest had gotten him into this situation, but found little or no help now in that fact. The insult had lost its force. What's wrong with me, wondered Jim? One kind word from her and I roll over on my back like a squonk.

However, it was a lot more pleasant being on friendly terms with her, like this.

At this point Squonk suddenly retracted its legs until they

were barely showing above its red feet, pulled in its neck until its head had disappeared, with the exception of its nose and mouth, closed its eyes and once again rolled over on its back. This time, however, it rocked back and forth a few times gently as its shell lost its momentum from the movement, and was still.

# C H A P T E R

# 18

"IT'S NOT DEAD, IS IT?" ASKED MARY.

"No," said Jim, "just sleeping. These squonks must go to sleep wherever the mood strikes them. Come to think of it, I'll bet the Laagi do, too—sometimes anyway. Remember the ones we saw near the entrance that had their legs, arms and heads all pulled in and were just sitting there like a cylinder on the floor?"

"But what makes you so certain it's sleep and not something else?"

"Because it's dreaming."

"Dreaming?" Mary hesitated. "You mean literally dreaming, the way you and I dream?"

"That's right. I can catch parts of it. It's like looking at a crazy recording made up of snippets from half a hundred different records."

"I wish I could reach the creature with my mind the way you do!" Mary said. "What's it dreaming about? Can you see what its dreams are?"

"If I try," said Jim. "Look, why don't you not say anything for a while, so I can concentrate on this? What it's dreaming about is clear enough; it's just that I have to concentrate all my mind to really see it. Not that any of it's so remarkable. All the dreams are about work."

"Work?"

"Work. Now, if you'll let me—"

"Sorry. Go ahead."

Mary fell silent.

Jim had been telling almost the complete truth. It was true that he had to concentrate in order to experience at second hand what Squonk was dreaming. But a deeper reason for his wanting Mary not to disturb him was that he wanted time to evaluate anything to be learned from the dreams, so that he could decide whether it might pay him to keep the knowledge to himself or not. The insult might have lost its force, but he was still determined to get away from the hold Mary had on him, if only to prove he could.

Squonk's dreams had a quality as alien as the creature itself. It occurred to Jim after some minutes that they might not be dreams in the human sense so much as some sort of sorting or memorizing process. But there was no doubt that they were, to say the least, pleasant to the dreamer. There was an emotion of strong satisfaction emanating from Squonk.

But the dreams were hardly more than flashes of episodes. Squonk cleaning *AndFriend*. Squonk cleaning the outer walls of a building. Squonk cleaning the pavement outside *And-Friend*, then carrying assemblages of parts from this floor to upper floors of this building. Squonk running a machine which cut segments from a living, green, flat creature; segments which Squonk and other squonks took out and laid down between newly built buildings to grow into pathways of the sort that it had traversed in coming to this building. Squonk hunting for something a Laagi had misplaced, a small part which was needed to fit in with other parts . . .

Interestingly, Squonk did not dream about being praised, either by the Laagi he had encountered on his way to this job or Jim's praising. In the dreams, however, there appeared at least three other Laagis who had put it to work at various things at various times. Jim got the impression Squonk would take orders from any Laagi. In fact, the relationship between Squonk and Laagi might be a lot less like the canine-human relationship Jim had been comparing it to.

But it was undeniable that Squonk existed here for the purpose of taking orders from Laagi. In fact, it was eager to do so. The kind of work did not seem to matter. It was the fact that there was work available that was the attractive thing from Squonk's point of view.

"By God!" said Jim suddenly.

"What?" Mary's voice seemed to pounce upon him.

Out of nowhere, Jim had been struck by a startling suspicion; this was that it was not the Laagi as individuals to which Squonk was attached, but to those aliens as suppliers of work. Work, it seemed, was Squonk's pleasure. Work that had been publicly acknowledged as having been done was the greatest pleasure of all. But Jim hesitated to pass this hypothesis on to Mary right now. For one thing, it might not be true. For another, it might contain the germ of something useful to him, privately, in making his escape from the hypnotic control. He chose instead something he had noticed about Squonk's dreams and which should be more interesting to her, anyway.

"You know," he told Mary now, "nothing in any of these dreams of Squonk's shows either Laagi or squonks doing anything but working. I mean, there haven't been any glimpses of homes or sleeping places or recreation areas."

Mary apparently thought about this for a minute.

"You mean that squonks may not be allowed into such areas?"

"That," said Jim slowly, "or maybe even the Laagi don't have them. They might sleep on the job, too, and do nothing but work."

"That's unthinkable," said Mary. "Unless all the Laagi we've seen so far are slaves, or something like that, tied to their work like galley slaves used to be chained to their oar. A technological civilization at all comparable to ours would have to have some reward for working that constantly. Otherwise there'd be no reason to develop a technology. To assume they do nothing but work doesn't make sense. The most primitive humans had more work than they could handle. It was the need to get in out of the rain and get free from having to be always gathering more wood for the fire that gave rise to technology."

"In our case," said Jim.

"Any technological civilization has to have been built in

response to a need. All right, you imagine a reason for being built at all, otherwise."

Jim tried, and found he could not, at least on short notice like this.

"All right, a technological civilization has to have rewards," he said. "Squonk sleeps, therefore the Laagi and other species here sleep. So there should be sleeping places—unless they do sleep on the job, as I said—and as our Squonk seems to be doing right now. And so there ought to be recreation areas . . . or at least nonwork areas, reward areas. For the moment, I'll agree."

"I don't know why we have to argue over everything," said Mary.

"Everyone's unique," said Jim. "I'm not you and you're not me. That means you're not going to see and do things the way I'd see and do them, at least part of the time. So there's always a difference of opinion."

"This much?" said Mary.

"Maybe."

"I really don't deliberately start out to argue with everything you say," said Mary. "It's just that . . . "

"I'm wrong."

"Well, yes. Frequently you're wrong, particularly when you're in an area I know something about. When you were driving *AndFriend,* I didn't argue with you, because that was something you knew something about. But in the areas of sociology and psychology, I know a lot more than you."

"Human psychology and sociology."

"The point is you don't know anything at all in those areas."

"The point is we're dealing with an alien culture where neither one of us is an expert. Correct? Where your human knowledge applies, you could be in a better position to make guesses than I am—maybe. But since we're both in unknown territory, the only thing that's certain is the fact neither one of us knows anything for sure. You could be right on the basis of what you've learned. But unlearned as I am, I could be right on the basis that I see things a little differently than you, being a different person, and I might just see something you don't see. So am I or am I not entitled to an opinion, in your opinion?"

It was a moment before she answered.

"You're entitled to your opinion," she said. "I'm entitled to tell you when you're wrong."

"When you think I'm wrong."

"All right, when I think you're wrong."

There was another pause.

"Now we're arguing about arguing," said Mary.

Squonk opened its eyes, rolled over on its feet, elongated them and stuck its head out once more. "Hello, world," it seemed to be saying.

"I'm sorry," said Jim. "I'll try to do better."

"Me too," said Mary. "Squonk's awake."

"It didn't sleep very long," said Jim. "Now what?"

For Squonk had just left the line of its fellows and was ambling back toward the rear of the building. It entered the eating room there, which was clearly divided into two areas, one for Laagi and one for squonks. In both the squonk and Laagi areas there were what seemed to be buffets, each against a wall at an opposite end of the room. In the Laagi area, groups of two to eight or ten were standing around pedestals on which sat what looked like large silver basins, eating to the accompaniment of a large amount of arm waving and alterations in leg and body size. Every so often one of the Laagi eating in a group would turn and leave and eventually a new Laagi would join a group, evidently bringing with him, her or it a double handful of materials from the buffet.

These, it dumped into the silver bowl and began, with the others, to eat the new mixture. It was plainly the mixture of everything in the bowl they were all eating, for occasionally a Laagi would reach in and stir the contents of the bowl.

Squonk had meanwhile approached the buffet at the squonk end of the room and was browsing along it, stopping to briefly intertwine tentacles as it encountered other squonks engaged in the same activity. This touching seemed more in the way of a perfunctory, if friendly, greeting or self-identification than anything else, since it was very brief and the two squonks, having touched tentacles, thereafter paid no attention to each other.

The buffet on the squonk side was considerably longer and contained more dishes—in this case, actually shallow pans about half a meter long and half a meter wide. The reason for the difference became apparent immediately, for instead of picking food from their buffet and carrying it off to eat it at pedestals, of which there were none at their end of the room, the squonks simply ate as they went along the line of the buffet. There was not as much variety as Jim had assumed at first glance. A number of trays of each item were set out in rotation. So that if Squonk was browsing at one and another squonk came along and found the contents of that pan interesting, it could simply move on to find one from which the contents were not currently being taken.

Jim's reaction to Squonk's eating was a touch of nausea. For the first pan the small, shelled alien approached had what appeared to be a mass of wriggling worms sticking their heads up out of a layer of moist earth; and Squonk immediately began to gather in tentacle-loads of worms and earth indiscriminately and start stuffing them into its mouth. Jim felt an echo of his nausea also through his mental contact with Mary.

"Watch the Laagi, ignore this," Jim said.

"Nonsense," said Mary. "I'll get used to it. I'm trying to watch both, to tell you the truth."

Jim, challenged, felt bound to get used to Squonk's eating habits himself. In addition, he reminded himself, he was at the moment more interested in squonks than in the master race that directed them. Watching Squonk feed through a variety of trays holding food, invariably live, but existing sometimes in what appeared to be earth and in others what appeared to be water or other liquids—unless the opaque ones were just water clouded with suspended material—Jim came to the conclusion that squonks were basically carnivores.

Unless what he was seeing were plant forms that had an animallike mobility. Bit by bit, he became used to both Squonk's diet and its methods of feeding. Privately, he bet himself that what was in the silver bowls of the Laagi was equally live, or live-looking.

A strange contrast, if he was right. Here was a ruling race that looked like adult, human-sized toys—almost as if they could be rather silly-looking pets, themselves—who nourished themselves on small animals that still had life in them when they were introduced to the mouths that devoured them. Shouldn't throw the first stone, Jim reminded himself. It was almost a foregone conclusion that a Laagi would be horrified by some . . . some? By *many* of the things done by humans, if that Laagi should ever find itself on Earth and watching humans act as they normally did.

Squonk finished eating and went off to the waste-disposal room. Jim made himself remember how once in Italy he had encountered a restroom toilet that was nothing but a hole in the floor with a tile edge on which one squatted. So it should not be so surprising to find a room filled with holes in the floor, here on the Laagi world. The holes were the same all over the room, but Jim noticed that they were laid out in two separate sections, with only a few squonks presently in the one part and a few Laagi in the other.

Squonk was returning up the line of other squonks to his former place in it, when Jim had an inspiration. Once more he developed an image in his mind of a Laagi talking to Squonk.

"Good squonk," the image was saying, "hard-working squonk. The ——" Jim envisioned *AndFriend* standing under its restraining, knife-edged arches. "It needs a special cleaning for special visitors. Good squonk, clean it up right away, will you? That's a fine, excellent squonk. . . ."

He continued talking, giving out the same order while holding the image in his mind . . . and Squonk continued up the line, past the place where he had waited before, and went out of the building.

"Where's it going now, do you suppose?" Mary asked.

"I'm betting—I mean I'm hoping—" answered Jim, "that it's going back to *AndFriend*. I'm trying an experiment to see if I can direct it."

"Jim! You think you can? If you can . . ."

"We'll know in a bit," said Jim.

After some distance down the green pathways had been covered it became apparent Squonk was indeed headed back toward the ship.

"Wonderful!" said Mary. "If you can make it go where we want to—how'd you do it?"

"It's a little hard to explain," said Jim. "I've been giving him mental pictures of a Laagi giving him orders, in a sense."

"How did you know how the Laagi give squonks orders?"

"I didn't," Jim answered. "I'm not speaking to his mind as much as to his emotions, I think. I just pictured a Laagi that spoke to Squonk the way I'd speak to a dog back home. Pet animals on Earth don't understand human words in the same sense we do, either, but they get the idea. So, evidently, does Squonk."

"But it's so surprising he didn't even question you," said Mary. "I mean, from Squonk's point of view you must have seemed like a ghost voice coming out of nowhere to tell it what to do. But you say that didn't seem to disturb it at all?"

"Yes," said Jim. "I really didn't have much hope it would work. But it did. Maybe we'll find out why, later."

"Animals," said Mary, "and even humans for that matter, respond to certain stimuli by reflex. There was that sad case just last year or so of a wolf who'd been raised as a pet, and seemed so friendly and gentle, just like a dog in every way. And then one day a very young child got into the back yard where it was kept, and the wolf killed it. They reconstructed the fact later that the child had unwittingly duplicated the actions of a wounded prey animal, and the wolf attacked it out of hunting reflex. It could be that work here is a sort of reflex for these squonks and you somehow triggered that reflex by what you did to it."

"Anyway," Jim said, "it worked. Here we are at the ship."

So they were. Mary's happiness and excitement over the fact that Jim had been able to send Squonk there, however, turned to dismay, when Squonk entered the ship and actually began cleaning.

"But it'll take forever if it goes over the whole interior of the ship again," said Mary. "Can't we stop it, somehow? This time could be used to a lot better advantage getting an idea of the way the city's laid out."

"I'm afraid to give a counterorder right away," said Jim slowly. "Squonk could decide that if he was told to do something, then told not to before he'd done it completely, then what he was hearing couldn't be real orders. We might lose whatever control I've got over him. Do you want to take that chance?"

"No! No, of course not," said Mary. "All the same . . ."

All the same, she was not happy about waiting. But they both decided that it was better not to take chances. The opportunity to control Squonk was too valuable to risk merely for the sake of saving a few hours.

They waited Squonk out, accordingly. As he was finishing up, Jim brought up the question what to do next.

"Have him take us out around the city in general," said Mary.

"I don't know that can be done—just that way," said Jim. "He only travels in order to get to some work or other. I think I'm going to have to give him a specific job to do that'll require him to take us where you want to go. And I don't know what kinds of work he might be asked to do. Let's start at the beginning. Think of a particular place you want to go to."

"Tell him to take us to the place where the Laagi rest."

"Too general," objected Jim. "Rest could mean sleeping on the job the way we saw those Laagi doing it."

"If they actually were sleeping," Mary said. "Maybe that was just something they do when they want to think undisturbed."

"After what we went through with Squonk?" asked Jim. "Squonk was certainly sleeping. I still say 'rest' is too general a command. Even 'the place where Laagi sleep' could be too general. Also we're assuming there is such a place—"

"I've got it!" Mary broke in on him. "Tell him to find something. Something that can't be found, so he'll have to hunt all over the city for it. Tell him he's to find a . . . a key, a regular metal key to a lock. Explain that the key is a part of this ship, that belongs with it, and he's to get the key and bring it back here and we'll show him where it fits into the ship."

"Umph!" said Jim—or would have said it if he had had a body with the vocal apparatus to make the sound. As it was, he was simply silent for a moment, in surprise.

"What's the matter?" asked Mary.

"Nothing," he said. "That's a very good solution you've come up with. I'm not so sure I know how to go about putting the idea of it across to Squonk, though."

"Why?"

"Again, it's too general. I'd have to make it specific, somehow. Then, there's the problem of how to picture something Squonk's never imagined before, using the materials out of its own imagination."

"Just picture the key to the lock on the front door of your

own quarters," said Mary. "That's alien enough and simple enough."

"Yes, but the trouble is he doesn't seem to see what I'm thinking, he just picks up whatever emotion I broadcast. For example, when I thought of Squonk cleaning this ship, I came down heavy on disgust at having the inside of the ship dirty and worry about someone important coming to see it. I think that's what he picked up—those feelings. How do you get across an emotion about something a squonk's never seen or imagined—wait a minute. I think I've got the answer. We don't have to. I'll just broadcast worry about something lost and a feeling that it may be in one of the buildings of the city and imagine that if Squonk went into the city, it could look for whatever it was. Then when Squonk goes and we see a building you want to go into, I'll broadcast hope that the whatever may be in it. I can even direct Squonk from place to place inside the building, for that matter. When you want time to observe in one particular place, I can broadcast a desire to search that place millimeter by millimeter."

"You know," said Mary after a moment, "this is insane, talking to an alien through emotions. The first assumption I'd have made about the Laagi, or any creature from one of their worlds—if there are other worlds where they live—was that our emotions would be so different from theirs that that was one element where we'd never match in any particular. Now you're saying we can feel so much the way they do that we can actually make a language in common out of the fact. It's crazy."

"You were the one who brought up the business of parallel evolution."

"That was referring to their developing a technology. But this . . . "

"On the other hand, maybe it isn't a matter of emotions at all. Maybe I'm communicating with Squonk in some completely other way. You know, when I do communicate with it, I don't think of talking to a squonk. I think of talking to a sort of dog—which is just a convenient way for my imagination to handle it, nothing more. Maybe pure mental communication's a universal language and it's only our bodies that make us not understandable to each other. People without a language in common can get their feelings across—"

"With sounds or facial expressions or body language," put in Mary.

"Well, the Laagi language seems to be just that—a body language. If it grew out of similar emotional roots, it could have end products that were like ours. After all, both we and the Laagi live in the same universe and relate to the same physical laws of that universe."

"You're guessing," said Mary. "I'm . . . I don't know where to begin to point out how many things could be wrong with ideas like that."

"Oh, hell!" said Jim. "Maybe it's all just black magic—my communicating with Squonk. Anyway, it worked to get the critter here. Besides, come to think of it, you've just given me a valid reason to interrupt the ship-cleaning beast—we've just discovered something's missing. Here I go."

Squonk had just begun his cleaning of the space suit locker. Jim pictured himself once more in his mind as a Laagi, gesture-talking to the small creature.

"Key? Where's the key?" he had the Laagi signaling. "The key's not here. Where's the key? It must be lost. Oh my, the key's lost. . . ."

"I thought you had all sorts of objections to using the idea of a key as what was lost?" said Mary; and Jim realized that in his concentration he had thought the words spoken by his emotional image out loud, as far as Mary was concerned.

He made a mental note to avoid making that sort of slip from now on. He had better get in the habit of delivering his orders to Squonk silently, as far as she was concerned. Otherwise he could let slip information he had intended to keep to himself.

"Well, I needed to picture something concrete for my own imaginational purposes," he said now. "Actually, once I thought about it, it doesn't matter what we send Squonk hunting for as long as he knows a Laagi—I mean me—is going to recognize it when he finds it. It's just like saying 'Rabbit! Rabbit!' to a dog you're about to take rabbit hunting. He'll perk up his ears and look around even though he hasn't heard or smelled a thing—"

"Would you hunt rabbits with a dog?"

"Actually no," Jim said, "so you don't have to sound horrified. I'm as squeamish as you are. I tend to identify with the rabbit. But it's not the dog's fault he gets all excited at the idea of catching and killing a rabbit—"

"Look! What's happened to Squonk?"

Interrupted, Jim looked. Squonk had come to a dead stop, just as it was, head nose-deep into the space of the locker, tentacles extended and poised. It looked like a toy the motor of which had just run down.

"What've you done to him, Jim?"

"You know as much as I do about what I've done to him!" said Jim, irritated. "You heard what I was trying to tell him. I don't know why he's suddenly gone paralyzed like that."

"He's been asked to do the impossible, that's what it is," said Mary. "It's my fault! I shouldn't have suggested using something completely out of his knowledge as the lost item. If I only hadn't said that—"

Squonk started to move again. Its head went completely in among the space suits hanging in the locker and the tentacles immersed themselves to their full lengths in the same space.

"There, you see," said Jim. "You were worried about nothing. He doesn't have the foggiest notion what a key is, but he's hunting for something loose in the locker—what did I tell you?"

Squonk had just backed out of the locker, with his tentacles holding a spare space suit oxygen-recycling unit. Jim hastily envisioned a Laagi being disappointed.

"No. Not key. Too bad. No key there. Where could that key have got to? Not on the ship. Maybe in one of the buildings of the city. Maybe we could go look in a building where it might be—"

Squonk carefully closed the door of the space suit locker and headed for the entry port.

"Now we can start to do things!" Mary's voice in Jim's mind was jubilant. "Jim, you're a wonder!"

"I am?" said Jim, startled, not so much by the concept as by Mary's voicing it.

She did not seem to notice his reaction.

"What I want to do first," she said, "is find some place where the Laagi are standing around doing nothing but talking. . . ."

# CHAPTER

# 19

"—NO. WAIT. STOP HIM!" MARY INTERRUPTED HERSELF AS Squonk headed toward the entry port.

Jim did.

"So," he said, "Squonk's been promoted from an 'it,' has he? Probably high time. I've been getting him mixed up with other 'its' every time I try to talk about him and things. Just remember it was you who renamed him, not me."

"Don't be ridiculous," said Mary. "Now, bring him back here."

For Jim had imagined Squonk being signaled to halt and he (to give him his new pronoun) had obeyed by going stone still.

"Tell him to move the temperature control all the way down to zero," added Mary.

"What?"

"Just do it, Jim."

"All right." Jim obeyed. He directed Squonk to the ship's interior atmosphere controls on the console, then to the temperature control among them, and finally to moving the temperature control to zero degrees celsius.

"Now up to twenty-three degrees," ordered Mary. "Now, down to nine degrees."

212

When the control knob brought the sharp point of the indicator back to nine on the scale, the whole area of the climate controls, which were mounted in the midst of the ship's controls vertically on the panel directly before the pilot's command position, fell outwards, showing themselves to be hinged at the bottom. Revealed was a dark recess, about half a meter square and of invisible depth.

"Very clever," commented Jim. "Turning a temperature control into the dial of a combination safe. Very clever indeed. Now what?"

"Now have Squonk reach in there and see if he finds anything."

Squonk, at Jim's orders, explored the aperture with the tip of one of his tentacles. It appeared from what Jim could see to be a recess about as deep as it was high or wide.

The tentacle came out holding nothing.

"Tell him too bad," said Mary, with satisfaction in her voice. "Apparently the key wasn't there."

Jim passed the message on.

"But do you mind telling me," he asked, "just exactly what's going on? Why all that trouble to set up a secret place and then have it empty?"

"It wasn't empty," said Mary, a little smugly. "Now that tentacle of Squonk's been infiltrated by a microtransmitter that'll broadcast anything seen or heard in his vicinity back to the ship's recorder."

"What recorder?"

"The same one that's been recording every noise and action aboard this ship since we started."

"Our mind-to-mind conversations, too?"

"No," said Mary regretfully. "It couldn't pick up the mind-to-mind talking. It's only recorded when you speak out loud through the ship's internal and external communication system, the way you talked to Louis Mollen and me when we were back at Base and you were first in *AndFriend*. Now, when we get out in that city, I'm going to start making notes on what I observe. We can't transmit those back to the ship via Squonk's transmitter, so I'll dictate them to you and you do what you'd ordinarily do to repeat them out loud over *AndFriend*'s internal communications system. Actually, you'll be repeating them out loud to the recorder."

For a moment Jim was silent.

"So," he said. "This was set up from the start, too, was it?"

"We only hoped, then, that we'd end up captured by the Laagi; but of course every contingency was planned for as far as we could imagine it," said Mary briskly. "Now, we've got to get going with Squonk. Will you tell him to head for the city buildings?"

Jim did. His mind was too full for words and Mary was evidently busy making plans, because they did not talk again until they were well in among the buildings on one of the green paths.

"Squonk's waiting to be told where to look," Jim said finally.

"I've been thinking about that," answered Mary. "We'll simply have to try various buildings until we find what I want; but I've been deciding what to look into first in this alien society. What we want, I think, is some place where Laagi get together to talk. Enough pictures of them signaling to each other ought to give the people back home enough information to break down their gestures into a language we can understand."

"Maybe," said Jim. "But if the way they think is completely different from the way we do, their language isn't going to make any sense, anyway."

"As I've said before, this is a technological civilization. There have to be parallels between its problems and their ways of handling them, and our own problems and solutions. Some sort of understanding has to be possible; and any sort of understanding, Jim, is a world of improvement over what we've had so far where they're concerned."

"Hmm," said Jim.

"You don't agree?"

"Oh, I agree," said Jim. "Yes, any improvement's worth the cost."

She was right, of course, he told himself. He found himself admiring her single-mindedness. Now that he was completely over his outrage at being drafted into this situation instead of being asked, he had to face the fact that he had had a chip on his shoulder where she was concerned from the first moment he had met her in Mollen's office, before she had ridden out in his gunner's seat in their successful effort to bring back *La Chasse Gallerie* and what was left of the mind of Raoul.

All right, she had her own shoulder chip, too. Hopefully, she would put it aside in time, as he was beginning to put his aside. A little wistfully, he wondered what she would be like if she did. He had never really let himself know her; and she, of course, had never really made herself available to be known. He had got his back up about her from the initial instant of meeting. First, because she was not a space fighter —not what Frontier pilots like him considered a space fighter. Second, because she was arrogant on the basis of her expertise in a field that he knew next to nothing about and thought even less of, and that arrogance rubbed him the wrong way. His own arrogance, he had to admit to himself, now, had been completely invisible to him.

Somewhere in that childhood of hers, she must have been forced into taking a turn toward toughness. He had always taken entirely for granted his own cheerful childhood, with plenty of friends his own age all through the growing-up years, with aunts, uncles, grandparents and likeable cousins —not to mention, now that he stopped to consider them, a remarkably happy set of loving parents. Loving to each other as well as to him. He could see why she might assume he had had a careless and easy ride through life, particularly since she had taken a thorough look at his life's records, which of course she had done as a necessary preliminary to using him as part of her project. About the only thing he had had in common with her was that they had both been only children.

The one element she would not have found in his records would have been his own private idealism, the determination to do at least one worthy and memorable thing in his life... though come to think of it, she must have sensed something of it, since there had been that moment just after they had *La Chasse Gallerie* safely back home and she had told him that his nature was that of a "white knight."

Which of course it wasn't. He might have white-knight-type dreams, but he was thoroughly practical, too. She would find out how practical when he broke loose of this hypnotic control she was using to keep him on a tether. But... even that really didn't matter, except as a principle, now that he understood and liked her better.

He wondered if there were some magic words that would make her open up about what had made her what she was.

From somewhere, he could not say exactly where, he had acquired a firm conviction that if she would just put aside her prickly armor for a moment, she would show him someone very good to know. He had become more and more sure that her combativeness was a shield behind which she hid her true self. Just like one of those people who go around warning the world how stubborn he or she is, while really only setting up a defense against the secret belief that anyone could talk him or her into anything. Mary's toughness, he now firmly believed, was a shield for a natural instinct toward a tenderness which she felt she must hide.

Again, he could not remember exactly how he had reached this decision. A number of small straws in the wind of their mutual adventuring must have pointed him to it.

It dawned on him suddenly then that somewhere along the way, she would need evidence of his own strength and abilities before she could be open with him. For her own reasons, some of which might be buried in that past she evidently disliked, she had a need to cling to the illusion that he was— what was it she had called him once? A featherbrained flyboy. That shielded inner self of her would need positive, undeniable evidence he was no such thing before she would permit herself to deal with him on an equal level. So one of the reasons for his breaking himself loose of her hypnotic reins would be to establish that he was strong enough for her to trust him and be relaxed with him.

On the other hand, of course, he could be dead wrong about all this. But, what the hell, it was worth a try. He woke up suddenly to the fact that Squonk was still coursing eagerly along the green pathway, waiting for instructions. Mary seemed to have gone off into her thoughts just as Jim had gone off into his.

"Squonk's still waiting," he said.

"I know that," she said. "I haven't been able to come up with any reason to pick a particular building to try first. Have you?"

"No," he said.

"I suppose we'll just have to try them at random."

"Looks like it."

"Will you tell Squonk to go into the next entrance we come to, then?"

He did.

Squonk carried them only a small distance farther down the path, therefore, before turning in through one of the typical doorways. This time they found themselves in what might have been an office building, if it had not looked so much like a honeycomb. Or perhaps it could be best described as a honeycomb taken over and made into an office building. There seemed to be innumerable floors, none of them higher in the ceiling than would comfortably accommodate an adult Laagi, with each floor having innumerable corridors and each corridor lined on both sides with openings into cubicles. In each cubicle was a Laagi, working a bank of controls, or simply standing motionless, staring at the bank of controls—and that was all there was to it.

"None of them are communicating," said Mary.

"At least, not unless they're doing it through that console in front of each one," said Jim. "Maybe it's some sort of information or control center."

"Anyway," said Mary decisively, "it doesn't offer me anything I can work with. If you'll just repeat the words after me for the sake of the ship's recorder, I'll make a brief description of it by way of a report, so that we can come back here, if what we learn elsewhere makes it worthwhile."

She did so, Jim parroting her words faithfully, a phrase at a time.

"On to the next building," said Mary.

But the next building was exactly like the one they just left. In fact, the next three buildings they tried were exactly like the first.

"They have to be the Laagi equivalent of offices," said Jim.

"So many of them?"

"Aren't our cities loaded with office buildings? What would an alien say if he could look into them and see people looking at screens and talking into receptors?"

"It's pushing belief past the limit," Mary said firmly, "to hypothesize that the Laagi have a business structure in their society that much like ours."

"All right," said Jim as they left the fourth building. "How

about this? Each one of those Laagi you see there is controlling some piece of automatic machinery somewhere else; and
the controllers are all gathered together so that their work can
be coordinated better."

"That's . . . just possible," said Mary doubtfully. "Anyway,
we can't do anything but keep trying other buildings."

But the next building was different. The upper floors were
honeycomb offices, but the ground-level floor was divided
into what seemed to be a large number of lofty, dome-cei-
linged auditoriums; and the likeness to an auditorium in each
case was increased by the fact that in each something resembling an audience of Laagi were working at very small consoles of controls on posts before them, while at the far end of
the room an actively gesticulating Laagi seemed to be having
an argument, or something like it, with the image of another
Laagi blown up to many times life-size in the tank of a screen
filling the wall behind the living gesticulator.

The floor was concave, from the entrance to the far end
where the screen was, giving all the Laagi in the "audience" a
good view of both the living and the screened individual.
These two seemed to take turns, one gesticulating for a while
while the other stood motionless, then the motionless one
would become active and the recent speaker would cease all
movement. The stubby fingers of the Laagi in the crowd flew
over their consoles as this progressed.

"An instructor and his students?" said Jim. "Or a conductor
leading a silent symphony performance?"

"We'd better wait until it's finished, whatever it is," said
Mary. "Tell Squonk to start searching the room. It's big
enough so that it ought to take him hours."

Jim did. Squonk scurried off to the nearby wall and began
a careful tentacle search along its base.

"My guess would be—"

"Don't bother me now," Mary interrupted. "I don't want to
miss anything that goes on."

Jim fell silent. He watched the crowd and the two Laagi up
front, the live and the imaged; but after a while his mind
began to give up on any attempt to make sense out of what
was happening. . . .

"Jim!" It was Mary calling him. He had lost a chunk of
time in what seemed to pass as sleep for him ever since he had

become a bodiless entity. He stared at the room. The two Laagi were still up front. The mass of the rest were as busy with their consoles as ever.

"Sorry," he said. "How long was I out?"

"Nearly four hours," she said. "Jim, there's a limit. This may go on for weeks, for all we know. The recorder must have a few hundred thousand gesture-bits from those two lecturers or whatever they are. I want to go and take a look at the rest of the city. Tell Squonk we're leaving."

"Want to look upstairs before we go out?"

"Just more offices. No, I want some place where there's a number of Laagi talking to each other. Something like a . . . a club or a restaurant in human terms. I don't suppose you can get the idea of a place like that across to Squonk?"

"I can try," said Jim.

He tried envisioning a room, of unspecified dimensions, but plainly larger than the cubicles they had come to call offices, and in that room a number of Laagi standing or sitting in groups and talking body language to each other. Squonk stopped still on the pathway. Jim read the creature's emotions as interested and willing, but puzzled.

"No go," said Jim.

"Maybe he knows of a place like that, but doesn't connect it with hunting for the key?"

"I didn't think of that," said Jim.

He introduced the image of the key to his mental image and added anxiety over finding it to his emotional projection.

Squonk was plainly still puzzled. But he started to move again. They went some distance and passed a number of buildings without the creature turning into any of them.

"I figured he'd understood the sort of place we wanted to search for the key next," said Jim. "But I didn't expect him to go this kind of distance. Maybe he was thinking of a place that's not in this city at all."

"All to the good if he is," said Mary. "We'll find out about their local transportation system."

Their destination, however, turned out not to require transportation to another city. After some distance along a complicated route through the pathways, Squonk turned into one more entrance.

It was as close to what Jim had envisioned as made no

difference. In an area almost as large as one of the auditoriums, but under a less lofty ceiling and upon a level floor, Laagi stood or sat in groups, gesticulating at others in the same group. Squonks were moving about and through the crowd. Those Laagi seated were perched on one of the cup-shaped seats, each on a slanted support, like those in the Laagi spaceships and elsewhere. About the only difference seemed to be that these particular seats were movable. Apparently at signals which Jim and Mary could not separate from the other movements of their body languages, a squonk would come scurrying up to the Laagi who wished to sit with one of the seats, the lower end of which seemed to adhere to the floor the moment it was set down. Abandoned seats were also picked up and carted away to the wall of the room by squonks.

In fact, squonks were everywhere, and included a group that seemed to be continuously at work doing nothing else but cleaning the floor and lower walls of the room. Jim could see now why Squonk had doubted that this would be a place to find the strange thing that the invisible Laagi commanding him wanted to be found.

"This is more like it!" said Mary grimly.

"If conversations between Laagi are what you want, it certainly is," said Jim. "It does look like some kind of club."

"Or political grouping."

"Or a think tank of some sort," said Jim.

"Well, whatever it really is remains to be found out," said Mary. "Why don't you go back to sleep or something? I'll be busy. I can wake you when I'm ready to dictate a report."

"Thank you," said Jim clearly and precisely, "but I'm not tired at the moment. Thank you just the same, though."

Mary laughed. There was as much excitement as humor in her mental voice at the moment.

"Bet you go to sleep anyway," she said.

Jim did not answer that. Mary evidently settled down to wordless observing, and Squonk continued his diligent search along the base of the wall.

Jim was left with leisure to take a better look at the place and its occupants himself. Light seemed to flood the place from all angles, so that there were no visible sources. It was the same deep yellow of the sunlight outside, so that it might have been daylight somehow piped in or introduced. The floor was a deep, rich red, much darker than the footpads of the squonks. The chair seats were a dark green and the walls started as dark brown at the base and changed gradually toward yellower and lighter shades as they mounted toward the apex of the domed ceiling.

There was a sudden horrendous clatter, to which no one in the room seemed to pay any attention except the unfortunate squonk which had been the cause of it. Certainly, thought Jim, Laagi must be absolutely without a sense of hearing; and probably the squonks were, too. What he had heard had been the very noisy result of two of the chair-carrying squonks colliding to send the chairs they had been carrying crashing to the floor.

What had happened had clearly been an accident. The tentacles of a squonk appeared extremely nimble, but there was obviously a limit to the amount of strength they possessed. One squonk seemed able to carry one chair comfortably by curling all its tentacles around the shaft that supported the seat. One squonk was also all that was needed to set the chair upright when it had been brought to the Laagi wanting it. The lower end of the support rod fastened itself by some invisible means firmly and automatically to the floor when the chair was set up. Apparently this adhesive, or otherwise self-fastening end, of the shaft of the chair being carried by one squonk had touched and fastened itself to the leg of one carried by another. Tripped up, or perhaps overbalanced by the unexpected double weight, both chairs and the squonk that carried one had tumbled to the floor.

One squonk hurried off, leaving things as they were. The other pushed itself back to its feet, using its tentacles. It then tried to pick up the chair it had originally been carrying and found it firmly attached to the other chair. After a few seconds of futilely trying to lift the awkward structure composed of the two joined chairs, the squonk put it down and scurried over to another squonk headed away after having just delivered another chair.

The second squonk stopped, the two entwined the ends of their tentacles momentarily, and the second squonk hurried away, while the first returned to the tangle of the joined chairs. After a few minutes, the second squonk—at least Jim thought it was the second squonk, since the creatures all looked so much alike that it was difficult to be sure—returned with what looked like a small rod with a sort of pistol grip at one end, held in one tentacle.

The second squonk touched the far tip of the rod to the point at which the chairs joined, both squonks took hold of a chair apiece and pulled with what seemed to be considerable effort; and the two chairs parted. Taking a chair apiece they trotted off and were lost in the crowd from the point of view afforded Jim by Squonk himself.

Jim watched them disappear, fascinated. It was the first time he had seen anything resembling communication or teamwork among the squonks. He continued to watch the room carefully, hoping for some further evidence of squonk cooperation, but no reason for such activity evidently occurred. He had seen, however, two squonks not only communicate, but solve a problem on their own without specific orders from any of the Laagi standing around; and that, he told himself, was food for thought.

# C H A P T E R

# 20

"Jim. *Jim!*"

"All right, all right," said Jim, "I heard you the first time. What is it?"

"You were sleeping again."

"I was not. I was thinking. Nevermind . . . what do you want now?"

"I want you to stop Squonk," said Mary. "Make him stand still—or better yet make him back up about two meters. There's a pair of Laagi I particularly want to keep observing."

"I don't know if I can," said Jim.

"Why not?"

"Well, I mean, I probably can tell him to stop searching, but I'm trying to think of a reason for it that'll make sense. The way we had to work out a way of sending him hunting for something, that made sense to him. Also, have you thought that if he suddenly just stops doing anything out here where he is, he may attract attention to himself?"

"What if he does?"

"If he attracts the attention of the Laagi, one or more of them might just come over to find out what he's doing here."

"We haven't seen any evidence that squonks can talk to Laagi," said Mary.

"No, but maybe there're other ways a Laagi could find out what Squonk's doing here. The Laagi might be able to identify Squonk as the one of his kind who's supposed to be cleaning *AndFriend* periodically and has a part-carrying job elsewhere; and so might wonder what he's doing here, instead. Even if the Laagi doesn't do any more than wonder, he might end up ordering Squonk back to his parts-carrying and Squonk might well listen to that Laagi and obey it, in spite of whatever I could say to him. Do you want that?"

"No. No, of course not." Mary paused. "But I've absolutely got to keep observing these two Laagi awhile longer. They're acting different from any others we've seen so far."

"These two right next to us?"

"That's right."

"All right," said Jim. He pulled the now familiar trick of imagining himself as a Laagi giving gesticulated orders to Squonk.

"Good Squonk," he thought. "Stop. Wait just where you are for the moment. I may have new orders for you in just a little bit."

Agreeably, Squonk froze in position, which at the moment was the one best adapted to minutely searching the open floor of the room along a line that was carrying him away from the two Laagi Mary had indicated.

"There. See?" said Mary. "There's no problem in stopping him."

"Stopping him wasn't what I was worried about," Jim said. "What I was worried about—"

"Will you please not talk for a few minutes?" said Mary. "These two are definitely unusual. I want to be able to concentrate on them and I can't do that with you jabbering."

On the verge of arguing, Jim suddenly realized what had really bothered him about the peremptory order had been Mary making sure she had the last word—as usual. He kept his silence accordingly and took a closer look at the two Laagi himself. They were both seated and they were by themselves —a group of two. Not only that, but the space around them was larger than around any of the other groups, as if the other Laagi were politely avoiding any intrusion on them.

The two also gave the impression of being very punctilious in their communication. When one gesticulated, the other did

not—of course that was the way it was also more or less, but
only more or less, among the other Laagi. But what was unlike anything Jim had seen between these aliens before was
that each time one of the two stopped talking, there was a
moment of complete motionlessness on the part of both individuals before the one who had not been gesticulating started
to reply.

"Did you notice how they pause?" Jim asked Mary.

"Of course," said Mary. "But there's more than that going
on here, different from ordinary Laagi conversation. If you
notice, the gestures of these two are slower and more deliberate than those we've been seeing."

"Maybe they're a couple of old Laagi," said Jim.

"Perhaps," murmured Mary quite seriously. "Also, their
gestures are more emphatic—look there!"

The one of the two who was currently gesticulating had
suddenly pulled his head down completely out of sight into the
top skin-folds of his body and ceased movement entirely.
After a long moment his head slowly came out once more.

Unexpectedly, Mary laughed; and Jim found himself with
the sort of feeling that in the flesh would have signaled a grin.
At the same time he was not exactly sure why what they had
seen had struck them both as so funny. He finally decided it
was the jack-in-the-box effect of the head pulling in that had
triggered off the sense of ridiculousness in both Mary and
himself. It was as if two human heads of state had been dis-
cussing a serious political matter with all the normal solemnity
of rhetoric; and one of them had suddenly stood on his head to
underline the point he had just made.

In any case, the one who had just pulled in his head—

"Call him 'A,'" said Jim thoughtfully.

"Call who 'A'?" demanded Mary.

"The one who just pulled his head in," said Jim, "and call
the other one 'B.' Now, it looks as if A's made his point and is
through arguing for the moment."

"How do we know they're arguing?" said Mary. "You're
right, though. Now, B's starting to talk."

B was indeed beginning to gesticulate. But its movements
were both slow and large, involving much lengthening and
shortening of its limbs and body. After a relatively small
number of gestures, B also swiftly and definitely pulled his

head down out of sight, kept it there for perhaps a full minute, and then stuck it out again. Both Laagi rose from their seats and went off in different directions.

"Some sort of conclusion achieved," said Mary.

"Or the breakup of a lifelong friendship over some matter of principle—" began Jim. But he was interrupted.

A squonk had come up to Squonk and was running the tips of its tentacles over Squonk's motionless body. Around them, it seemed that every other squonk in view who was not burdened with a chair or otherwise obviously occupied, was also headed in Squonk's direction.

"Squonk, go back to what you were doing!" said Jim hastily.

Squonk started to move. He lifted his head, exchanged a brief tentacle-touch with the other squonk who had been feeling him over, and went back to his careful search of the floor before him. The squonk who had been examining him went away. Those others in the distance who had been headed toward them also turned off in other directions.

"You see?" demanded Jim. "The minute a squonk—or a Laagi—stops doing anything, it attracts attention."

"You're right," said Mary briskly. "However, it's all fixed. Now, I've got a report to dictate. Are you ready?"

"Ready as I ever will be," said Jim.

Mary began dictating. There was some general data on the other Laagi she had observed in communication, in the room they were now in; but the bulk of her report, once she got into it, was to all effects almost a gesture-by-gesture recounting of the exchange between the two Laagi they had just been watching.

Mary's reports, Jim had noted, came out in short, declarative sentences. The words she chose were simple and the meaning unmistakably clear. She did not ramble. She must, thought Jim as he carefully repeated after her, have had considerable experience dictating such reports. The thought, for some unknown reason, reminded him of a question that had occurred to him from time to time lately. He waited until Mary was done to ask it.

"Tell me," he said then, "when do you sleep?"

"When you do," answered Mary.

"Oh?" Jim thought this over. "And why don't I ever catch you doing it?"

"Because I don't sleep as much as you do," said Mary. "I never did sleep much. I could get by on four or five hours a night indefinitely when I was in my body; and I think I can do a lot better now, if I want to. So I just wait until you're asleep before dropping off myself—and only then if there's nothing going on I want to observe."

"That still doesn't explain why I've never woken up and caught you at it."

"When you wake up, I wake up," said Mary. "I set myself to do that, and it works. Also, it always takes you some few minutes to come to when you do wake up, so you don't realize I've just woken up, too. Of course, most of the time, even if I go to sleep after you do, I wake up long before you wake up."

"Score another one for you," said Jim.

He had been joking, but the tone of Mary's answer was completely serious.

"If you say so," she answered absently. Jim was nettled in spite of his earlier good intentions.

"Tell me," he said, "did it ever occur to you it might be to your benefit to make friends with the people you work with?"

"Why?" said Mary, almost fiercely. "That's right, why? The job's the thing. If the work gets done, who cares how the people doing it get on together?"

Jim took a few seconds to absorb that.

"I think you really mean that," he said at last.

"I do," said Mary. Suddenly one of the changes in her that was as astonishing as the sort of attitude Jim had just been questioning her about seemed to take her over. "Sorry, Jim. I don't deliberately set out to be hard to coexist with. It's just that what we're involved in here is one of the most important things any members of the human race have ever tied into; and something like that is so much more important than friendship, or sleep, or anything else, that there's no comparing them."

"It's also true," said Jim slowly, "that it's a job as big as the Laagi race itself. It's not the sort of thing that's going to be done by one person, or two persons, alone."

"Whoever comes after us is going to build on what I do

now," said Mary. "I owe it to give them as much as I can. That's that. If you don't like it, you can lump it!"

Mentally, Jim opened his mouth to answer her, then closed it again. It was no use. He and she seemed to talk different languages.

But it started him on a new line of thought.

There had been something approaching a violence in the emotion he had felt from Mary just now; a violence he had not felt from her before. It was nearly as if she was reacting to him as a competitor, or even an antagonist. He compared that emotion in her with his memory of her, when he had first come out of his trance, to find himself in hypnotic shackles with *AndFriend*, locked down on the surface of this alien world.

She had been entirely different then. She had seemed honestly regretful at what she obviously felt she had had no choice but to do, and apparently honestly concerned at what it had done to him. Now she was all claws and teeth. Why? Unless—wild as it seemed—there was something about studying the Laagi that had triggered off the change in her.

He tried to imagine what that might be. It could hardly be the example set by the Laagi themselves. So far they had seen no sign of anything even approaching violence of emotion in the Laagi, let alone any evidence of brutality or worse; and even if they had, why having observed it should cause Mary to change her attitude toward Jim was a mystery. Like the squonks, all the Laagi did, apparently, was work. Work and keep working.

The only connection between that unceasing activity and either Jim or Mary was the fact that Mary was also a worker. But even she could not work around the clock, seven days a week, for a lifetime; which was what—so far—it looked like the Laagi did. Could she really get by on four hours' sleep a night, indefinitely? Jim himself had occasionally found it necessary as a Frontier pilot to go on five or six hours' sleep out of each twenty-four for spells of up to several weeks; and the lack of sleep had wrung him out. Of course, different people had different requirements as far as sleep went. . . .

More to the point, had she really been able to do her sleeping only when he was sleeping, and wake before or at the moment he woke—

"Jim!" She was calling him now. "What're you doing with Squonk? I don't want him to go back over there to the wall again; I want him to keep on working through the crowd out here in the middle of the floor. Jim!"

"I didn't tell him to do anything," replied Jim. For Squonk had suddenly turned and was headed as Mary said, toward the wall, the base of which he had searched some hours past. "Squonk! Good Squonk, don't go that way. Come back to where you were."

But Squonk had reached the wall by this time. He leaned up against it, shortened his legs, fell over on his back and lay rocking gently on his shell, with his two red feet facing upward toward the distant ceiling.

"Well," said Jim after a moment. "Apparently when it's time for him to sleep, he sleeps."

"Can't you wake him up?"

"How?" asked Jim.

"I don't know. You're the one who runs him. Think of something. There must be something—some sort of emergency signal that'd bring him to."

"Maybe there is," said Jim. "But don't you think you'd better just let him sleep when he's used to sleeping, if you want to keep him in good shape for your own use? How would we go about getting another squonk if something happened to him, or he got so tired he stopped paying attention to what I said to him? The way he didn't listen to me just now, when I told him to stop going toward the wall."

She did not answer. He thought he again felt a deep anger in her, anger at him as well as at Squonk. But he could not be sure. It was difficult for him to do much more than guess at her emotional state unless she spoke, and then her feelings came through loud and clear as an overriding quality on the words she said. He told himself that he might have been imagining it in this instance; but from then on he watched for a number of things during the time that followed after Squonk came out of his brief period of sleep and responded to Jim's commands in his old obedient manner.

In the weeks and perhaps months of local time that followed—the day here seemed to be somewhat longer than twenty-four of Earth's hours, although without access to the ship's instruments, it was impossible to compare the two until they got back to *AndFriend*—they saw, and Mary dictated, reports on an astonishing amount of information about the Laagi.

They penetrated to the city's outskirts, and discovered that there, it stopped abruptly with the last building and beyond this was a scrub-brush type of open country with hard-packed sandy soil, bushes, or perhaps small trees that seemed capable of pulling up their roots at will, moving slowly to a new location and putting them down again. This open country was also plentifully sprinkled with evidence of more primitive life forms, from conical mounds that resembled large ant hills several meters in height, to communities of smaller mounds no larger than a human fist, from which in the daytime emerged a number of small trotting, flying or hopping creatures, possibly insects, that apparently fed off the vegetation or each other.

They ventured a short distance out into this countryside, until Squonk became too upset to go farther. But once they were well out from the buildings, a kilometer or more, both Mary and Jim had thought they caught glimpses of moving forms as large as Squonk or larger, among the vegetation in the distance.

" . . . it was impossible to be sure," Mary dictated after their return to the city, "whether it was fear or a sense of having abandoned his proper place or duty that made Squonk so eager to return to the city. It may have been both. . . ."

Within the city itself, they eventually found the equivalent of a transportation terminal, with both atmosphere and space-going craft resting there, taking off, and landing upon it.

"Strange they wouldn't keep *AndFriend* here, instead of someplace else in the city," commented Jim.

"Questions like that can be speculated on later," said Mary.

Nonetheless, it was a question that continued to bother Jim. He wished he knew whether Raoul's ship had been kept here at the field for regular space and atmosphere traffic.

They also witnessed the Laagi equivalent of long-distance communications. The Laagi they watched operated a set of controls that consisted of buttons on a vertical rod, which, in addition to being pivotable about its base in the floor, was capable of being pulled out to greater length or pushed down to shorter, as larger sections slid backwards or forwards over

adjoining shorter sections. The stubby Laagi fingers meanwhile played with studs set into the rod itself.

While the Laagi they watched was doing this, it watched
the screen of a three-dimensional tank in which the image of
another Laagi moved and gesticulated. It took only a little
thinking to realize that the live Laagi before them was operating the movements of an image seen by the Laagi being communicated with; and that that other Laagi was controlling the
movements of the image that the live Laagi was watching.

"Call it phoning," suggested Jim. "You might as well; and
it's less confusing than to talk of it as a form of alien communication the way you are."

Mary did not answer. But in her reports from then on she
did use the word.

But they found no recreational areas and nothing resembling separate homes, dwelling places, or even dormitories—
with the exception of one place that seemed pretty obviously
the equivalent of a hospital.

They did discover a maternity area at the hospital, with
evidence that at least some of the Laagi—it was impossible to
tell by looking at them—were capable of bearing young. Although whether these were the result of bisexual, asexual, or
some other engendering process, they did not find out. Certainly, they saw no Laagi in the act of sexual coupling. In fact,
Laagi almost never touched each other, except for the faint
touches that went along with the vibrating arm gestures such
as Squonk had received from the Laagi he had sought out and
been praised by when they had first left the ship. Laagi in
conversation with each other sometimes used similar arm vibrations. But this was the closest to touching that Jim and
Mary were able to observe.

The young Laagi were evidently carried to term within the
adult Laagi, just as a human child is within its mother; and the
pregnant adults, apparently, came to the hospital-equivalent
for delivery. This took place within minutes of the pregnant
Laagi being admitted to a maternity ward, which led to Mary's
suspicion that those so admitted had at least some conscious
control over when the delivery was to occur.

The baby Laagi, however, which on delivery had all its
limbs and head tucked inside its peripheral flesh folds, was
immediately taken away by one of the hospital staff; and the

formerly pregnant Laagi got up, left the hospital immediately and went back to work.

Apparently, parent and offspring never had anything more to do with each other after that. The young individual was taken to the equivalent of a nursery, where, gradually, during the next week or so, it began to essay small emergences of its limbs and head from their hiding places. Within two or three weeks it was up on its feet and mobile, and was taken out of the nursery to be put into what was apparently a school; where it began to work, or perhaps play at working, almost immediately and almost without instruction.

" . . . Natural selection on this planet, assuming that this is the only or originating planet of the Laagi race," dictated Mary in one of her reports, "seems to have specialized in communal life forms. If this turns out to be so, it may well be that the Laagi are a communal life form that evolved into an intelligence equal to humans and built a comparable civilization, one adapted to their own special requirements and so differing from our own.

"The result seems to be that while in many areas of activity they react according to racial imperatives, in which the needs of the community are all that is considered, in more modern and technological areas they react as individuals. Although I've been unable to find any hard evidence of a government and individuals acting as leaders, both I and James Wander feel strongly that there must be such things somewhere in the social machinery of the Laagi. . . ."

The adult Laagi ate at whatever communal food source was handy and slept at their work when they had reached the point where sleep was necessary. The greatest concession they made to the need to rest was, like Squonk, to get out of a general traffic area before going off to sleep. Also, their sleep was at best a matter of an hour or two and was taken at no set pattern of intervals.

One somewhat unpleasant discovery was that the Laagi also died at their work. Occasionally one of them who had pulled in its limbs and head in what seemed normal sleep simply never woke up again. Death was signaled, apparently, by the fact that head, legs and arms emerged slightly from the skin folds into which they had withdrawn themselves and showed a limpness that was otherwise uncharacteristic.

When this happened, sometimes the dead Laagi's former coworkers would carry it off. Sometimes its former coworkers ignored it and after a while other Laagi came to remove it; and, then or shortly after, a living Laagi took its place.

At Mary's insistence, they followed such a removal team and found that the body was simply dumped onto the equivalent of the garbage pile from the nearest food room, from which a squonk-operated mechanical trash gatherer gathered it up along with the discarded food materials and took it off to be disposed of elsewhere.

All this, Mary meticulously reported via Jim back to the memory banks of *AndFriend*. Meanwhile, Jim himself was occupied in two other activities.

One of these was determining if it was possible, through Squonk, to get access to tools and the assistance of other squonks on a joint project. This particular research on his part came to Mary's attention when Jim deliberately ordered Squonk to lift and move a piece of metal scaffolding that was leaning against a wall in a building half-factory, half-offices that they were in at the time. The scaffolding was far too heavy for Squonk alone to lift. But Jim concentrated strongly on the image he broadcast to Squonk of wanting the scaffolding moved, for its own length down the wall against which it rested.

The results were an unqualified success. Squonk, ever-obliging, trotted off and rounded up three other squonks who were either passing by or for other reasons did not have their tentacles engaged at the moment. The four of them returned to the piece of scaffolding, lifted it with the strength of their combined tentacles and shifted it as Jim had envisioned.

They made no objection at all to an order to immediately move it back again, once the original move had been made. Then they dispersed.

"What's happening? What's Squonk doing now?" Mary's voice woke Jim out of a self-congratulatory mood. "I wanted him to stand still so I could watch the Laagi on this assembly line."

"Sorry," said Jim. "Just an experiment to see if I could get him to make use of other squonks for us, if necessary. I'm trying out a few things in the way of controlling him."

"Well, let me know beforehand, after this," said Mary. "It

may not always be the best time for you to pull him away from what I'm studying. Did you think of that?"

"I didn't. Sorry," said Jim. "Back to the assembly line, Squonk."

And that was that. The other activity with which Jim was concerned was studying Mary herself.

In the time since he had first met her he had gone from being irritated with her to an active dislike, and from there to a tolerance during the long period of getting him ready to become a part of *AndFriend*. From that point he had developed into a cautious partnership that was beginning to approach a genuine liking. But this had been swept away by his outright fury on discovering how he had been tricked into his situation here on the Laagi world. Now, however, he had made a step beyond that.

The fury in him had faded and with it, curiously, all the negative feelings he had had at one time or another toward her. Somehow, working deep within him and underneath the surface changes in his emotions, something like a fondness and a genuine concern for her had developed. She no longer had the power to make him seriously angry. He liked her and he was worried about her; and, as the weeks grew into months on this alien planet, that worry about her grew.

The Laagi, he and she had now pretty well established, lived to work—as did the squonks and probably most of the other communal species of life forms on this planet. They worked until they could work no longer, then they died. It was a world in which work was everything. Nothing else had any meaning.

And Mary, herself, was a worker. She lived to work, and as far as he had learned, nothing else for her had any meaning. But what was natural for the Laagi was not natural for her, a human. Still, she was now caught up in an environment in which her ability to work no longer set her apart from anyone else—anyone but Jim himself, whom she had long since dismissed from any possible use as a yardstick. With most people such an environment would not pose such a threat. But Mary, Jim had concluded, had grown a protective shell about herself.

He had checked up on her claims regarding the small amounts of sleep she needed. It was true to a certain extent that she was phenomenal at keeping going on what would normally be a very few hours out of Earth's twenty-four. But beyond that there were a few holes in what she had told him about herself.

For one thing, she did not sleep only when he was sleeping. He had watched the same things she had watched and later repeated for recording the reports she made on them. There had been things done by the Laagi that Jim had seen—things that he now knew her well enough to be sure she would have made part of her report if she had seen, that she had not reported.

If she could not tell the difference between the periods when he was silent because he was asleep and those when he was silent because he was thinking, neither could he tell that difference in her—except by this sort of omission from her reports. The interesting question was whether she could herself. He had not realized at first, after becoming part of *And-Friend*, when he had been asleep. It might be Mary could not either. She might quite honestly believe that she slept only when he did. Out of the body as they both were, the physical signals customarily felt on waking were mostly missing.

He concentrated on training himself to be aware of what small signs there were in himself that would tell him he had just woken after a period of sleep. Slowly, he began to identify them. There was a faint lassitude—not the physical heaviness that the body normally reported after being slowed down by the process of slumber, but a short space in which the mind had to rouse itself to the different process of thinking consciously again, after having abandoned the conscious for the unconsciousness of dreamland.

There was also, as he came to recognize the existence of his sleep periods, as sleep periods, an awareness that he had not realized he possessed. It was an awareness of a period of inactivity, in the conscious area of his mind, a blank stretch in the memory record. And with his recognition of this, he began to remember the dreams he had had—just as someone who makes a point of writing down his memory of dreams on awakening becomes conscious of them.

Remembering the dreams, he became able, after a fashion, to measure the length of his sleep period by the amount of his remembered dreams. It was very imprecise, but it gave him something on which to estimate the length of his sleep.

In the process of doing this, for the first time, he came to realize that there had been a refreshment for him in having slept. His mental machinery had gotten some relief that it needed from its constant activity in the conscious state. This much realized, he made a final step forward and began to be aware of the mental fatigue signs that signaled him sleep was needed. It was a strange awareness, a feeling that was in no way a bodily feeling—something like the tension of a stretched rubber band and like that of the jittery nerves that in some people preceded a headache. It was very faint, but it was there, when needed; and he found that all that was necessary once he became aware of it was to look away—remove his conscious attention from the scene he was watching or any particular concern that had been occupying his mind—and he would fall asleep immediately.

Finally, now that he had discovered this much about himself, he had a rough system for measuring time under these abnormal conditions. He set himself to seeing if he could further train himself to become aware of signs in Mary's behavior that also signaled tiredness and the lassitude of just awakening. If what he had begun to suspect was true, she was killing herself.

# C H A P T E R

## 21

"...ALTHOUGH NOTHING MUCH MORE THAN GUESSES ARE possible on the basis of the small amount of observation we have been able to make of the Laagi in this short time," dictated Mary, "some possibilities might be considered as reasons for elements of Laagi behavior that have been unexplainable until now.

"Such Laagi actions as those by some of their fighter spaceships on the spatial Frontier they share with us. For example, the occasional but not too infrequent situation of a large number of their space fighter craft turning and retreating from a much smaller number of human ones; or—conversely —a mere handful of their ships attacking a much larger number of human ones they have just encountered, even when such attack seems suicidal and therefore reasonless."

She stopped dictating, and there was a long moment in which Jim began to wonder if she would begin again.

"Therefore . . . therefore," she went on again abruptly, "we may consider as a possibility that the apparently unreasonable actions of the Laagi in the fighter ships just referred to were examples of reactions governed by a system of racial imperatives we humans do not have, and so do not realize exists. In other words, what seems unreasonable to us humans is reasonable to the Laagi, under certain special conditions.

"From what I've seen, and from what Jim Wander, who is with me on this observational incursion into Laagi territory, has seen, the Laagi may be more strongly influenced than we are by the inherited reactions that promoted survival in their prehistoric forebears.

"The Laagi, as I've pointed out a number of times before this, seem to be at base a communal race, in the sense that a hive of bees or a hill of ants is a communal race. But for a communal race to develop a technology comparable to our own requires that at some point it must have allowed the development of a certain amount of individuality in its members. Technology requires invention. Invention demands originality. Originality is a faculty of the unique individual who is different from all his fellow individuals. The Laagi, as I have mentioned before, have no recreational areas or recreational activities. This is because their work is their recreation. Even our host member, whom we have named Squonk and who belongs to a local alien species of lesser intelligence than the Laagi, is actively unhappy unless he is constantly working during the hours he is awake. So with the Laagi themselves. They are born to work; and they do work until they die at their job—just as the worker bee literally works itself to death. I ..."

Her words trailed off once more. After a few seconds, she went on.

"...I have made a number of attempts to determine whether at this time the Laagi's occupation is still determined genetically, as that of the worker bee is. But so far, I've been unable to gain any solid evidence, one way or another. However, the impression both Jim Wander and I get is that the present-day, civilized Laagi does not have his occupation genetically selected for him at birth."

Squonk stumbled suddenly, backed up several steps and then began again searching the same area of floor he had just gone over, in the room where Mary and Jim were currently observing. The small alien was still singlemindedly in search of the missing object that the invisible Laagi within him would recognize when he, Squonk, found it. This was not the first time Squonk had so stumbled and backed up to search again over an area he had already examined. He had done it for the first time three days before. Jim was concerned. Mary had not seemed to notice.

" . . . if we use as a model for a typical human being one who has a base of instincts and reflexes based on those instincts, this overlaid by a pattern of cultural reactions and behaviors acquired from the community of humans surrounding the youngster as he grows up, and this in turn overlaid by a set of habitual actions and decisions, plus current decisions engendered by the conscious processing of previous experience plus the influence of the two lower layers of reaction, we have a three-layered structure for human action and response to a given situation.

"By contrast, the Laagi appears to respond according to a two-layer structure of which the older, instinctive one is dominant under some conditions, but under others the newer, conscious layer can control. To create a hypothetical example, suppose that if a Laagi encountered another Laagi that showed a particular form of sickness, his older instinct would force him to destroy the sick one, even if consciously he did not wish to do so. But if the other Laagi showed some slight difference in that form of sickness, then his newer, individual consciousness would be allowed to use its discretion about killing the other Laagi or taking him to one of their hospitals."

Mary stopped abruptly. It was marvelous, thought Jim admiringly, what she had been able to deduce from observations alone of a totally alien race. Sherlock Holmes would have been proud of her. When she went on, though, her voice was ragged with fatigue.

"Note again that what I have just suggested is a purely imaginary model, by way of example. We have not witnessed one Laagi killing another for any reason at all. We have not seen a fight or even what we could be absolutely sure was a serious disagreement between two or more Laagi . . ."

She ran down and this time did not resume talking, although her usual pattern with reports was to wind them up with a clear statement that the report was ended.

"Mary," said Jim, after she had been still for a long moment, "you're worn out."

"I'm fine," she said.

"No, you aren't. I've been watching you get more and

more exhausted. No matter how much you think you can work steadily at something and just get by with an occasional snatch of sleep, you're running downhill, and you ought to recognize that yourself."

"What are you talking about?" demanded Mary. "We've got no bodies to run downhill. That's a purely physical phenomenon. I can work as long as I like. The mind doesn't get tired."

"Sorry. Yes, it does—evidently," said Jim.

"What would you know about it, anyway? You haven't had to do anything but ride along and redictate my reports."

"And watch everything that goes on," said Jim, "with the result I see some things you seem to be missing, lately. About Squonk, for one."

"What about Squonk?"

"You've been overworking yourself, so consequently you've been overworking him; because he isn't built to know when to stop for his own health and safety."

"You're insane!" But there was a note of concern for the first time in Mary's voice. Concern—but disbelief as well. "He can take a nap anytime he wants to, and we always let him."

"He doesn't want to nap," said Jim. "He wants to find that nonexistent key we've had him hunting for for months. He's begrudging himself sleep more and more because you're begrudging yourself sleep. He'll stop and find a place to roll over and snooze, but only when we don't seem to be in the middle of something—such as when we've just given him a new order to search somewhere he hasn't searched before. Or when we're talking like this."

"You think he can hear us?"

"He can hear me," said Jim. "At least the part of me that gives orders to him; and for all I know he can feel my emotions as much as I can feel his. If he can do that, too, he's been picking up the backwash of the urgency I echo whenever you order a change in place or direction, or anything like that."

"I don't believe he's being overworked. That's what you're saying, isn't it, that I'm overworking him?"

"That's right. I know you aren't doing it deliberately; but all the same you've been setting up a situation in which, to

take a leaf out of your own deductions, his racial imperative to
work himself to death is controlling him."

"I don't believe it. This is some plan of yours to wind up
my work here, so I'll turn you loose to get back to Earth."

"Sorry," said Jim. "If you won't believe me, you won't
believe me; but I think you've forgotten who controls Squonk.
Me. He needs rest and he's going to get it. Have you thought
what kind of situation we'd be in if he died? I don't know how
we'd go about switching to another squonk or getting back to
*AndFriend*."

He broke off and spoke directly to Squonk through his
usual Laagi image.

"Squonk, good Squonk, you can stop searching now. Time
to sleep, Squonk, then we'll go right back to finding that key.
But for now, Squonk, time to rest."

(?) said Squonk's emotions.

It was the first time the creature had done anything like
trying to communicate directly with the invisible Laagi he
now obeyed, and Jim read the unusual action as a sign of
considerable confusion and upset in Squonk.

"Sleep!" said Jim. "Squonk, go sleep!"

Squonk, who had stopped searching at Jim's first communication, hesitated. He put his head down, backed up and
began searching again over the floor ahead of him, then
stopped and stood uncertainly. He looked over at the nearest
wall of the room and back at the floor.

"Sleep!" ordered Jim.

Squonk turned toward the wall. He wavered a little on his
feet as he went, and as soon as he bumped into the wall itself,
he pulled in his head, legs and tentacles all at once and literally fell over backwards. He rocked for a moment and then lay
still.

"—What are you doing?" Mary was storming at Jim. There
was fury, pain and outrage all at once radiating from her.
"You're doing this deliberately to slow me down. I don't believe a word of what you say—"

"Mary," said Jim. "Squonk's asleep. There's nothing more
you can do until he wakes up, except observe from against the
wall, here; which you already did, when we first came into
this place. So why don't you sleep, too?"

"Sleep? Why should I sleep? Who're you to tell me when I

need or want to go to sleep?" An explosion of mixed emotions was riding on her mental voice.

"I'm sorry," said Jim, "but I'm not going to let you kill Squonk and I'm not going to let you kill yourself. You've already done a mountain of work here. Face it, it actually is time we headed back to Base and Earth."

"That's what all this is about!" Mary's voice was raw with anger. "It's all a ploy of yours to get me to turn you loose, so you can phase-shift *AndFriend* out from under those metal arches they've got her pinned down with. Well, it's not going to work. We're staying here until I decide my work's done enough to leave. We'll stay years if we have to. We'll stay a lifetime, if necessary."

"Don't say that," said Jim as gently as he could. "You'll force me to find a way to get *AndFriend* loose and take her home without paying any attention to what you still need or want to do."

"Don't try it!" Mary's mental voice was savage and a welter of emotions. "Don't try to fight me, Jim, or you'll find you've bitten off more than you can chew. I mean that! I was only six years old when I knew what I wanted to do—and that was something that had some meaning to it. Can you understand something like that?"

Jim decided not to answer but simply let her talk herself out. And in a moment, sure enough, she went on without needing an answer from him.

"When I was six years old—the age for first grade—I was already beginning to understand what my parents were. Do you know what they were—my mother and father? My mother spent her time killing time with other women as empty-headed as she was. My father was just as empty-headed. He was a real estate salesman, and made money at it—lots of money. And they put in their lives trying to pretend that what they did was of some use, that it made one damn bit of difference to the world. Actually, if they'd died at birth the world would never have gained or lost a thing—except for the fact they had a child."

She stopped.

"Why don't you say something?" she demanded. "All right, don't answer. I know you're listening. You have to listen to me whether you want to or not, so you might as well learn something. When I was six years old I'd already made up my mind that whatever I did with my life, it'd add up to something. It'd matter to the future of the world whether I lived or died. I wasn't going to be a cipher like my parents. I was going to be someone who did something."

She paused again. Jim still said nothing.

"And I've stuck to that decision ever since. And I've done what I said I'd do. That's why I couldn't wait to get away from my family and begin to build something on my own. I picked a work and I worked at it. And I built it until it brought me here. And here is where I'm going to stay until I've answered all the important questions about the Laagi. Do you understand that? And you're going to stay with me, and so is Squonk, because I need you both. So don't try to go against me, Jim. I've spent my life taking care of whatever got in my way; and if you get in my way, I'll take care of you. Think of that. And keep thinking about it!"

She stopped. This time it seemed for good. Because she said nothing more; and, after a time, the sensitivity that Jim had been developing to her sleep periods seemed to indicate to him that now, finally, she slept.

As for himself, he had had to take what she said at its face value. She was determined to stay until she killed herself; and end by killing herself, she certainly would, because the job of understanding the Laagi was not something that could be done by a single human, or even by a generation of humans, studying that race. It would take millennia, perhaps, before humanity would finally be able to say that it understood these people with whom it had been locked in battle for over a hundred years. If Mary would only stop to recognize the fact, she would realize that she had already left her mark on the history of the human race by what she had done here so far on the Laagi world. It was not necessary for her to try to do the impossible.

But, clearly, she was not about to recognize that; and she was not willingly going to free him to take *AndFriend* home. That meant he must decide himself what to do to get the ship loose and with both of them aboard it, in spite of her and against her will. No more than she doubted herself, did he doubt he could find a way to do that. But there was a lot yet to be thought over and worked out.

Two days later, Laagi time, Squonk stumbled and fell in the process of searching along the wall of one of those enclosures Mary and Jim had come to call "discussion rooms" from the fact that they seemed to have no other purpose than to provide a place for the Laagi to gather and communicate. Such rooms had become favorite observation places for Mary.

Squonk immediately got back on his feet and resumed searching. But he seemed confused; and, after a moment, he straightened, backed up several times his own length and began to search again over the base of the wall he had just covered. But before he could complete a second search of the same area, he drifted away from the wall and began searching apparently at random out into the open floor where the discussions were going on.

"Squonk!" ordered Jim sharply, "rest. Time to sleep. Stop!"

Squonk obediently rose, headed back toward the wall, pulled his limbs in as he usually did when preparing to sleep, but checked himself before he had rolled over on his back. He extended his limbs again and started blindly searching the base of the wall beside him.

By this time, other squonks in the room were converging upon him. Jim again ordered Squonk to sleep, but now Squonk did not seem to hear him. A moment later, other squonks had surrounded Squonk and were feeling him over with their tentacles.

Fumblingly, Squonk began to search them back, as if they were part of the wall he had just been exploring. The surrounding squonks wrapped their tentacles around his legs and head and tried to push them back into the skin folds on his body from which they emerged. But Squonk struggled to keep these body parts out where they were, his tentacles meanwhile searching, searching, up and down the very tentacles that were trying to compress his body together.

The cluster of squonks had finally attracted the attention of some of the nearby Laagi. One of these left his discussion group and came over, pushing his way among the squonks, who made room for him as soon as they realized the superior life form was there. The Laagi stood over Squonk, and from the waves of emotion Jim picked up from Squonk, he guessed that the Laagi was giving Squonk orders.

"What's the Laagi doing? What's happening?" Mary was asking in the recesses of Jim's mind.

"Hold the questions for now, will you please?" said Jim irritably. "Squonk is being ordered to sleep by the Laagi, but he's not responding, any more than he was responding to me."

The Laagi turned and reached toward one of the nearby squonks, who immediately stretched out his neck and held it there, while the Laagi vibrated his arm above it, undoubtedly sending some kind of order in the same sort of feather touches Jim had first believed were only a form of praise, when on their first leaving the ship, Squonk had sought out a particular Laagi for what Jim had then thought was only attention. Now Jim suspected that the faint touches of the vibrating Laagi arm were used far more to order than to praise. In fact, their most common use, he now strongly suspected, was to make a major alteration in the current work orders under which a squonk had been operating, and to put it on an entirely new job.

The Laagi waded out of the crowd of squonks and returned to his group. The squonk he had touched dashed off. The other squonks continued to surround Squonk, although they had now ceased to try to push his legs and head back into his body and simply contented themselves with stroking all of his body that was not protected by the shell on his back.

This stroking seemed to have at least a partial calming effect on Squonk, although he still tried, erratically and feebly, to search any surface that came within reach of his tentacles. The squonk that had left returned, riding a sort of flat-bed truck or raft which floated just above the floor, held there by some force, perhaps antigravity, perhaps something that merely repelled the floor's surface.

The other squonks coaxed and pushed Squonk up onto this raft and the squonk which had brought it drove it off, with Squonk now trying to search the bed of the raft.

They left the building, moved down one of the green pathways and through a tangle of other, connecting paths into a hospital building. Here, the raft was driven to a large, dormitorylike room Jim and Mary had not found in other such hospitals they had visited—although they had never really searched any of them in detail. Their destination now was a ward, plainly, for squonks only. Long rows of rafts with unmoving squonks on them, like the one on which Squonk was being carried, floated just above the floor of the room; and the driver of their raft maneuvered it into position on the end of one row. The driver then departed, leaving the raft there, with Squonk still mindlessly searching the surface of the vehicle's platform.

Almost immediately another squonk appeared, carrying what looked like a large piece of mosquito netting, and threw it over both Squonk and the raft. Looking out through the meshes, which were so large and flimsy they barely obscured the view, Jim noticed what he had been too concerned with Squonk to notice before; and that was that a good share of the other vehicle-beds had their occupants enclosed by similar nettings.

Almost immediately, the netting began to radiate a mild heat, and this seemed to have a calming effect on Squonk. He pulled in his extendible body parts, stood for a little while unmoving, then rolled over on his back and abandoned wakefulness.

"He's asleep?" asked Mary. It was the first word she had said since Jim had peremptorily shut her up in the discussion room.

"Yes," said Jim. "Which means we're all right for the present."

"Why only for the present?" Mary echoed.

"Because Squonk'll either die or get well," said Jim. "If he dies, we're stuck in a dead body—and we've seen what they do with dead bodies here. We'll probably end up in some trash pit or incinerator—I'll bet on the incinerator rather than the pit."

"And if he lives?" Mary's voice was controlled and even.

"If he lives, I can imagine some Laagi checking up on what made him sick enough to end up here. I've no idea how detailed the information might be that a Laagi can get out of a squonk. Have you? But if the Laagi learns that all this time, Squonk's been searching for something that's missing from *AndFriend*, and that he's been getting his orders from a Laagi that's not there in the flesh, what do you think's going to happen?"

"I've no idea," said Mary, still levelly. "But I imagine nothing good—for us. You were right and I was wrong about overworking Squonk. Aside from that, everything I said earlier still goes. And now, since there's nothing much for me to observe here, and because I really could use some sleep right now, I'm going to fold up. Wake me if you need me."

She stopped talking, and a moment later Jim felt sure that he was once more picking up the mental signals from her that indicated she was truly slumbering.

He himself was wide awake with no desire to sleep at all. It was strange to be so alert, while his two companions were out of it, so to speak. They were asleep, around him all the other invalid squonks were asleep and no squonk attendants were in the room. He was literally alone with his thoughts.

He let them run free, accordingly. They flitted from speculation over how long Squonk would take to get rested, and how long Mary would take to rest up; and ended up speculating about things he and she had observed in their exploration of this Laagi city. Eventually, they ended up in speculation about the Laagi themselves.

There was something driving the Laagi, as a race, Jim thought. They were concerned with something more than just survival and increasing their population by settling more worlds. Perhaps, he thought, they had some sort of racial vision, some sort of dream that was strong enough to drive them all—perhaps strong enough to drive them forever.

They were too advanced, too civilized, not to be headed somewhere. The war with the human race, the endless work, all that was a product of the older part of their brains. But there was more to them than those obvious things. Both he and Mary had come to feel that the rooms in which many Laagi sat and observed one of their number apparently in conversation with the picture of another Laagi on a screen, as well as the "clubs" where they gathered and communicated in anything from pairs up to small groups, had to do with learning and decision-making; and almost surely, if those first two were present activities, with speculation as well.

Like humans they must wonder where it all led to, and what was the right way to go. And if they attacked that question with the relentless effort they brought to everything else they did, they could have made admirable progress, even by this time, possibly in some ways humanity had not even considered.

He found himself admitting to himself that he had come to

admire the Laagi in certain ways, just as he had come to
admire Squonk in some of the attitudes and efforts which that
little creature showed. Mary was right. He and she must observe and deduce and come to understand this alien race. Just
as technologically-advanced races on Earth had at first been
blind to what could be learned from races who appeared technologically backward until they began to learn better in the
twentieth century, so it would be easy now to be blind to what
the Laagi must have discovered and put to use that humanity
had not even imagined.

Whatever the Laagi were, they had things to teach us. . . .

Somewhere along the way with that thought, Jim himself
fell asleep. He continued to sleep and think, alternately, as
time passed and he waited for Mary and Squonk to recover.

After all, there was nothing else he could do. There was no
possibility in any case of going anywhere without Squonk,
and Squonk was clearly in no shape to move. They all waited,
therefore, for the better part of two days.

Once a day, as closely as Jim could figure time here, one of
the squonks who acted as attendant in the ward would come
around with a container filled with pink cubes about the size
of a child's toy block.

These looked rather as if they had been made out of straw-
berry jelly. The attendant squonk gave one to each of the pa-
tients, including Squonk. Squonk ate it with every appearance
of appetite and seemed to be fully satisfied as far as food was
concerned until the attendant came around with another cube
the next day. Jim used the visits of the attendant with food as
one of the means to estimate the passage of time here indoors.

He remembered that it had been late afternoon, local time,
when Squonk had been carried to the hospital. Jim made his
best estimate of the hours that had gone by since then. In the
situation they now found themselves, if anything was to be
done once Squonk was able to move, Jim wanted to do it at
night.

Twice—according to Jim's reckoning, it was during the
early morning hours—a Laagi came through the room and
examined each squonk that was a patient there. Most he
merely glanced at. In about a dozen cases the squonk he examined was able to stretch its neck out in the customary action
of one of its race waiting to accept orders. When this hap-

pened, the visiting Laagi vibrated his arm above the proffered neck; and, in two instances, the squonk so spoken to got to its feet, stepped down off the raft that had been its hospital bed, and left the room. In all other cases, the squonk touched went back to sleep.

There was one incident, however, that varied from this usual pattern. During the second Laagi visit—Jim had no way to tell if it was the same alien as the first time—at one of the beds, the Laagi stopped to look at its occupant, but without extending his arm, the squonk lying there began to struggle to move and managed to get up on its feet, although its legs were still not extended. The squonk shakily stretched out his neck toward the Laagi and reached out fumblingly with his tentacles to encircle the Laagi's arm. Most of the tentacles slipped off, but two managed to maintain their grasp on the Laagi's arm. Effortfully, the squonk pulled the arm into position over his extended neck.

For a second the Laagi merely stood there. Something about the way he stood seemed to signal to Jim—he did not know why—a feeling of sorrow or sadness. Then he began to vibrate his held arm over the extended neck, and as he did so the squonk shivered ecstatically and one of its legs managed to extend itself slightly. It was only then that Jim saw that the hand at the end of the other arm of the Laagi was stealthily approaching the underside of the extended neck, dark thumb stiffly upraised like the end of a blunt club. As the squonk seemed to bask under the vibrations of the Laagi arm above him this thumb came to within inches of the underside of the neck—and suddenly thrust upward.

The blow was a more violent one than Jim had expected, testifying to a strength in the Laagi arm he had not suspected those aliens of possessing. There was an audible crack, as of something breaking in the squonk's neck, and it suddenly dropped, to lie still with its head at an angle to its neck.

Two of the attendant squonks that were presently in the ward had started forward when the bedridden squonk had first started to struggle to its feet, but halted when the Laagi extended his arm over the sick one's neck. Now the Laagi turned away, and they came forward, lifted the obviously dead body between them and carried it off.

The Laagi moved on to examine the next patient. It may

have been Jim's imagination, but it seemed to him the Laagi still radiated sadness, an emotion Jim had never before seen in one of the aliens. He found himself happy, for some obscure reason, that Squonk—their Squonk—had slept through the whole incident. In fact, Squonk had been unhesitatingly obedient in composing himself again for sleep whenever he woke up and Jim urged him back into slumber.

Squonk had been awake when a visiting Laagi had entered the room the first time, but Jim had urged him then to go back to sleep; and in docile fashion, Squonk had. He was therefore still asleep when the visiting Laagi got to him. The Laagi gave him a quick glance and went on. Jim had not been holding his breath only because he had no breath to hold; but a great relief washed over him as the Laagi moved on to the next patient.

For a second Jim was almost tempted to wake Mary—who had also slept through it all—to share that relief and the story of how they had escaped a closer examination of Squonk. But prudence held him back. He let Mary sleep on.

The second day when the Laagi—or some Laagi; it was impossible to tell if it was the same one that had come the day before—entered the ward, Mary was awake and witnessed the death, and Jim was able to tell her how the previous visit had gone. Once more he was successful in convincing Squonk to be asleep when the visiting physician, veterinarian or whatever, came by.

" . . . But that," said Jim to Mary after the Laagi had left them, "is probably the last time I'll be able to make Squonk sleep when that visitor comes. Squonk's definitely getting slept up and beginning to feel restless. He may not be ready to go back to work, but he certainly feels like it. That means we have to make a break for it tonight."

"Why tonight?" asked Mary. "Why not right now?"

"I want to be sure that Laagi who inspects here has left this part of the hospital for the day. He just might be able to identify Squonk from other squonks, and remember that our Squonk was supposed to be in this hospital. At the same time I want us to have as much time as possible to be free before he comes again and finds Squonk's bed empty."

"What're you planning to do once we get out of here?" Mary asked.

"Go back to *AndFriend*. Maybe we can get the Laagi to

assume that Squonk's been doing his regular duties if they come looking for him and find him back, cleaning the ship—or even trying to clean her. Or, once back at *AndFriend* we might decide to leave Squonk to go his own way and rejoin the ship itself—temporarily, at least."

"Why?"

"I'm not sure. We're going to have to make decisions as we go along. Maybe the ship'll turn out to be safer for us. Maybe Squonk won't be able to do any more than get us back to her before he dies. Maybe just about anything. Don't ask me for answers now. Let's get out of here and then see what the situation is."

"All right. Call me when time for decisions . . . " Mary's voice trailed off, and within seconds Jim was sure she was asleep again.

From the first, since Squonk had been carted off to the hospital, she had woken up suddenly, like someone startled out of a nightmare or roused by the internal signal of some habitual duty clamoring against the need to oversleep. Lately, the occasions of her waking had been less frequent; and the time she was awake before sleep took her again, becoming shorter. It would be too much to ask, thought Jim, but wouldn't it be wonderful if she slept all the time it took to get them back to *AndFriend*?

He waited until he felt it must be dark outside the hospital building, then roused Squonk, taking as much care as was possible to do that with the image in the back of his mind and not think out loud, as it were, which might rouse Mary.

He succeeded.

"Good Squonk," he mentally whispered at the awakened creature. "Is Squonk able to get up from this place and go somewhere else?"

Squonk stretched his neck and flailed his tentacles about affirmatively.

"Good," said Jim. "Quietly, then, so that we don't disturb these poor, sick squonks all around us. Get up off this thing you're lying on and we'll leave the building. Oh, and pick up a container of those food cubes on the way out."

He steered Squonk out of the room. They had to hunt around, but eventually they found a room containing a number of empty baskets and a machine ending in a large hopper that was filled with the pink cubes. At Jim's order, Squonk filled a basket and, on his own initiative, balanced the basket on his shell, holding it in place with three of his tentacles. They left the room and went down the most deserted corridors they could find until Jim saw a doorway that gave on to the outside of the building. But he still did not let himself relax until they were safely out on one of the green pathways and the hospital was being left behind among its fellow structures.

He considered Squonk. As far as could be told from the way the other was covering ground, the small alien was in as good shape as ever; but Jim suspected that, like Mary, Squonk had recovered only a portion of his normal energy and might easily collapse, once that was used up.

"We're going to the ship, Squonk," Jim said. "The ship needs cleaning again. Go slow and if you start to feel tired, just stop. Do you understand? Stop if you start to feel tired."

Squonk made affirmative physical signals and they proceeded. But he did not stop, or perhaps he did not feel the need to stop, until they were once more back inside *And-Friend*. Jim sighed mentally with relief as the ship's port clanged shut behind them; and Mary woke.

"Where are we?" she asked.

"At the ship. Go back to sleep. Squonk's got to rest and so do I," said Jim.

The last bit was a lie. He intended to do anything but rest.

"It'll be hours yet before anyone at the hospital notices Squonk is missing," he said, "and I don't want to start him on the cleaning too soon, even if he's physically up to it. It'll be best if anyone hunting for him comes in and finds him actively at work here."

"Oh. All right. . . ." Mary was off to slumberland again.

So was Squonk. The urge to wake the small alien was strong in Jim, but he made himself hold off. There was no telling how the trip here had taken it out of Squonk's recovered physical powers, and these would be needed, later. He let the others sleep for half an hour by the ship's time-keeping system.

His first act after waking the little alien was to have him store the cubes of food where acceleration forces could not send them tumbling around the interior of the ship. The second was to teach him how to use the system installed aboard for the disposal of human waste. It was a difficult and trouble-some task to teach Squonk how to make use of what was to him the unnatural apparatus, but it turned out not to be impos-sible, which was a relief to Jim. He had been afraid that he might not have time later on for giving such lessons, if they turned out to be necessary.

With that much done, his next move was to transfer his point of view back into the structure of *AndFriend*. He had nothing to go on but guesses as to how this might be done, and he had planned to have Squonk put his tentacle back into the same hidden drawer in which it had picked up some of *AndFriend*'s substance, so that Jim and Mary could become part of the small creature instead of the vessel. He had con-ceived of the switch back as an all-out effort of will; and he had tried, without success, to come up with some plan that would let him make such an effort without waking a sleeping Mary, which he was sure it would.

To his surprise, however, there was nothing to it. Once back in the ship, he found himself naturally wanting to be part of it again, and, having wished, found himself where he wanted to be. It was so easy that he decided to gamble on trying it again. He found it almost as easy to slip back into Squonk and, having done so, to once more return to being part of the ship.

It was so easy, he found himself being suspicious of it. The only reason it could be so little trouble, he finally decided, was that, in effect, he was actually in both places at once at all times, since the material of *AndFriend* was both in the form of the spaceship and in the flesh of Squonk; and it was merely a matter of his own internal point of view which host body he looked out of.

Happily, he discarded the effortful plans he had thought might be necessary to get back to Squonk long enough to give their companion his final orders. While he was still part of the ship, he took his time, and ran a complete check of the work-ing equipment aboard. Only then did he slip back into Squonk, who had fallen asleep once more as soon as Jim had left him.

That slumber, in fact, suited Jim very well. He had planned to let Squonk sleep until roughly three hours from daylight, but the little alien surprised him by waking after only about a couple of hours' sleep and immediately beginning to try to clean the interior of *AndFriend*.

"No, Squonk. Good Squonk, but there's something that needs to be done first. Come outside with me."

Hoping that Mary would stay asleep, he led Squonk out into the night and away from the ship until they could stand back and see it all clearly under the moonless, but starbright, sky.

"The ship has to be moved forward about its own length, Squonk," said Jim. "And to do that we've got to cut loose, temporarily, those arches that hold it down. You'll need other squonks to help you, and tools. Can you do that, Squonk, noble Squonk?"

Jim had no idea what kind of tools or methods would be used to unfasten the base of the hold-down legs from the concretelike surface underfoot, so he simply envisioned a number of squonks clustered busily around each arch-base for a moment or two, and then the base coming loose and rising upward some two meters above the surface. Squonk turned and started eagerly back toward the city.

Jim shifted his point of view back inside *AndFriend*. He watched the small alien move away until the night made the bobbing back-shell too hard to separate from the surrounding dimness. Then, at last, Jim let himself relax into just being *AndFriend* once more, although he was careful to stay awake. Mary, thank God, had never stirred from her sleep even during the shifts he had made from ship to alien and back again. There was relief in knowing that, but right beside it a strong feeling of guilt. The task he had sent Squonk on was one that only Squonk could do; but the doing of it might prove too much for their faithful servant. He might very well, Jim told himself grimly, have sent Squonk to his death.

But . . . he had not. He kept a watch through the outer surface of *AndFriend*'s hull, and less than an hour after he had watched Squonk leave, the other returned, followed by either seven or eight other squonks—it was difficult to count them accurately as they scuttled around in the darkness.

This squonk team, including Squonk himself, went immediately to that base of the front arch that was to the right of *AndFriend*'s forward section. What they were doing there, Jim could no more make out than he had been able to imagine definitively how they would go about freeing the connection of each base from the pavement beneath the ship.

But, one by one, the bases came free and floated up, each with a chunk of pavement attached, to what would have been about the height of Jim's head, if he had been out there in the body to use himself as a measuring stick.

Jim shifted momentarily into Squonk.

"Good Squonk. Good squonks!" he projected. "All the others can go now, Squonk. You tell them."

Squonk scurried around, touching tentacles with the other squonks, who headed off and were swallowed up by the darkness.

"You come back on board with me," said Jim to Squonk, once the others were gone. "Now you can start cleaning up in there."

He shifted back into *AndFriend*, opened the port and let Squonk in. Then, using the same ability he had discovered in himself when he had awakened in *AndFriend* back at Base, he lifted the ship lightly in the air and pointed it at a slant upward toward the stars now hidden behind the cloud bank that had since drifted in to further darken the night.

The moment he was back inside the ship with the entry port closed behind him, Squonk had determinedly begun his postponed cleaning of the ship's interior.

# C H A P T E R

## 22

"WHAT'S GOING ON?" SAID MARY, WAKING UP. "OH, YOU'VE
moved us back into *AndFriend*. You should have checked with
me before you did that."

"Why?" said Jim. "Since I was going to shift us over anyway? That's one of the things you don't control—what body
or thing we're in."

"You're right," said Mary. "I'm sorry. It's just habit speaking in me."

Jim was stunned by the mildness of her reaction. Suspicion
woke in him. Why, he asked himself, was she suddenly being
so reasonable? Was the reasonableness only a cover for some
plan she had cooked up to catch him unawares?

He was tempted to tell her that they had left the Laagi
world. Her reaction to that news should reveal how she was
really feeling about what he had done. They were, in fact,
already almost into interstellar space. He had been accelerat-
ing at a steadily increasing rate until that rate was well beyond
what a human body would have been comfortably able to support. Then he had remembered Squonk and realized that while
to him and Mary in their present conditions such acceleration
might not make any difference, it was literally life-threatening
to their small alien companion. He looked for Squonk now,

and saw him painfully trying to continue work in spite of the
effect of essentially having his weight almost doubled. A little
ashamed of himself, Jim backed off to an acceleration only
slightly greater than the gravity Squonk was used to normally.
Even at the lesser rate, they were putting distance between
themselves and the Laagi world in gratifying fashion.

It was not the distance-eating travel of phase-shifting. But
they were rapidly losing themselves in an increasing volume
of space that was already large enough to sorely trouble even
the large number of ships the Laagi could put into space in
pursuit.

"Why exactly did you move us back into the ship from
Squonk?" Mary asked. The tone of her question was entirely
reasonable. "I'd think we could always have shifted over if the
need arose—if some Laagi came out here to *AndFriend*, or
something like that."

Facing the fact of telling her, now, Jim found himself uncomfortable with the need to do so, even though he was still
sure inside himself that he had done the right thing.

"I had to be in the ship so I could operate her," he said. "I
got Squonk to round up some of his friends and cut loose the
arches that were holding us down. Then I used my own, personal, nonship powers—the same ones Raoul used to drive *La
Chasse Gallerie* all the way through Laagi territory to get
home—to take us off. We've left the Laagi world."

She said nothing. He waited.

"I know," he said, "you're feeling I betrayed you. Well,
maybe I did. But you were working yourself to death and
you'd already done anything anyone could have expected you
to do back there—and more."

"So we're in space now?"

Aside from an emptiness and a strange impression of distance, as if she had physically withdrawn from him, her voice
was calm and he could feel no explosion kindling in her in
reaction to what he had just said.

"That's right. On the equivalent of ordinary drive, which is
all I can manage on my own, but moving away steadily."

"I suppose we could go back if we tried?"

"Yes," said Jim. "But I won't. If you'll just cancel that
hypnotic lock you've got on me, so I can work the ship and

phase-shift, we'll head out around Laagi territory and go home."

"No," she said. "I'll never do that. Not as long as there's a chance of our going back to the Laagi."

The continuing utter calmness of her voice and emotions held an inflexibility that gave no hope of its being changed.

"Then we'll have to take our chances, this way," said Jim.

"The Laagi'll catch us long before we can reach the Frontier and any human protection," said Mary.

"Maybe they could," said Jim, "maybe not. But I'm not headed up-galaxy toward home. I'm headed down-galaxy toward the fly-swatting territory. I think it'll take the Laagi a little while to figure out *AndFriend* might go in that direction; and any time gained is a plus for us, in this case."

"I see," said Mary. "All right. Understand me. I've had a chance to get some rest now. My head's clear. You were right. I'd worked myself to the point where I wasn't thinking straight. But I'm thinking straight now; and there's work back there I've left unfinished. If you'll turn back and let the Laagi catch us again, I'll promise you we'll leave within a quarter of a year, their local time."

"No," said Jim.

"Is a quarter of a year going to make that much difference to you after the time we've spent there already?"

"It's not that," said Jim. "I'm afraid I don't trust you. If you could go back there, a quarter of a year would become half a year, then a year. By the end of a year you'd be back again in a condition where there'd be no point in trying to talk sense to you about leaving, ever."

There was another extended silence from Mary. In the picture of her he carried always in his mind now, put together from bits and pieces of memory, he imagined her with the right corner of her lower lip caught thoughtfully for a moment between her teeth as she searched for the words most likely to move him from his position. It was a fetching, even in a strange way an endearing, picture; but he could not afford to give in.

"So you're going to try taking us home in spite of the odds against it?" she said at last.

"The odds wouldn't be so much against it if you gave me back the ability to phase-shift *AndFriend*."

She ignored what he had just said.

"You realize," she said, "if the Laagi shoot us on sight, instead of simply trying to capture us, you're risking the loss of everything I—we've found out about them. That information will never get back to Earth then; and it means everything to them, back there."

"Give me phase-shifting ability and there's a good chance the information will get back."

"Good?" she said. "No. Only a little better. Let the Laagi capture us again, let me work with them awhile longer; and maybe I can get to the point where I can talk to them. You've been repeating every note I've made but you don't seem to have understood what those notes meant. The Laagi are only fighting us because we've triggered off a genetic, territorial response in them. Their reflexive assumption is that the only reason we could be in their territory—and they think of it as their territory, not ours, where our ships first met in space—is that we mean to move in and take their worlds from them. Their inborn reflexes can't imagine any other reason for our being there."

"So?" he said.

"So, their reflexive system can't—but maybe their upper, civilized minds can—accept the fact we wouldn't want their worlds, even if we could have them. Their atmosphere's unbreathable by us and there's probably a limitless number of other things wrong. But we can't tell them that until we can talk to them; and I have to stay there until I can talk to them."

"Or maybe we can send a whole expedition back, knowing what we know now," said Jim, "and they can find out how to talk to them."

"And meanwhile your friends on the Frontier are being killed daily; and so are something like the same number of Laagi; and both races are going broke building warships and defending their side of the Frontier."

Jim winced. She had hit him in one of his vulnerable areas. But the fact remained he dared not trust her.

"You want to keep on gambling," he said. "I want to take the chips we've won so far and run with them, to come back and try to break the bank another day. I'm not going to change my mind."

"Neither am I," said Mary. There was sadness in her voice.

"So you'll have to do what you're trying to do without phase-shifts."

They drove on without talking for some time. There was no sign of pursuit yet, as far as Jim could see. But that meant nothing, when a Laagi vessel could phase-shift into existence within a thousand kilometers of them without a moment's warning. More to the point, now that he was back on board, he had access to time-keeping equipment. As best he could figure by estimating the time left until dawn when they had taken off from the Laagi world, the ship's clocks gave him as much as an hour yet before *AndFriend*'s absence would be visible to those traveling the green pathways that gave a view of the place where she had been anchored down on display.

How long after that it would take the Laagi to organize a pursuit and get ships into space was something he could not guess. But on Earth, in a parallel situation, it would be a matter of four to six hours at least, and probably it could not be done much more speedily by the Laagi.

After a long time, Mary spoke again.

"Why did you take Squonk along?" she asked. "Wouldn't it have been kinder to leave him back there? Or did you want to try to bring out a living specimen?"

"No," said Jim. "But without us to give him orders he'd go immediately to the first Laagi he saw who could give him some, and ask to be put to work. Doesn't it seem to you that that Laagi would want to know what a squonk had been doing up until then, and why he was free for other work now? And what's your guess on the possibility of the Laagi being able to find out from Squonk what he's been doing for us—and perhaps learning that *AndFriend* had brought at least two invisible alien intelligences on their world?"

"I see," said Mary. "It was self-protection you had in mind."

The words could have been said with her earlier sharpness. But, once again, there was a sadness that seemed to be underlying them; it was as if, thought Jim, in some way he had disappointed her.

"Yes," he said. "But there's a certain kindness involved in bringing him, too, whether you believe that or not. He's been involved in everything we've done. For months he's been hunting that nonexistent 'key.' You might say it's become his lifework—like your own determination to make yourself of use to our world."

The pause before Mary answered this time was shorter than the others had been, but long enough for Jim to hear his own words echoing in his mind.

"That was a rather brutal thing to say," said Mary.

"Maybe it was," said Jim. "But Squonk's given us everything he had to give; and what he'd tell you he wanted most, if he could tell you anything, would be that his wish would be to die working. As soon as he finishes cleaning the ship, which was the excuse I had to use to bring us here, I'll let him go back to searching the ship for the key. I've even had the ship's robot tuck a couple of dozen small objects in corners about the ship for Squonk to find. Of course, when he does find them, we'll tell him they aren't what we're looking for, but it'll keep the hunt alive in his mind."

"Until we reach Earth. And if we don't, which is most likely, he won't either."

"He won't reach Earth in any case," said Jim.

"Why not?" asked Mary, and then answered herself. "Are you planning on putting him out the entry port while we're still in space—"

She broke off.

"You mean you don't think he'll live until then?"

"That's right," said Jim. "I don't think he will."

"Why?"

"I don't know," said Jim. He searched for the words to describe what had given him the impression. "It's just something I feel from him. He's been very close to dying for some time, I think. He can't last much longer."

Neither one of them said anything more for a minute.

"Look at him," Mary said then; and Jim realized she must have been spending the small interval watching Squonk. "He's working away just as he always does. What makes you so sure of this feeling?"

"Only the fact I've got it," said Jim.

They drove steadily down-galaxy, not saying very much to each other. A couple of days, Laagi-time, went by. Squonk finished cleaning the interior of *AndFriend* and was set to work hunting for the nonexistent key, ignoring the fact—which did not seem to bother Squonk either—that he would be searching the very areas he had just finished going over so meticulously in the process of cleaning them.

The third day two Laagi fighter ships appeared off *AndFriend*'s right bow at a distance of about eight hundred kilometers. They moved in to within less than a kilometer and one of them disappeared—phase-shifted off to someplace else. The one that remained kept station beside *AndFriend*, following her toward the Laagi down-galaxy frontier, simply paralleling her course and waiting.

"I wonder why the other one left?" said Mary.

"Why do you think?" Jim answered. "His friend here was left to keep an eye on us while he went to get more ships. They'll be planning to do exactly what we did with *La Chasse Gallerie* when we brought her home. Lock on to *AndFriend* and phase-shift with her attached, so that she has to come along with them."

"Take us back," said Mary.

"Yes."

"What are you going to do?" she asked.

"That depends on you," he answered. "I can let them take us, or if you give me back the ability to run the ship, I can make a phase-shift jump—one long enough and at an angle that'll confuse them until I can make a few more and get beyond their frontier in this direction—into fly-swatting territory. As much as they might want *AndFriend* back, I don't think they'll follow her there."

"You know I won't give you back anything."

"Think about it," he said. "Think it through—what'll happen if they take us back?"

"I have," she said. "I'll study them for another year, that's all. Then I'll set you free and you can take us home. But I've got to have that year back on the surface of that Laagi planet."

"You'll never get it," he said.

"Why? Because you'll start fighting with them some way using what mind control you have over this ship; and they'll destroy *AndFriend* completely when they find they can't stop her just by cutting her up?"

"No, there's no way I can fight *AndFriend* unless you turn me loose. But suppose we just do let them lock on and carry us away. Stop and think of it. They'll never let you down on the surface of that world of theirs again."

She did not speak for a second.

"You're crazy," she said finally. "You're so determined to get away, you're imagining things."

"No," he said. "Think. Think it through."

"I have," she said. In his imaginary mental image of her, he watched her eyes narrowing. "Why wouldn't they take *AndFriend* back down on the surface of their world?"

"They've had two human ships," Jim said. "They've picked up and taken home two human-made ships with no humans aboard them. The first one just up and left on its own and made its way back to the human Frontier and beyond. So they tied down the second one when they got it home, so that it physically couldn't take off. But it's not only taken off, anyway, but got some of their own squonks to cut it loose so that it could. And in each case, as far as they could tell, there was no human on board. In the case of *AndFriend*, at least, they'd even had the entry port open at one time, so that there was no atmosphere inside to support Earth life."

"All right," she said. "I can see where they'd be puzzled."

"Puzzled isn't the word. Frightened, I think, would suit the way they feel, better. Somehow, either human ships can operate without any living thing aboard—and Laagi ships aren't able to do that. Or else humans have some way of being invisible and undetectable inside their own ships. In which case, who knows what's been done by whatever humans might have been aboard *La Chasse Gallerie* and *AndFriend*?"

"Hmm," said Mary. "I see."

"In any case," went on Jim, "whatever harm's been done has been done. But they're certainly not going to take the chance of any more human intrusions on their home world, or one of their home worlds—whichever the one we were on is. Once they lock onto us, they're going to take us out into interstellar space, well inside their territory, but far, far away from any of their worlds, and effectively nail us down out there. They'll post guards on us to see we stay where we've been put, and kept that way until they've figured out the answer to how we did what we did—which may take them a few thousand years or more. Meanwhile, what you've learned so far isn't going to be getting back to do any good on Earth."

"It might be like that," said Mary thoughtfully. "All right, we'll just see. We'll let them come and take us away; and if they put us out in space somewhere the way you think they will, I'll set you free, and you can take us home."

"Then'll be too late," said Jim.

He imagined her staring at him, the brown eyes wide now.

"Are you talking absolute nonsense?" she demanded. "Even if they've got guards watching, once you're free you can phase-shift *AndFriend* up to ten or fifteen light-years at least, in any direction, can't you?"

"I suppose," said Jim, "it's not your fault you don't think in terms of a military action in space. You didn't think I meant they'd just put a couple of ships beside us wherever they left us, and then the rest of them would all go home? We wouldn't do anything as stupid as that if the situation was reversed; and nothing on the Frontier's indicated the Laagi are any more stupid than we are. There'd not only be guard ships beside us, but we'd be boxed in for as far as we could jump in any direction by sentinel ships with instruments tuned to track us if we suddenly went off by phase-shift. And there'd be other space-forces on call near enough to keep us tracked, and close in on us within a day at the outside, no matter which way we went or dodged about." He snorted. "For that matter, they might just come on board and remove our phase-shift engines."

"Of course," said Mary slowly, "this is all just a theory of yours."

A two-person Laagi warship phased in not a hundred meters from *AndFriend*'s right side.

"Woops," said Jim. "That was close. A fortieth of a decimal point farther, and he'd have been in *AndFriend*'s space when he came out of phase—and that'd be all there was! Bet you a snap of the fingers that whoever commands his flight is jumping down his throat, right now."

"These are aliens. We can't be sure of how they think," said Mary.

The Laagi ship which had just appeared rolled over on its side, revealing what appeared to be two long bars, like skis, attached to its hull by struts several meters in length. Both struts and runners were thick and heavy, firmly bonded to the body of the craft. As they watched, the bottom surface of the runners that was facing toward *AndFriend* began to turn pink, and the pink color darkened until it became obvious that the surfaces were warming up toward a white-hot heat, at which temperature they would weld themselves firmly to *And-Friend*'s hull at a touch.

Another ship appeared on the other side of *AndFriend*, but in this case it popped into existence a much safer four or five kilometers off. But it, too, had attachment runners and the face of these, also, began to heat up as they watched.

"Maybe two more ships yet to come, to cover us completely," said Jim. "Time's getting short, honey."

"Clear all, Jim Wander! Clear all—go! Go!"

As the words erupted from Mary's mind, Jim felt control of *AndFriend* return to him. Two other Laagi vessels with runners had appeared and the first two were drifting in close. He had programmed the shift down-galaxy in his mind long before. It was an automatic thing to feed it to the phase-shift mechanism.

They shifted.

All at once they were alone in empty space with strange stars burning all about them.

"How far did we come?" Mary asked.

"At least three light-years," said Jim grimly. "I think we've taken them by surprise, and maybe we'll be able to make it to fly-swatter territory."

He calculated and shifted, shifted again . . .

He was scanning space in all directions around them, gratefully once again using the powerful distance vision of the ship's equipment. "Look at that, I think we're beyond the fly-swatter range—there are those G0-type stars we saw before. Maybe that's what Raoul meant by Paradise—"

He broke off. The interior of the ship was suddenly aswarm with invisible life.

# C H A P T E R

## 23

IT WAS UNBELIEVABLE. NOT ONLY THAT, THOUGHT JIM, IT WAS just about indescribable.

He and Mary and Squonk were surrounded by what could only be described as a host of innumerable invisible fireflies. To call them fireflies and at the same time to say they were invisible was a contradiction in terms, but it was the only way of describing them. They were invisible to any physical sight —even *AndFriend*'s instruments did not register their presence. But his mind saw them very clearly indeed as multitudinous living points of colored lights—lights whose colors changed constantly, so that it was like standing in the midst of a rainbow in the process of sorting itself out from an endless number of tiny component parts.

And they were constantly in motion.

Not only that, but they were not only in the ship but all around it. They were in the interior space of the ship, they were partway through the hull of the ship, they were outside the ship, swarming in space and stretching off into the interstellar distance like the tail of a comet.

"—They see us! Like the other one!"

"—That one doesn't."

"—But these two do. It's lovely to see and be seen by you."

Their voices rang in Jim's mind, each one different and memorable. Each one audible separately for a moment before they were drowned by a perfect roar of greetings from what sounded at the very least like hundreds of thousands of such voices, all entirely individual.

"Who're you?" asked Jim.

"I'm me," said the chorusing host of different voices.

Jim shook his head, stunned.

"If you'd speak just one at a time," said Mary, "we could hear you better."

"Of course, if you wish. But what kind of hearing is that?" said one voice. "We loved your friend. We'll love you, I think. Why aren't more of you lovable?"

"I don't know what you mean by what kind of hearing," said Mary. "In what way are we lovable?"

"Are there different ways of being lovable?" asked a different voice.

"I asked you a question first," said Mary.

"No, you didn't," said the voice that had agreed to talk one at a time. "I asked you a question first."

"Got you," murmured Jim to Mary.

"What is 'got'?"

"Look here," said Mary determinedly. "What do you mean, 'what kind of hearing?' and in what way are Jim and I lovable?"

"There really is only one way to hear," said the most recent voice to speak to them. "Just like there's only one way to see. The small hole that's your other friend doesn't see or hear us."

"You mean Squonk?"

"There it is again," said the voice resignedly. "You're just like your friend who could see and hear us. It's very painful for us when a person won't, of course. That's why we told your other friends not to come any nearer. We only let this one come with you because you two can see and hear us, and we wanted to talk to you. But you're just like your other friend we loved dearly, who was here before. He'd start to tell us something and then he wouldn't say it. You just did that. You said 'you mean . . . ' and then you stopped."

"I didn't stop," said Mary. "I said his name was Squonk."

"You're doing it again. You say 'I said his . . . was . . . ' "

"I think," said Jim, "that we've got a communications problem. When we say 'talk,' we're referring to what we usually make as physical sounds in the air—"

"Of course!" said the speaker. Jim had privately named him ?1 and, seeing there were so many more of them, had privately decided to think of all the others as simply ?plus. "Of course, you garble it up very much, but I think I understand you now. You make changes in your hole in order to converse. But why do that when you can talk?"

"I was starting out to say when you interrupted me—" began Jim.

"I'm sorry. I did interrupt you."

"—Yes, he's very sorry."

"—Very sorry, indeed."

"—We're all sorry with him."

"—We would have interrupted, too, because we didn't know you couldn't talk and listen at the same time."

A roar of apologies and explanations, all in different voices flooded in, then was cut off abruptly as the single voice spoke again.

"From now on, I'll wait for you to tell me when you're through speaking."

"That might get a little clumsy," put in Mary. "Why don't you just wait until one of us pauses? We always pause when we're ready to listen."

"Good. I'll do that. So will everybody else. Did you ask me a question last, or did I ask you one?"

"Don't you know?" asked Mary.

"Of course I know, but I'm being nice."

"Jim was trying to explain that what you call talking we call thinking—"

"There you are," said the voice sadly. "You were just about to tell me what you called something when you said . . ."

"Go on," said Mary, after a moment of complete silence.

"I was not saying what you didn't say," said the voice of ?1. "What I meant to say was that you said nothing, you said a blank."

"Let me suggest something," said Jim.

"By all means," said ?1.

"As I said, we're having a communications problem."

"You did say that," put in a ?plus. "There's really no need to say it again."

"Sorry," said Jim. Now I'm doing it, he thought, a little crazily. "I've got a suggestion to make that might give us all a solution to this communication problem."

"Good," said ?1.

"It's this. I'll start to talk and explain as fully as I can about Mary and myself. When I'm done, I'll tell you so. I'll say, 'I'm through.' Then one of you will answer me, telling me how much of what I said was heard by you and how much wasn't. That way we may be able to figure out where the communication breaks down, and why. With your permission, I'll now start talking. You'll all listen without saying a word until I say, 'I'm through.' Then one of you will answer me, and Mary and I will do nothing but listen until that one of you says, 'I'm through.' Then I'll speak again until I say, 'I'm through.' You answer under the same rule, and so on. Agreed? I'm through."

"Agreed. I'm through," said ?1.

"Good for you, Jim," said Mary.

"Thanks," answered Jim. "Tell me that again, later, will you—when I've got time to appreciate it?"

He turned his attention back to their invisible/visible audience.

"All right, then," he said. "I'll begin. We seem to be able to talk to each other to a limited extent, but wherever the concept behind our thought isn't known or understood by the listening party, nothing comes across. Instead, the listener hears what seems to be a blank, just as Question Mark One— as I've named the one of you who's done most of the speaking to us—said.

"As a result, there are undoubtedly going to be a lot of blanks in what I now say to you. Hopefully, finding out where these blanks are will help us establish the areas in which one of us doesn't understand the other, and we can try to fill those blanks with meaning by trying to describe these unknowns.

"Just to give you something to start working with, I'm already aware that you don't understand the difference between us and some of those you call our friends. The third living thing aboard this ship, which you call a hole for reasons I don't understand, is actually something different from Mary and myself. Mary and I call ourselves humans. We have bodies with two legs, two arms and a head. The individual we call Squonk, which is the third living thing here, has two legs, a head and six tentacles, but no arms.

"Mary and I come from a planet orbiting a sun a long way from here, on the other side of the territory of the living things we call Laagi. Squonk is a less intelligent, servant species used by the Laagi. The Laagi are those you call our friends, but who can't see you and whom you told not to come any farther, with the result that they sat in their ships and died at the edge of your territory. Mary and I came here without our bodies to study the Laagi. The Laagi don't know that we can live outside of our bodies. Since you have no bodies most of what I have just been saying probably made no sense to you. So I will stop here, although there's a lot more I could say. I'm through."

He stopped. There was a prolonged silence.

"I will begin," said ?1, "since you mentioned me—why are you radiating surprise? I'm through."

"I just thought the name I'd given you would be one of the things you couldn't hear. I'm through," said Jim.

"I don't know what that blank is you said you just gave me, but you identified me as you began speaking, so I'm answering. Shall I continue? I'm through."

"Yes. I'm through," said Jim hastily.

"I'll continue, then. Speaking for all of us, I feel that our responsibility in this case is greater than yours, since we had already talked to your particular beloved friend who was here before you and found his speech also full of blanks. Although I must say, regretfully, that there seemed to be some problem about his thinking, as well. In fact, forgive me for saying . . ."

?1's mental voice had sunk to a confidential whisper.

" . . . but he sometimes saw things that weren't there."

?1's voice went back to its normal tone and volume.

"However, we have had experience with a person such as you and clearly you have had no experience with persons such as us. Therefore we . . . and I most certainly . . . in any case, thank you. It is, as you apparently understand, very hard to guess what might be found in the blanks that occur in your talk when you speak to us. Let me try . . . therefore to recapitulate what you told us.

"You said that the holes of some of your friends were different from the holes of your other friends. Therefore there was some larger or general difference between you and them. We were left with the possibility that the friends who are holes different from you do not understand why you sometimes do not take your personal holes with you when you go to visit them—I refer strictly to your personal holes, not the somewhat larger hole you and your nonseeing, nonhearing, speechless friend here, whose hole is in some way different from yours, are currently wearing. The question arises why do any of you, similar friends and different friends, wear holes at all? I'm through."

"Fine," said Jim. "Already we're making some progress. When you talk about holes, I think you're referring to what we call ships, or bodies. Were there a couple of blanks in the last few words I said? I'm through."

"There were," said ?1. "Apparently you have a different conception of holes than we do. I'm through."

"You tell me what you think holes are. I'm through."

"A hole is hard to define. A hole is a hole. It is a place that isn't. I'm through."

"Isn't what? I'm through," said Jim.

"Isn't the universe. A hole is any place where the universe ceases to be because the hole's there. I'm through."

"When I say 'space' do your minds hear 'universe'? I'm through."

"In a way," said ?1 cautiously. "There's both something extra and something less in what you say when you say hole than when we say it. I'm through."

"When I say 'think,' do you hear me saying 'say'? I'm through."

"Certainly. Did you intend to say something different? By the way, do you suppose we could stop saying 'I'm through' so much, now? We believe we've come to understand the rhythm of your end-of-speech pauses."

"Fine. I'll be glad to stop saying it. It was a clumsy way of taking turns talking anyway."

"Very clumsy."

"All right," said Jim. "With that much out of the way, let's try this. When I say man, woman, ship, Squonk, Laagi, Earth, moon, what do you hear me saying?"

"You're just," said ?1, "repeating the word hole, over and over again."

"Aha!" said Mary.

"Yes," said Jim. "Aha, indeed. ?1, I think we've got a real problem here. We aren't hearing what the other is saying at all. We're hearing the closest thing to it that our minds can find in their own experience and understanding."

"Then you don't really know what a hole is?" said ?1.

"We don't know what you mean when you think the concept that our minds translate into the word 'hole.' On the other hand, you use 'hole' as a sort of general term for a great number of things that our experience teaches us are entirely different."

"I'm distressed!" said ?1. "How can this be? A hole is a hole!"

"A hole, if I understand you correctly," said Mary, "is any place space isn't. You make the distinction, but apparently you can travel through holes as easily as you can travel through space."

"Why not?" said ?1.

"I'll tell you why not. Because we can travel through space but we can't travel through what you call holes."

"I see. Well, that makes sense," said ?1. "A hole can't travel through a hole without one absorbing the other. We've seen little holes run into big holes and become part of them. —Forgive me. There is an exception. Sometimes, if the holes are about equal size, they both break up into a lot of smaller holes which go off in all directions."

"Like two asteroids crashing together," said Jim.

"That's what I said—two holes hitting each other," replied ?1.

"The point is," said Jim, "that we all need to understand that what we're doing is thinking at each other, not talking; and that what's received may not really be what was sent."

"No, that's not right, either," said Mary. "What you mean to say, Jim, is that what ?1 thinks may appear to be something we understand, when actually we aren't understanding it at all; and vice versa. The blanks in speech are when a sent concept finds no common experience to relate to in the receiver at all. So there's two problems. One, how to tell the other side about something they've never known and have no word or description for; and two, how to be aware that when the other side seems to understand a thing you mention, they're not confusing it with something else they know about, or see entirely differently."

"Good for you, Mary," said Jim.

"Well, I thought what you said could use a little straightening out."

"Er . . . yes. I suppose. Well, ?1, what do you say to what Mary said?"

"It had relatively few blanks. We appreciate it. But I will ask a question of you both. Why do you keep identifying yourself, each other, and even me?"

Jim found himself unexpectedly at a loss as to just how to answer that.

"I think he's referring to our using names, Jim," said Mary. "We do it so that everyone present will know which one of them is being spoken to."

"But isn't that obvious? You identify a person by speaking to her."

"You referred to me just now as 'her.' How would you refer to Jim, then?" Mary asked.

"I would just refer to him as him," said ?1.

"Are you bisexual yourself, then?"

"I beg your pardon, but what you asked me if we were came through as a blank."

"Why do you say him to Jim and her to me, if you have no concept of sexual differences?"

"The kind of differences you referred to came out as a blank," said ?1. "But to answer your question, I simply referred. I identified no difference between you in referring."

"You see," said Jim, "that's exactly what I was talking about. They can say something that comes through loud and clear but doesn't necessarily mean what we think we hear—or receive, rather. ?1 just said whatever he said, and when we thought he was talking to me we heard what he said as 'him'; and when we thought he was talking to you—"

"He *was* talking to me," said Mary.

"—we heard it as 'her.' ?1, what do you hear when I call you '?1'?"

"You say 'you,'" answered ?1. "I must say you seem moved to say it a lot more often than is necessary."

"How many of your friends—I mean your own people—are listening to us talk right now?"

"I would assume," said ?1, "as many as are interested."

"Sorry," said Jim. "I may have phrased that a little badly. Let me ask you instead how many of your people are here, in and around the ship, listening to us talk?"

"As many as want to be, I assume," said ?1. "I don't understand what you're striving to elucidate."

"How many of your people are there, all together?"

"Many," said ?1.

"Can you count?"

"I'm sorry, but what you asked if we could do came out as a blank."

"Mathematics unknown. Do you know how what you call holes—large holes—move about?"

"Certainly. The movement of hole material has always caused a web of forces throughout the universe. By these forces are the holes moved, and the forces generated by their movements move other holes. It is the primary dance—not one of the prettiest, but quite wonderful in its own way."

"When I say 'stars,' does the concept come out as a blank to you?"

"Oh, no. We understand you quite clearly when you say 'stars.' They are individual holes of somewhat larger size."

"Also hot—I see what you're driving at, Jim," said Mary.

"Well, more hot than you are, or this larger hole you have around you. Your holes would be changed on coming into contact with a star."

"They would indeed," said Jim. "Luckily, there's no star here. Do you know if there ever will be—here, where we are now?"

"One will pass through this point in the universe in four million, five hundred thousand, eight hundred and twenty-nine point four seven six six two eight years," said ?1.

"There will, will there?" said Jim. "And that brings us back to what we're driving at. If you don't recognize mathematics, how did you decide exactly when a star would be here? And where did you learn the concept of 'years'?"

"The concept of what?" said ?1. "I merely told you when the hole would arrive where we are now."

"Oh," said Jim.

"Yes, it's dancing in this direction and therefore it'll be here then. That's the way the dance works out. But of course you'll have moved in four million, five hundred thousand, eight hundred and twenty-nine point four seven six six two eight years, won't you?"

"You can count on it," said Jim.

"We suspected you would. By the way, we are enjoying talking to you very much."

"We," said Jim, "are enjoying talking to you."

"In that case," said ?1, "may I suggest one thing? We have nothing against holes, but they really are somewhat uncomfortable compared to the universe itself. Would you be agreeable to moving outside this somewhat larger-than-you hole of yours, so that we can talk under more natural conditions?"

Jim hesitated. Mary evidently was also hesitating, for she said nothing also for a moment.

"I beg your pardon?" said ?1 anxiously. "I haven't offended you by that suggestion?"

"No, no," said Jim.

"It's just that I don't know if we're able to move outside the ship," said Mary.

"But I see nothing attaching you to this hole," said an obviously puzzled ?1.

"That's right," said Jim. "There isn't anything attaching us to this ship. So, why not?"

"Squonk," he told the small alien, who had continued to work steadily all this time—they had him searching for the bits and things Jim had caused the ship's robot to hide about the vessel's interior so that Squonk could continue his hunt for the "key" that he had been put on to begin with—"I've got to go away for a little while. But keep searching until I get back."

Squonk signaled an affirmative with his antennae, and broadcast an eagerness to continue with his mind. Jim returned to the question of how to leave the ship with these invisible mental entities.

He imagined himself—his mind only—stepping outside the hull of *AndFriend*, free to roam the universe as a nonphysical thinking entity, alone. Nothing happened. He got angry and tried again, forcing against whatever held him back.

There was a strange sensation, a sensation that he thought

later was what it might have felt like to be a living cork and feel himself be pushed out of the neck of a bottle of champagne, because the bottle had been shaken and too much gas pressure, released from solution in the wine, had built up beneath him. He found himself outside the ship.

"There we are. Nothing to it," he said. "How do you like it, Mary . . . Mary? Mary, where are you?"

He had suddenly become conscious of a sense of loss, and that loss was of the identity of Mary, which had been so close to him all this time.

"I'm right here, Jim. Jim, where did you go?" He heard her voice. "Jim, I'm in the ship, but I'm not part of you anymore. Where are you?"

"I'm outside the ship now. Evidently when we travel as free spirits, we travel on our own. Come on out, Mary. Just be determined to come out and join ?1 and me and all the rest. You may have to push a little—I did—but it can be done."

"Push? How? Jim, I don't know—"

"Ah, well," said Jim. "I guess it's just something you may not be able to do. I didn't have any trouble, but maybe it just isn't possible for you. Don't get yourself all worked up trying, if—"

"What do you mean?" snapped Mary. "If you can do it, of course I can do it! I can do whatever . . . there! I'm out."

And she was, too. He could tell by her voice, somehow, that she now was near to him, rather than apart, or inside him as he had grown so used to her being. He was bothered by an odd sense of abandonment, and he reassured himself by summoning up the picture of her in his mind. It comforted him. There she was, as bright as ever.

"Quite a feeling, isn't it, Mary?" he asked.

"It is." Her voice was unexpectedly soft. "You're right beside me, aren't you, Jim?"

"Absolutely right beside you," he said. "Invisible but present and able."

"That's good," she said.

"You find it strange not to be in a hole?" inquired the voice of ?1.

"Very strange," said Mary, still with that unusual softness in her voice. "Very strange, but lovely."

"Do you, too, find it lovely?" said ?1, and Jim understood

without needing to be told that he was the one being addressed.

"You could put it that way, I suppose," he said.

"It is the natural way to be, of course," said ?1. "Sometime, when we can understand each other better, you must explain to me why you chose to live in holes in the first place."

"Where did you people come from?" asked Jim.

There was a strangely long pause before ?1 answered.

"We don't know," he said. "It never occurred to us to wonder about that before. Do you suppose we started out in holes, too, and found our way out?"

"Can you think of an alternative?" Jim countered.

"We could simply have sprung spontaneously into being. . . . No, that's ridiculous," said ?1 thoughtfully. "No," he went on, obviously addressing someone besides Jim and Mary, "and I find it hard to believe we existed before the universe did, let alone created it. Of course, we might have created it—until the facts are known, any hypothesis is possible, but most of us don't believe that."

"You speak for yourself most of the time, but then you suddenly start speaking for all the rest of your people—all that're here, anyway," said Jim. "Are you just guessing how they feel or do you actually know?"

"I was not hypothesizing," said ?1. "Of course. Agreement or disagreement is obvious. Can't you feel those reactions yourself?"

"Feel is not the way we generally communicate agreement or disagreement, particularly when we're wearing our holes," said Jim.

"That's strange," said ?1. "This time you said 'hole,' but it had a larger meaning."

"I actually said 'hole,' not one of my own words that you translate into it," answered Jim. "I'm learning from you."

"How happy of you!"

"No need to get all excited," said Jim uncomfortably. "Learning's a natural process for any thinking mind, isn't it?"

"Ah, but the will to learn! To exert that will is a compliment, in addition to all else. I must exert myself to learn from you, in turn!"

"Well . . . ," said Jim. "Thanks."

"There is no need to thank me for a pleasure which you make possible to me," said ?1. "Now that we're all back in the universe again, would you care to dance? Or is there something else you'd prefer to do?"

"Like what?" asked Jim.

"I've no idea," said ?1, "since I've no experience in what pleases you."

"Let's just go on talking," said Mary.

"No," said Jim. "We can always talk—am I right about that, ?1?"

"How could it be otherwise?"

"Then, for now can we go and visit some of those G0-type stars and land on any planets they may have? I want to see if any of them live up to what Raoul was talking about with those references of his to 'paradise.'"

"Would this be pleasurable also to you?"

"Of course. I just said—"

"I think he was asking me, Jim," interrupted Mary. "Yes, thank you. Even though Jim suggested it, I'd be interested to see any planets of those nearby G0 stars."

"What do you consider nearby?" queried ?1.

"Those we can see," said Mary.

"I can see six million, two hundred thousand and forty-nine holes of the type you concept, with planets orbiting them."

"Oh," said Jim. "Well, let's just start with the closest one to where we are now and go on from there. All right, Mary?"

"Fine," she answered.

"Then we go," said ?1.

# C H A P T E R

## 24

THEY WENT. IT WAS A MAGNIFICENT BUT SURPRISINGLY BRIEF trip. Outside the ship as they now were, they were at the head of the comet's tail of invisible yet rainbow-colored fireflies that were those of ?1's race which had chosen to come along. They went like a comet's tail to the nearest yellow pinpoint in the firmament surrounding them—but not directly

For aesthetic reasons, Jim found himself understanding through some wordless channel of communication, they approached the star of their destination in a delicate curve. He was a little disappointed that they arrived there almost as quickly as if the star in question had been no farther away than the length of *AndFriend*.

A few minutes later, they were hovering just above the soil of a very Earthlike world. One which looked as if, with no more than relatively simple terraforming, it could be made habitable.

But the portion of it they could see, at least, was disappointingly far from qualifying as a paradise in any human terms. They appeared to have landed—if that word fitted the situation—on a dry, desertlike surface of black sand with some awkward, green-brown growths poking up here and there through the soil to no more than three or four meters in

height. Above, the sky was cloudless, bright blue, and a five-
to- ten-knot wind was blowing, which did not seem to be
enough to cause perceptible motion in the stout, rather bul-
bous trunks or leafless limbs of the growths.

"What do you see?" inquired ?1 anxiously.

Jim described what the place looked like to him.

"I am vastly relieved," said ?1, and a sort of busy murmur-
ing from the host of his fellow creatures that were still with
them echoed and appeared to approve his reaction. "It was
here that your poor, beloved, special friend saw things that did
not exist."

"Oh?" said Mary quickly, before Jim could react.

"Yes. It was here he saw what he called Christmas trees—"
?1 broke off suddenly.

"Yes? Go on," said Mary.

"Did you hear me?" demanded ?1 excitedly. "I used one of
the blanks your friend said and because I knew what it looked
like to your friend, I could hear myself saying it. 'Christmas
tree,' 'Christmas tree . . . ' I'm beginning to speak your
blanks! Not only that, but I think I may have some understanding of this one, because of what we saw in your friend's
vision. Were these Christmas trees green and pyramidal and
with things of bright colors about them that were not part of
their natural appearance as a hole?"

"Yes," said Jim.

"And snow, and carols and presents . . . "

Jim could see it, himself, suddenly, as the longing mind of
Raoul Penard, already crippled by distance and loneliness and
being lost, had seen it. The dry desert flatland with its strange
growths transformed into the uplands of Canada. The holiday
season, the packed church, the people coming and going, the
snow and the plumes of breath in the frosty air . . .

Without warning, he found himself ready to weep for
Raoul Penard, alone and lonely at that time, wanting so badly
to get home—and he could feel Mary sharing the vision and
the emotion with him, so that they saw and felt it together
inside themselves . . . and meanwhile, ?1 was chattering on . . .

" . . . But it works! Because we all see the same thing, it
works. Now we can talk together and fill in the blanks and
understand each other. And all because you picture what you
speak of. You're giving us wonderful pictures now. Just think

—what a marvelous solution, just because we see the same things . . . "

"No, ?1," said Jim. "Forgive me for contradicting you"— I'm picking up the way they talk now, he thought a little wildly, not for the first time—"but it's not that we see the same thing, it's that we feel the same thing. Just as, right now, Mary and I were feeling for Raoul, when he was here with you."

"Feel! Of course, feel! How obvious!" fizzed and crackled ?1. "A solution to all incomprehension—to feel alike. How simple. How easy. How natural! I'll learn to feel as you feel, dear friends—for you are dear friends, obviously—and there'll be no end to the wonderful conversations between you and us—"

"There'll have to be at some time in the future," said Jim. "Mary and I are going to have to get back to our people, if we can make it safely around the Laagi."

"The Laagi are your friends—I apologize, your not-quite-the-same friends—the living holes we had to tell to not come any farther this way? Why would they not want you to go to a place that moves you as deeply as you and Raoul were moved? Surely they would be moved as well?"

"Almost certainly not," said Mary. "They live on a different world and see things differently."

"But we live on no holes at all and see things very differently from you; and we were all deeply moved just now that you should be so moved by what you and Raoul saw."

"It's hard to explain," said Mary. "To begin with, Raoul did see what you felt us reacting to. But we were just imagining what he saw, not really seeing it. Also—"

"But you made us see it all over again, what we saw Raoul see that was not there."

Mary hesitated and Jim stepped quickly into the moment of nonconversation.

"At a guess," he said, "you either had what you'd seen through Raoul's mind triggered again in your own by our feelings; or you took our feelings and associated them with the picture you remembered picking up from Raoul."

"Nonetheless, we do have a tool for understanding between us, do we not? Isn't that true?"

"Yes," said Mary and Jim together.

"Marvelous!" said ?1. "That was very well answered. Are you beginning to learn to talk and listen at the same time, then, as we do?"

"I doubt it," said Jim drily. "That was an accident. We just happened to answer you at the same time. That sort of thing happens because we can't read each other's mind, instead of the opposite."

"I'm so sorry."

"It's not your fault," said Jim.

"Nonetheless, we're sorry. We're all sorry you should be so crippled and deprived."

"Thank you," said Mary. "But as it happens we humans prefer it this way."

"Prefer to be crippled!"

"We prefer the privacy of not having our fellow humans reading our mind all the time."

"Another blank," said ?1 sadly, "just when I thought I was doing so well in understanding you."

"I've no idea what blank you mean," said Mary.

"I think he's talking about 'privacy,'" said Jim.

"What is this concept, 'privacy'?"

"It's the pleasure of being alone, and the right to be so," said Mary.

"But you like being together! Just like we do!"

"That's true," said Jim, "but we also like being alone, sometimes."

"How can you have pleasure in company when you also have pleasure in isolation? Doesn't one cancel out the other?"

"You see," said Jim, "we humans are individuals—"

"But so are we—I'm sorry, I interrupted."

"As a result," said Jim, "when we're alone we often want to be with others and when we're with others, we can want very much to be alone."

"You baffle me completely," said ?1. "Such a mixed-up existence! However, let's let the difficult question of how you enjoy two diametrically opposed states wait until we understand each other better. I think I understand 'Christmas tree' better now. But what is 'snow' . . .?"

So, for some little time Jim and Mary were busy trying to give meaning to the vision ?1 and his people had picked up from the battered mind of Raoul when he had been with them.

"Is the rest of this planet's surface all like this?" Jim asked ?1, once they had done their best with explanations.

"By no means," said ?1. "Every part of it differs, of course."

"Why did you bring us here, then?" asked Mary.

"But I thought that was obvious. It was Raoul's favorite place."

"Did he have other favorite places?" asked Jim.

"Not on this planet. But many on other planets. Do you want to see them?"

"Yes," said Jim.

So ?1 and his friends took them to the other places Raoul had cherished—the places he had referred to later as Paradise.

They were spots on some twelve different Earthlike worlds —and three of them were indeed so Earthlike that if the atmosphere had been adequate for humans and there were no unknown dangers hiding undiscovered there, it was conceivable that humans might have landed on them the next day and started building. The rest were such as to require terraforming —as much, in some cases, as it might take to clear the cloud cover from Venus, lower that world's temperatures and turn it into a green and fruitful planet. Four of the worlds they visited were almost all ocean.

But each had at least one spot that had triggered off in Raoul a vision of one of the fondly remembered scenes from the Canada of his youth. In most cases his mind had had to play tricks with the local scenery to make it into the place of his memory. But some came so close to being Earthlike that only the imaginative equivalent of a squinting of the eyes was necessary, even for Jim and Mary, to see it as a part of their home world.

A tree-filled valley, a steep, bare cliffside, a riverside, a lake—even one area of desert, filled with wind-sculpted rocks, which Raoul's imagination had transformed into the appearance of the houses and buildings of his own home town. All these were shown to Jim and Mary by ?1 and their innumerable escort of living minds. And as they went, Jim found himself getting more and more able to see in the alien realities of these locations the familiar shapes and outlines Raoul had imagined in them.

In proportion, ?1's understanding of what went on in Jim

and Mary's mind improved with remarkable speed. Steadily, the immaterial alien found more and more words with which to talk meaningfully to them and seemed to grasp ever more quickly what they meant by the words they thought at him. Privately, Jim was amazed at ?1's ability to learn. He was strongly tempted to compliment the alien on it, calling on Mary to back him up—except that Mary had grown more and more silent as they went along; and, having had some experience with her now, Jim hesitated to draw her into a conversation unless he knew certainly that she wished to be drawn. On the other hand, he had become more and more convinced that there were things he and she needed to discuss.

He decided to bull ahead.

"The subject of privacy and our human desire for it came up awhile back," he said to ?1. He was finally getting used to the idea that if he thought of himself as speaking to ?1, that alien immediately realized he was being spoken to. How this understanding was managed, Jim did not have the slightest idea, but since it seemed to work there was no reason not to use it. Accordingly, he had fallen into the habit of doing so, to the extent that occasionally he forgot and thought at Mary, without remembering to specify that it was her he was addressing.

"Yes, I remember, of course," said ?1.

"Tell me, would there be some way in which I could talk with Mary privately? That is, without at the same time talking to you and your friends? Maybe I'm not putting it clearly enough. What I'm trying to say is that I want to talk to Mary, now, and not have anyone else hear what we say."

"If you like, of course," said ?1, "none of us will listen. If you speak to Mary, alone, it becomes obvious to the rest of us that it would be very unkind—indeed, unthinkable—for one of us to listen."

"Oh . . . good," said Jim. "I'll just keep in mind, then, that I'm talking to Mary alone, and you tell me that none of the rest of you will hear what we say?"

"Naturally," said ?1.

"What is it, Jim?" asked Mary.

"Well, I . . ." Jim would have liked some reaction, some signal from ?1 and the rest in the comet tail, that they were really not listening to what he was about to say, but evidently that was so unnecessary that none of them, including ?1, thought to make it. It was rather like the finding that it was unnecessary to say "I'm through" when a speaker was finished talking and ready to listen to an answer.

"Well," he said again. "About these worlds we've been looking at. They aren't the paradise Raoul's mind made them out to be, of course; but they could certainly be settled by humans, a few even without terraforming. But with the same kind of thinking, it's easy to see that the Laagi could settle them just as well with about an equivalent amount of terraforming to make most of them habitable to their race."

"Yes," said Mary. "Of course. What of it?"

"Why, it brings up a question of our responsibility toward claiming these worlds as soon as possible for our own race," said Jim. "I'm sorry—I don't mean to sound pompous; but these are, literally, worlds that both we and the Laagi can use; and we're presently on speaking terms with the race that controls them, even if they don't have any use for them, themselves. The question is what should we do about it?"

"If you want my opinion," said Mary, "I certainly think we ought to tell our present friends we badly need the worlds and we'd like to settle on them, and find out if our settling on them would disturb them. But that's just my opinion. I'm going to leave all the dealing with ?1 and the rest up to you."

"Me?"

"That's what I said."

"Why me?"

"I'll tell you why you. Jim, I've had time to do a lot of resting and a lot of thinking since we ended up in that Laagi hospital—"

"Yes, but what I'm talking about right now—"

"Let me finish. Be patient, it'll all tie together when I've had my say. To begin with you were right. I'd been overworking."

"Well . . ."

"More than that," said Mary determinedly, "I'd lost my perspective. I've learned a lot from you and Squonk—yes, from Squonk, too. You were right when you compared me to him. Part of me was like him, and like the Laagi, in general. That's why I did so much better a job of understanding them from the first than you did."

Jim thought of saying something, then decided not to.

"You were right. I live to work, and they live to work; and I liked them for that. I admired them for that. And, toward the end, this started to affect my judgment. Unconsciously, I was out to prove that I and they were on the right track and all the rest of the human race was wrong. I began wanting to justify everything they did; and I began to anthropomorphize. I began to find human reasons and emotions in them that weren't there, just to prove how right their way of life was."

She paused.

"Do you remember that Laagi in the hospital who killed that squonk that was asking to be put back to work, when it wasn't able to work and never would be again?" she asked. "Remember the Laagi made the sort of gestures for praising a squonk and giving it orders, then killed it at the very moment when it was being most happy over being sent back to work after all?"

"I remember," said Jim.

"Well, when he killed that squonk, part of me was shocked beyond words, because he'd lied to the squonk by essentially promising it what it wanted while all the time he was planning to kill it. But at the same time another part of me was agreeing with him for putting out of the way a worker that wasn't any use anymore. I missed the real meaning of what was going on in his mind. He killed the squonk not because it couldn't work anymore, but because it was in misery for that reason; and he praised it and gave it a work order just before it died so it would be as happy as possible at the moment he ended its life. So that it died happy. Do you understand?"

"Yes," said Jim. "Yes, in fact, that part I understood then, when it happened."

"All right. I didn't until later, when you told me our Squonk couldn't live much longer and he'd be happiest hunting for that nonexistent key as long as he lived. It was then I faced up to the fact that I could approach an understanding of the Laagi and squonk reaction to work, but I'd never really understand it, even if I worked myself to death, trying. It's a different order of things. So I saw my limits."

"Limits've got nothing to do with it," said Jim. "You did a magnificent job there on the Laagi planet. I used to be amazed watching and listening and seeing how you put things together and understood them."

"Limits have got everything to do with it. We've got to face the fact that each of us, individuals that we are, can have a particular knack or gift or ability for understanding a particular type of alien that other humans don't have. I had it for the Laagi. You've got it for ?1 and his little friends."

"Oh, I don't know that I'm any better at it than you are . . ."

"Let's not play polite games!" said Mary. "You're better here, and you know it. I know it. I was the best one of the two of us to investigate the Laagi and you're the best to investigate the . . . the mind-people. I don't know why. Maybe the fact you've always been fascinated with space gives you something in common with them I don't have; but I've been listening to you and watching you; and I'm the one who's been amazed at how quickly my partner is picking up information —putting two and two together to get four where I can't."

"Hell!" said Jim.

"What's that supposed to mean?"

"It means I'm bowled over, if you want to know. I never thought . . . " Jim ran out of words.

"You never thought to find me admitting somebody else was better at something than I was, let alone you being that person."

"Er . . . yes."

"Well, now you have. And now, let me tell you something more about talking to the mind-people about humans on these worlds of their territory. What I dictated to notes through you, back on the Laagi planet, were facts. I kept my conclusions to myself, partly because I wanted to sneer at you for not being able to make them for yourself. I've no direct evidence, but my own strong personal opinion is that the Laagi live on only one home world, too—just like we do."

"You think so?" Jim waited for an explanation and when none was forthcoming, prodded for it. "Why?"

"For a number of reasons. We're overpopulated on Earth to the breaking point. People are cheap. But it takes all our people, working like beavers, to keep enough manned fighting ships on the Frontier to match the Laagi there. All the evidence that I could glean seemed to add up that the Laagi have fewer cities on a much less rich world than Earth—but their population per city is much, much higher than ours. And both they and the squonks have a work ethic we can't match, plus not having the internal dissensions that still go on, even in our present-day United World, where no nation fights nation, or group fights group, anymore because the battle with the Laagi comes first. But in spite of this the battle on the Frontier hasn't resulted in their winning, any more than it has in our winning. In short, the Laagi are only able to produce enough ships and personnel to match our production. One planet's worth. So they need to expand to other planets as badly as we do; and in fact that's why they've been hammering so hard in our direction after finding they couldn't come down-galaxy this way, because of the mind-people."

"Whoof!" said Jim, which in thought-language came out rather like an invisible exclamation mark.

"So, I suggest—I only suggest, mind you; the actual decision's up to you—that if the mind-people are willing to have these planets settled by us, we might even suggest that one or more of them be opened to the Laagi, too, provided we can reach an agreement with them. Then we could go back to the Laagi, and after we'd found out how to talk to them, tell them that through friendship with us, only, they had a chance to settle on the new worlds they've always wanted, down-galaxy. There's no hurry about getting all this done. The worlds for the Laagi are going to have to be terraformed for them as much as most of the worlds we get are going to need to be fixed up for us, so we've got plenty of time to hammer out a way to talk to them. But if that idea works we'll have peace with them, as well as new worlds for both our races. Plus, from our viewpoint, we'd have two other intelligent races as friends and neighbors in case we run into a really unfriendly one, later on."

Jim thought about it.

"What about this business of ?1 and his friends finding it painful the way the Laagi can't see or hear them?" he asked.

"I don't know," said Mary cheerfully. "You're the expert in this area. I'll leave it to you to come up with an answer to that problem."

"Thanks," said Jim.

"You're entirely welcome," answered Mary. "Now, hadn't we better be getting back into contact with ?1 and the others?"

"I guess we should."

He paused for a second, puzzling over just how the getting back in contact should be accomplished. Finally he decided it couldn't require much more than simply announcing that he and Mary were once more ready to engage in general conversation.

"?1," he said (or thought), "are you there?"

"Of course," said ?1. "Though I'm not sure I fully understand what you mean by 'there.'"

"Neither do I," said Jim. "So let's not get into that. The point is, you're close enough so that we can talk, now that Mary and I are through with our private conversation."

"You have completed your private conversation? Excellent. We welcome you back into conversation with us. Happy! Happy!"

"We say 'hurrah'—or at least, some of us say 'hurrah!'"

"I fail to see the difference between that and 'happy!' However, if you wish—'hurrah!'"

"Come to think of it, I guess there isn't any difference," said Jim. "Happy! Happy!"

A general chorus of "Happies!" poured in on his mind.

"On this subject of 'there,'" said ?1, "you seem to relate it to being physically close enough so that speech is possible. But speech is possible at any distance in the universe. How otherwise could the large holes, and the congregations of large holes, be able to tell each other which way they were dancing?"

"Say that again?" asked Jim.

?1 good-naturedly said it again, word for word.

"To my way of thinking," said Jim, "you seem to be confusing physics with communication."

"But isn't all dancing a form of communication?" said ?1. "Forgive me if my limited capacity to understand confuses this subject between us."

"No, it's not you." Jim tried to think of ways of explaining what he meant. Then he thought of human dancing, real dancing, and he had to admit to himself that in essence, it was communication in a sense.

"But large holes have no minds," he said. "Therefore they

don't communicate the way we do. If I understand what you mean by their dancing, it's simply that they're moving in response to the forces acting on them from the rest of the solid matter in the universe. All the other holes, I mean—from the very beginning when there was only one big hole that's since broken up into all the other ones."

"Was there only one big hole in the beginning? How interesting," said ?1.

"Well, we think there was. You mean you people don't know? I was under the impression you knew everything there was to know about the physical universe, holes and space and all."

"Oh, no!" said ?1. "We understand very little. That's why we're so eager to indulge in the pleasure of learning from you."

"We're—well, I'm complimented," said Jim. "But I have to admit we don't really know how the solid universe started, either. We only have theories—hypotheses—like the one I just told you."

"A hypothesis, only?"

"I'm afraid so."

"I'm devastated. Nevermind, though. Perhaps it will prove to be a fact."

"Yes," said Jim, "and since we're on the subject of facts, I meant to ask you about your stopping the Laagi—those you call our other friends—from coming down into your space, here?"

"You'll remember I explained that," said ?1. "They would not see or hear us; and, this being very painful, we told them not to come any farther."

"You say it was painful," Jim said. "Let me suggest another concept that might fit it better. 'Uncomfortable'?"

"No," said ?1, "that approaches the concept as we know it, but only partially, as your concept 'painful' approaches it only partially. Surely, you must know what we mean, though. Is it completely unknown to you and your friends, the effect of being not-seen and not-heard?"

"Well, yes and no," said Jim. "It's been used as a sort of punishment by social groups among us probably since we first began to band together in social groups. To be ignored and cut

off from all communication is unpleasant for an individual. I
think I know what you mean."

"Yes," said ?1, "to an extent I think you do know what we
mean. We are extremely sensitive to that sort of unpleasant-
ness, ourselves. It disturbs us all greatly when we must use it
to discipline one of our own members."

"You do that sort of thing to one of your own?"

"Alas," said ?1. "Every people must have their rules."

"What could one of you do to the others to require that
kind of reaction?" asked Jim.

There was a momentary hesitation on ?1's part.

"I don't think it can be explained to you," he said finally,
"at your present stage of understanding of us."

"I suppose," said Jim.

He thought he could imagine what it must be like for one
of these eagerly friendly little creatures to be suddenly treated
by all the others as if he or she or it did not exist. "How long a
session of that does it take to bring one of them back to proper
behavior?"

"Oh, forever, of course," said ?1. "Once we have ceased to
see or hear them, they no longer exist for us. Even their memory is put away."

Jim felt the mental equivalent of an unexpected chill on the
back of his neck.

"You don't mean you shut them out permanently?" he said.
"What do they do? Where do they go?"

"Who knows?" said ?1. "Since they no longer exist, in
fact, what does it matter? But you wished to talk to me about
these friends of yours called Laagi?"

"Yes," said Jim. He was still shaken by the idea of some
living thing like ?1 being shut out from the society of its kind
forever. There was an indifference in the attitude of ?1 which
reminded him forcibly, suddenly, of how alien the other mind
he spoke to was.

"You see," he went on, "like us the Laagi are holes who
live on one of the larger holes called a planet; and you have
planets in your space on which either they, or we, could live,
after the world had been changed some physically—they and
we would change a world to suit ourselves in different ways,
you understand. So probably the reason they were headed this
way was to find other worlds on which they could live."

"You think so? How interesting! But it makes sense—being holes, all of you seem to prefer holes as environment. I should say, being physical beings, you seem to prefer physical environments. Did I get that right?"

"You did, indeed," said Jim. "Now, the question I wanted to ask was whether, if they or we occupied the surface of some of these planets, that would bother you, in this not-seeing, not-hearing way."

"I don't know," said ?1. "Possibly not . . . yes, we think possibly not, since they and you would be part of the holes—but of course, you do see and hear us, so the question doesn't arise."

"You're seeing Mary and me out of our bodies—out of our personal holes—" said Jim. "The rest of our people are still in theirs. Maybe, as physical entities, they won't be able to see or hear you either."

"No, no!" said ?1. "Your own ability to see and hear us reached out through the hole where you were with your third friend who did not see or hear us. You radiated to us, and of course we radiated back. As you are, so must others like you be, I'm sure. If so, you wouldn't bother us at all occupying any of the planets in this area of ours. But to answer your question, even your Laagi friends might not bother us once they were a part of a planet, since by definition, such a hole is outside our universe. But why do you ask me this?"

"For a rather complicated set of reasons," said Jim. "You see, the Laagi have been having a war with us—"

"A what? Even improving as I now am in experience with your way of thinking, that last came across as a complete blank."

"Say, a serious disagreement," suggested Jim.

"Ah, a disagreement. Yes, and therefore—"

"Well, therefore when we arrived here, the Laagi had just been chasing us. Tell me, how did you get them to stop right at the border of your space like that?"

"Oh, we simply told them to stop. You must remember, I've already given you that information."

"And they just quit? Gave up coming any farther?"

"Oh, yes. Of course."

Jim thought that behavior of that sort did not seem to fit what he had seen of the Laagi. He returned to the question.

"Just because you asked them to stop where they were?"

"Dear friend, I have told you twice now," said ?1, with distress rather than anger, "we did not ask them to stop where they were. We *told* them to stop there."

Suddenly, Jim understood. The chill that he had felt earlier when ?1 had talked about his race refusing to see or hear one of their own kind who had violated a law of their society should have prepared him for this, but it had not. Now it was back—but a hundred times stronger.

"Jim, what is it?" said Mary.

"If I had a body to do it with," answered Jim greenly, "I think I'd be sick."

# C H A P T E R

## 25

"WHY? WHAT IS IT?" MARY ASKED.

"Our butterflies have fangs," said Jim.

"What do you mean . . . oh!" said Mary.

"?1," said Jim.

"Yes?" said ?1.

"Were you listening?"

"Of course not," said ?1. "It was determined, if you remember, that when you and Mary exchange concepts we do not hear you."

"Good. Thanks. We've got a few more words to say to each other and then we'll be back in conversation with you."

"I look forward to the prospect."

"Jim?" said Mary.

"Yes?"

"What is it about their stopping the Laagi that upsets you so much? It's not just what you said. I can feel you're upset."

"I guess it's because I've been a fighter pilot," said Jim. "I can put myself in their place."

"The place of the Laagi who were told to stop?"

"Yes. I've fought them; I've seen them fight when they hadn't a hope until we killed them; and now I've seen them on

294

their own world. I can guess how they follow orders. I can imagine how it was for them, those who got stopped."

"How was it, then?"

"You studied them. You know as well as I do. They live to work; and for a Laagi fighter crewman what he does is his work. You can imagine for yourself what it must have been like to have the combined minds of our bodiless friends here tell them to stop."

"I'm sorry, Jim. Maybe it's because I never was a fighter pilot; but I still don't see why hearing about this upsets you so much."

"Maybe you're right. Maybe it's just me. But picture it for yourself. Those Laagi went out under orders to follow their version of the centerline down-galaxy. They were under those orders when the contrary order of the combined minds of these people told them to stop. And they stopped. That's why I said these little friends of ours have unexpected fangs. You remember how ?1 didn't seem to care what happened to one of their own people after that particular mind-person was cast out—ignored?"

"Yes. How does that tie in?"

"Don't you see? Somehow these mind-people can set up a—they'd probably call it a concept—that says any living being that can't see or hear them has to stop at a certain point in space; and it's a concept that overrides anything else that being's been told or wants to do. When they say stop, they mean literally *stop*. And that's just what those Laagi crewmen did."

"You mean that's why they halted their ships where they were, why they didn't go back to their world to report what had happened?"

"I mean they couldn't go back. They couldn't do anything but what they'd been overridingly ordered to do. So they did it. Think of them, driving along. And an overriding order suddenly tells them to stop their progress, shut off their power, do nothing more. So they do it. They obeyed, because they weren't able to do anything else. They stopped . . . and there they sat, in the case of those ships we looked into, until we came to see what was going on. You've seen how the Laagi can't stand being idle. But they had to sit there and die. And there they'll sit until Judgment Day, them and all the rest who brought ships close enough to this zone in space that our mind-people've taken over for their own. You and I could see and hear them, so their order to stop didn't affect us. But otherwise you and I, Mary—we, too, we'd have been sitting there now, dead."

"I . . . see," said Mary.

"Think of those Laagi then, sitting there, not able to move, waiting to die; and finally, dying. Sitting there dead, killed by these nice, fluffy little friends of ours, here. No wonder they've been able to keep these worlds and this part of space to themselves for however long they have. And no wonder the Laagi are looking for other worlds to live on in any direction but this one."

"Are you saying we shouldn't want the worlds that're here, either?" There was a hardness in Mary's answer.

"I'm not sure what I'm saying. But we don't want to bring people in here to live under the nonexistent noses of aliens who can suddenly just order them to stop what they're doing until they die in place, do we?"

"No. You're right about that. But what can we do to make sure they'd be safe, though?"

"I don't know. I've got to get more of a handle of ?1 and his friends. Let's go back and talk to them some more.—?1?"

"Yes. Happily, you are with us once more, both of you."

"And we're very happy to be back."

"That makes us all happy together. What a fine thing."

"Yes. About the Laagi. I may have told you we were being chased by them when we came here."

"Don't you recall telling me that?"

"I think so, but I'm not sure."

"How strange. You seem very forgetful."

"I guess I am."

"However, be assured you did tell us that."

"Thank you."

"It's a pleasure to assist your failing memory."

"It only fails in little things, as a matter of fact," said Jim. "As I was saying, about the Laagi. Now, you were telling me they couldn't hear or see you, but when your whole race spoke to them, telling them to stop where they were and not come any farther, they stopped. So they actually were able to hear and see you, after all."

"But my dear friend! I didn't say they *couldn't* see or hear us. Any other intelligent mind should be able to do that. I said they *wouldn't*. They refused to see or hear—which was very insulting and extremely painful. There was no excuse for such behavior at all, since we'd never met them before. So we shut them out; and they've stayed away even from the place where we told them always to stop, ever since."

"I see," said Jim.

"We are glad you understand. But of course, we knew you would, being a gentle, courteous being yourself."

"Thank you."

"We do not merely compliment you. It's the truth."

"Thank you, anyway," said Jim. "Now, before we escaped from the Laagi, who had us as prisoners for a while, we learned something about them. I don't wish to make you, my friends, at all uncomfortable, but from what I know of the Laagi, it occurs to me there's a chance you might have misjudged them."

"Oh, no. That's impossible," said ?1.

"It is?"

"Absolutely. . . . What makes you think we misjudged them?"

"Tell me something first," said Jim. "When they intruded on you, why didn't you just go away from them, instead of doing something to stop them?"

"But this is the best spot for dancing in the galaxy. Beyond any question the best spot! Should we give up the best spot of all to dance because some impolite beings intrude on us, there? We were here first. We didn't intrude on them—they intruded on us!"

"Just a minute," said Jim. "I'm afraid there's something I didn't understand as well as I thought I did. You told me you didn't like holes, and that the movement of the holes in relation to each other in the universe was a dance. But since you didn't like holes, I assumed you had no particular feeling for their dance, so—"

"Oh, no! No, no, no, no! No such thing. The dance of the holes is not something to be either liked or disliked—you're right. It merely is. But by itself it has little to recommend it. A hole—forgive me, dear friend, because I know you have a personal small one around, somewhere, though you show your good taste by being out of it at the moment—is not a pretty thing. However, we use the lines of force that is the dance of the holes as threads upon which to weave our own beautiful dances. The possibilities are limited only by creativity itself. That way, this web of natural forces can be made into a beautiful, a shining thing; and here, at this point, is where the possibilities for such creative effort are greatest. We have always lived here because at some time our ancestors found this the best place for dancing. We will allow no intrusion upon it."

"But I mentioned my people might like to live on some of the holes in this area—"

"Their being there would not affect the dance in any way. It is a small, polite gesture on our part to allow such as you to do what you want on and with the holes, themselves."

"The Laagi would not disturb the dance either by living on some of these holes," said Jim.

"No, but they would disturb us greatly by coming through this space and refusing to see or hear us."

"That's bad, I know," said Jim, "but was it sufficient provocation for you to kill them?"

"Forgive me," said ?1. "I am baffled. We are baffled. You have come up with a blank of which not even the edges of meaning am I able to grasp. What was it you said we did to these intruders?"

"Kill. Make die. Cause to cease living," said Jim.

"None of this makes any sense at all. Forgive me, dear friend, but as I said, we are baffled. Completely baffled."

"Tell me," said Jim. "Do you live forever?"

"Do we never cease to exist? Of course, any one of us could wish to cease existence sometime. But none of us know when, just as we do not know how we came to be as a people."

"No, I mean, do you, ?1, expect to never cease to exist?"

"Oh, I don't see how that would be possible. Even if I wished to exist forever, I don't believe anything can do that. Of course, long before it was forever, I'll probably get tired of living and go out."

"Out where?"

"Just out into the universe by myself. There've been speculations of a different sort of existence once one has gone out, but such speculation is generally considered idle among us. If one is tired of this existence, why would one want more?"

"Does anyone ever put anyone else out?"

"How could they? But in any case, what an unthinkable concept! The undiluted rudeness of putting another out of present existence!"

"You may have been responsible for the Laagi going out of present existence—the ones you stopped, I mean."

"Oh, no," said ?1. "In the case of the ones we stopped, after a while their minds left their holes and went off somewhere, back the way they had come. Their minds were very much in existence when last seen . . ."

There was a pause.

"I am informed that we noticed that their minds when they left were completely unformed. Like new minds, who have to learn everything. You don't mean to suggest that our stopping them was responsible for their minds to lose acquired form—that it was a kind of putting-out?"

"I'm suggesting," said Jim, "that possibility."

There was another pause before ?1 spoke again.

"If so," said ?1, "that was an unplanned result, which we regret. Nonetheless, they brought it on themselves by stubbornly refusing to answer us when we spoke to them in a polite and friendly manner."

"That may not have been their fault," said Jim. "You see, there are drawbacks to being formed as a mind when that formation takes place within a personal hole."

"What drawbacks could stand in the way of polite response?"

"The fact that they may not have believed you were there."

"Not there?"

"That's what I said," said Jim.

"But you can't be serious. As intelligent minds they had to perceive us, let alone the fact that they became very disturbed after we had spoken to them, which they had not been until that moment. Certainly that effect augurs a cause which would be that they were aware of us."

"I'm sure they were," said Jim. "But you ran up against a particular sort of conditioning imposed on them by the holes within which their mind had been formed. Mary and I, now, grew up in personal holes that communicated by causing vibrations in the gases of the large hole on which our people lived. Our reception of these sound waves was what we call 'hearing'; and because of that early training, even though we know now it's a case of our minds receiving the concepts your mind gives them, we conceived of what you say to us as sound vibrations heard in a gas medium, like that in which our minds were formed to adult intelligence. The Laagi, on the other hand, were formed in personal holes that communicated by distorting the shape of those personal holes in various subtle ways to convey concepts to each other."

"This is strange and wonderful," said ?1, "but I fail to see where it might be leading us."

"Hopefully, to a better understanding of the Laagi," said Jim. "You see, when your people first spoke to the Laagi in the ships that approached your territory, they confronted those Laagi with a situation that the Laagi knew could not possibly be, but which was nonetheless undeniable."

"No such situation is possible!"

"I'm afraid it is possible. That was the trouble. The Laagi knew what they were seeing—receiving from you in the way of a message—could not possibly be delivered as it was being delivered. At the same time their mind gave them no choice but to believe it was being so delivered."

"I don't wish to offend you, dear friend," said ?1, "but you're the one who's making no sense."

"Let me try to give you an example of what it must have been like for them. Do you know what I mean when I mention the concept of carbon dioxide gas?"

"You're speaking of a gas which is a familiar component in larger holes, and even in some smaller holes."

"You're also familiar with it in its solid form?"

"Of course."

"What would you think if you saw a block of it in solid form floating in the atmosphere of a very hot star?"

"It could not. It would take on its gas form, immediately."

"But what if you saw it as I said, in the heat of the star's gases but itself still in solid form."

"I could not."

"Now," said Jim, "if I saw such a thing and knew the chunk of frozen carbon dioxide to be actually that, and the gases of the star to be actually as hot as I've said they were,

I'd consider that I was having what my people call a hallucination."

"You are saying you would be less than healthy. You have not really thought you saw such a thing, have you?"

"Rest easy," said Jim. "No. Of course not."

"I am so relieved. If you had, you would be sick and we would be forced to shut you out. I should imagine your people would do likewise?"

"Not exactly. We've got other ways, ways of helping people with hallucinations not to see them anymore rather than shutting them out."

"You must tell us sometime how to do this. But, I understand. You're using this image of a block of carbon dioxide remaining in ice form although in the midst of heat more than sufficient to change it into a gas, as an example. We fail to see its application to our simply speaking to these Laagi."

"I'll explain," said Jim. "Just as in order to make sense of your thoughts, Mary and I must imagine we hear them as words, that is, as sound waves through a conducting medium —under the same sort of conditions one of the Laagi you spoke to could only conceive of receiving your message as if it were visual signals from another Laagi."

"Visual signals?"

"Yes," said Jim, "distortions of the shape of another Laagi hole. Specifically, the signals had to be given by some other Laagi, since their signal system is built on the shape of their particular personal holes and that form's unique capabilities for distortion. Therefore, what the Laagi receiving you thought he saw was another Laagi—in a ship where there was room for at most the two that were already there—saying something to him he could not understand, because first, there were gaps in what he heard—these being concepts the Laagi did not know—and second, what did reach him implied a people and situation that were inconceivable from his point of view. He could only conclude that he was doing the Laagi equivalent of hallucinating. Naturally, since he thought the one of you speaking to him was merely an aberration of his own mind, he did not reply. He rejected the reality of the image—as you rejected the possibility of a cake of carbon dioxide ice—'dry ice,' we call it ordinarily among our people —floating in a hole of high temperatures."

From ?1 there was an extended moment of silence.

"What you tell us is almost impossible to believe," he finally answered.

"Don't take my word for it," said Jim. "Some of you go to the large hole the Laagi inhabit—it's just up-galaxy a handful of light-years from here—and observe for yourself them talking to each other the way I've described."

"It would be distasteful for any one of us to go to such a place and do such a thing, so I will volunteer to do so," said ?1.

There was a silence following his last words that went on and on for perhaps a minute and a half, at Jim's estimate. Then ?1's voice spoke again.

"Yes, it's true," he said. "My friends are all astonished. If I had not witnessed it myself, they would have been unable to conceive of such a thing. Your insight in this case is worthy of the highest praise. But we were certainly right to tell them never to intrude upon our space. How could anyone ever communicate to any purpose with such creatures? And what benefit could be gained by such communication?"

"Possibly, great benefits, the existence of which you don't even yet suspect," said Jim.

"Come now, dear friend," said ?1. "The fact that you are ordinarily a hole, yourself, has made you over-indulgent toward these Laagi. Say what you will about our misunderstanding of their reaction when they came this way first, the fact remains that they approached us in the persona of their personal holes, which you and Mary had the politeness not to do; and in any case, what could they have to tell us that we do not already know?"

"We're to take it then that your people already know everything?" Mary asked.

Since she had said nothing for a very long time indeed, her reappearance in the conversation jolted Jim and seemed to throw even ?1 and his friends momentarily for a loss. There was a perceptible pause before she was answered.

"Not everything, of course," said ?1, "but anything that's at all important."

"Important to you, that is?" demanded Mary.

"Of course, what is important to us . . . I see, you're implying that there may be knowledge which is important, even though it doesn't concern us directly. As a theoretical possibility, that could be true. But even if it were true in any practical sense, why should we concern ourselves with it if it's unimportant to us?"

"Because it may become important to you," she said.

"In the memory of our people, that has never happened."

"Doesn't mean it couldn't happen," said Mary.

"There is really nothing new anywhere—"

"Oh, you've encountered people like Jim and me before?"

"No. Of course not. But in the sense of something new and important—if we should simply shut you and the Laagi out, how could our own way of life in any sense be affected?"

"It might," said Jim, "if, after you had shut us out, you suddenly discovered that one or more of the large holes in this area of the galaxy that you like so much had been moved from its accustomed orbit, with the result that the dance of the holes in this area as a unit had been altered. Wouldn't that cause some alterations in your own dancing with the local pattern of those forces?"

"WHAT?"

The voice was still the single voice of ?1, to Jim and Mary's perceptions, but it was as if that voice had suddenly increased to incredible proportions.

"I think we got the attention of all of them at once with that question, Mary," Jim said.

"You can't move large holes from their orbits," said the voice of ?1, back at ordinary volume.

"I'm not so sure," said Mary. "We're holes ourselves, remember. We know things about holes that were unimportant to you and so you never learned them, while we're learning more every day. I'd say it won't be too long before we're able to move even the largest of holes from their orbits."

"You would have absolutely no right, no right at all to do such a thing!" said ?1.

"Perhaps not. It depends on your definition of what's right and what isn't," said Jim. "In any case I don't think a people like ours would ever do such a thing. Mary just brought that up as an example of information that you may have considered unimportant, but which might turn out not to be so, after all."

"These Laagi," said ?1, "do you suppose they might eventually be able to move large holes?"

"We'd only be guessing if we tried to answer that," said Jim. "But of course they're holes, themselves, just as we are, so they'd be interested in the same sort of information."

"We must find out this information at once," said ?1.

"Can you?" said Jim. "We holes don't actually have it, ourselves, yet, as I say. But even if you did find out, it might be that being nonholes, you might not be equipped to understand, let alone use, such knowledge."

"But this is terrible! Perhaps we should go to the world of these Laagi right away and command them to never leave their planet again, just as we commanded them never to come any closer to our area of space."

"Are you sure that would work with a whole race?" said Jim. "Forgive me. I don't mean to trouble you with unpleasant possibilities, but when you stopped them from coming any closer before, there were a lot of you speaking to just a few of them. Would your command be so powerfully effective, do you think, if you were speaking to just about as many minds as you are, yourselves?"

"Oh, there's no doubt of it. None. I'm sure there couldn't be any doubt of it. Not to be successful commanding them is practically unthinkable. Practically . . . "

"Well, then, you can do that. I'm sure there wouldn't be any bad consequences," said Jim.

"What bad consequences? How could there be any bad consequences from an order given and obeyed?"

"None, of course. None I can think of anyway," said Jim. "Though the Laagi are a little on the combative side, by nature. After all, they've been fighting us for quite some time over a frontier situation rather like the one you have with them. I was just thinking, if you commanded them and it didn't work, and afterwards they found out how to shift the larger holes . . . Well, of course at the moment they don't know you exist, but if you commanded them not to leave their planet and it didn't take, they'd know you were here and would probably come not only to get at the empty planets in your area, but to find out more about you so they could pay you back for what you did to them earlier."

"But we did nothing at all to them, but tell them to stay out of our territory. They couldn't resent a small thing like that, surely? You, dear friends, none of your race would let yourselves be bothered by a little act like that?"

"If any did," said Jim, "I assure you, I'd be the first to put your view of the situation most strongly to him or her."

"There. You see? And yet, it was these Laagi friends of yours you were suggesting we allow in here to settle on some of the planets of our space!"

"It just might be a good way to keep them under control," said Jim.

"Keep them under control? But how?"

"Well, of course," said Jim, "I'm assuming, as I said, that we also had some of our own people also settling on planets here at the same time. I'm not sure, mind you, that there are some of our people who'd be willing to do this. But if there were, and once we got able to talk to the Laagi, using the method they use to converse since they can't converse our way, those of us who were here could watch the Laagi settlers and point out to them that what they were doing was wrong, if it turned out to be something that might be undesirable to you."

"You say," said ?1, "you don't know if your people might want to come here? But as I remember, you earlier suggested that they would be eager to settle on some of our planets."

"Did I use the concept 'eager'? Forgive me. I was actually just exploring the possibility with you first, before we go back and suggest it to them," said Jim. "I think you and I got off on other topics and I never did get around to explaining that I'd have to ask them, first. You see, the rest of our people don't know that we've found livable worlds here. Oh, they know it's possible we might, and if by some strange chance we never went back to them, they'd eventually get around to sending other individuals to see what the situation is as regards livable holes, here; but at the moment they don't know definitely about these planets, and they most definitely do not know what a wonderful people you all are. I'm sure they'll take to you at once, from what we'll be able to tell them, and want to come. I just don't have the right to say certainly that they will come when I haven't yet talked to them."

"But you would talk to them?"

"It'd be the first thing we'd do, on getting home."

There was a silence on ?1's part that extended for some seconds at least.

"Jim," said Mary softly, in this moment, "have you any idea what kind of forces would need to be involved in moving a star out of its orbit?"

"Shh," said Jim. "Little pitchers . . . "

"What?"

"Small fireflies have long antennae."

"But he said they wouldn't . . . oh!"

"Exactly."

"I understand. A verbal promise only. . ." said Mary. "You're right. But, by the way, you called them butterflies last time you described them."

"Did I? 'Fireflies' is better."

"Actually," said Mary, "I think you're right about that, too."

"We must, I believe," said ?1, breaking in on them, "think this matter over. Meanwhile, will you dance with us?"

"Dance?" said Mary and Jim together.

"You hesitate? In all our memory, out of the millions of dances we have done, there are five we remember as classic. We will do one of those, together."

"Forgive us," said Jim. "But we aren't hesitating because we don't want to dance with you. But you should be told that I, at least, don't really know what you mean by 'dancing.'"

"I'd realized there was somewhat of an ignorance on your part where dancing was concerned," said ?1. "But I did not understand it could be so complete. You really are not aware of what dancing is? I told you, it is a weaving of patterns around the threads of force set up by holes in their movements through the universe."

"Yes, but that only defines it," said Mary. "What Jim means is we've got no conception of how you weave such patterns, let alone an appreciation of them. We've never seen such things in all our experience."

"You really have not? It's incredible!" said ?1. "And yet you seem like such dear friends and nice people. Tell me, aren't you aware at this moment of the skein of developing and shifting forces about and through us, at this moment?"

"No," said Mary. "Jim?"

"Neither am I," said Jim. "I'm sorry."

"Unbelievable! But it's so hard for me to grasp that you're basically holes, in nature. You seem so rational, so intelligent, so nice, that I fail to keep your limitations sharply in perspective. Do you really feel nothing of the forces? Look at that white star over there. Don't you feel the powerful, moving pull of it like a great arm sweeping through all of the universe?"

"Hold on," said Jim. "Let me concentrate. Maybe I can feel it."

"I'll try, too," said Mary.

Jim honestly tried. He was a competitor by nature, and his first reaction to this sort of situation was that if someone else could do something, he could do it, too. Feel . . . he told himself, concentrating on the pinpoint of light that was the white star, *feel* . . .

"Yes!" he said finally. "There's something there, a sort of soft pressure—Mary, you know how it feels when you've been in the shadow of a cloud and it passes away from the sun, and you feel the warmth of the sunlight as it creeps across you?"

"Yes. I've got it myself, now," answered Mary. "Just a touch, though. And if I tried to do anything else but concentrate on it, let alone whatever you call dancing, ?1, I'd lose it."

"Quite incredible," said ?1. "It's obvious one of our great dances would be entirely wasted on you. Five of them, can you understand that tremendous fact? Five great dances winnowed out of millions, over a time equal to all the memory we as a people share between us? These five great patterns of movement that reflect the greatness of accomplishment of our race! You must understand at least a little of what that means."

"I think we do," said Mary seriously.

"In any case, as I say," said ?1, "any of those five would be wasted on you. But we can carry you, as we carried you to look at the places that Raoul saw differently and loved, through one of our simple little dances that we have for the new-budded minds among us that have everything yet to learn. Will you come? Are you ready?"

"Why not?" said Jim to Mary. "Shall we dance?"

"I'd love to, thank you," said Mary.

# C H A P T E R

## 26

"...BUT IT'S LIKE SKATING!" SAID MARY, "LIKE SKATING AT A billion miles a second!"

"Like riding a bobsled down a bobsled run!" shouted Jim. He had no need to shout. It was the excitement in him making him do it.

"Like skating down a bobsled run, then," Mary shouted back, "without having to worry about hurting yourself!"

A yellow point of light in the far distance grew almost instantly into a huge golden sun as they dived toward it, then swept past, with the galaxy full of stars pinwheeling around them, toward a white giant of a sun past which they curved in turn. It was indeed like traveling at unimaginable speeds, for they were literally in motion. It was not like phase-shifting where you ceased to be at one point, were spread out throughout the universe and reassembled at a different place, all in literally no time at all . . . but it was fast, faster than imagination could believe.

And it was in fact a dance, all graceful swirls and turns across enormous spaces, as if they actually danced in a mighty ballroom where the stars were lamps. But it was more than just a dance. The creativity of it reached into Jim and woke all sorts of emotions and yearnings in him, building him inwardly toward an understanding of he knew not what. Also, he was actually beginning to feel the skeins of gravitic forces reaching out through space, the natural forces about which the dance was woven; like a piece of silk with threads so fine as to be invisible, woven on a magical loom that could be known, but neither viewed nor touched.

> *I'm skating out here with the stars,*
> *In space with the stars, with the stars . . .*

. . . sang Mary.

"Jim!" she cried. "I'm making my own music to go with it. Are you doing that, too?"

"I'm doing something—or it's doing something to me!" Jim shouted back.

The dance built to a climax; and in Jim's mind a realization broke like a shower of colored lights from a skyrocket bursting far overhead. It came to him suddenly that he had found his blue mountain. For a long time now the Forever Road had been inclining upward; its steepness had increased without his noticing that he was going uphill. But now he understood that he had, and understood why. Because the road had brought him not only to his mountain but to the very top of it.

For the blue mountain was the universe. Not just this one galaxy, but the whole universe; and he stood at the highest point of it. From where he was he looked out and down in all directions to the universe's end. He was at the point he had searched and traveled to come to—and, then, just as he was beginning to believe that he could see the shape of the dance and the forces it was woven about, it crescendoed. It completed its statement. It ended.

And they were back at the point where they had first started to dance.

"There you are," said ?1.

"?1, that was truly lovely," said Mary softly. "Thank you."

"It was indeed," said Jim. "Thanks."

"It was nothing. Or, actually, it was a dance so simple and small that if I had not known how limited you were, I'd have been ashamed to show it to you. But you did respond to it, didn't you?"

"Oh, yes," said Mary.

"Now you can understand, perhaps," said ?1, "why one of us would spend all his available existence dreaming and working to create one really great dance, if what you saw was only a small one; and why this space we need in which to create is so precious to us and has to be protected at all costs."

"Yes," said Jim. "I understand that a lot better, now."

"Meanwhile," said ?1, "we've thought it all over. We will help you if you and your people will help us. We will both have to trust each other a little, since we can never really know holes and you can never really know us. But after thinking it over, we believe if we both try hard we can work together. So we will let you bring your people in to live on the planets of our stars, and we will also let the Laagi in, once you can find some means to show us clearly that they understand enough about us that they won't destroy this precious place or the labor we live to do. Is this agreeable to both of you?"

"To me," said Jim.

"And to me," said Mary.

"Then we are agreed," said ?1.

"And in that case," said Jim, "we ought to be getting back into our hole that we brought with us—the one we call our ship. If you'll show us where that is."

"You are there," said ?1. And, instantaneously, they were. At it, but just outside its hull.

"Hmm," said Jim, disgusted. "I could have found it, come to think of it. All you had to do was think of it, to find it. Isn't that right?"

"Quite right," said ?1. "But, since you asked, it was no trouble to do it for you."

"We're obliged," said Mary.

"I don't quite understand that concept, but I suppose you're expressing some sort of appreciation for being brought back here. As Jim has pointed out, you could have done it for yourselves, so appreciation is hardly necessary. Farewell—"

"Wait a minute!" said Jim.

"Yes?" answered ?1.

"We've got to get back inside the ship so I can move it toward our home planet. But I'd appreciate your help on the way. We need to find a Laagi ship with at least one Laagi inside and take it back with us, with the Laagi in it unharmed. You can help us with that, can't you?"

"You mean," said ?1, "by ordering those within it to make their ship accompany your ship?"

"You understand exactly," said Jim.

"I suppose this is an undertaking that will help us all toward the situation both our races most deeply desire?" said ?1.

"That's right," said Jim. "We've never been able to bring back a live Laagi prisoner before, so that we could work out any method of communicating with that race. If we can bring one home now, we can get to work right away at solving the communication problem. Will you help?"

"Certainly. We've already established the fact our two races will help each other. This merely executes that decision. Shall we go find what you wish right now?"

"Give us a few minutes alone with each other and the ship here, first. I'll call you when we're ready to go."

"Agreed," said ?1; and suddenly not only was he gone, but there were none of the firefly colors of the mind-people anywhere around. They were alone with *AndFriend* and the galaxy.

"I wish we had our bodies," said Mary dreamily.

"I know what you mean," answered Jim. "I do, too."

They were both silent for a long moment.

"But I can see you perfectly well, you know that?" said Jim. "Isn't it funny? When I had you around in the body I never really looked at you; and then, all this time, with no one to look at, got me started digging out the old memories of you and putting you back together, piece by piece, until I had you all complete in my mind's eye. So that now I can see you as clearly as if you were standing in space, right here in front of me, beside *AndFriend*."

"You can't. Not as if I was really here."

"Yes, I can. I tell you, I literally couldn't see you any clearer if you were actually here in the body. I've got every part right, all built back together, a bit of nose here, a touch of smile at the corners of your mouth, there and there, all complete."

"Oh, Jim!" She laughed.

"It's sober fact," he said. "I don't know why I didn't have the sense to take a good look at you when we were on the

ground, back at Base. Because you're beautiful. You've probably heard that so often it doesn't mean anything to you. But
you really are; and I just wanted you to know I've finally
realized it. I don't know why I didn't have the sense before.
Anyway, you understand, don't you, Mary?"

She did not answer.

"Mary?" he said. "You understand, don't you?"

Still, there was no answer.

"Mary?" he said. "Hey, Mary! Ahoy! Jim, here! Mary, do
you read me? Answer me, for anybody's sake!"

"Hadn't we better be getting back into the ship?" she said.
Her voice was utterly cold.

"Certainly. Right. But I was asking you if you could understand why it took me so long to realize—"

"Why don't you shut up for once—just for once?" she
said. "Everything has to be a joke to you, doesn't it? A lovely
moment like that dance and you have to turn it into a clown
act. Let's drop the subject, shall we, and get back inside? The
sooner we get back to Base the better I'm going to like it!"

Jim felt as if he had been punched in the stomach. His
mind whirled, baffled.

"If you want to," he said at last.

"I do."

He thought of the inside of *AndFriend*—and they were
within the ship.

"If we're going back into Laagi territory to look for one of
their ships, you'd better start charting a flight plan—" Mary
broke off suddenly. "Oh, no!"

Jim had already seen what she had seen; and the blow this
time was in the same category as the one of a moment before
—which was still baffling him.

Squonk half-lay, half-leaned against the com-seat of the
pilot's position. On the deck just before the seat and under the
controls panel, where the pilot's boots would normally rest,
were lined up all of the small objects Jim had caused the ship's
robot to secret about *AndFriend*'s interior. All except one.
That one, Squonk still held.

His legs were extended by slightly different amounts, but
approximately enough to raise him to the height necessary to
let him rest his body's weight on the edge of the seat; his neck
was extended, his head rested on its left jaw upon the seat and

all of his tentacles but one lay loosely about. He was unmoving and limp, except for that one tentacle. This also rested on the seat by his head; and the end of it was tightly curled, holding a large, shiny metal hex-nut, probably had been the last of the objects he had found; and hopefully, Jim thought, the one that had finally represented to him the long-sought "key," which he had located at last.

Mary said nothing; but Jim could feel, as if it was something tangible, the outpouring of emotion from her. The image of her in his mind was crying; and all his upset over her reaction to him just now outside the ship was swept away by the pain in him at her pain.

"Mary, don't," he said. "He didn't even know you or I existed. It didn't matter from his point of view whether the 'key' was real or not. He probably died happy, thinking he'd found it. In any case, he died the way he wanted to, working."

"Leave me alone!" said Mary . . . and he could get no more from her than that.

Yielding at last to things as they were, he turned back to the demands of duty. Taking mental control of the ship, he ran an automatic check of *AndFriend*'s equipment, internal and motive, and laid out a series of phase-shift jumps back into Laagi territory, close to the Laagi galactic centerline, and did the calculations on the first shift.

Having done that, he put out a call.

"?1," he said. "Where are you? We're ready to travel now. Could you come here, please?"

A single invisible firefly light showed up before his nose.

"You didn't specify where 'here' was to be," said ?1. "If you'll do so in the future, I'll be, as Mary says, obliged—and I hope I was right in guessing that it implied gratitude of one kind or another."

"It does; and you're welcome, which is one of our standard answers to that polite phrase," said Jim. "Now, about what we're going to do: if you can help me in finding a Laagi ship, it would help a lot. Also, how will you be going about issuing your command to those aboard it to follow this ship? Can you act as a speaker for a large number of your people, or do they have to come with us, or can they just show up once we've found a Laagi ship, or what?"

"Yes," said ?1, "I believe we can help you find one of

those holes you call Laagi ships. I will travel with you; and when needed, I can utter an order with the full voice of my people. It's not necessary for them all to be there, in person. To ask you a question in turn, how are you planning to take this ship with you when you go?"

"It takes us," said Jim.

There followed a rather confused discussion between the two of them in which Jim tried to explain both phase-shifting and ordinary drive to a mind that was completely unused to thinking in physical terms at all.

" . . . Suppose we leave the matter at this," said ?1 at last. "You tell this hole of yours to move to a certain place and it goes there. Can we agree on that?"

"Yes, although—"

"Please!" said ?1 firmly, "no more explanations. Holes, particularly holes without a spark of life or intelligence, are profoundly uninteresting to me. Is my statement essentially correct?"

"It is," said Jim. "All right. We're going to make our first phase-shift to approximately the area of your frontier with the Laagi, the area where you first told them not to come any closer. From there, we can look farther into Laagi territory and see if they've set up some kind of watch to catch us, if we cross back more or less where we originally came in."

"Very well," said ?1.

"Right, then," said Jim, "here we go. Shift number one—" He shifted.

?1 disappeared.

It was a full minute before he reappeared.

"I apologize!" he almost spluttered. "I most sincerely apologize. We all apologize and confess. When you spoke about moving stars, we had some doubts that you might have been talking of something you could never really achieve. I will be absolutely truthful with you; we only half-believed you'd ever be able to do any such thing, no matter how long you tried. Not that the mere possibility alone wasn't reason enough for us to take action. But when we see now that you've already achieved the instantaneous repositioning of smaller holes . . . Well, we apologize for our doubts, which you must have guessed we had. Believe that you can count on our full cooperation from now on—in every possible way."

Jim was suddenly very grateful that he was not in his body at the moment and that in any case ?1 would not have been able to read the expression on his face. Mentally, he pounded his fist against his forehead. Of course! Why couldn't the same mechanics founded on the Heisenberg Uncertainty Principle, which had birthed the phase-shift technique, be used to shift other, larger things—even stars? It would be a huge job to find the proper means and be a tremendous undertaking to actually shift something that large. But when he got back to Base, it would be well worth suggesting just that as a line of research.

"Well, thank you," he said to ?1 now. "And think nothing of the fact you were doubtful. We'd expect anyone to be."

"The Laagi also use this method to move their smaller holes—ships, I mean?"

"I'm afraid they do," said Jim gravely.

"Let us hurry and find one of their ships to take back to your world so that you can get started immediately discovering how to communicate with them."

"Right away. Let's first see," said Jim, "if they've got any ships out there, watching for us to come back from your side of the frontier."

"There are no ships there. None!" said ?1. "I will let you know if any concentration of their ships seems to be moving in your direction. Just a little way off, there is a single ship of theirs. You can take that one."

"Farther off? Where?" asked Jim, for to the limit of the viewing of *AndFriend*'s instruments, no other vessel was being reported.

"Why, right there—nevermind!" said ?1.

Suddenly the space around *AndFriend* was filled with fireflies once more and her screens, as well as Jim's view of the firmament from all sides of the hull, showed the galaxy pinwheeling around them once again. Suddenly, everything was stable once more.

"There!" said ?1.

And there, indeed, a two-person Laagi fighting ship was, fifty meters away, completely within collision range, but floating as easily alongside as if invisible bonds already bound it to *AndFriend*.

Jim's mind leaped at the controls and he put an instant, safe five kilometers between his ship and the other one.

"What's wrong?" demanded ?1, puzzled.

"We might have collided!" said Jim. "It could have destroyed both ships."

"Naturally," said ?1 stiffly, "we would have seen that no such touching occurred."

"No doubt," said Jim. "Let's just say that for the comfort of my own personal sensibilities, I prefer us at least this distance from them. Now will you please tell them to follow us wherever we go?"

"We already have, naturally," said ?1. "We also ordered them not to do anything unfriendly to your ship."

"Thank you," said Jim.

"You are, as you say, entirely welcome. Now, do you intend to make your own way home with this companion ship, or shall we assist you in that action, also?"

Jim thought. It had not occurred to him before, but getting safely out around Laagi territory and back to Base might be greatly helped by having ?1 and his people along as guardians. On the other hand, sheer luck had given him a considerable prize in the mind-people's reaction to seeing the phase-shift in action. It might be better to act as if he did not need any help. An idea occurred to him.

"What we're going to have to do," Jim said, "is go at right angles to the direction by which we came here, until we're clear out of Laagi territory. Then we'll turn and head straight out from the center of the galaxy again until we get level with our area of space, which is beyond the Laagi territory. If you and your friends would stay with us on the first leg of the trip, at least until we were out of Laagi territory, then if a number of their ships find us, you people could command them to leave us alone."

There was a moment's pause, which Jim had come to understand indicated that ?1's people were talking the matter over.

"Why don't you just reposition yourself directly at your home planet?" ?1 asked.

"Well," said Jim, "you see, there's a drawback to the phase-shifting system, so far. Holes of all kinds have their limitations, as you know—"

"Oh, yes indeed," said ?1.

"Yes. Well, one of the limitations in this instance is that the mathematics required to figure out our destination point, even using the best of hole-type means we can put in these ships to figure it out, has a built-in percentage of error. The farther we have to go to a new position in one shift, the greater that error becomes; until at a repositioning of much over fifteen light-years the possible error becomes as large as the distance to the new position. That means, in practice, that if we shift a distance of fifteen light-years in one jump, we could end up in a position that would be as much as fifteen light-years off from where we want to be. The result is that we move in shifts, normally, of no more than five light-years at a jump."

"It seems so clumsy and ridiculous," said ?1.

"It's both," put in Mary unexpectedly, "but there's nothing we can do about it."

"I really don't understand. Why should there be error? If you can see your destination out there, why not go straight to it?"

"Well, the fact is, we can't see it," said Jim. "We find it by using a theoretical line running from our star to the center of the galaxy—"

Jim tried to explain human methods of navigation and found himself back in the same tangle of misunderstandings and inability to understand on ?1's part that he had encountered in trying to explain phase-shifting.

"Nevermind!" said ?1 at last. "Just tell me this. You can't see your star, you say?"

"See it? Of course not," said Jim. "It's somewhere between a hundred and two hundred light-years from here."

"I can't believe such limitation in a people who can do what you do," said ?1. "I was simply going to ask you to point it out to me, and then I'd tell you how to follow the pattern of forces that would lead you most directly to it. But how do you intend to get to it if you can't see it?"

"That's what I was trying to explain to you just now," said Jim. "The direct route would be up the line from our star to the center of the galaxy—and the ship's instruments, which have kept track of each movement and change of position it's made, can tell me where that is from here. But if we find that and follow the direct line of it up-galaxy, we'll have to run right through the center of Laagi space; and they'll be sure to find us. So we want to go out and around."

"Please," said ?1, "take your ship to this centerline and I'll accompany you."

"That's back to where we might run into other Laagi ships," said Jim.

"If you do, we will protect you," said ?1. "Please, just take this hole and your captive one to this line you talk about."

"All right," said Jim.

He made the calculations and the shift.

"Now," he said to ?1, when they had arrived, "we're on the line. Straight out away from the galactic center, straight through the heart of Laagi territory, brings us eventually to human space and about fifty light-years farther on we come to our sun, a G0-type star."

"Can you indicate the line?"

"I can orient our ship along it."

Jim did.

"All right," said ?1, "looking out along the line the long axis of your ship now indicates, I can see a G0-type star directly in line with it at a distance of roughly—what is that barbarous form of measurement you use—a hundred and twenty-three times the distance light travels in what you concept as a 'year.'"

"A year is the amount of time it takes for our planet to orbit its star."

"I see. That's a rather important planet you seem to inhabit if you're planning on measuring the galaxy in terms of one motion of its local dance—but, forgive me, as holes I mustn't hold you too accountable."

"We have other measurements. A parsec—"

"Please. One such clumsiness is enough. Moreover, it's beside the point. Your ship is now pointed at your destination and you know how far away it is. Make one shift to that destination. That will put you past and out of Laagi space."

"And we'll probably," said Jim, "find ourselves a hundred and twenty-three light-years away from that destination in some other direction—or perhaps a multiple of a hundred and twenty-three light-years—and possibly lost."

"If you do, I will direct you back to your star, helping you correct your errors until you finally reach it. Do as I say. Shift a hundred and twenty-three light-years."

"Too close," said Jim. "If by sheer bad luck we happen to end up right on target, we could land in the center of the star itself."

"The center of a star has its interesting points. I have examined several at odd times. You might find the center of this one worth looking at—this once, anyway."

"No doubt," said Jim. "But our ship wouldn't; and the Laagi ship, to say nothing of the Laagi inside her, wouldn't. I'll shift one hundred and twenty-two light-years. Then we'll only run the random risk of error putting us in the center of some other star."

He set the ship's equipment to calculating the jump.

"What are we waiting for?" asked ?1.

"The ship has to . . . " Jim found himself on the edge of another discussion in which he would not possibly be able to explain mechanics to ?1. " . . . get itself ready before it shifts. It just takes a matter of minutes."

"I see. I am missing out on a considerable amount of dancing, with all these delays. Forgive me. It's uncharitable of me to mention it."

"You're forgiven."

"Never in the history of our people has anything outside our own pursuits been allowed to use up so much of our valuable time and attention."

"Sorry."

"One can hardly blame you. You're only holes after all; and your understanding of the importance of dancing is limited—"

"We're ready to go," said Jim.

"Then by all means do so."

Jim shifted. This time ?1 stayed with him, but the Laagi ship disappeared.

"We've lost them—" he was beginning, when they suddenly appeared alongside.

"It slipped my mind to tell them where you were going, so they would go, too," said ?1. "A minor oversight, which might have been complicated by the fact that it was only I, speaking to them, alone. The error has now been rectified."

Jim looked out from the hull. Sure enough, there—and

larger to be seen on his screens inside the ship—was a beautiful yellow sun.

"Home! And we hit it right on the nose!" he said happily. "I don't know how to thank you, ?1."

"You can thank me and all of us by getting into communication with these Laagi right away and explaining to them what they should do," said ?1. "You've been . . . let us say, interesting—for two people who are essentially no more than living holes. We may meet in the future. Meanwhile, farewell!"

He disappeared.

"Jim!" It was Mary speaking urgently to him. "Look at the instruments!"

Jim looked. He stared.

"Laagi ships!" he said. "Two coming up at a hundred and forty by thirty-two degrees from down-galaxy—and one coming from sixty-one by ninety-seven degrees, from up-galaxy? How can that be, here in our own territory? What's happened? Wait—"

He hastily checked the instruments.

"The spectrum's not right!" he burst out. "That's the wrong sun! And ?1's already left us. ?1! ?1! Answer me, will you? Come back, ?1! You took us to the wrong sun. *?1*!!!"

An invisible firefly appeared in the center of *AndFriend*'s cabin space.

"What do you mean, calling me back after all this?" demanded ?1. "And what do you mean, I took you to the wrong star? I told you where the star was on the line you gave me to look along, and that's the one you went to."

"Well, it's not our sun. We had an error, just the way I warned you we might!" said Jim. It just happened we landed near a sun that's almost a duplicate of our own."

"Nonsense!" said ?1. "We went right out the line you indicated. I can assure you of that, since, unlike you holes, I know where I am by reference to the galactic pattern."

"Well, it's the wrong star, all the same," said Jim. "Not only that, but there's three—no, there's four now, according to the instruments—Laagi ships closing in on us fast. If you don't want to see all our plans aborted, you'd better get your people here to command the Laagi aboard those incoming ships to turn around and go away, before you do anything else."

"Oh, my!" said ?1. "I can't—I absolutely can't intrude on the dance time of so many of our people to help you again, after all the attention they've already given you. Even if I did, most of them would probably refuse to let themselves be interrupted like that once more."

"Then get us out of here, fast!"

"Why don't you just get out on your own?" demanded ?1.

"Because I don't know which way to go!" shouted Jim—or at least he would have shouted, if he had had a voice to shout with. "All right, if you won't help us, we'll simply make a blind jump away from here of at least five light-years and try to figure how to get home after this. Obviously your pattern-sensing can't be right, since this definitely is not Sol—our star!"

"I tell you," said ?1 exasperatedly, "it's impossible for anyone not to know where that person is by reference to the pattern. If you only had a decent capability for sensing it, yourself, you'd see how ridiculous it is to think you could get lost, anywhere in the galaxy—"

"No time to talk anymore," said Jim. "I'm programming the shift!"

"Very well. Act in a completely foolish manner—just a moment," said ?1, "you did say your sun was a yellow G0-type star, on this line?"

"Yes! But so what, now? Those Laagi ships'll be in firing range in seconds; and, judging by the way they're acting, whatever your people told whoever's aboard our captive ship, it didn't stop them from letting these others know they were being held prisoner, as soon as the others got into instrument communication range. Those ships coming at us are out for blood—"

"Ah, as it turns out," said ?1, "another sixty-one of your light-years farther out this line of yours there just happens to be another G0 star very much like this one . . ."

"What? Where? How far?"

"Sixty—"

"Nevermind. I heard you the first time. I'm setting up a shift for another sixty light-year jump straight ahead, right now. In fact, we'll jump it on rough calculations. Better to be in larger error at the far end than take any more timeow—"

They shifted.

This time the Laagi ship that was their prisoner came with them. So did ?1. But this time Jim paid neither of them any attention. His view was on the instruments panel, examining the spectra of the new yellow star that now lay before them at a distance of less than a light year. ?1 had evidently been rather cursory in his estimate of the distance; but once again they had shifted to what, for practical purposes, was their exact aiming point—which was something to think about when there should be time to think about it. Two miracles of phase-shifting in a row became suspiciously something more than miracles.

"It's all right," Jim announced. "Thank God. The spectrum checks. We're home."

# CHAPTER

## 27

HE SPOKE TO AN EMPTY CABIN. ?I HAD NOT EVEN BOTHERED TO say farewell, this time, before departing.

Jim checked his instruments.

"There's Earth," he said. "Alarms'll be sounding all over the world right now, seeing we've got a Laagi ship beside us. I'll give them a call."

Mary said nothing. True, what he had just said, himself, did not particularly ask for comment, but he would have welcomed a word or two, from which perhaps he might have judged how she was feeling. Evidently, she was still angry with him for some reason—if angry was the word for it. Oh, well . . .

"Base," he said through the ship's equipment in broadcast to that location, "this is ship XN413, your lost baby from a far country. I'll leave our location sounder on, so you can send out an escort to bring us in. We've got a prisoner—he's harmless, so don't come loaded for bear—and he'll need an escort. Also I need to talk to Louis One. Repeat . . ."

He ran through the broadcast several times. He had barely finished before the first half-dozen fighter ships began to appear around him and began to englobe *AndFriend* and her Laagi prisoner.

"Welcome home, XN413." A voice on the ship-to-ship circuit filled the interior space of *AndFriend*. "Since we're being formal, this is XY1668, Wing Cee for the pack you see around you. You want to slave to me and we'll carry you in? How about your prisoner, is he slave to you—and is he alive?"

"Very much alive. Handle with care," answered Jim. "Not, repeat not, slaved to me, but will follow. I slave to you— now. Give prisoner in particular lots of room and drive regular. He'll follow. Land him, but do not disturb further. Also do not disturb me after landing. You'll probably get added orders on both of us from Base—but everything clear for now?"

"Clear. Here we go."

The escort moved off, with *AndFriend* and the Laagi ship traveling as if held in invisible bonds in the center of their formation.

"Mary?" said Jim softly, speaking mind to mind.

She did not answer.

"Mary?" he asked again, still softly.

"What is it?" Her voice was no longer cold, but neither was it warm. It spoke to him with the remoteness of disinterest.

"We're home," said Jim. "This is your territory, again. How do we go about getting back into our own bodies?"

"We'd better wait and see if they're ready to have us reenter, first. Louis will be calling us, shortly, won't he?"

"I'd expect so," said Jim, knowing that short of death, nothing was going to keep General Louis Mollen from being on the phone to them as soon as he heard they were back.

"We'll have to ask him to check with wherever they've been maintaining the bodies, and make sure the technicians there are ready for us to reanimate them. When he gives us word they are, we can go ahead."

"How do we do it? I mean, how do we go about moving back into our bodies?" Jim asked.

"When I was in Raoul's mind in *La Chasse Gallerie*"—her voice still sounded remote, disinterested—"after I found I couldn't move the ship by myself and also I couldn't communicate with him any better, I finally felt I was wasting my time there. Then I wanted to be back in my own body—and as soon as I wanted to, I was. Evidence is that where you most want to be, your identity is—remember how you got into

*AndFriend* in the first place? How you wanted to be with her, and so, you were."

"If you and I could just stay here in the ship, together, I'd want that," said Jim.

"Suit yourself," she said lightly. "As soon as we get word the bodies are ready, I'll be leaving."

He did not try to say any more and she did not say anything. The formation of ships proceeded Earthward at one gravity of acceleration, reached midpoint, flipped end for end and decelerated, still at one gravity. Time passed; and Earth became visible as a blue globe, though still small, on *And-Friend*'s close screen.

"—XN413, this is Louis One. Answer, XN413. This is Louis One. Are you hearing me all right—"

"Hearing," said Jim. "Both of us."

"It's wonderful to hear you. Mary?"

"She's here, too," Jim said, since Mary could not talk aloud except through him.

"Terrific! We'll save the talking until you're down. Anything you need right away?"

"We've got some live Laagi in the other ship we brought in and the body of a dead alien subspecies on board here. Be sure to note that the atmosphere in both ships at landing will be that of the Laagi world."

"Right," said the general. "Anything else?"

"Tell Louis to have our bodies checked," said Mary. "Have the technicians standing by for reentry."

Jim repeated her words aloud.

"Reentry when?"

"Tell him as soon as he can tell us they're ready for us, down there," said Mary clearly. "We don't have to wait until our transportation gets there."

Jim repeated.

"Oh! I understand," Mollen said. "Hang on, then. I'll check on that and be back to you as soon as I can. Shouldn't take more than a few minutes. Hang on."

The voice of General Louis Mollen ceased.

"Mary?" said Jim.

She did not answer.

He dwelt in silence until Mollen's voice came back into *AndFriend*.

"Ready at any time over in the body shop," said Mollen's voice.

"Thanks," said Mary.

"Thanks," said Jim.

"Mary," said Jim, on their private mind-to-mind level, "let me just tell you something before you go. I just want to say I'll always remember this crazy business of being just a couple of minds together all these months. I learned a lot—"

He broke off. His words were sounding emptily to his own mind in the hollowness of *AndFriend*'s interior. Mary was already gone. Gone, he realized now, from the moment she had answered Mollen's message that their bodies were ready for reoccupancy. He had been talking to someone who was no longer there.

Mentally, he shook his head. There was no reason for him to stay any longer, either. He stepped out of *AndFriend* as he had stepped out of her with ?1 and started toward the surface of Earth, and Base.

That face of Earth holding the North American continent was toward him and the sensible thing was to go there in a direct line. But for some reason, for old time's sake with the ?1 and his kind, Jim found himself choosing to come in on his destination in a soft, looping curve. There was no hurry in any case.

I must look like an invisible firefly myself, he thought, or would, if there was another loose mind around to see me. It was a definite pleasure to swoop along the curve he had chosen rather than go directly. He was enjoying a last time of being out without a ship, without a body, without anything but himself, alone with the stars.

He felt the pleasure of it . . . and, it came to him suddenly, after a fashion he could actually feel the pattern of forces ?1 had talked so much about. Certainly, he could feel the strong bar that was the pull from the Sun; and, now that he was this close, the even stronger one from Earth, like two threads of the celestial tapestry. It was strange, although he could feel the one from the Earth to be stronger because he was close to it, something in him recognized it as one of the most minor of minor threads in the galactic warp; and he thought he could faintly see some of the skeins from the other planets and even some from the nearer stars.

And it was true what ?1 had said. It would be impossible to lose one's way because even a piece of the warp implied the pattern of the whole. Down-galaxy, the direction toward the mass of the galaxy's center was as plain as if a street sign stood in the void, pointing to the midpoint of all the great whirl of stars and dust and cosmic debris.

But, he was entering Earth's atmosphere now; and he said farewell—as ?1 had said it at least once—to the stars. Below was the continent he aimed for, below were the mountains surrounding Base. Below was Base itself.

And then he was there. And the building, the room, the bed that held his body, drew him to it, for—in another way—it, too, was part of a pattern.

It looked rather uncomfortable, his body, with all those tubes stuck into it. But he would do something about that, just as soon as he was back inside.

He slipped into it, and then he had moved the muscles that opened his eyes and was looking up into the faces of people in white medical clothes who stood staring down at him, as if he was some kind of Egyptian mummy returned to life . . .

What followed turned out to be a long period of getting him and his body back into operation together.

To begin with, although they had kept the body very carefully, and cleaned it and fed it and turned it and even exercised it, it was out of the habit of operating under its own power and it had lost not only muscle strength, but the habit of use.

Added to that was the fact that, after having been a free mind with no physical weight to clog his senses and weigh him down under gravity, he had to learn to love his body all over again. That was not easy. His first feeling, on finding himself in it, had been almost like that of a child shut up in a closet.

He had felt trapped.

Grimly, he had fought that feeling down. A body was a great thing, he told himself. Not only that, but it was a necessary thing. Stop. Think. There were things possible to a body, smells and sights and touchings and a whole host of others, of which the mind alone could not even conceive.

Also, although there might not be much importance to it now, somewhere Mary was also back in her body; and only as another body could he ever have anything to do with her again, however transiently.

So he told himself that his return to flesh was just what he wanted. He did what the technicians told him, let himself be weaned from intravenous feeding back through liquids to solid food, let himself be exercised until he was able to take over the business of making his body exercise by his own will. He worked his way up the long slope of effort against the drag of gravity to being an ordinary human being again.

Just another hole—in top hole shape.

Mollen had been in to see him a number of times as he recovered; and of course Jim had been debriefed by a large number of interviewers. These had come, one at a time, of course, to stand at his bedside, or beside his exercise bike, or walk and finally run beside him. They had emptied him of every memory and thought he had had while he was gone, except those he had kept private to himself; and he gathered, from Mollen as well as from what reached him through the gossip channel of his attendant technicians, that work was going busily forward with both the Laagi ship and the two Laagi he and Mary had brought in. Squonk's body was never mentioned, but he was sure that it, too, had been thoroughly investigated with scalpel and microscope, by the time he was ready to walk out of the building where they had kept his body.

By that time he was ready to accept Mollen's invitation to a full scale wrap-up of the trip, in the general's office. It was to be a private session with just Mollen—and, he hoped, Mary. He had not seen her since he had reentered his own body, though when he asked about her he had been told she had readjusted well. In fact, she had been up and around, evidently, before he had been able to stand on his own feet. She was someplace other than the rooms that they had him in. Naturally, they did not tell him where.

The day finally came on which he left for good the building in which he had regained his body, and headed for Mollen's office. It was one of those sparkling clear mountain days in summer that he had used to love, and now for the first time again he found himself appreciating the body with which he responded to it. The major acting as receptionist in Mollen's outer office was a trim, fortyish woman with light gray hair whom he did not know.

"Colonel Jim Wander," he said. "The general's expecting me."

"Yes, Colonel. If you'll sit down for a moment . . ."

It turned out to be indeed only a moment. Which was just as well. The receptionist's office, in a building that had not existed when Jim and Mary had left the Base, was high-ceilinged but entirely within the building and therefore without windows. Jim had become sensitive to being enclosed since his return to his body. He got to his feet and put down the magazine he had been holding open without really reading the print before his eyes. He went into Mollen's private office.

Mollen's room had the same high ceiling but was easily four times as large as the reception room. There was a floor-to-ceiling vision screen on the wall to Jim's right. The other wall had a large painting which made no sense to Jim but was probably something expensive for important visitors to notice. Happily, however, the wall at the far end of the room, opposite the door by which Jim had entered, was all one large window with heavy floor-to-ceiling curtains drawn and tied back as far as they would go on either side, taking away all of Jim's mild new claustrophobia. In between him and the window was a lot of thick carpeting, overstuffed chairs, bookcases, a bar, and a large desk a couple of meters before the window and facing the room's entrance, a desk behind which Mollen sat in another overstuffed chair.

Mary was there, too, but she was in one of the chairs that was to the side of, but beyond Mollen's desk, closer to the window. She was in civilian clothes, wearing a gray-green dress, and her chair was so angled that she looked out of the window. Her face was turned away so that Jim, after all these days, could not see it. Mollen had swiveled his own chair around and was talking to her as Jim entered. He swiveled back to face Jim; but Mary did not turn.

"Sit down, sit down, Jim!" said Mollen. He waved Jim to a chair in front of and facing the desk. Jim sat, frustrated to be forced into a position where Mary's face was still hidden from him.

"Well," said Mollen, "you're looking well. I hope you're feeling as good."

"As holes go, I can't complain," said Jim.

Mollen laughed.

"Yes," he said, "I've read the results of your debriefings on the mind-people. Sobers me up to realize all I am to them is a hole in the continuum. Still, the human race has got on that way for millions of years, so I suppose we'll continue to struggle along in the same fashion. You two did a marvelous job out there. Better by a long shot than anything we expected. You come back not only with new worlds for us and the means to a way of dealing with the Laagi, but with news of another race yet, and a couple of Laagi prisoners to work with."

"How're they doing?"

"Just fine," said Mollen. "We've got them in a separate building in pretty much the same kind of set-up we had your ship and *La Chasse Gallerie* in Mary's lab. We sweated a little over how to keep them fed. But we made a guess they might be able to subsist on the same thing your little friend Squonk was fed in that hospital. We built a special room around the entry port of their ship, flooded it with the same sort of atmosphere that was in your ship, and left a container with some of the original cubes you'd brought along for Squonk, plus some we'd made up after analyzing one of the cubes."

"You were able to duplicate them?" asked Jim.

"Oh, yes. Chemically, at least. Of course, God knows what our version tastes like to a Laagi; but we knew the two in the ship were watching us outside their hull with their ship's instruments; and, sure enough, after we'd left them alone for a while with the extra room and the two containers of cubes, one of them ventured out, picked up the container of original cubes, plus one of the duplicates we'd made and took it all back inside. Evidently our version went down all right; because they eventually came out, got the rest of our cubes and ate them."

"Not a very happy life, being prisoners," said Jim. He looked over at the back of Mary's head, but it did not move and she did not say a word.

"No. But then you can't expect it to be," answered Mollen. "We're making good progress toward being able to talk with them, using that notion you passed on in your debriefing, by the way, Jim. You know, the idea of one of us with a picture box strapped to his chest showing the image of a Laagi; and whoever it is speaks to a Laagi and the picture box translates his words into the image in the box, making the body movements that translate his words."

"And you're close to this, already?" asked Jim.

"Close, no," answered Mollen. "I said it was a final goal, and it is. But right now we're still working to really grasp that body language of theirs. You've heard of the 'third language' technique?"

"No," said Jim.

"Essentially, it means that if you've got two people, neither of whom can possibly ever speak the other's language, you invent a third language they can both speak. It's an outgrowth of the invented languages we were teaching chimpanzees and other animals as far back as the twentieth century, in order to communicate with them. There was a sign language, and a language of symbols different researchers used with different animals, and so forth. . . . Well, that's what we're trying to develop to use with our two Laagi, a third language."

"And it can be done?" Jim asked.

"It can be done if both sides have enough elements in common. For example, as I say, it worked with chimpanzees and dogs and elephants and a few others, but they've never been able to make it work with cetaceans like dolphins and killer whales. Too different environmentally. We're just lucky that the Laagi've developed a technological civilization not too different from ours. We may not think the way they do, but we've got enough problems in common—like how to get from one star system to another by spaceship."

"They're already talking about space flight with the Laagi?"

"Nowhere near that, yet, I'm afraid. First we had to build a sort of Laagi-instrument, in line with your idea. The technicians came up with a picture of a Laagi figure that could be made to make body movements the way they do. The movements were made by punching specific keys on a keyboard below the picture. Then we built a transparent section into the wall of the room we'd added around the Laagi port; and set the instrument up outside the window with a human operator seated at it, punching keys and making the figure move. Meanwhile, we were trying to isolate from the pictures you'd

brought back of Laagi talking to each other at least a few
body-movement words that our prisoners would recognize as
attempts by us to talk to them."

"You're using pictures from whatever got stuck to
Squonk's tentacle, I suppose," said Jim. He glanced over at
Mary. But she still had not moved. Her face was still, hidden
from where he sat, and there was no sign she was even listening to the conversation.

"That's right," said Mollen, "we've got pictures of nearly
every place you went in that city. The first big step was breaking the arm and body movements down into something
roughly equivalent to action-units inside a given three-dimensional space, action-units small enough so that we could be
sure each was all, or part of, no more than a single signal—
you follow me?"

"No," said Jim.

"The point was to get down to the basic building blocks of
their body language. Where there were simultaneous movements of more than one part of the body, that was taken into
account, too, but one way or another, all recorded body signals were listed and compared—thank God for thinking machines—then handed back to us in order of frequency, related
to the conditions and situations under which they were being
used, and so forth."

"I figured something like that would have to be done," said
Jim. "It must have been a big job."

"It was," said Mollen. "But, little by little, the technicians
began to pile up associations. You know—this movement
goes with beginning to speak to someone else, this one with
ending a conversation with that person. This one goes with
greeting someone; this, with leaving an individual. Et cetera.
And from all this we put together what should have meant 'we
want to talk to you.' We gave the Laagi a screen and keyboard
in their outside room hooked to the screen and keyboard they
could see through the window of that room, then had a technician sit down at the keyboard and type out 'we want to talk to
you.'"

"Where were the Laagi at this time?" asked Jim.

"In their ship, of course," said Mollen. "Where they'd
gone the minute we sent men in space suits in to set up the
screen and keyboard for them. But we figured they'd be

watching on their inside screens what went on in the outer room we'd made for them. Anyway, the technician kept sending the same message over and over."

"What finally happened, sir?"

"One of the Laagi came out to the keyboard and screen in their outer room, spent several hours learning which keys to punch, and finally sent back a message we couldn't understand."

"And the techs were stuck."

"No, because they figured on that happening. They sent another message. This one said, 'we want to talk to you with these,' and the screen showed some of the symbols for the artificial language they'd set up as the best bet to try to bridge the communication gap between us and the Laagi. The two of them took to the idea like ducks to water; and from there on it's been like teaching an artificial language to an animal—but a very smart one, of course."

"And this worked?" Jim said.

"After a fashion. The artificial language's very limited, of course—you could guess that much. But now the technicians've been able to begin adding in movements of the Laagi figure where the symbols wouldn't convey precisely what we wanted, or they thought they understood a Laagi movement well enough to use it in something like the way it should be used. The Laagi caught on, as you might expect, and started correcting our errors; and from then on it's been progress."

"How much progress?" asked Jim.

"We're just beginning to learn to talk to them, still, of course," said Mollen. "Nobody knows how long it'll take; but I must say those two Laagi are cooperating. When one leaves the keyboard the other sits down at it."

"Of course," said Jim.

"Why 'of course'?" asked Mollen curiously.

"Because they live to work. I told the debriefer that and Mary must have told hers the same thing. If you'd left them there much longer as simple prisoners with nothing to do, they'd probably have died. Now you've given them some reason to live."

"At any rate," said Mollen, "it's just a matter of time until we can really talk with them. Then the big job starts."

"Getting them to understand that there's no point in both

our races exhausting themselves in a war that'll do neither of us any good?" asked Jim.

Mollen looked him over.

"You've been thinking about this," he said.

"I've had months to do it in," said Jim. "Learning to communicate with the Laagi is one thing. Getting them to see things the way we see things is something that may never be done."

"You? Pessimistic?" said Mollen. "That's a change."

"I'm not pessimistic. Just realistic. We had trouble getting humans to agree with humans before this war with the Laagi started and we all had to work together. And the Laagi think a lot more differently from the way we do than any fellow human ever did. Also, they're not likely to change the way they think because of anything we can tell them. The most we can hope to do is sell them something."

"Sell them something?" Mollen stared at him. "Jim, what makes you so sure about all this?"

"?1 and his little friends," said Jim. "With one race of aliens to deal with, it's possible to make a whole lot of false assumptions. With two, it's possible to see from the bad guesses they make about each other where we could be making a bad guess or two about either one of them."

"Those mind-people you ran into?" said Mollen. "Mary told us all about them."

"With all due respect to Mary," said Jim, looking at the unmoving back of her head, "I think she'll agree that while she's the expert with the Laagi, I'm the expert with the mind-people—in fact she said so once. Didn't you, Mary?"

"He's right," said Mary, without moving. "You should listen to him, Louis."

"I'll listen to anyone; but you'd be high on the list in any case," said Mollen, throwing his heavy body back in his padded chair, so that the chair creaked and tilted slightly away from the desk. "What're you saying?"

"That I think the best we can hope to get out of being able to communicate with the Laagi is to offer them a deal where we help them to find the worlds they need so that they'll temporarily suspend trying to take over our world."

"Oh—that," said Mollen. "The business of giving them

worlds in the mind-people's sector that you arranged with the mind-people."

"It's far from arranged," said Jim. "We can easily overlook the fact that the Laagi aren't built to give up on trying to take our world for living room for themselves; and we're just as likely to assume that what the mind-people agree to today they'll still be in agreement with tomorrow. Both those notions about another race can be traps because they're based on the way we think ourselves, not the way the other race thinks."

"I don't think I follow you." Mollen's thick eyebrows came together.

"Remember how we used to wonder why a single Laagi ship would sometimes attack a whole wing of our fighters when it ran into them; while at other times a whole wing of them would turn and run from one ship of ours under practically the same conditions?"

"Yes. What about it?"

"The answer was simple. Tell him, Mary."

Mary said nothing.

"All right," said Jim. "I'll tell you, then. In both cases the drivers of the Laagi vessels were doing what they'd been told to do, not what reason would dictate they do."

"But that's stupidity!" said Mollen. "They're too bright to be that stupid."

"No, it's not stupidity. It's a whole world of difference in thinking. If they'd been told to use their own judgment, they'd have done so. But in the cases I'm talking about they'd simply been given a general order. What they did was no different from a human following orders even when he personally disagrees with them—with one exception. It's only under certain conditions that a Laagi allows himself to disagree on any subject; and one of those conditions isn't when he's at work. And what holds true for a Laagi individual holds true for the whole race. What I'm saying is that the Laagi could very well take a million habitable worlds, if we had that many to give them— and still keep on trying to conquer humanity so they could have Earth."

"Why?" demanded Mollen.

"Because getting Earth was something they started out to do. It was a job they started and haven't finished."

"You're telling me," said Mollen, "that even though events

proved what they'd been doing wasn't necessary, they'd keep right on doing it?"

"That's what I'm saying, General. Finishing a job isn't something a Laagi reasons about. It's something that's built into the primitive part of their brains—just like a territorial response is built into us humans. It's so deep in us, we react to it according to the patterns of our various cultures, without even realizing why we stand a certain distance apart when we talk, why we avoid looking or deliberately look into the eyes of people when we talk to them. Built into the Laagi is the fact that there's no reason for his existence unless it involves doing work of one kind or another. And a job's not abandoned until it's finished. Any unlimited number of Laagi may have to be used up finishing it; but whatever the job needs to get it done, it's going to get. They're a race that never quits and never backs up, because they can't."

"Man!" said Mollen, "you're telling me we can never make peace with them."

"That's right," said Jim. "Never."

"All right," said Mollen. "Then you tell me. What're we supposed to do?"

"We can't make peace with them as they are now," said Jim. "But maybe we can arrange an indefinite pause in hostilities that just happens to last until they develop a different attitude—and that'll take generations. We've got to use the fact that the mind-people are there as leverage on the Laagi to keep the indefinite pause going, while at the same time we use the presence of the Laagi to make the mind-people keep their promises to us and the Laagi."

"And how do you plan to do that?"

"Set ourselves up," said Jim, "to the Laagi as the only force that keeps the mind-people from stopping them from working; and to the mind-people as the only people who can talk to the Laagi and explain how they mustn't get in the way of the art that the mind-people are spending the lifetime of their race developing—and it actually is one hell of an art, General. It may turn out to be greater than all our arts put together."

"All right," said Mollen; and while there was nothing in the general's tone to give it away, Jim had the uncomfortable feeling that Mollen was humoring him. "You want to set up a

THE FOREVER MAN / 337

sort of triangular, three-race agreement that makes both the Laagi and the mind-people do what we want, out of a combination of benefit and fear. Assuming you could show each of those races reasons to act that way to each other, why would they want humans in on the deal? What do they need us for, anyway?"

"As interpreters," said Jim.

# CHAPTER

# 28

"INTERPRETERS?" MOLLEN WAS FROWNING, BUT JIM NO LONGER seemed to read any inclination to humor Jim in the general's voice.

"That's right," said Jim. "Stop and think about it. We can talk to the Laagi—just barely, so far, but we can talk. And we can talk to the mind-people, but as far as mutual understanding goes, what we have there is just barely, too."

"Right. What about it?" asked Mollen.

"But the mind-people and the Laagi can't talk to each other at all. It's worse for them—much worse than the problems you mentioned they had with teaching artificial languages to dolphins. The Laagi and the mind-people don't have anything in common—no common ground at all. The only way they'll be able to communicate is through us humans."

"Go on," said Mollen.

"For example, we've got bodies and a technological civilization, at least, in common with the Laagi. And now we've got the ability to move around as free minds, thanks to Raoul Penard, in common with the mind-people. There's other things on both sides. We've got a work ethic—not one as basically ingrained as the Laagi have, but we've got one in common with them. We've got a concept of art, which is

338

expressed entirely differently from what the mind-people express in their 'dancing,' but at least we can begin to understand how they could be that attached to the dancing. What do you want to bet that one of the concepts we'll never be able to get across to the Laagi, even when we come to be able to talk with them pretty well, will be the concept of an art?"

"That's all well and good," grunted Mollen, "but what happens when the Laagi learn to free their minds from their bodies the way Raoul, you and Mary've done? Once they do that they can talk directly to the mind-people. And since, according to your information on the debriefings, the mind-people talk mind to mind directly and can be understood directly that way, the Laagi'll be able to make their own agreements with them."

"Well, to begin with," said Jim, "I don't think, unless and until they develop a much larger attitude toward existence than they have now, that the Laagi are going to be able to get any of their minds free of their bodies. Our experience is you have to want pretty badly to leave your body before you can do it; and for a Laagi to do it, if one of them moved his mind out of his body, on the instinctive level he'd be abandoning the only tool with which he can do the work that justifies his existence."

"But suppose one of them did manage it?" said Mollen. "They could deal directly with the mind-people then."

"I don't think so," answered Jim. "So many of their concepts would be incomprehensible to the mind-people, and so many of the mind-people's concepts would be incomprehensible to them, that both sides would be hearing mainly blanks when they tried to talk to each other. Mary and I just barely managed to establish an understanding with the mind-people and they'd already had Raoul to practice on; plus, as I say, we've got a lot in common with them that Laagi don't have— that the Laagi can't have, without violating their own picture of the universe. Can you imagine yourself trying to describe a symphony to a Laagi, as I say?"

"But what we call art isn't really what the mind-people are concerned with," said Mollen.

"No. But it's close enough to their dancing so that it gave Mary and me a concept in common with them, even if we both used it to mean largely different things. It gave us something to build our communication on," said Jim. "That's the point I'm trying to make. We're like enough to the mind-people so that there's something there for us to build on. And like enough to the Laagi to have something to build on there, too. But I can't see anything the Laagi or the mind-people have in common, enough so that their two races could build a communication on it. But even assuming it turns out I'm wrong and they can, they're still both going to communicate better with us than they do to each other; which still gives us a chance to mediate between them."

"Mary?" said Mollen, looking over at her.

"I'm sorry, Louis," her voice came back at him, "but I'm afraid he's right, at least as far as the way the Laagi seem to look at things. Of course, we've really only scratched the surface of getting to know about them, so far. But if I had to go on what I know so far, I'd have to say he's right."

"I see," said Mollen. His face had become thoughtful. "By God, if you actually are right and the human race can act as a broker between two other races like that . . . "

His eyes, which had been focusing thoughtfully on nothing, came suddenly and sharply back on Jim.

"Even if it's possible, there's the question of how to do it, what to offer who," he said. "Which brings me back to one point, Colonel. You weren't sent out with any authority to go making treaties or arrangements with races we'd never met before. What do you mean threatening these mind-people with the possibility that the Laagi, or even we, could move stars? That's the wildest piece of impossibility anybody ever offered anybody else!"

"With due respect, sir," said Jim. "I was on my own out there and had to do something right away. I had to play it by ear. Also, why don't we check with some of the people who'd know about such things? We're an engineering race; and so are the Laagi. Sooner or later, we've been able to move anything we tried to move; and the Laagi've been comparable to us in all sorts of other ways. You might just suggest to the people you talk to on this that we look into the possibility of moving a star by using phase-shift physics on it. You know it takes only as much energy to shift a command ship as a fighter ship; and once the shift is set up and activated, no more force is needed to move either one of them ten light-years than ten inches, because in effect, in a physical sense, no mass has been moved—it's just been defined as having a different position in the universe. Why shouldn't we be able to do the same thing with a star?"

Mollen looked fiercely at him.

"Do you know what a box of demons you're proposing to open?" he said. "If it became possible to move a star—or a planet—anyplace you wanted it, you'd have . . . I'm not even going to try to speculate on what you might have!"

"Well, maybe it's not possible, particularly in practice. Or maybe there'd be too high a price to pay for moving it. But I thought it was something that could be mentioned to the experts as a possibility, anyhow. Besides, we don't really want to move any suns about. In fact, I've got a hunch that as we come to understand what the mind-people call the dance of the holes in the galaxy, we may not want to disturb that dance under any circumstances because of what might result. All we really want to do is have the mind-people considering that we—or the Laagi—might eventually be able to do such a thing."

"Oh, of course," said Mollen. "Well, now, if that winds up the firecrackers you've got to set off under my nose today, let me give you some idea of what you'll be doing from here on out. You and Mary are going to be working separately from now on—"

"If you'll forgive me for interrupting, sir," said Jim, "just one more firecracker."

"One more?" Mollen stared at him. "Nothing on the order of what you just hit me with, I hope."

"It might be," said Jim apologetically. "In fact, it might be even bigger."

"Holy Jerusalem!" Mollen threw himself back in his chair. "All right. Go on!"

"The mind-people can't get lost anyplace in the galaxy, evidently," said Jim. "Maybe they can't get lost anyplace in the universe, but I don't really know about that. But they're definitely oriented anyplace in our galaxy because they see what they call the 'pattern' of gravitic forces set up around them, at least, by the larger bits of matter like stars and planets, and maybe right on down to dust fragments. It's that pattern they weave their 'dances' around and they can use it as well to find their way from anywhere to anywhere. Also, they seem to be able to see things of any size at light-years of distance, possibly across the whole width of the galaxy."

"Can they?" said Mollen. He stared at Jim for a second. "That's something, if true. All right, I'll give you credit for having had another firecracker equally big up your sleeve. Now—"

"I'm not finished yet, sir," said Jim. "The firecracker's yet to come. I think we can learn to see that same pattern, too. That means we could give up this business of navigating by a theoretical line to the center of the galaxy's mass, and phase-shift any distance in one jump, hitting our target point right on the nose."

Mollen simply looked at him for a long moment.

"I'm afraid to ask," he said at last. "But I will. What makes you think that if there actually is such a pattern, we can see and use it, too?"

"Because both when the mind-people took Mary and me dancing and when I came in from *AndFriend* to Base, I thought I could see the pattern around me. Particularly, coming in from *AndFriend* to my body, I could see or feel—it's hard to describe what the perception of it's like—the threads or skeins or whatevers from the Sun and Earth, in particular."

"I think," said Mollen, "I'm going to want to have the psych people look you over and give me a certificate of sanity on you; not only for my own use, but to have in hand before I pass along to anyone higher up these things you've been suggesting. Mary, did you see anything like this pattern he's talking about?"

"Not coming back into Base from *AndFriend*," she answered. "But during the dance with ?1 and the others, I thought I did."

"So it could really exist. As to seeing it better, and maybe in the long run using it to navigate the stars . . ."

Mollen threw up his hands in the air.

"Even if you've got something more up your sleeve," he said to Jim, "don't tell me. Save it for the next time. Let's go on a little longer pretending it's business as usual. What was I just about to tell you when you sprang this last surprise package on me? Oh, yes. You and Mary are going to have to work separately—

"I don't think that'd be the wisest idea, General," said Jim. "I'd like to have Mary with me."

"No," said Mary.

"You can't have her," said Mollen.

They had spoken almost in chorus, so promptly had the negative responses come from both of them.

"You see, what needs to be done just as soon as one of those Laagi you're teaching to communicate reaches the point where he can understand when we tell him why we're doing something," said Jim, ignoring what both of them had just said, "is for Mary and me to take him back into the territory of the mind-people and introduce the two races to each other with us translating. Start the ball rolling early, in effect."

"I told you if you had anything more up your sleeve to keep it there," said Mollen. "Not only that, but you just heard the answer to your continuing to work with Mary. It was 'no.'"

"Let me talk to him, Louis," said Mary, still facing away from Jim. "Jim, whatever you might come up with in the way of plans, I'm not going to be part of them. That's because I don't want to be part of them, or connected with you in any way."

"Come to think of it, I just thought of something I have to step out of the office to take care of," said Mollen. "I'll be back in a minute."

"No, Louis. Please stay," said Mary. "I want you to hear this, too, even though you know what I'm going to say. Jim—"

Jim half rose from his chair.

"Sit down, Colonel," said Mollen. "And listen."

Jim sat down.

"This isn't easy; but it has to be said." Mary's voice came to his ears strangely from her turned-away face. Somehow the fact that she spoke with the back of her head turned to him put an unnatural distance between them. "Jim, listen to me. I've explained this to Louis and he understands. I'm not a nice person. I never have been, and I never will be. I felt for you when we had to put you through those months of hell to get you to where you wanted *AndFriend* more than anything else on Earth; and while we were out together in this last trip, I came as close to . . . enjoying being close to another human being as I ever have with any other person in my life. But it's no good."

"Mary," said Jim, "if you'll listen for a second—"

"No. It's your turn now to sit and listen to me," said Mary. "The trouble is we're two different people. Worse than that, we're the wrong kinds of two different people, too wrong to ever get along. I'm what I am; and you—you're an idealist. You're even worse than that. You're an idealist who insists on acting as if his ideals were reality. You're so caught up in seeing the universe as if through rose-colored glasses that you're going to change the universe's color to rose, if necessary, to make it so. Well, that sort of thing doesn't work, particularly with people. Sooner or later you'll run up against reality as it actually is; and since you can't back down—in your own way you're as stiff-necked as I am, or Squonk was, in his own fashion—you'll go right on refusing to believe; and the reality'll kill you. If I let myself stay around you, what would happen would kill me, too. And I don't want that."

"Mary . . ." Jim got to his feet again; and again Mollen rose from behind his desk.

"Colonel," he said. "You stay where you are. The lady wants it that way."

"I'm sorry, Jim, but I do want it that way." The back of Mary's head was immovable. "You don't believe me, do you?"

"No," said Jim. "Because it's not true."

"It is. Oh, it is." Mary's voice was bitter. "You don't see even what's right under your nose. Instead, you shift it around until it suits you; and you're so good at it you don't even know you're doing it, most of the time."

"No," said Jim. "If anyone sees things to suit herself, it's you. You're so determined to justify the shell you built up around you that you'll cut off your nose to spite your face."

"Yes," said Mary, "that's the way you'd work it, wouldn't you? You'd blame it on me, instead of yourself. Well, it doesn't matter. I've told you what I set out to tell you. I won't work with you. I don't want to see you again, and I don't want you to try to see me."

"You don't want me to try to see you—" Jim began to walk toward her and Mollen moved to get in the way. But while the will to stop Jim physically if necessary was there in the general, there was also the knowledge of the twenty years between them that left no doubt that if Jim really intended to force his way in to face Mary, the other man could not stop him. And he did so intend—both he and Mollen knew it.

Mary saw Mollen moving to intercept Jim and knew it, too.

"All right," she said. "If you won't be warned, you'll have to find out the hard way. Out in the ship you told me you'd put together an image of my face in your mind. Let him come, Louis—was this the face, Jim?"

Mollen stood aside and Jim reached her, just as she rose and turned. He looked down into her face, and there it was, with the same blue eyes, the same reddish blond hair, the straight lines at the side of the face coming in to the small, square jaw—just as it had been ever since he had walked into Mollen's office and seen her there for the first time in ship-wear coveralls.

He frowned, letting out his breath in one great gush of relief.

"Thank God!" he said. "I thought something terrible must have happened to your body while we were gone—not that that would make any difference now that I know you mind to mind. But what're you talking about? You look the same way you always have; even if I never really did get around to seeing it properly until I had to put that picture of you back together in my mind, out between the stars. You're still the most beautiful woman I've ever seen."

She stared up at him. She stared for a long, long moment. Then, slowly, her mouth crinkled at the corners, and the crinkles spread their way out into a wide smile that made her look, Jim thought, even more lovely. She threw back her head and began to laugh; and Jim found himself laughing with her. They laughed together until, at last, still gazing into each other's eyes, they gradually sobered.

"I am now," she said.

She put her arm through his, still smiling.

"Forgive me, Louis," she said. She turned, still arm in arm with Jim, and they went out together.

# MORE SCIENCE FICTION ADVENTURE!

# ACE
# SCIENCE FICTION
# SPECIALS

Under the brilliant editorship of Terry Carr, the award-winning <u>Ace Science Fiction Specials</u> were <u>the</u> imprint for literate, quality sf.

Now, once again under the leadership of Terry Carr, <u>The New Ace SF Specials</u> have been created to seek out the talents and titles that will lead science fiction into the 21st Century.

|   |   |   |
|---|---|---|
| __ | THE WILD SHORE<br>Kim Stanley Robinson | 88874-7/$3.50 |
| __ | NEUROMANCER<br>William Gibson | 56959-5/$2.95 |
| __ | IN THE DRIFT<br>Michael Swanwick | 35869-1/$2.95 |
| __ | THE HERCULES TEXT<br>Jack McDevitt | 37367-4/$3.50 |
| __ | THE NET<br>Loren J. MacGregor | 56941-2/$2.95 |

---

*Available at your local bookstore or return this form to:*

**ACE**
*THE BERKLEY PUBLISHING GROUP, Dept. B*
*390 Murray Hill Parkway, East Rutherford, NJ 07073*

Please send me the titles checked above. I enclose _____. Include $1.00 for postage and handling if one book is ordered; add 25¢ per book for two or more not to exceed $3.50. CA, NJ, NY and PA residents please add sales tax. Prices subject to change without notice and may be higher in Canada. Do not send cash.

NAME_____

ADDRESS_____

CITY_____STATE/ZIP_____

(Allow six weeks for delivery.)